INTO THE SUN

or *The School*

DENI ELLIS BÉCHARD

milkweed
editions

© 2016, Text by Deni Ellis Béchard
All rights reserved. Except for brief quotations in critical articles or reviews, no part of this book may be reproduced in any manner without prior written permission from the publisher: Milkweed Editions, 1011 Washington Avenue South, Suite 300, Minneapolis, Minnesota 55415.
(800) 520-6455
www.milkweed.org

Published 2016 by Milkweed Editions
This edition is printed by special arrangement with House of Anansi Press Inc., and published simultaneously in Canada.
Printed in Canada
Cover and interior design by Alysia Shewchuk
Cover photo/illustration by Ellerslie / Shutterstock
The text of this book is set in Garamond Premier Pro.

16 17 18 19 20   5 4 3 2 1
First Edition

Special underwriting for this book was contributed by Barry Berg.

Milkweed Editions, an independent nonprofit publisher, gratefully acknowledges sustaining support from the Jerome Foundation; the Lindquist & Vennum Foundation; the McKnight Foundation; the National Endowment for the Arts; the Target Foundation; and other generous contributions from foundations, corporations, and individuals. Also, this activity is made possible by the voters of Minnesota through a Minnesota State Arts Board Operating Support grant, thanks to a legislative appropriation from the arts and cultural heritage fund, and a grant from the Wells Fargo Foundation Minnesota. For a full listing of Milkweed Editions supporters, please visit www.milkweed.org.

Library of Congress Cataloging-in-Publication Data

Names: Béchard, Deni Y. (Deni Yvan), 1974- author.
Title: Into the sun : a novel / Deni Ellis Bechard.
Description: First edition. | Minneapolis, Minnesota : Milkweed Editions, 2016.
Identifiers: LCCN 2016013644 (print) | LCCN 2016013702 (ebook) | ISBN 9781571311146 (hardback) | ISBN 9781571319241 (Cloth)
Subjects: LCSH: Kabul (Afghanistan)—Fiction. | BISAC: FICTION / Literary. | FICTION / War & Military.
Classification: LCC PR9199.4.B443 I58 2016 (print) | LCC PR9199.4.B443 (ebook) | DDC 813/.6—dc23
LC record available at http://lccn.loc.gov/2016013644

Milkweed Editions is committed to ecological stewardship. We strive to align our book production practices with this principle, and to reduce the impact of our operations in the environment. We are a member of the Green Press Initiative, a nonprofit coalition of publishers, manufacturers, and authors working to protect the world's endangered forests and conserve natural resources. *Into the Sun* was printed on acid-free 100% postconsumer-waste paper by Marquis Book Printing.

Advance Praise for Deni Ellis Béchard's *Into the Sun*

"Ambitious, elegant, and filled with a kind of ferocious intelligence."
— Roxana Robinson, author of *Sparta*

"An intimate portrait of people willing to die for their hungers, consumed by the romance of being narrators and saviors. As they try to find their outermost edges, every act is contemplated, every cruelty somehow unavoidable, and everyone destroyed by what they seek in a land where foreigners are thrilled to be hunted and only natives long to escape. We wake from this book as witnesses to Kabul, to America, and to the crimes of men who need destruction to find definition and women desperate to understand."
— Benjamin Busch, author of *Dust to Dust*

"A riveting mystery-thriller that also probes deeper into the nature of war and the ways in which it attracts and transforms some people."
— David Abrams, author of *Fobbit*

Praise for *Vandal Love*

"Béchard has reinvented the generational novel with innovative brilliance."
— Robert Olen Butler

"Reminiscent of Proulx and Doctorow in both sweep and grace of prose."
— Dagoberto Gilb

"The word 'masterpiece' is not to be used lightly, but one is tempted in the case of *Vandal Love*. . . . Its muscular use of language conjures a young Faulkner, García Márquez, or Steinbeck."
— Katherine Min

"Prose that's both lyrical and gritty, able to evoke big emotions with exquisite intimacy."
— *O, The Oprah Magazine*

"Masterful storytelling and heartbreakingly beautiful writing."
— Loung Ung

INTO THE SUN

Vanity of vanities, saith the Preacher, vanity of vanities; all is vanity. What profit hath a man of all his labor which he taketh under the sun? One generation passeth away, and another generation cometh: but the earth abideth for ever. The sun also ariseth, and the sun goeth down, and hasteth to his place where he arose. The wind goeth toward the south, and turneth about unto the north; it whirleth about continually, and the wind returneth again according to his circuits. All the rivers run into the sea; yet the sea is not full; unto the place from whence the rivers come, thither they return again. All things are full of labor; man cannot utter it: the eye is not satisfied with seeing, nor the ear filled with hearing. The thing that hath been, it is that which shall be . . .

— *Ecclesiastes*

. . .

Khorasan is the name by which the Afghans, Baluch, and Brahui designate the region known to Europeans as Afghanistan and Baluchistan. It is a softened pronunciation of Khoresthan, or country of the sun or the place of light . . .

— Edward Balfour,
The Cyclopaedia of India and of Eastern and Southern Asia, Volume 2, 1888

PART I

KABUL: MARCH 2012

美智子

WINTER WAS PREMONITION. We knew something was going to
happen. We saw it in the desolation and poverty, the gusting
indeterminate scraps, the men pushing trash carts, their figures like engravings of the plague, heads wrapped in tattered
keffiyehs; or the smog of traffic, wood fires, and diesel generators — the effluvium of four million souls desperate to heat
concrete and earthen homes — mixing with dust in the thin,
chill mountain air and hanging over the city in blunt journal-
istic metaphors: shrouds, palls, and, of course, veils. Snow fell,
churned into mud that rutted and froze. Pipes burst. Handymen
returned to our doors, grim and extortionate, like doctors.

Despite our predictions, the country became so inhospitable that the war itself ground to a halt, the passes closed, the
Taliban waiting. As we edged into spring, storms tottered on
the horizon and swept down over the rooftops without precipi-
tation, gusts scouring up filth, lifting it in long drifting curtains
the color of distant rain. At last the downpours came: hailstones
as big as bullets, gutters gorged, streets flooded, a season of trash
and excrement rising to the surface. Then the roses bloomed; we
sighed, even sunbathed, and the fighting season began again.

On the night of the attack, spring was still more than a
month away, and the taxi carrying Alexandra, Tam, and me

3

worked its way over ice and gouged earth, its shocks creaking, the street dark until we came to the compound's red metal gate.

Alexandra had asked us to join her, as moral support, because she was meeting a man at a party, a security contractor and former soldier. In our circle, there was no less appealing object of desire. No one I knew dated military contractors. The ratio of women to men was so in favor of the former that, for an evening's company, they could pull from a bevy of preening journalists and aid workers.

If a lesser woman had revealed interest in a mercenary, we'd have mocked her, but Alexandra was so assured and private that her attraction seemed like parlor intrigue. She was a human rights lawyer who defended women in prisons, putting in twelve-hour days to file reports of abuse. She told us about girls incarcerated for fleeing forced marriages and how they'd repeatedly given birth during their years behind bars. At parties, she cited studies to diplomats and reporters, naming those in the government intent on rolling back protections for women and those crusading for them. She spoke so decisively that we forgot she'd only just arrived and had learned everything from books and NGO reports.

Though I doubt anyone thought of her as an impostor, we all wondered if her taste in men proved a lack of values and a true nature aligned with the occupation we criticized.

"America's number one export to Afghanistan," Tam once declared at a dinner, "is its rednecks." We spoke of contractors as second-class expats. We abandoned bars when they showed up and stood drinking, staring with reptilian eyes at the women among us.

The contractor's name, Alexandra told us, was Clay: pleasingly American, an evocation of the frontier, of a man coarse, blunt, hewn from the land. I was eager to see him so Tam and I could discuss the situation later: What did Alexandra like about this kind of man? How did it feel to be the object of her singular attention?

I'd had a taste of it earlier, at their house, while I was waiting for Tam to get home. Alone with me, though I barely knew her, Alexandra described Clay: magnetic, present, different from other men here, reserved and in control — the sorts of things one said after first impressions. She'd asked me to go with her to the party, touching my hand. She was normally so undemonstrative that the gesture seemed erotic with vulnerability, as if the story she'd become involved in wouldn't make sense without me.

Tam arrived on her motorcycle as the taxi pulled up, and she agreed to come along. I knew we were thinking the same thing, not just about Alexandra's fascination with rough-grained American types, but that she was already involved with one.

For the past few weeks, she'd been seeing Justin, a born-again Louisianan so bearded Tam had nicknamed him the Mullah. He was here to teach English — a teetotaler who disdained all expats other than Alexandra and almost never left his school. People thought he was boring. A weirdo. A loner. A religious fanatic in that way of Americans from the Deep South. At a dinner party, we speculated why, when all the men in Kabul were throwing themselves at her, Alexandra had picked the dullest. We confectioned theories: she could control him; she enjoyed being the interesting half of the couple; she suffered from self-loathing, like many attractive women. The only thing she seemed to have in common with Justin was an all-consuming sense of purpose and an inclination toward solitude.

We didn't expect to see Justin that evening, not at a contractor party. Tam mumbled about slumming as we followed

Alexandra like bodyguards through a living room, where people were serving themselves at a bar, to the doorway of a lounge. Alexandra pointed herself at a man — not coarse as I'd imagined, less hewn than carved — who was talking to someone just out of sight, and she smiled as he — he had the magnetism of a warrior, aesthetically, at least — smiled back, his hair dark and his eyes such a pale green they seemed to glow like the pupils of a wild animal at night. She took two steps farther, into the doorway, and froze.

The person Clay was speaking to was Justin — almost as tall, nearly as military in build — his dispassionate face now aimed at her dissolving smile. Clay and Justin had known each other in the US. They hated each other, according to Alexandra, though they'd once been friends. We'd come to the party to witness not just a desirable woman's poor taste in men but, it seemed, the opening round of a love triangle. Our only regret was that the men weren't more high profile — neither established journalists, nor diplomats, nor seasoned humanitarian workers, and therefore hardly fit story fodder in our circles.

I was nearest to Alexandra. Her black hair and pallor, and the severity of her expression, lent her a European air, though she was from North America. At a distance, her face was an emblem: the clearly defined jaw, just long enough to be elegant, the faint rising slant of her cheekbones. She met Justin's gaze, her poise intact. Her bones seemed to hum beneath her skin like struck crystal. Her stillness gave the impression she was listening for this sound.

Tam turned as if on cue, and I followed her back into the living room. She wasn't tall, only five-six, but had the carriage of a boxer — an authority that caused people in crowds to shift aside. When we were far enough away, we let our laughter go.

"If the Mullah thinks he can keep Alexandra, he's delusional," she told me, "but how did he end up here?" We agreed that Clay should have warned her with a text message, unless he'd invited Justin himself, staging the situation in an act of one-upmanship and using her like a weapon.

Tam slipped her scarf back, its ends brushing the floor, and let herself come in for a hug, one of her rare moments of public affection — maybe because there were no hard-hitting journos to impress here — before moving away and self-consciously touching her hair, which she wore in a tight braid.

At the bar, I poured her a vodka tonic. I wasn't sure who the host was. Someone had put on Lana Del Rey. We weren't bored of her yet. Talk of her invented persona, plastic surgery, and rich dad paying her way to rock-and-roll fame had yet to reach us.

As I glanced toward the lounge where we'd left Alexandra, the space my body occupied contracted. My breath was knocked out of me and my ears ached, as if someone had simultaneously shoved me and slapped them. We were all lying down, like toy figurines on a bumped table, glittering with glass.

I couldn't breathe. I pushed myself to my knees. It should have hurt, but pain was a faraway sensation, small shards biting into my skin. Someone began wailing. I gasped, but smoke made me gag. The large windows had been blown out. People were fumbling about, shouting, their voices muted by the thud of my pulse and the ringing in my ears.

I crawled to the balcony, my head a primitive camera, a box with a hole punched in. There was no me, none of my fear, just details: an intact beer stein and tumblers on the floor, shattered glass so thick and white on the leaves of potted plants it resembled snow. I lifted my head above the concrete edge of the balcony.

At the end of the driveway, the gate was blasted open, barely connected to its twisted frame. A man stepped through it, and my body retracted and curled, my head jerking away from the sound at my ear: a hummingbird's passing. Small puffs of atomized concrete spurted from holes in the ceiling of the room behind me. I heard gunshots.

EXPLOSIONS, SHRAPNEL, INDISCRIMINATE BULLETS — so many expats had died over the years that I couldn't help but picture my own end: in a restaurant garden one evening, after telling a near-death story, or in a bar, a guesthouse, any of the places foreigners sipped wine, whiskey, and cocktails, smoked pot or snorted methylphenidate — knockoff Ritalin shipped in from Iran or Pakistan, and sold without a prescription.

The deaths of expats were rarely fully explained. They'd been caught in the gears of war, the overarching historic machinations, plots cooked up in the Federally Administered Tribal Areas, funded by Islamabad or Riyadh, or power struggles between Kabul and Kandahar, between Afghanistan and America — the circle jerk of politicians, generals, businessmen, warlords, opium kings, and transient diplomats. They were bystanders near someone important, or targeted directly, in strikes against the occupation's colonial machine. Even journalists were threatened, for publishing propaganda — stories the Taliban hated and we loved — about brave Afghan souls risking everything to be Western: the athletes and musicians and actors, and, above all, the women.

Thinking back on the attack, I wondered which of us had drawn the Taliban. Of the twenty-one people in the house — Americans, Canadians, Australians, Brits, and so on — most were behind-the-scenes office types or neophyte reporters.

Security contractors were generally killed opportunistically while guarding a target. Justin taught Afghan women, but in a school too obscure to inspire such an organized assault; someone would just shoot him in the street. And like Justin, Alexandra was new here, the women's rights organization she worked for one of many.

Tam was perhaps the best known among us, but though she'd told stories about being targeted for her exposés, the police or government were usually her antagonists, not the Taliban. Besides, before we'd started dating, I'd heard expats debunk the plots against her, chalking them up to vanity, self-promotion, and a dash of paranoia from having lived here too long.

Later, security video footage sold to CNN would reveal that a man had run by the front gate and thrown a duffle bag loaded with explosives against it. After the blast, I lost track of Tam, not sure if she'd stayed where she'd fallen or left me there. On the floor, my body was a flare of adrenaline. Behind the ringing in my ears, Lana still crooned, but softly, as if the attack were her doing, and she was whispering to us, calling us somewhere.

I don't know why I went to the balcony. In my shock, my brain had become less a thinking organ than a recording device. Bullets whirred past and thudded into the ceiling.

"This way," a man shouted behind me. "The safe room is back here."

I scrambled inside and across the living room. Downstairs, there was the clanging of a metal security door closing.

We all followed a burly man with a golden crew cut — definitely ex-military, certainly a security contractor — back to the lounge, a small room with two couches, a wall-mounted flat-screen TV, and a steel trunk for a coffee table.

"Anyone missing?" he called from the doorway, to no one in particular. The safe room remained open, and people were shouting, "Close the door! Close the fucking door!"

"There's no rush," he said. He wore a black button-down and jeans, and appeared a young forty. He must have been our host, his accent British or Australian. A piece of pulverized glass shone on his lapel like a diamond.

The gunfire rattled on, with enough lulls to suggest that people were moving about and the guard was returning fire. From the balcony came the sound of an occasional bullet ricocheting. Another explosion, in the courtyard this time, heaved the air and hit us with a wall of sound, resonating in the safe room like an ocean wave slamming into a cove.

The host went out and came back hauling a young man by the arm — a German I'd recently begun noticing at parties. He'd hidden in the bathroom, spots of urine on his pants.

"Check if anyone's missing," our host said. Alexandra, Justin, and Clay stood near the wall. Tam was fiddling with her iPhone, selling the story before it had finished happening.

"Everyone here?" he asked and then shouted into the house, "Last call!"

He reached into the door frame, slid out a slab of iron, heaved it shut, and locked it with a lever. The sounds in the room became muted, like those on an airplane. Faraway gunshots popped, quiet as pebbles tossed at a window, as if the attackers had come here to court us.

With the safe room closed, I realized the silence wasn't that of an airplane at all, but of a bunker, far beneath the earth.

"Let's have a look," he said and took a remote from its holster on the TV. He changed channels, from ESPN to Al Jazeera to a replay of *Friends* to a grainy colorless image of the compound yard, the guard booth obliterated and a dead man lying where he'd taken cover near a Toyota 4Runner riddled with bullet holes. Then he switched to a feed showing the metal security door at the house's entrance. Three bearded men in *shalwar kameez* and body armor were inspecting it.

A woman in the back of the room called out a question, her voice a fearful chirrup. It took me a moment to realize she'd asked whether the men outside were Taliban.

"They are now," he told her and turned from the TV. "Come on, everyone, there's no need to be scared."

"I'm not," Tam said, holding up her phone. "I'm trying to get reception. I need to tell my editors what's going down."

"Now this is a proper safe room," he replied as he made his way to an iPad console. "The walls are too thick for much cell reception, but we've got Wi-Fi. Password is *end of the world*, all one word."

"Thank you," she said. "And what is your name?"

"Steve Hammond."

"And you're from?"

"South Africa."

"And is there any reason you would be targeted?"

"I have twenty foreigners partying at my place."

This was what I envied about Tam: she had the presence of mind to ask questions others would consider only once their survival was guaranteed. She was already trying to deduce the target, an activity I'd engage in later, recalling memories as vivid as frescoes.

The room was crowded and hot, and we repositioned ourselves, easing out of our protective huddles. In the back, two people helped a woman who had glass in her eye.

"And this safe room is secure?" Tam asked, pausing from

her typing to assess me and the few other journalists among the guests.

"Secure as it gets," Steve replied. "There's no access to us but through two steel gates on the ground floor and this one here. I've already put out a call to the police. And for those of you who are feeling queasy, there's a bathroom behind that sliding panel."

Tam was studying him.

"And what do you do for a living?" she asked.

"I sell safe rooms, among other things."

A few expats actually laughed with relief, their voices unnatural, nervously hysterical as they touched each other for reassurance.

Steve unlocked a cabinet. I expected guns, but there were four bottles of Macallan 30 and one of Hendrick's gin. He ignored the gin, cracked the whiskey, took out a stack of plastic cups, and asked who was drinking. Those who didn't accept at first soon did, seeing others calm a little but also realizing we might not get a second chance to taste Scotch this old or this expensive.

Tam motioned me to the space on the couch next to her. Specks of glass glittered in her hair, like a party girl's sparkles, and her eyeliner was smudged. If I were American, I would have boasted that an attacker had shot at me. He'd seen me peering over the balcony, and I'd felt the wind of a bullet at my ear.

Everyone was engrossed with the Taliban on the screen, and though I sensed the fear around me, I felt emptied of my own. It had suddenly become a pointless emotion, unable to offer me anything.

The woman who had something in her eye rinsed it out — Steve had the place stocked with water, food, and first aid kits — and her eye was fine, only a little red. She admitted that maybe it was just dust, "though it felt like glass," she said. "I'm pretty sure it was glass."

"Fuck!" the German shouted. On the TV, one of our attackers had taken a brick from a green backpack, the kind schoolchildren wear. He attached it to the front door, lit a fuse, and ran. Tam studied Steve, who sipped his drink, observing the screen. A few men and women held their heads, squealing until they were out of breath. The blast took out the camera near the entrance. It sounded like someone slamming a door in an old house. The floor vibrated.

Steve switched to a different feed. In the yard, the three insurgents held their Kalashnikovs at the ready and ran through the blackened doorway.

"How many doors left to go?" Tam asked.

"One on the first floor, at the bottom of the stairs," Steve said, "and this one here."

Something deep in my head seemed to contract, and everything in the room, the lines of the walls and ceiling, the TV and the expats, became sharp, as if a razor had cut away the dullness. Tam's eyes, the crystalline departure at the iris's dark blue edge, their whites slightly gray — a side effect, she believed, of nine years in Kabul's pollution, and a source of insecurity — were now infused with light.

I've often returned to my memories of that evening, when death was no longer an ending but an opening into a shadowless world, and each glimpse felt like a lifetime. Among the images that haunt me are those of Alexandra, Justin, and Clay. The people in the safe room — a few ex-military types, NGO workers whose security Steve's company handled, and independent journalists or videographers for hire who went to any party that would have them — had formed groups on the couches or the floor, holding hands, whereas Alexandra and Justin stood apart, staring at the TV, their expressions beatifically blank.

Clay also stood alone, the tallest person in the room, at once compact and long-limbed, hard-faced like a fighter but not blunt, the lines of his skull crisp, his brown hair cropped short. He appeared detached despite the feral green of his eyes.

At the time, I made only cursory note of these three. The two men and her desire for them, so uncouth as to seem illicit, had become irrelevant. I noticed Justin and Alexandra because I saw in them the purity of what I felt, and I evaluated Clay's strength as I asked myself who would protect us if the safe room was blasted open.

I might have forgotten their love triangle altogether — its only purpose, perhaps, to underscore the foolishness that brought about my near death — had they not died two days later. Though expats would fail to find a connection with the attack on the safe room, months of my own investigation would reveal that we were all nearly killed because of that very love triangle: a convoluted story of pettiness; less a plot than a conjunction of character flaws.

"The help is here!" Steve shouted. He'd switched from the camera downstairs, where one of the insurgents was setting up a round of explosives at the next door, to the camera in the courtyard. Afghan Special Forces were coming in, stout men in uniforms and body armor. We admired the determination with which they crossed the yard under fire.

"We're going to be fucking okay," Steve called out. "Who needs a refill?"

TWO DAYS LATER, I was in a private taxi, on my way to an early interview at the Inter-Continental. The young driver — cleanly shaven and so doused in cologne the car smelled like a duty free — was enjoying the largely empty streets, swerving around potholes, racing into intersections, veering and braking when yellow-and-white public taxis cut into our lane, glittering calligraphy spelling the names of Allah in their windows.

Suddenly, he slowed. I'd heard a thud and thought nothing of it, but he was scanning the horizon. A white cloud rose above the rooftops and drifted toward the river, trailing a line of darker smoke.

"Let's go take a look," I said.

"No," he told me. "It is dangerous for you."

"It's not. Let me out here. I'll walk."

Both of his cells were ringing. News spread quickly among Afghans when there was an attack. He pulled over, and I dropped eight dollars on the front seat.

The absence of fear I'd felt two nights before was still with me as I followed the road's scant shoulder. Though my features allowed me to pass unnoticed as a Hazara — an Afghan believed to be descended from the Mongols — this was the first time I'd walked here so at ease, my mind unobstructed by visions of danger.

A crowd was forming in Abdul Haq Square, near the Dunya Wedding Hall, men skirting pieces of smoking metal. The bomb had been in a car, its doors blown open and its paint blackened. I'd anticipated the scorched bodies of bystanders, but the attacker seemed to have targeted an empty roadside or just the car's occupants.

The interior was on fire, and the victims — much of them at least — must have been in that cloud, drifting across the river.

I lifted my chin, considering sentience — memories, intentions, dreams — and this wind-pushed smoke. As far as having your ashes spread, it might not be a bad way to go, if a little unexpected.

I'd been in Afghanistan for more than a year, and only in the last week had I seen any attacks. When I moved here, my mother had put money in my bank account for body armor, but few expats used it, with the exception of paranoid diplomats or security contractors on duty. Kabul wasn't what people saw on TV. When foreigners died, my mother would hear about it on the news, and I would reassure her that they were just unlucky.

Cars were stopping, hands holding cells out windows to snap pictures. I hadn't been dating Tam long enough to know whether the stories were true and she really did make it to every major attack in Kabul within twenty minutes. But then I heard her motorcycle, and she pulled up, dressed for an Armageddon road movie: head wrapped in a white-and-gray *keffiyeh*, torn jeans over black yoga leggings, a scuffed leather biker's jacket with a vest of yellow sheepskin from Oruzgan, its ruff warming her neck. I waved, but she drew her Nikon D4 out of a holster and began shooting. A few dumbfounded traffic police stood around in oversized suits. Green pickups started arriving with more police crammed in their beds.

Wind and a brief icy rain the previous night had purged the smog, and even distant mountains appeared close, hanging above the horizon. The parking lot and street had filled. Horns blared. More men came through the traffic. The cloud of incinerated lives was already dissolving over the frozen streets — just something else Kabul's inhabitants would have to breathe.

As I edged out of the crowd, I came to a circle of men with their backs to me. They were gazing down, and I walked along their perimeter until one peeled away and I took his place. My stomach clenched and my knees pulsed, a feeling like when an elevator reaches a floor, an airy sensation in the joints, of being buoyed and dropped at once.

A hand lay on the asphalt, on its back, the skin pale and intact, its fingers curled slightly, as if it had been severed in the moment of receiving an offering. It was probably a woman's, though Afghans are generally small, and a bloodless hand must decrease in volume.

I prided myself on being able to look, and then turned away. I'd seen similar things when I'd left the safe room, but in my euphoria, they hadn't bothered me.

Tam was busy interviewing people in Dari, her camera set to video. She'd already published two pieces on the safe room: a photo-essay of the attack featuring pictures I hadn't noticed her taking with her phone, and a witty story about how it feels when the people on TV are trying to kill you. Soon, she would have a car bomb article, a slide show, and a video report ready so that when the police announced the victims she could plug in their names.

I hailed a taxi and continued to the Inter-Continental on its hill overlooking the city. For a travel piece, I interviewed the manager about its history back to 1969, when people sipped champagne on the terrace and women lay in bikinis by the pool. I ate lunch there and fished online, but found nothing about who'd died in the bombing. I settled into a chair with a view. At a distance, Kabul bore no trace of any attack, except for maybe 9/11, which had drawn the world's attention here and transformed a modest capital into this sooty, sprawling metropolis.

I intended to write about the car bomb, but the details I'd witnessed were generic — no different from hundreds of other events like it. I took *Humboldt's Gift* from my backpack and tried to read, but the morning's events made it impossible to concentrate. I felt both as if I'd come here to experience these attacks and as if nothing I'd lived here mattered. My persistent state of alertness was at once potent and disconcerting.

That evening, when I opened my door, Tam was reading the collected works of Gertrude Stein on my bed, near the *bukhari*, a cylindrical metal woodstove that, once lit, immediately radiated heat. She was alone, a crimson scarf spooled on her shoulders. In the next compound, the Afghan death metal band was rehearsing. I'd written a piece about them and gone to a few of their parties, but since the success of their album, they were no longer as friendly and I'd begun to resent the noise.

I lay on the bed next to her. This was something she liked when we saw each other — not talking, just touching. As she rested her cheek on my shoulder, I had the impression that I was with a superhero's vulnerable alter ego.

The reverberations of the blaring music ceased, and I undressed her, kissing her skin. She was conscious of her hips since it was hard to exercise in Kabul, so I slowed for them. She had dozens of tiny poppy tattoos, one for each person she'd seen dead. They clustered on her shoulder blade, circled a biceps, framed her heart, and otherwise freckled her in random spots: an ear, a knuckle, a breast. She lay with her chin back as I kissed up along her chest. I moved my fingers over her throat's long lines and her collarbone.

"I read a passage today that made me think of you," I told her. As I took the book from my backpack, she kept the fingers of one hand on my waist. I'd found a stash of Saul Bellow novels in an expat's home and become obsessed with him. His awareness and self-examination, his study of others, was addictive.

The Americans I knew seemed to have emerged from a civilization that had since declined.

I leafed through for the passage that reminded me of when I'd met her during a dinner at the *Wall Street Journal* house. She'd been drinking gin and tonic, a ceiling light shining on her sculpted clavicle as she told me that though her father was Manhattan high society, her mother, a model from Alabama, had named her Tammy after a favorite aunt. When the dot-com bubble imploded, they moved to Burlington, Vermont. Tam, then a teenager, asked if she could change her name before enrolling in her new school. Attentive for the first time in her life, her father suggested Tammany, for New York's Tammany Hall, but she read about its corruption and would have refused if not for the original Tammany: the Native American chief who made peace with the English settlers. She was a child of the nineties, a chic hippie educated in a Manhattan Montessori, from whose vantage the earth appeared in a golden age, and the name suited her idea of what America was meant to be.

As I searched through the novel, her cell chimed. She swung her legs down and crossed the room, her hips curving deeply, the rice-paper lamp at the bedside casting her shadow.

She read the text and was suddenly haggard. I put the book aside, and she returned to lie against me, her hand with the cell on my chest.

"Tam?" I said. The way she touched me had changed. Her tears ran along my throat.

"It's Alexandra," she told me. "She and Justin were in that car."

My grief was slow in coming, my emotions stunned. I could sense the mechanical intonations of the city beyond the room — the battering of a truck motor, a motorcycle's whine — more clearly than whatever was happening inside me.

She shifted onto her back, her gaze abstracted, as if the low smoke-dimmed ceiling was the night sky and her attention moved along the constellations.

EVENTUALLY, we went to Tam's house, where she and her friends gathered — hugging, crying, or sitting, their heads lowered like those of people fathoming an impossible equation.

A plainclothes officer, a well-groomed man in his forties, came by with an escort of two green Ford Rangers. He sat with us, holding the tea Tam had served as he explained that there had been three people in the car. The scant remains offered few clues, but the car belonged to the school where Justin taught. Justin and Alexandra were missing, as was one of his students, a young man named Idris, who was Justin's driver. The Taliban had tweeted that the victims were killed for immoral contact with the Afghan girls they were subjecting to Western educations. Justin must have been the target, since many mullahs forbade men from teaching girls after puberty, but Alexandra had recently become involved at the school as a mentor, so her death wasn't incidental.

After the officer left, we discussed why the Taliban would bomb a car when they could have stormed the school and killed its teachers and founder, a septuagenarian named Frank Alaric who'd been in Kabul since the American invasion. Tam phoned Frank, offered her condolences, and then mostly listened.

"I would love to do that," she said finally, "but I'm starting a documentary on the US Special Forces. It's a long one ... Yeah, a month of embeds at different bases ... I leave this week, but I'll come see you as soon as I'm back. I'll do a feature. I promise."

Even when grieving, Tam existed to create stories. She hung up and said Frank sounded almost proud to have been targeted. He vowed he'd never shut down his school.

By 2 a.m., the last of our friends had gone, leaving Tam and me alone in the house she'd shared with Alexandra. We decided to get some rest, and in bed she pulled close.

When I'd moved to Kabul, I'd tried to shift from travel writing to journalism, selling pieces to a Tokyo online zine that distributed to cell subscribers. The editors liked having a correspondent in Afghanistan, and I liked the idea of being one. The title served me well, and I sent in short articles about culture and social life, even about conversations overheard in bars.

The people I met in the expat scene — journalists and aid workers who'd spent decades abroad and had personas big enough to contain their restless lives — fascinated me. At parties, we laughed about those who'd become unhinged in their quest for purpose while we quietly worried about our own. I'd been drawn to Tam because I wanted to understand where she found her courage. She was both ruthlessly ambitious and emotionally fragile, and I learned more than I expected from her. After the safe room, I realized what kept her here. I'd seen the attack I'd lived through anatomized in the online news and repeatedly played on CNN. I'd experienced the connection to something bigger that came with living in a war zone.

Tam's bedroom felt hot and closed in, and I had the impulse to get up and shut the *bukhari*'s flue, but the air was cold on my damp skin. I became aware of the house's silence, my heart banging with the desperation of a trapped animal. My thoughts no longer moved in an orderly progression. The vacuum I'd existed in since the attack was gone. The room seemed to contract, the dark thick and smothering.

What I was feeling took its time rising and then did all at once, with a pulse as long and transfixing as a seizure — a sense that something else had to happen, that none of this made sense if it all ended here. The Taliban habitually claimed responsibility for foreign casualties, but the targets of the car bomb and the school itself were inconsequential — trivial in the scope of the war. Justin and Alexandra had also been in the safe room, so the two attacks must be linked. The first had been so substantial and calculated that far more than the lives of two unknown expats had to be at stake. I felt certain there would be another attack.

I was sweating hard. I tried to lie calmly and not wake Tam. The suddenness of my panic terrified me. All along, behind my tranquility, a hidden part of my mind — the autonomous, atavistic kernel of my cognitive organ — had been at work. The incompleteness of the violence felt like jagged edges in my brain.

And then an image came to me — of me setting to work, investigating the event that almost killed me — and my heart began to relax. I was almost back in that awakened, accepting space that I'd briefly thought would be mine forever. The siege during the party and the car bomb had to be pieces of a larger plan that was still in the works. More people could die.

Though I was conscious of the manic energy behind my thoughts, I didn't care: I would uncover the plot behind the attacks and write it into a major story — my first in English, for a big American magazine like *Rolling Stone* or *GQ*. I'd prove the Taliban claim untrue and solve the murders. I'd say something more meaningful than the articles that were instantly published on the heels of carnage, their conclusions interchangeable, their perfunctory insights borrowed from the previous week's news. I would make my readers experience what I had — the way chaos could suddenly engulf a life and the desire for agency that arose from that. Justin's and Alexandra's faces returned to me: the look of mastered stillness that they'd shared was common in Japan.

Tam's breathing slowed. She worked so hard, fueling herself on caffeine, that her sleep was sudden and deep. I slipped my leg from beneath hers, took her wrist, lifted her arm, and placed it on the warm bed. I pulled on my pants and shirt, and let myself out. A USB wall charger gave her forehead a blue, mortuary glow. I carefully closed the door.

I listened, reassuring myself of the silence. My heart had steadied. I wasn't passively awaiting the next attack. This investigation was the only thing I could imagine doing, and my restored equanimity seemed proof that it was the right choice. I crossed the hallway to Alexandra's room.

There seemed to be two kinds of expat dwellings: those that were overdecorated, the concrete walls covered with personal photos, artwork, and movie posters, the bookshelves crammed with novels and DVDs; and those as stark as jail cells, as if being here were doing time, an obligation to society or necessary duty for some future career. Alexandra's was unadorned — plastic on the windows, old rattan blinds lowered, a desk with a laptop, a bed with a blanket and small pillow.

I wanted to touch everything, to slide under the covers. I smelled the clothes hanging in the closet. They held a faint fragrance of lavender, a remnant of fabric softener.

No one had known her well, except as an expert on a subject she'd schooled herself in from a distance. That was part of her allure. But the hint of defensiveness in her suggested she'd fought to prove she was more than her appearance and that accepting admiration would be surrender.

Alexandra's laptop, a very old HP, was open on her desk, and when I touched the mouse, the screen lit up. It had been asleep, not password protected. Maybe she never stopped working and saw no reason to impede her efforts. I began forwarding emails to myself. Years of her typing had worn the letters off the keys, smoothing or hollowing them ever so slightly. I pictured her working with a straight back, too pragmatic to worry about getting a new fashionable computer as long as this one functioned.

I permanently deleted the messages I'd sent to my account, logged out of her email, closed her browser, and shut the computer off, but left it open. Makeup removal wipes were on the dresser, and I ran one over the keyboard. From the bottom desk drawer, I took out a large leather book — a journal. There was also a heavy plastic ring, the kind from gumball machines, and I slid it on my finger. I suddenly felt nauseous. I pulled the chair out too loudly and sat. I held my face, cooling it with the skin of my fingers.

The hand. Where was it? In a bag in a police refrigerator? In the trash? On its way to Montreal? It had to be Alexandra's. I'd barely known her, but I wished I could go back to the circle of men at the site of the car bomb and see the severed hand as more than a sign of the random brutality of war.

A growing awareness of time muted my thoughts, and though I wanted to inspect every pen, every scrap of paper, to discover more about her and find something that justified my presence here, the risk had become too great.

A nightlight's glow strayed along the wall. I made my way to the bathroom, where I examined the journal, its cover worn dark and scuffed. The entries — some only a line, others pages long — were in French, the dates going back eight years. The printed letters were squarish, tight and determined. I put it on the highest shelf, behind a row of towels. I dropped the wipe in the toilet, flushed it, and turned on the faucet. I was still wearing the blocky ruby-colored ring. I hid it as well and washed my hands. I studied myself in the mirror.

A young Afghan woman once told me, at a party, that even with oppression, sexuality found paths, not because of individual will but because of the laws of nature, like the insistent flow of water or seeds sprouting beneath stones. These were her metaphors. The last few years of my life, negated passions had been rising within me. Until now, I'd never attempted an investigation this big. Though my actions felt urgent — all that stood between me and an imminent, unknown violence — they were also a release from stasis, from waiting for my life to have an objective that mattered.

Tam fit against me as soon as I was back in bed. As with an infidelity, in a few decisions, I'd locked a part of myself away.

THE SCHOOL WAS two stories of rain-streaked concrete. The other buildings on the street hid behind walls, but the school's upper windows were exposed, close enough to throw a stone through, or a grenade. It had been built during the hopeful years I'd heard about, just after the American invasion, and not amended for the hard reality that followed. Despite its modesty, there was arrogance in those two panes of glass — righteous provocation.

Frank looked well past seventy, not just rawboned but meatless, his liver-spotted skin like parchment on an angular skull that might have been handsome encased in flesh. And yet he had the glow and gravity of a man facing terrible odds, the authority of one who has been the target of America's enemies. He smiled as I came in the door, his hand wrapping mine, transmitting by touch an anatomical sense of bone and tendon.

When I'd called and told him I was doing a feature on the personal missions of expats who'd lost their lives, I'd expected him to be wary, but he'd appeared eager to talk, less about

Justin and Alexandra than about his school — to make it sound worthy of their deaths.

He walked, gesturing into rooms, tapping his steel-frame glasses into place with the knuckle of his index finger as he told me about the free classes offered and how he was creating a future for Afghanistan. His violet shirt betrayed few suggestions of the body beneath and, if not for the belt cinching his slacks, might have flapped like a sail. His gaze was direct, appraising, unapologetic; he had the smile of one accustomed to sales and elections.

"This is the office. Just a sec."

Seven teenage girls sat, glancing from beneath headscarves to determine whether I was Hazara. Frank checked his laptop, on a desk right in the middle of theirs, and I tried to make sense of this aging American man surrounded by Afghan girls. From speaking with Alexandra, I knew the place was a prep school of sorts, where Frank handpicked high school– and college-age girls and the occasional boy for his program. He led me next door to another office and motioned to a folding metal chair.

From the way he looked at me, I could tell he was seeing a demure Japanese, not a *bijin* — I am far from that — but maybe a hint of the *ojoosama*, the naiveté of the *hakoiri musume*, and above all the patient *ryosai kenbo*, the part of our tradition that, in step and posture, evokes the values of service, embodied, as we believed for centuries and still largely believe, in a woman. I let my headscarf slip. The skin around my eyes relaxed. I didn't employ this skill often, but I'd seen it used daily in Tokyo.

"I don't know what to tell you about Justin," Frank said, though his demeanor called to mind a sprinter at the starting line. "When I interviewed him for the job, I played skeptic. If someone can't convince you he should be doing something, he has no business doing it. But he was too convincing, the kind of kid who should have had his own school and been playing by his own rules. I said yes only because this place needs classes morning to night. We need to be a factory in the best sense of the word."

Frank faltered, his hand hanging between us like a pale spider. The moment increased in focus as if a faint incandescence gathered in the room. What I'd sensed — the story — it was here. Frank wasn't searching for words. He was trying to restrain himself. I nodded, my headscarf slipping a little more.

"'America,' Justin told me, 'is asleep. We have no clue where we're going or why we're doing what we're doing. Half of us say we need to reclaim what we lost, and the other half say we need to forget about it and move on, but neither of those options are any good. I can't use a gun, so I figure I might as well educate as many kids as possible.'

"'That's the way to do it,' I placated him, and he said he'd read that every insurgent we shoot inspires five more, and every one we educate will make five less. I agreed it was a plausible theory. I suspected he was a kid who'd done well but had reached the point where whatever had driven him still anchored him. He'd come to the end of his chain like a dog running across a yard. It had to hurt. I saw this in people. I'd felt it myself. Why else does a man come back from Vietnam, spend decades building businesses and selling them, marry a good woman and have four daughters, and then, when he's supposed to retire, pick up and head back to a war zone? After that first war I'd seen so much destruction I was hungry to go home and build, and after thirty-some years I'd evened things out and there wasn't enough destruction left in my memory to keep me building. So I came to Afghanistan. My wife remarried. She did so four years ago.

It took her five to realize I wasn't coming back. My daughters have all exceeded my expectations, and I have another decade of raising girls here."

Frank adjusted his glasses.

"For the first few years," he said, "I helped run the American University of Afghanistan, but the vision was buried in the details. There's nothing wrong with grammar and math, and I know it takes time to nail all that down, but a country needs more than translators and accountants. I kept thinking about a school built on a vision. Who wouldn't be changed just by sitting and talking to a man who'd been through war and who'd invested in society? An entrepreneur who'd played a hand in his country's local politics? I remember one day asking myself: What's the worst that can happen? And having the thought: some talented young people will get to learn from me.

"So I rented this place from two expats who went home. That's when expats were beginning to leave. The golden days of the occupation were ending. Everyone was ready to drop what they were doing and run. The nice thing about being seventy-five is you get gunned down in the streets of Kabul and you die happy. I've had a fuller life than anyone I know.

"Since then, I've brought in more than two dozen volunteers, most of them just staying the three months of their visas and teaching what they could, when it suited them. But Justin was sending me syllabi and curricula before he even arrived."

Frank chuckled — a dry, mirthless sound in his throat.

"I remember his look when he walked in here. 'If it were an ivory tower,' I told him, 'we wouldn't need you.' He just asked where his room was and who was responsible for what, and we've all had headaches ever since. Until a few days ago, I guess. Well, no, the car bomb, that's been the biggest headache of all."

Frank hesitated, guilt obscuring his glow of pride. He no longer seemed so primed to voice his conflicts with a recently dead man.

"Would you like to see his room?" he asked.

"Yes, please."

He led me to the door and opened it for me. I stepped in and turned.

"Can I have a moment alone?"

His small bloodshot eyes focused in on me briefly from behind his glasses.

"You knew him?"

"I did."

"Well, I don't see why not. I'll just be in my office."

I closed the door and breathed. I needed a moment after Frank's oration. I'd felt caught in its rhythm as the story poured out of him.

I sat on the bed and placed my hand at the compressed center of the foam mattress. The closet shelf held a bottle of contact lens solution, a hand mirror, and neatly folded shirts, pants, and underwear, their colors dark. On the desk: books on pedagogy, English as a second language. A Bible lay on the sill. A notepad was empty except for a Kabul phone number that I copied. His laptop was shut. A drawer with pens also held a 32 gig zip drive.

I took the drive and paused. His room was even plainer than Alexandra's, the line where the tile floor met the concrete wall uninterrupted but for the unadorned desk and bed. Had he lived with the minimum so he could test his loyalty to the spirit? His brief relationship with Alexandra made little sense. He'd appeared less a lover than a priestly chaperone.

Frank was waiting in his office, stick-thin legs crossed, one hand holding his glasses, his mouth chewing with a ratlike motion on the part that hooked over the ear. The plastic had been gnawed off, the metal serrated with teeth marks.

"Justin wanted to save the boy," he told me as soon as I sat.

"The boy?"

"Idris. Most of the students here are girls, but we do have a few boys. Justin and Idris were usually together. Idris was there when that party was attacked."

I had no memory of Idris in the safe room, though I did recall from other occasions the young Afghan man who'd driven Justin around Kabul.

"Idris was in the car," Frank said. "At least that's what the police told me."

"He and Justin were friends?"

"Well, that's not quite right. Justin thought he could be Idris's savior, and Idris used him." Frank was speaking more deliberately. "That's how he met Clay."

"Clay?"

"Clay and Justin were old friends, from Louisiana." Frank pursed his lips, wrinkles bunching around his mouth.

"What does Clay have to do with the car bomb?"

"Clay disappeared that day as well. The company he worked for thought he'd been kidnapped. They checked the security feed outside his compound. It showed him getting into the car with Justin and Alexandra and" — Frank looked me in the eyes now, as if to say he needed to tell somebody and had no one else — "and Idris. Idris was driving. But there were only three bodies, what remained of them anyway. The security company never went to the police. They asked me not to in a, well, not very friendly way."

"If you will permit me," I said, "I would like to approach the security company."

"You?" Frank stared at the ashen carpet cut to fit below his desk and chair, to damper the cold from the concrete.

This was the story I'd been looking for. Clay's presence in the car with Justin and Alexandra reinforced my conviction that the bomb wasn't Taliban retribution for teaching girls.

"Did you know them all well?" I asked.

"Clay not so much, but Alexandra a little more. I met her through Justin. I asked her to come and speak to the girls. We need female mentors. I'd go so far as to say . . . well, no . . ."

"Pardon me?" I eased my tone, sounding confused and in need of guidance, concealing my excitement that Tam would be doing an embed and everything I'd just learned was mine.

"If you ask me — I'd never go on record with this, but — she's the tragedy. The others . . ." He shrugged. "Anyway, I hope you have all you need from me for your article. The bit about the security company is off the record. Don't mention my name to them. But if you have other questions or if you find something out, just come by whenever."

"Thank you," I said, wondering if he would ask me to be a mentor as well.

He walked me downstairs. The school's driveway was empty, and we went out the gate and stood in the street. I'd imagined Justin and Alexandra propelled by their missions, reeling incautiously toward a point of combustion, but the story was more complicated.

"Why," I asked, "did Justin think he had to save Idris?"

Frank's jaw went crooked. "Everybody who comes here believes he's got to save someone. I remember telling him, you don't fix a country overnight. It must have been his third day. He was already assigning homework, and the girls complained to me. I told him they were too busy for homework. They all had jobs, accounting for a pharmacy or a clinic, translating and typing. 'Think in decades,' I said."

He appeared to be trying to pick up where he'd left off in his monologue, to regain the conviction to finish the polemic he'd been harboring so he could drive his verdict home. But he'd waited too long. He fumbled at his pocket and took out his wallet, as though to pay for my taxi. He pinched at a worn leather fold, removed a card, and extended it to me.

"You know," he said, half his face contracted as he squinted off down the muddy street, "people tell me I've had a good run and it's time to head home, that I'll be next. But that's how you lose a war. You turn tail. You show them their barbaric tactics work. So let them target me. What was it Tennyson said of the aging Ulysses? *Made weak by time and fate, but strong in will.* I know what I'm doing, and so did Alexandra. She told me that everyone she worked with talked women's rights and wrote up reports, but had almost no contact with Afghan women other than a few who came through the office. She wasn't the one visiting the prisons and seeing the abuses. Meeting the girls here changed her. She said that Afghan women aren't as weak as people think, and she was right. The strongest women I've ever met have studied in this school, and if I have to die to see that they have their freedom, that's a small price to pay."

At that, he blinked and lifted his gaunt palm, and I got in the taxi. As it pulled away, I inspected the card. On its back, a number was written, the pen strokes angular and uneven, like tiny cuts, but too wet, blotting. I flipped it over. Printed in a stern font were two more numbers, an email, and a name: *Steve Hammond.*

ALL THAT WEEK, Kabul was quiet — traffic jams and construction and impromptu checkpoints, but quiet nonetheless. Spring
arrived in sunlit days. Afternoon showers stripped dust and
smog from the air, and tamped it into the earth. The nights
hovered at freezing: brittle stars, drafts at windows, and the
creaking of metal as the fire took in my *bukhari*.

I sat next to it, working my way through Alexandra's scuffed
journal with the help of an iPhone French-English dictionary
and Google Translate, searching for what compelled her into a
love triangle like a Wild West standoff between a hayseed missionary and a gun for hire. In expats' speculation about who
had died, Clay was absent, and I enjoyed his mystery as I read
her entries, anticipating his arrival.

During high school, I studied French. Its sound evokes
refinement for the Japanese. My professor said the history of
France and Japan is a love story between aesthetics, each finding in the other the embodiments of ideals. But I knew nothing
about French Canadians.

Je n'ai pas le choix, she wrote before leaving Montreal for
Kabul. "I have no choice. I have to go. I am afraid. I have no
affinity to that place or its people, but going will help me move
on." The dramatic tone surprised me. I said the first line out
loud: "I have no choice." Tyranny is a poor metaphor for inter-
nal struggle, and yet it was a feeling we shared.

In Justin's emails to Alexandra, he described the importance of educators in the civilian surge, whereas she was more
interested in justice for women. They sounded intoxicated with
their ideas, as if, in the space of writing them, they'd transformed Afghanistan.

His emails mentioned Idris: *If we're going to create change,
we need to change those in power. The men have power. We must*

not marginalize them . . . He wrote about Frank: *He believes he can shape a culture by choosing its leaders; rather, its leaders must choose us. They must see in us a representation of values they can aspire to.*

Though I'd intended to pen a seminal article and expose the plot that nearly took my life, I read with a growing sense that I was onto something bigger: a tale of power and a doorway into America, where all passions seemed justified.

Hour by hour, the reasons for my interest seemed to rise up, promising and bright on the horizon, before evanescing like mirages. When I'd come to Kabul, I'd planned to become a war correspondent. I read Ernie Pyle, and longed for World War II's grit and simple glory, a clear enemy, two options: heroic victory or destruction, not endless games of attrition played in secret. I read Michael Herr: *you couldn't find two people who agreed about when it began . . . might as well say that Vietnam was where the Trail of Tears was headed all along . . .*

And yet, as I learned about Justin, Alexandra, and Clay, my imagination nourished their stories with the journeys and characters in the American novels I'd grown up reading. Increasingly, I pictured myself writing in that form. I was fortunate to have a mystery, a plot, a missing person, maybe even a murderer.

That evening, Tam came over. She'd been preparing for her Special Forces embed, doing paperwork and preliminary interviews on bases in Kabul while wrapping up edits for previous projects. Each time I saw her, she talked about Alexandra's death. She never mentioned Clay, only Justin's obsession with Idris, his conviction that Frank was using him. "But what disgruntled student embarks on a suicide mission?" she asked. She, too, was skeptical of the Taliban's claim — unless Justin had been proselytizing. Converting a Muslim was one of the worst offences here.

Kabul was a haven for conspiracies. Sooner or later expats explained away even the most random killing. If a Westerner was shot, a rumor arose that he was feeding information to an embassy or a diplomat, and someone put out a hit. If the deceased was a journalist, people said his writing had been critical of a warlord, when in truth it was hard to write anything about Afghanistan without mentioning warlords or being critical. Some days, we agreed on the incompetence of the Afghan security forces. Others, we believed they had precise information about everyone and would do anything to maintain the status quo, even kill us.

The conspiracies gave us the sense that we were players in a vast intrigue whose chaos hid its order. In this way, they made us feel safe. If we accepted that much of what happened was random, how could we go out our front doors? We repeated stories that stripped others of their innocence so as to enshrine our own and live more fully in its protection.

If I told Tam about my investigations, she would think I was encroaching on her territory, but just gathering this information and building it into a story diminished the uncertainty I sensed around me.

Embers glowed inside the *bukhari*'s open hatch. Beyond the compound wall, an engine raced, tires spinning loudly against the ice.

I closed my eyes. Bodies immolated, blown apart. What made everyone so sure of who was in the car? Did the police simply count the pieces? Death was too common here for them to do more than that.

I stroked Tam's hair until she fell asleep. I traced her throat, her collarbone. She drew closer, pressing against me, breathing softly.

I OFTEN REPLAYED the attack in my head, a looping reel the details of which I sorted through to determine who I'd seen before and after we'd gone into the safe room.

Once we were locked inside, Steve Hammond told us he used the room to showcase his product: a lounge space insulated in every way, with AC and Wi-Fi, a bathroom, liquor cabinet, and iPad console, a TV to monitor the outside from wide-angle cameras, and an iron door embedded in the wall, impervious to light explosives.

"Is this a setup?" Tam asked. "Are you staging this to make us buy one of these?"

"I'm sold," the young German called out. "When can I move in?"

No one laughed. Justin and Alexandra remained entranced by the screen. They didn't comfort each other, and they didn't accept the Scotch. There was something private and reverential in their attention to what was happening outside.

The Afghan Special Forces had staked positions in the yard, and Steve switched cameras so that one moment we were watching the soldiers shooting into a dark window and the next we saw the insurgent crouched just inside as bullets blasted grooves in its frame.

"Shall we place bets on which one lasts the longest?" Steve asked and turned back to the room. "Aw, come on. Is this how you want to live — huddled up like rats?"

"We have to name them first," Tam said.

The insurgent threw a grenade into the yard, and the soldiers leapt for cover.

"Jesus!" someone cried out in a breathy, terrified voice.

"Okay," Steve told us. "That one's clearly Jesus. They could be twins except for the body armor. What about this guy?" He switched channels.

"Moses," Tam replied. This was typical Kabul humor, at once proof and negation of the human spirit.

"And number three?" Steve asked.

"I know, I know," the German called out, "how about —"

"No!" we interrupted, drowning out his voice.

"But there are no Afghans here," he said.

"Have some respect, you fuckin' infidel," Steve told him.

"How about Elijah?" Tam suggested.

Everyone agreed, habituated enough to the circumstances to put down twenty dollars on the insurgent of choice. I picked Elijah because he held back and let the other two take risks. As Jesus was rigging up explosives on the steel door at the bottom of the stairs, he caught a bullet in the throat and detonated them. This time we felt it: the lights flickered and there was one less camera, the others capturing only drifting smoke. Although Jesus had been a favorite, no one was thinking about the heap of twenties.

Lana Del Rey hadn't stopped singing, now crooning "National Anthem." Steve went to the iPad mounted on the wall, brought up her image — that classic retro mug shot — and changed the song to "Born to Die."

For an hour, the last two Taliban held out as the Special Forces worked their way inside. The German, an aspiring videographer, mourned not having his gear and recorded with his phone, asking questions like, "Do you regret your decision to take a job here?" and "What are you feeling right now?" He was repeatedly told to fuck off until Steve — who paused from switching between feeds that revealed his home being system-atically disfigured — simply said, "Come on, mate, quit being a cunt."

The terrified people were eating up the bandwidth, tweet-ing and IMing, making work hard for the journalists who were seeing their Afghanistan payout. A young American named Holly, who was often at social outings and worked at a shelter that rehabilitated Afghan street dogs, bawled on Skype with her mother, saying she loved her, though the line kept cutting out.

"Tell her the connection is overloaded," Tam said. "Each time the call drops, she probably thinks you've been killed."

"Tell your mommy the bad guys will be dead soon enough," Steve reassured her. "Have a drink before it's all gone and, hell, sit back and enjoy the show. You'll never see another one like it."

Though the attackers were just outside the safe room, the gunfire sounded more distant than I'd expected.

Steve's coolness gradually waned. Maybe the show had gone on longer than he'd planned. To calm his guests, he anatomized the door: a ten-inch-thick slab, essentially an iron box filled with concrete and sliding on ball bearings in an iron frame built into the wall.

He unlocked the metal trunk that served as a coffee table. It held four handguns and three short rifles. He gave a rifle to Clay and to another contractor, and asked who else knew how to shoot. Tam said she used to go to firing ranges with an ex in the States. The woman who'd had glass in her eye told us that as a teenager she came in second in the state fair for skeet shooting.

"These aren't skeet," Steve told her, "and adrenaline is a dif-ferent game." He handed her a pistol, the people near her inch-ing away. Tam and two men also took guns.

We arranged the couches into a barrier. On the screen, Elijah was setting up explosives on our door. We crouched shoulder to shoulder behind those of us holding weapons. Everyone had gone pale. Someone began throwing up in the bathroom. Justin was praying, and Alexandra was looking at Clay as if she'd put her bet on him.

Two members of the Special Forces crept in from the living room and got Elijah under crossfire. There was a resonant boom. The floor shook, reverberations clapping in the room. Our ears rang and a little smoke rose from under the door.

"I told you we were safe," Steve said.

The people who had money on Moses tried to divvy up the pot, but their hands shook so badly they kept dropping the bills until they finally gave up and hugged each other.

"Imagine," Tam said, "they could have cleaned out twenty foreigners in one go."

My mind refused to consider what had just happened. I was too busy forming memories that instantly seemed like artifacts. But four days later, after talking to Frank, I studied those memories: the young German attempting his blasphemous joke and then insisting there were no Afghans, and Tam making her comment about how many foreigners would have died. Idris, who was supposed to have driven Justin to the party, definitely wasn't there.

When the last Taliban fell beneath a volley of bullets, we cheered.

The whiskey was gone and Steve told someone to crack the gin. We poured it in cups and knocked it back.

"Finish the gin! Finish the gin!" I'm not sure who started the chant, but even Holly drank. She was crying uncontrollably. On the screen, the security forces were scanning the building, carefully moving through. We clapped as Holly shook and wept and tipped the cup back, gin dribbling from her chin and spotting her shirt. Weeks later, I would hear her at L'Atmos, where she stood at the bar and described the firefight as the greatest thrill of her life.

I think it dawned on all of us then, as we turned from Holly to the door, that we would have to open it and walk out and see the granular images from the screen become flesh, the remains of men who'd died or blown themselves to pieces.

Steve was smiling, his hand on the lock.

PART 2

KABUL: JANUARY/MARCH 2012

美智子

EACH TIME I left my apartment after the attack, I felt the city in a way I hadn't before — its hunger, that primordial urge become urban panic. People charged, tromped, scurried with postures of determination, drudgery, or rage. Men full as ticks passed others so thin muscles twined bones, their loose, ragged clothes not masking the inequity, their profiles like glyphs. They were on their own trajectories and hardly noticed me. I saw that now.

Where the asphalt ended, I followed the dirt road up through the square, earth-colored houses crowding TV Hill — one of the ridges above Kabul, its slope a suburban ziggurat and its summit loaded with the eponymous antennae and red-and-white striped communications towers.

I was here without another expat or Afghan — friend, interpreter, or fixer — and I didn't squint down at Taimani and find my house, measuring the time it would take to backtrack to that speck of walled safety.

I sat on a stone with a splotch of white paint on its edge, a marker from demining years back. Wind whistled through the transmission towers, and the sun bore down out of a winter blue sky. *Azan* echoed over the rooftops, the *muezzin* shrill in the minaret speakers. At dusk, Kabul coalesced inside its geologic cauldron, headlights sparking, wide avenues cutting it into provinces, into eras, divides as clear as evening's shadow from the mountains.

I never intended to come to Afghanistan. It's odd how little we learn from experiences and choices, that we can wake up in Afghanistan and go about our days, forgetting that something of consequence had driven or lured us. Our paths of longing rarely lead where we expect. I used to think I had nothing in common with my mother, but eventually I realized that I shared her frustration, her inability to belong to the world she craved.

She wanted to be part of respectable society. She spoke rarely, so I never knew what set her alienation into motion. Solitude, I'd learned as a child, is not a static state in a singular element, but a movement, even a journey, that can go in as many directions as we imagine.

My mother was born in 1964, a reckless child of the economic boom that seemed to be lifting Japan toward global economic domination. I never met my grandparents. She raised me in a one-bedroom apartment in Tokyo and worked nights as a hostess. Her job seemed respectable when I read about it in magazines and discovered that a few hostesses had become celebrities of a sort. I was relieved to learn that hostesses weren't prostitutes, though some people perceived them as such. Maybe her career explained the familial rupture, or maybe she'd found her job after a fall from grace. She did go on dates with certain clients, and on occasion she didn't come home. I suspect she desired a few of her suitors. Their gifts piled up: fur coats, jewelry, chocolates, and perfume.

I was raised like an envoy back to the people she'd lost. She managed my outfits and schooling, helped me with my homework. As I got older, I realized how educated she was. That was the reason wealthy men wanted to relax in her company as she poured drinks and discussed politics and history. Even as her beauty faded, her mastery of the art of listening and polite conversation retained its value.

She never told me I was different. The Japanese are conditioned to find discordance, and it was from children at school that I learned I was *haafu*. I asked my mother what it meant, and she explained that, yes, my father was American. Who was he? Where was he? Could I find him? These were questions I asked for years. But she knew little. He'd grown up in California, lived in New York, and visited Tokyo. She'd been nineteen and had met him in a club. He was a *wan naito sutando* — a one-night stand.

As if to console me, she said that children with mixed blood were often stars in Japan, models and actors — symbols of beauty. When we walked in the street, she pointed to posters of women advertising clothes or shampoo, and at the magazine covers on the racks.

When I was nine, I realized that *haafu* was the Japanese pronunciation of *half*. I had made English my passion and felt a sense of ownership over the language. I was drawn to it before it was offered in school. I watched English TV, read magazines and eventually novels. I was soon better at speaking English than my teachers. But science, my mother told me, over and over, was life's highest calling, and languages would not earn me the respect I deserved.

When I got a little older, I sensed another difference within me. There was a misalignment of desire that I couldn't verbalize but felt in the way I gravitated toward girls, how talk of boys didn't interest me. The girls ignored me, sensing they weren't entering into an alliance for a mutual goal but were the goal themselves. Just as my mother wasn't part of the society she craved — though she could evoke it to the satisfaction of power-ful men in hostess bars — I saw my people in American novels and TV shows, and counted my days.

To please my mother, I excelled in science, through uni-versity and into a respectable job, synthesizing lab reports on DNA studies. One day I learned that she'd been writing letters to her parents for years, and one had finally been answered. They wanted to meet. We had a long tense dinner at which a gray-haired man with pouches below his eyes asked me about my work. My mother had two siblings whose photos were on the walls, and I learned about them and my successful cousins. Hearing my mother and grandparents speak, I realized what I should have long before — that I was her fall from grace, that the family's last shared memories dated to her pregnancy.

After dinner, at her home, she wept, thanking me, and then I went back to the apartment I'd recently moved into. The next day I couldn't get out of bed, couldn't go to work. All my life I'd lived under the weight of something I was unable to name, an array of fears — of difference and failure — and now I saw that my life was invalid in my culture. My story — if it were to be told — was that of a mistake attempting redemption.

After a week, I accepted that I could no longer pretend. I slept and spoke to no one, and in the times when my mind cleared, I read American stories — of defiance and adventure for the sake of self-invention. Until then, my fate had been to fashion myself in an image established by a society under the domination of toad-like old men with teenage mistresses and three-thousand-dollar suits. I craved leaving behind the hyp-ocrisy and setting out for a frontier where I could prove that my confused beginnings were the prologue to something great.

Of course, when I did cross the Pacific, to San Francisco,

the place I found was no frontier. The America I'd composed in my brain was a country of the past: the memories or inventions of dead authors. I was frightened by the uncertainty before me and realized how much fear I'd been harboring, how much it had locked me into my previous life. Every decision now was laden with expectation and consequence, and yet I gradually realized that when I was making the decisions, selecting my challenges, the apprehension that had overshadowed my life became manageable.

Though I floated through my travels, my choices at each juncture encouraged me. Exploring the West Coast, I wrote travel pieces, mapping the area by its tourist venues, trendy hotspots, and gentrified streets.

As my writing found an audience in Japan, I was offered assignments abroad. I composed testimonies to the luxury of a new generation of Gulf State hotels, or the splendor of parks in Africa and Asia. When an editor asked if I would go to Afghanistan, my dread seemed to erase me, and this compelled me to confront it — to let it purge me of myself.

I was hired to write about Bamiyan, one of Afghanistan's safest provinces and the historic home of the Hazara people I resembled. When I arrived there, at an altitude of eight thousand feet, the spring air was cold and the trees barely budding. I visited cathedral-high niches in the cliffs, where the Taliban had dynamited the ancient towering Buddha statues, and I climbed to the crumbling mountaintop turrets of Shahr-e-Zohak, the red fort at the entrance to the Bamiyan valley. I visited Afghanistan's first national park, Band-e-Amir, a chasm holding six sapphire lakes separated by natural travertine dams.

In the guesthouse, listening to journalists and NGO workers on R&R from Kabul tell stories, I felt a twinge of recognition, as if the characters from the novels I'd grown up reading had appeared in the flesh. What I found familiar wasn't just their love of adventure — that is universal enough — but an obsession with testing boundaries and reinvention. They sounded excited by their own words — the experiences they described not finished but still having effect on them, like a catalyzed chemical process or an initiated life cycle.

A few days later, in Kabul, as I met more expats in cafés, bars, and hotels, my impression grew, a sense that they had stepped out of history's shadow and knew it — that their thoughts and actions actually mattered. They seemed aware of their fears, capable of describing them, and yet able to survive here. I delayed my flight, found a room among expats, then a studio apartment, and my articles began edging away from the subject of travel.

For a year, as I navigated unease in my new environment, the dangers of daily life illuminated parts of my old self that I hated. The attack on the safe room forced me beyond a fear so old it was a current — a river I had always swam against, moving closer to its source. I found myself in a quiet, powerless space, where what *was* was: material, unmoved by my mind, unclouded by emotions and ideas. In the weeks after, tiny pieces of glass emerged from my body, from my knees, from my palms, from healing cuts I'd barely noticed.

In the dusk, as Kabul's lights came on, I decided that I'd sufficiently tested my courage. I made my way down rainwater gullies or in the dirty patches of snow to keep from slipping, moving aside for a taxi struggling home, its mismatched yellow and white panels rattling.

I called my *chowkidar*, the guard who cared for the apartments in my compound, and asked him to light my *bukhari*. By the time I arrived, the studio was warm, and I sat at my desk.

When my job had been to read reports of genetic studies, I'd seen so much of what makes us human broken down to code: the impulse to love or hurt, the lust for dominance and conquest. As I read imagined lives crossing the American continent, I recognized the workings of our heritage, the ticking of destiny in hungers and needs, our insatiable quest to claim more territory and dominate others in every way possible, even if under the banner of civilization, or salvation.

Though I understood that we create fictions to transform the perpetual rising of animal desire into human stories of fulfillment, I struggled to give myself the authority to invent. And yet I'd reached the limits of journalism. Reading about Alexandra, Justin, and Clay, I had the sense that I'd come to a forgotten temple in a dusty, ruined America and, while trying to decipher the civilization portrayed there, had seen the same figures repeatedly etched upon a wall: characters like those I'd read about since I was a child, the bearers of a language, as if, in a myth, they'd met me at a river and taken me across, illuminating the dark country beyond with their bodies.

Among the copious Word files on Justin's zip drive — most of them syllabi and curricula — was one entitled "Notes," a record of his life in the form of — I didn't see this right away — sermons. He revealed glimpses of his life behind biblical lessons: boarding a plane in Dubai, excited by the brightness of the sky. It seemed that he harbored ambitions as a preacher and thought his life might be a source of inspiration. The prose was so overwrought that reading it felt like spying on him through a dense jungle.

The story I found there was a personal fiction of omissions — guilt and obligation whose origins were not mentioned — and as I sat at my laptop, I hunted these blank spots in my mind. Though he had no impact on what happened in the safe room — made none of the memorable remarks — he was the least incidental of those who might have been in the car. Without him, Clay and Alexandra wouldn't have met, nor Idris and Clay.

He remains clear to me from the safe room, handsomely indifferent despite the judgments on him or from him — he disapproved of almost everyone and was considered a pedant and zealot. He had short auburn hair, sun-bleached to red in places, and a beard as abundant as those of the men outside to kill us. Though the beard and square cut of his hair drew attention to his nose, making it appear long and vaguely prophetic, it wasn't an unusual nose in itself, and faint rosy spots on his cheeks suggested that, shaved, he'd look like a boy.

He echoed this perception in his notes, wishing to see his reflection in the plane window as he neared Kabul, afraid he lacked poise, and at once knowing that his readiness depended only on his faith. This is how he comes back to me, peering into the window to see my evocation of a face shining as if lit in a niche, staring in thrall, craving what he saw.

JUSTIN

IN COUNTLESS CYCLES, a dream sequence that refused to finish, the plane turned, the horizon's curve glowing the saturated blue of an LCD screen. Justin leaned close to the window.
It must be time. He had a sense of floating, motionless above
the gray field.

Over the intercom, the pilot explained they were circling
high above Kabul, waiting for the cloud ceiling to lift. Every
few minutes, the airliner tilted as it turned, windows on one
side going dark as those across the aisle brightened, silhouet-
ting turbaned heads and beards.

The discharge from Justin's sinuses worsened. He blew his
nose. The two men who'd begun the flight next to him had
found seats farther up. Across the aisle, a bulky man with a
mop of beard glared.

The blue vanished, dense clouds battered past the small passenger jet, and altitude losses jolted the wings. The landing gear
dropped, the wind shear palpable as Justin's seatbelt tightened
against his hips. The plane vibrated through rough air like a car
going over a rumble strip.

He checked his mind for fear. His arrival was only a way-
point. Death would be meaningless. If he trusted the knowledge that came to him in the seconds between waking and full
consciousness, or in that confluence of daydream and vision,

he would have the years he needed for everything he'd lived to have meaning.

At the front of the cabin, a cell bleeped: the text message alert of an early Nokia no longer used in America, a repeated double pinging that had become of another era within a decade. One by one, throughout the plane, other cells echoed — two, four, almost a dozen — so that, though clouds gusted and muscled at the window, he knew the ground was just below.

Brown lines of wet roads appeared in glimpses, framed by dirty snow. A white hill emerged then dissolved in mist. The city's sprawl came into focus, two-dimensional at first, thousands of square rooftops in a maze of streets. The wheels thudded, the wing flaps went up, the plane rocked and then pushed hard against the tarmac.

Buckles clicked and men crowded the aisle to open overhead bins as the plane slowed, as if they were on a bus. They pulled out their bags, their beards angled upward. Some shouted into cells.

The edges of his nostrils burned. As the others were rushing out, he touched the drink napkin to his nose and stood. In the aisle, a black cloth lay in a heap. He stooped and lifted it, a headscarf maybe. The material felt smooth and synthetic between his fingers.

Just inside the airport, a woman stopped as the men hurried past, a few of them looking her over. Her back was to Justin, her brown hair cut below her shoulders. His sinuses ached, and he blew his nose.

He passed her and turned. He'd been told not to speak to Afghan women in public. She stared slightly up and beyond the ceiling, her black eyes unfocused. It took him a moment to realize that they seemed so dark only because her pupils were dilated. The thin rings of her irises were actually amber. One of her hands lingered at her shoulder, her fingers in her hair.

Did you drop this?

She focused on him, her pupils contracting. She was breathing fast.

Oui! Merci. Thank you. It is mine.

You're French?

She took the scarf carefully, appearing at odds to control her fingers, and looped it over her head.

Québécoise. Thank you for finding this. I just realized.

As they walked together, Justin's apprehension faded. He made himself confident to reassure her. Only his cold undermined his arrival.

What brought you to Afghanistan? she asked.

I'm volunteering at a school. A prep school, basically.

Side by side, like a couple, they approached the officer checking passports. They had their fingerprints scanned, headshots taken, and passports stamped. Her passport was Canadian. Why hadn't she said that?

Outside the open doors of the baggage claim, the wet parking lot was threaded with melting snow. Men stood packed together at the inert conveyor belt. Justin asked what she did.

I'm a lawyer. I have a contract with an organization that defends women in prisons.

The conveyor began to chug and creak. His headache had worsened, and his back ached.

I'm finishing my doctorate in education, he told her. At the University of Houston. I was offered an academic director position here.

He didn't want her to think he was just a volunteer, but he disliked how his words came out. He hadn't meant to cut her off to state his superior credentials. The sense of the journey he'd lived through his prayers grew distant. He should be able to follow the truth without needing to tell another.

When they'd retrieved their bags, they walked out together, following the Afghans who pulled their suitcases across a road and through a gate into a parking lot where groups of people waited: families, women in headscarves, and taxi drivers, many of them in Western dress. Those in *shalwar kameez* had chosen tan or brown, a few blue. No one was in black, and none of the foreigners — except Justin — were dressed like locals.

Is it okay for us to be talking in public? she asked.

I don't see why not.

Is this your first time?

As he said yes, she glanced down at his black Afghan tunic. With a few steps, she put space between herself and him, as if realizing he was not only new here, but possibly dangerous.

The sudden shifts in her carriage — the lengthening of her stride, the redressing of her shoulders and neck — gave her the air of someone on a routine visit. Lifted, her forehead was clear. There were faint determined lines on either side of her mouth, like those of a woman who didn't want to be disturbed.

A man wearing a casual suit and trim goatee approached her and extended his hand. His accent was faintly British.

Ms. Alexandra Desjardins, welcome. I am Hamid. Please let me take your bag.

She thanked him and then observed Justin warily. Hamid was poised, appearing ready to lunge between them.

It was a pleasure meeting you, Justin told her.

Yes. Good luck. She smiled with only her mouth — her pupils suddenly tiny, her irises thin golden bands — before walking away.

A few taxi drivers called to Justin. Through a growing buzz of adrenaline, he realized how cold he felt, his jacket much too light.

IN THE DAYS before his flight, Justin had perfected his appearance: a fist of beard, close-cropped hair, and the black *shalwar kameez*. Ahmad, the Dari teacher he'd found on Craigslist, a grocery bagger at Whole Foods, had stood next to him before the mirror at the tailor's.

You will do very well, Ahmad had said.

Justin was still confusing the *shalwar* and the *kameez*, one part of the outfit loose pants with narrow ankles, the other a tunic that hung to his knees. As he studied himself in the mirror, he envisioned his arrival in Kabul: his calm blue eyes contrasting with the auburn beard.

During his layover in Frankfurt, he began to sniffle. By Dubai, his nose was stuffed. On the flight to Kabul, his back muscles ached. When he took his window seat, the young Afghan next to him smiled. He wore black jeans, an ornate leather jacket, and had gel in his hair — clearly the son of an affluent family. Justin pictured himself having dinners with them, discussing politics and the parallels between Islam and Christianity. He tried out his Dari — *Chettor hasten?*

Khub hastam, the young man replied and then switched to English. Do you lift weights?

Yes, but only to stay in shape.

Then you must know Hamidullah Shirzai? He is one of Afghanistan's great bodybuilders. There is a film about him. I believe he must also be famous in America now.

Justin's sinuses throbbed with the drumbeat of his heart. Discharge stung the edges of his nostrils, gumming up his mustache. He put a drink napkin to his nose and blew.

The young man went rigid. He stood, walked up the aisle, and leaned to speak with other passengers. Afghans glanced back at Justin. By the time the plane landed, he was alone in his row.

He'd imagined his arrival as a new beginning, but now, feverish, he could see only risks: that he wouldn't be able to communicate, that he'd be harassed for being an American, or even kidnapped — or that the Taliban would shoot down the airliner. How could it be safe to land in the capital around which America's longest war had been spiraling for years?

As Justin waited in the parking lot, he thought how reassuringly familiar Alexandra had been — even if she was French and from Canada, a country that called to mind only his father's stories about Vietnam and the men who escaped north to flee the draft.

He began to shiver, his muscles like icepacks.

Mr. Justin?

The young man wore jeans, and a belted jacket hung on his frame like a bathrobe. He had the starved look common to people who hadn't recovered from being underfed as children.

Yes. That's me.

I am Idris. Mr. Frank sent me.

If not so thin, Idris would be striking with his black hair, his cleft chin with a few sparse hairs, his unwavering dark eyes set against milk-pale skin.

You had a good voyage?

Long but good, Justin lied as they crossed the parking lot to a white Corolla. The car had mud all over it: on its panels, on the bottom of the trunk where he put his bags, on the floorboards. He'd expected dust, and the mud's familiarity felt intrusive.

Idris pulled onto the main thoroughfare, the lanes packed with jockeying Corollas, some of the drivers steering on the left, some on the right.

Justin asked why there were so many similar cars — and why some of their steering wheels were on the left side and some on the right. Idris said that most of Kabul's vehicles were shipped in from Japan, where people drove on the left. This made Afghanistan's traffic treacherous, since most drivers couldn't see oncoming traffic when they tried to pass.

Idris asked about Justin's education, where he grew up, where he'd studied.

I'm from Louisiana. I did my undergraduate at Louisiana State in Baton Rouge.

So you wanted to be a teacher?

I wanted to be involved in education. Yes, I teach, but . . .

There was no easy answer, so Justin explained he'd done two master's degrees, in English and education, and had nearly finished his PhD dissertation. Idris asked about university programs and scholarships for foreign students, but Justin admitted he didn't know much.

Idris drove them past embassies with blast walls and guard posts. The main roads were sound, though the side streets were filled with mud and pond-size puddles whose ice had been smashed. As dusk claimed the unlit street, a convoy of dun armored vehicles passed — Justin recognized them as MRAPs — their headlights blazing over the traffic ahead. The thrill of being in a war zone arose in him, accompanied by a vague nostalgia for the days when he'd dreamed of being a soldier.

There are so many ways to use words ending in *ing*, Idris said. Would you be so kind as to teach me this?

Sure.

Justin reluctantly looked away from the convoy. He was still giving examples when they came to a highway under construction. Idris jammed the accelerator, and they shot through a gap in the yellow taxis and cargo trucks with flat-faced cabs and flowery paint jobs.

Justin put the tissue to his nose and blew. He'd been breathing through his mouth and could taste the dust, gritty on his tongue and between his teeth.

Your explanations are very clear, Idris said. You will help many people here.

That's why I came, Justin replied.

Three muddy unpaved roads later, Idris pulled up to a nondescript house with a low compound wall, a metal door, and a dented gate with a scrawl of rusted barbed wire above.

May I give a suggestion? Idris asked.

Of course.

I am not bothered, but for many Afghans, this problem with your nose — this blowing of the nose — it can be insulting.

Why? It's a bodily function.

Many bodily functions are not done in the company of others. Maybe it is like, for you, releasing wind.

It's that bad?

Releasing wind for us is even worse than for you, so how can I know?

Briefly, Justin relived everything that had happened on the plane.

Frank is waiting, Idris told him, and pressed the horn twice.

The gate shook, and a short, bulky man with olive skin and blond hair pulled it open.

He is the guard, Idris said as he drove the car inside. His name is Shafiq. He does not speak English, but he is a very dedicated bodybuilder. Even though he is not so tall, his muscle is very good.

Justin had expected talk of God or war, at the very least politics, but instead he'd already had two conversations about bodybuilding.

Shafiq greeted Justin, squinting like a man reading a distant street sign. Weightlifting calluses scratched Justin's palm as they shook hands. Shafiq's forearms bulged, and swollen veins thinned at his wrists before spreading out again like roots.

I know the place doesn't seem like much, Frank said from the doorway, waving him in, but if you put away your preconceptions and remember this isn't America, I'll give you the tour.

The school's leanness — its sparse furnishings and undecorated spaces — seemed an expression of Frank: tall, even compared to Justin, but so fleshless he appeared a relic.

On the first floor, the dining and living rooms doubled as classrooms. There were mismatched chairs, dry-erase boards on easels, a shelf of espionage best-sellers, and a few mauled classics, Twain and Defoe. The kitchen held a blackened gas stove and some upside-down pots and pans. A low basement had been turned into the girls' dormitory, rickety bunk beds lining the walls, their tops only about a foot from the ceiling. The girls were out, but a woodstove was going strong, and the air retained a hint of perfume.

You teach these kids, Frank told him, and they'll make a difference. Today, we all read about changing our lives, but self-help doesn't come close to what the military has been doing for years. You tell someone he's a leader, he becomes a leader. You give him a role, that's who he'll be. I built this school because we need to empower young people to change their country.

Frank's smile was gone, replaced with a sudden theatrical

earnestness, like that of a pastor who speaks cheerfully from the pulpit only to become stern and deliver a moral.

I don't need to be explaining this, do I? You're the first volunteer who's treated the job like a paid position. If something's worth doing, it's worth doing well. Everyone's heard that. Just working for a paycheck is biding time. The real pay is personal satisfaction.

Justin's department administrator had forwarded the email about the school and, even though the position was voluntary and applicants had to pay their own way, Justin had given the cover letter more care than his PhD applications. The school wasn't what he'd expected, but he reminded himself that learning should take place in the most meager buildings.

Frank showed him the top floor — a few couches in the wide hallway, two bedrooms, two offices, and a bathroom. The concrete walls exuded cold, the basement's heat imperceptible.

Your room has a view and lots of light. There's not a day I've woken up wanting to be somewhere else. A few weeks getting used to this air, and you'll be unstoppable.

Before leaving him to unpack, Frank patted him on the back, his hand so bony Justin felt like he was being reassured with a cooking utensil.

Justin's bags were already near the bed, and he began to close the door. Idris was leaning against the wall near the stairs, his arms crossed. Justin nodded, and Idris tipped his head before walking away.

Justin unzipped his roller bag. The narrow room held an electric heater, a closet with a shelf and row of hangers, a particleboard desk, two ladder-back chairs, and a narrow bed with a foam mattress whose center had been compressed to the plywood. Outside, the backyard was yellow. It contained a few brambly trees and leafless bushes, and Shafiq's guardhouse.

Justin sat at the desk and took a notepad from his pocket. It held a phone number he'd transferred from a gum wrapper. For a moment, he wished it were Alexandra's. He pictured her haloed pupils and then deprived his desire of thought until it receded. He'd come here for the school and was impatient for his new life in Kabul to begin.

And yet he'd brought this number. He studied the foreign assemblage of digits: three zeroes, a nine, a one . . . It had been written while he stood on a quiet Lake Charles street during his favorite season: when gulf winds blew the humidity away and pecans ripened and fell against rooftops, when the crisp shadows of branches draped the pavement and children rode bicycles from school, and a few lanes over black boys tossed footballs. A woman he hadn't seen in a decade had given him the phone number. Elle was no longer pretty in the way she'd seemed when he was a teenager — but trashy, with her tattoos and jean shorts.

Justin, she'd called out, recognizing him despite his beard. She asked how he'd been, and he said he was finishing his PhD and leaving soon to be the academic director of a prep school in Kabul called the Academy of the Future. She'd written down Clay's number and said, Make peace. It would be good for both of you. He never intended to hurt you.

Encountering Clay's mother after so many years had felt like a mistake, and yet the synchronicity, before his departure, now seemed fated. Clay was here, as if, all along, destiny had been carrying them in a similar direction. Justin had spent years with a sense that something had to be done, but now he wondered if there were things back then he hadn't understood.

He took his toiletry kit and opened it on the desk. He

pressed his thumb beneath his right eye, against the ridge of bone, and pushed down his lower lid. With his index finger, he pinched the front of the eye and pulled it from the socket.

美智子

THREE DAYS AFTER my first visit to the school, I returned. When I rang the bell, the muscular guard answered, and we exchanged a few easy words in Dari before he showed me inside.

"I'm trying to learn more about Idris," I told Frank. I had yet to call Steve. Once I contacted him and divulged that I knew four people had gone missing and left only three bodies, I'd enter an entirely new realm of ambition and danger.

"Idris," Frank said, holding his chin in a big hand webbed with sinew and veins. "He knew how to manipulate. Americans are innocent. The bell rings, and we salivate and run to the dish and eat to our satisfaction. The Afghans have never had that. They know the value of a meal. They hear the seconds ticking until the next war, the next foreign invasion. If America fell apart, we'd sit in our living rooms and wait for the lights to come back on."

He hesitated, and I did too, wanting to redirect the conversation but fascinated to see two impulses at odds in him: condemnation of Idris and proof of his empathy for the Afghans. Or maybe by establishing himself as an authority, he thought he had the right to judge.

"Who was Idris manipulating?" I asked.

"Idris?" he said, his voice trailing off. I nodded, no longer trying to act demure. His interest in strong women had made me rethink my initial ruse, although it had seemed to open him up. He moved his mouth a bit, appearing to feel the rhythm of what he wanted to say so he could convey it with his voice.

"Everybody comes here with a mission, even if they aren't aware of it, and Idris knew how to manipulate people to make them think he was the one they should save."

"What is your mission?"

"What was my mission?" he replied, as if he'd already accomplished all he'd intended. He kept moving his jaw with that faint ruminating motion.

"These young people come from America thinking they're going to change everything. They complain about the food or the lack of heat or the power outages. When I came here ten years ago, this neighborhood was a wasteland. It had been shelled to rubble by the *mujahedeen* after the Soviets pulled out, and the Taliban hadn't rebuilt it. The American invasion had left craters all over the city. Outside the window of my first house, a sewer had been blown open by a bomb and become a cesspool. The air tasted like shit. Pardon me for saying it. My food tasted like shit. I had the smell of shit in my nose all the time. I took antibiotics for months to keep myself together. I lost twenty pounds and began to bleed from the inside. I was finally looking my age. So I retreated to the US and got proper treatment, and as soon as I was better, I announced that I was going back to Kabul. My wife had put dinner on the table, mashed potatoes and pork chops — I'd told her I wanted to eat pork every day for a month — and she said, 'I want a divorce.' I asked if she was sure, and she was. 'The girls will be upset,' I told her, and she said, 'They'll get over it.' Just like that. 'Okay,' I told her. 'Sit down. Let's eat. The food's getting cold.'

"We ate, and we slept in our bed that night. She's the best

woman I've ever known. I don't expect to know another, but some things are more important. A man wasn't made to stay home and find hobbies. *It little profits that an idle king by this still hearth . . . matched with an aged wife.* Ha! I never heard my father talk about retirement. We were farmers. The closest he came was when he was eighty-seven. He called my office and said, 'I can't do it no more. Maybe something's wrong.' Eight hours later my plane landed in Nebraska, and I rented a car and drove to his house. He was dead in his recliner. That was retirement.

"I remember once asking him where our name came from. I'd gotten into Vanderbilt, and students talked about that stuff. 'Alaric?' he said. 'It's American.' But everything comes from somewhere else, I told him. 'Sometimes people's heirlooms do,' he said. The way he told it, when his people were asked to write their names at the courthouse, not one of them knew how. He said their accents were so thick they had to repeat their names a dozen times. 'If an American farmer who can't spell tells his name to an American clerk, and that clerk writes it down, I think that makes the name American.'

"When he told me this, I wasn't impressed, but years later, when a salesman came to my door selling genealogy, I repeated the story. I had my father to thank for not letting college turn me into someone else. By then I understood. Who we were wasn't what we were called. It was what we did. That's why I built businesses and sold them, and that's why I came here. I don't blame my wife for not waiting. I couldn't even promise I'd come back."

As he spoke, I expected his tone to soften with regret or nostalgia for a marriage to which he'd given half his life. Instead, he sounded brash, prideful of his nature. His was the voice of a type of man I'd never known, who stated a truth and followed it, like a samurai submitting to his leader. I wanted to track this voice to its source — the duty and vision confounded, the Go West, young man — to stand by the broken-down cabin, ferns growing from its walls, or a crumbling sod house on the plains, and feel the wind, listen to the rarefied nature and amplify it in my mind and imagine the world that had woven this voice from the cultures crossing that vast America.

"My first years," Frank said, "the Afghans were eager for a new start. But then the US got tangled up in Iraq, and the support dried up. The Afghans kept building, but the momentum was slowing. The people here began going back to their old way of being, taking as much as they could before things got bad again. As far as changes go, it wasn't good for human relations.

"For a while, I developed programs at American University, but my students applied themselves less with the intent of helping their own people than with the goal of getting a visa out of here. And I didn't hear my coworkers talking frankly enough about the real job at hand. They were more interested in generous overseas pay and vacations in Goa. So I came up with my plan. The school would be free. We wouldn't give certificates, and we wouldn't pick our students with tests. They'd have to have ambition, and if they showed drive, I'd do everything in my power to help them. But I wasn't going to push anyone. Those who worked hard would move up. Those who didn't would do what deadweight does.

"Justin didn't understand how this place works. He wanted to see change overnight, by holding people's hands or bullying them into learning more than they were ready to. I would have kicked him out, but he had education and was willing to work for satisfaction instead of money. When another man gives you his time, you have to leave a little space for his ambition. So I told him to go ahead and save Idris."

Frank lowered his eyes to mine, perhaps wondering who he was revealing himself to. His voice — even if it was an affectation or an inheritance — got into my head: his purposed cadence, the conviction that allowed him to speak of personal goals and the future of a nation in the same breath.

"I'm going to Louisiana in a few days," I told him. "I've decided to visit Justin's family. Have you sent back his belongings?"

He gestured to two roller bags in the corner. "I had to clear out the room for a new volunteer. If you don't mind, I'd like to send Justin's parents a letter."

"I'd be happy to deliver it."

"It's not ready yet. Can you come back tomorrow?"

"Of course."

JUSTIN

THE COLD WOKE Justin. He had a sense not of a dream but its imprint, the phantom glow on the retina after glancing at the sun. He'd curled on his side under the old woolen army blanket, his mouth open and an acrid film on his tongue. He checked his watch: 10 p.m. He'd lain down to rest and must have drifted off.

The air had a foreign taste: thin, singed — dirty and slightly metallic, like a tarnished penny. His lungs itched, and he suppressed a cough. Before his arrival, he'd run across a blog post that anatomized Kabul's dust, claiming it to be sixty percent human fecal matter — from the contents of septic tanks dumped in nearby plains only to dry during the summer and blow back into the city; or simply from open sewers, the tires pummeling the filth in the unpaved streets, the movement of the millions Kabul hadn't been built to accommodate.

Since 2001, the city's population had grown from half a million to more than four million as refugees returned from abroad or fled war-torn provinces. The mountains held in the emissions of traffic, generators, and construction, the demolition and mixing of concrete, as well as the smoke from wood, diesel, and kerosene. Also lacing the dust was the pulverized remains of the thousands of mortars that had rained down during the civil war, the depleted uranium bullets and armor-piercing rounds, the streets and buildings incinerated by American bombs.

Justin had prayed for the strength to live in such a place and bring healing to it.

He laced his boots and went into the silent school. Frank's door was dark around the edges. The first office held desks and a few old mainframe computers, though Frank had told him the girls now had laptops and took them downstairs at night. On a shelf, Justin sorted through sooty American textbooks with swollen pages. The other office had a cabinet of stationery.

In the bathroom, he rinsed the grime from his hands with rust-colored water that smelled faintly of sewage. The scum lines along the inside of the tub resembled the growth rings of trees.

He explored downstairs: kitchen cabinets with plates, cups, mugs, and utensils, all laminated with a mixture of dust and the grease deposited from cooking fumes. The labels of spices were yellow and peeling, a bag of brown flour disintegrating, bouillon cubes melting through their wrappers. He felt like someone searching through the debris of a shipwreck to build a life.

There was a door to what he thought must be a pantry, but it was locked. He went into the dining room. Idris was at the table with an open book, the room unlit but for a lamp.

What are you working on?

Idris touched the book as if he'd forgotten.

Grammar. Mr. Frank told me that when my English is perfect, he will help me get a scholarship in America. But I have been through this book many times, and through two others.

In the US, almost none of the foreign students speak as well as you do. You should read novels. Your ear will learn naturally.

My ear, Idris repeated, testing the phrase. You must understand that Mr. Frank finds the girls jobs in NGOs and in his friends' businesses while I change lightbulbs. He does nothing for the boys. The girls here know they are safe, and they get what they want. Every day this week, I have driven them to the mall.

The mall?

Yes, Idris said, his expression hard to read — either anger or determination. It's very Western, very fancy. One of my jobs is driver. Mr. Frank tells me not to disturb him. If a girl wants to be driven, I should take her. He tells me that if American girls can go to the mall, why can't Afghan girls? But you cannot imagine the traffic. People drive badly. I must pay attention. Then I wait while the girls are inside. I am too tired to read. I do grammar exercises to stay awake. And driving is not all. The circuit breakers go out often. Sometimes in the house. Sometimes in the street. I fix them. I replace everything that breaks. The boys used to live in the basement and the girls had their own dormitory down the street, but when Frank could no longer pay its rent, he kicked the boys out. Only rich boys come here now, and me. Frank does not bother the rich ones.

So, where do you live?

Sometimes here. There is a closet next to the kitchen. Frank calls it the pantry.

Justin remembered the locked door. A dog barked in a nearby compound, the noise amplified within concrete walls like a shout through cupped hands. The silence of the neighborhood reinstated itself, not calming as in some natural setting, but full of apprehension.

Other times, Idris went on, I stay at my uncle's house. But the girls have never had to do an exchange for their education. Mr. Frank told me I have more opportunity because I am a boy. I do not see this opportunity. I think he wants a girls' school. They are very popular for foreigners.

Then why didn't he make one?

Because if Afghans learn that an American man sleeps alone in a house with Afghan girls, they will be angry. And he cannot run the school by himself. He does not have much money left. So he gives me promises. I am sure he will send Shafiq away, and I will be the guard.

I'll talk to him.

Thank you, Mr. Justin.

You don't need to say Mister before my name. Justin is fine.

Are you sure? I am not so comfortable with that.

We do not say Mister before a first name in America. We rarely ever say Mister.

I see. Thank you, Justin. Thank you for your honesty.

Climbing the stairs, Justin paused. The school's quiet was monastic, his *shalwar kameez* like the robes of a monk. With his fingertips on the chilly wall for balance, he envisioned himself as an ancient devotee habituated to deprivation. But his mission, his calling, was worldly. He'd read online that Americans sometimes abused their power overseas. He would need to curb Frank. Only prayer purified the mind so that one's actions didn't serve the self.

In his unlit room, he knelt. *For we maintain that a person is justified by faith apart from the works of the law. Or is God the God of Jews only? Is he not the God of Gentiles too? Yes, of Gentiles too, since there is only one God.* And, yes, of Muslims too.

Faith had brought him here. After he'd lost his eye, he'd lived in a barrage of anxiety, a smudge of lost time, daylight barely reaching him. Fear stalked him for years, receding only as his faith grew. In his devotion to God, Justin had found his mission. As for the chance encounter with Clay's mother on the street? It must be connected somehow, also divine. Clay had set him on this path unknowingly, his violence as random as a lightning strike.

Traces of the city's ambient glow sketched the room's contours. Justin plugged the heater in and its elements lit up, the warmth as palpable as a hand on his cheek. Beyond his window came a cracking, like a stick breaking, and the heater shut off.

He knelt a moment longer, contemplating the space between faith and life, the discipline required to diminish it, and whether the cold could be endured in the spirit of abnegation. He stood to call Idris, but outside, the metal compound door was already clanging.

ALL THAT WEEK, Justin taught, struggling not to blow his nose and wondering if Afghans viewed this privation as a small cost for dignity. He read an article suggesting that such offences might be behind some green-on-blue attacks, Afghan soldiers simply unable to bear the endless insults from the crass Americans they worked with. Though he asked Idris to buy him heavier blankets and a better jacket, his infection worsened, inflaming his throat and vocal cords.

Despite being ill, he got to know the girls. They were a varied group from across the country, all from poor families, some with excellent English, like Zahra and Sediqa, and others shy, struggling to patch sentences together. A few were beauties and knew it. Sediqa was one, and she pried his gaze away from others with her own, asking about his life or for help with grammar.

There were only four young men on the attendance sheets, compared to nearly forty girls. Justin was curious to see if Frank treated the boys differently, as Idris had told him. But Frank spent his days in his office, writing emails to potential donors while the girls who lived in the basement sat around him with their laptops, chatting on Facebook.

When Justin finished teaching for the day, he retreated to his room, intent on adapting his curriculum to address the various levels of the students. But before he could begin, the door pushed open, and Frank's cadaverous hand gripped its frame. He invited Justin to come out to L'Atmos — L'Atmosphère, he explained — his favorite bar. Friday was the Muslim holy day, he explained, so expats partied on Thursdays. Justin insisted he had too much work, but Frank asked if he was afraid and expounded on the safety of Kabul — that one should never do the same thing at the same time every day, but other than that, everyone was free.

Throw your shoes on. Spending time around people your own age will pick you up.

Idris already had the Corolla running, the inside so warm that Justin became sleepy almost immediately.

As Idris drove, Frank talked about how Afghanistan was changing, how seeds planted now would shape generations. Oncoming headlights flashed through the windshield like a series of snapshots: Idris rigid, clutching the wheel; Frank's glasses glowing, his hand lifted in a gesture that appeared historic. Justin dozed, opening his eyes only once, when the car braked sharply. A dog was lit up, its rangy form clipped from the night: long back legs, a narrow waist, a bulging rib cage.

When Justin woke, the car was next to a concrete building, where a man with a Kalashnikov was talking to the driver of a green police truck. Frank and Justin got out, and the guard pounded on a metal door. A peephole opened. They were let into a room with only a metal-frame cot. Another guard had been sitting on it in a rumpled gray uniform, his rifle next to him on the mattress. He frisked them and banged on a second door. They were let into a courtyard and followed the path to a bar with misted windows.

Frank plunged into the crowd. Justin went to stand by the *bukhari*. He overheard a man say, The Americans keep making Karzai dance like a puppet. He was bound to turn on us.

The crowd was mostly young: men in their twenties and thirties with spruced-up hair, fashionably short beards, or none at all — and others, grittier, in drab pea coats or khaki jackets, standing hunched, holding whiskeys or beers. The young women had more presence, points of stillness among gesticulating hands, bobbing heads. They'd hung their headscarves with their jackets or wore them around their necks. The pulsing music was loud and impersonal.

Frank was in the corner, holding a beer, his listeners offering up resigned nods. To live here for so long, Justin thought, with so few means, maybe Frank needed an audience to convince himself daily of his purpose.

Justin moved closer to the *bukhari*. He had the cell Idris had bought him and was debating whether to call and ask him for a ride home. He rubbed his hands in the heat and scanned the room perfunctorily. In the uneven radiance of dim lights — the lamps at tables and the bulbs near the bar — the fine bones of Alexandra's face gained definition. She interrupted her conversation, placing her hand on the arm of a sturdy redhead, and walked toward Justin.

I didn't expect to see you here, she said.

I didn't expect to be here.

You didn't cross the planet to join a club of people who've spent their lives searching for a club that's worthy of them?

She smiled so faintly her skin hardly creased. She was

different than at the airport, but then again, he'd met her only
briefly, in a stressful moment.

I was about to leave, she said. Be a gentleman and walk me.
I'll call you a taxi from my place.

People in the bar watched them go. Justin followed her
through the courtyard, grateful to be out of the bar even if he
regretted being back in the cold and was wary of the pleasure
he felt in her company.

She looped her scarf over her head and turned right along
the dark street.

I didn't expect it to be like this, she said.

Like what?

For everyone to be so self-satisfied. These people are all so
proud of themselves.

Shouldn't they be?

Not like this. They've already decided what this experience
means to them. They might as well stay home and lie about it.

She found a path along the heaped earth beneath the walls.
She lifted her hands for balance but never reached for him. The
street made him think of an exitless corridor. He considered
asking if she was afraid. Anyone driving by could shoot them.

Are you afraid? she asked, as if reading his mind.

Justin didn't reply, aware of a car behind them. It had slowed
on a cross street and veered in their direction, thousands of tiny
airborne particles glinting against the headlights.

I think you're afraid, she said.

I'm not. Where's your house?

Three streets over. There's a shortcut through the alleyway
we can take.

Their shadows lengthened as the car crept up behind them.
He squinted into its light.

The car wobbled and jerked to a stop, the driver only now seeming to realize they were in the way. It revved its engine and swerved around them, into the middle of the street, and plunged through a puddle three times its length, a chunk of ice banging against its fender.

They cut into the alleyway, where silhouettes of concertina wire spooled above them. He asked Alexandra why she wanted to walk like this, and she said that she didn't come to Kabul to live in a box — that there must be expats who led normal lives, eating in places without guards, speaking the language and doing good work.

You don't say much, she told him.

I'm thinking, he said. She'd described how he wanted to live in Kabul.

I'm sorry. I must be doing what I see others here do. This place makes people anxious. They talk too much or laugh too hard, or get so angry.

Suddenly, she whispered in French — a breathy, urgent sound, like a curse.

Look. She pointed ahead. Do you see them?

Where the alley joined the next street, the darkness shifted and rippled.

His heart was racing. He made himself step past her.

There was faint rustling, the sound of padding through mud, followed by a low growl. She backed against the wall and into a doorway, and Justin joined her. His fear emptied him of everything but faith. He squatted and felt around for a rock.

Three dogs appeared, followed by more than a dozen rangy mongrels, their heads down as they sniffed at the ground. Alexandra turned on her cellphone's flashlight. The dogs jerked their heads, wincing like old men. Their eyes glowed green or blue, their lids red and crusted. Their coats had bald spots and tufts, piebald from filth or injuries, from scabs, mange, and scars. An occasional growl came from the pack. There were at least twenty dogs now, some as broadly built as rottweilers. Others were painfully thin.

Two slowed, one with strips of muddy fur hanging from its flank. Alexandra shone her light in its eyes, and it drew its lips back from its teeth before filing past.

It's as if they know better, she said. They're afraid of people.

As they began walking again, Justin wanted to touch her and feel the warmth of her skin. He knew nothing about Quebec. He saw Canada as a great northern backwater, freeloading off America's hard-earned liberty. Louisiana had French history too, though Cajuns had never seemed very different from normal Americans.

As a muddy UN Land Cruiser passed, Alexandra knocked on a gate so softly he didn't think anyone would hear. But the peephole slid open on two eyes. The bolt snapped back, and a small man in a leather jacket let them in.

Thank you, Fahim, she said. This is Justin.

They shook hands. Fahim smiled and retreated to his guardhouse.

Two dogs ran up and pushed their muzzles into Justin's fingers to be petted. They resembled those in the street, yellow with squarish heads, but friendly and clean.

When I was a girl, she said, I spied on neighbors. I hid in their yards. I liked watching people who were alone best. I could see them relax. It made me wonder how the world would be if we lived alongside each other the way we are when we're alone.

It would still be messy, he said.

But peaceful. That's how you looked in the bar. You were

aware of yourself, but then you'd forget. It was more honest than in the airport.

Justin never felt alone. He always sensed others beyond his wedge of sight, and an invisible eye mapping his life. He thought of the car in the street, the dogs, and her calm. He was certain Alexandra must be profoundly spiritual.

God protected us this evening, he said, and she shook her head, seeming to come to.

Do you want me to call you a taxi? she asked.

No, I'll call my driver. When he took out his cell, a furrow appeared between her eyebrows, giving the impression she regretted speaking so quickly.

Justin asked her for the address, repeated it to Idris, and hung up. She said they should exchange numbers. The car soon approached outside. The speed of Idris's arrival made Justin realize how short a distance they'd walked.

As she let him out of the gate, her lips were pursed, disappointed. In the light, she called to mind a lean tribe on a Breton coast. She thanked him for his company and said good night.

Idris asked if they should go back and wait for Frank at the bar, but Justin was too tired. He angled the heat vents toward himself. Relaxing into his seat, he recalled how, as a doctoral student, he'd gone through a period when he would wake up in a sweat, unable to control his desire except through prayer. He was haunted by the bodies of young women who attended his classes in yoga clothes or skirts, or those on the covers of fashion and men's magazines, or the conversations he overheard — two TAs talking about sleeping with undergraduates, how, in bed, one had referred to her implants as sweet-sixteen breasts, propping them in her hands for him to admire. Justin had visited the university chapel where the boyish pastor asked if he'd given any thought to marriage. Justin told him he preferred the greater battle: devotion and resistance to the oceanic darkness against which he could measure his faith.

美智子

TWO DAYS BEFORE Tam left for her embed, her emotions were still oscillating. She alternated between her usual boasting and wondering about the car bomb. She reminisced about Alexandra — how confident she'd seemed, like someone who'd been here before or who'd read every Kabul expat blog — and the first time we'd seen her with Justin, in L'Atmos, the place packed, people turning as she crossed the room to go to the big bearded stranger, as if he belonged to her. And then Tam cried and admitted she would find our time apart difficult, and I held her.

When she went to take a shower, I said I'd join her in a moment. The water hissed as I sat next to the *bukhari* in my underwear. I hadn't told her I was going to America. I didn't feel guilt, just an unwillingness to share. I didn't yet know how to spell out what was driving me to investigate the lives of those who'd died in the bombing.

The knobs squeaked, and water splashed the floor rhythmically as Tam wrung out her hair. I pictured her skimming water from her body, the way she usually did, moving her hands rapidly over her skin before reaching for a towel.

"You didn't join me." She stood naked in the bathroom door, a cut below her knee, the watery blood glossy and thin — a dramatic flourish, like her scarves.

Wicker blinds hung in the bottom two-thirds of the windows, exposing segments of fading sky. The final call to prayer had begun, the *muezzin*'s reedy voice resonating in the walls.

"Are you okay?" she asked. "You've been different."

"I'm just tired," I told her. "Kabul. You know how it is."

"The winter's hard." She knelt and put her arms around me. In the fire's heat, she was already dry, just a faint humidity where the top of her chest pressed into my ribs. I ran my fingers through her hair to soothe her. It felt like frayed wet rope.

Later, as she slept, I lay restless, panic rising in me each time I stopped thinking about the story. Reporters were trained to offer bright glimpses into a situation, but more often than not their pithy lines reduced it. I was no longer envisioning an article in an American magazine. Such an investigation would end where I wanted to begin. I would write a novel instead.

That night, I dreamed that I picked the hand up from the street and walked through a field of skulls knowing I would recognize Alexandra from the beauty of her bones. I dreamed that she spoke to me, fire inside her mouth, a perfect sun behind her teeth. I awoke, haunted by my memories of the car, the indiscernible mass of burning plastic and humans cremated in full consciousness.

The next morning, after Tam left, I examined the card Frank had given me. Calling would cast me into the story I'd been imagining. I would no longer be a bystander. I chose the handwritten number on the back.

I recognized Steve's voice instantly. I'd considered various introductions. If I told him I was a journalist and knew about Clay's disappearance, it would give me a sense of authority, but it might also carry a threat for him and danger for me.

"Hi," I said. "I'm sorry to bother you. I was a friend of

Alexandra." I paused to see if he'd make a sound of recognition, but he didn't. "She was involved with Clay. I've tried to call him, but his phone has been off. I was wondering if you would be willing to put me in touch."

"Where did you get my number?"

"From Frank," I said, since there was no other plausible explanation. "I was there during the attack, at your place."

"Well, damn," he said. "That was quite the party. Which one were you?"

"Michiko. I don't believe we met."

"Yeah. I remember. You were with the pretty redhead. Why don't you come over?"

"When would be good for you?"

"Now," he said, and hung up.

An hour later, when the taxi let me off outside a new gate and freshly plastered walls, I asked the driver to wait. The guard opened the door to a courtyard containing a 4Runner without evidence of bullet holes. My heart sped up, my pulse throbbing in my throat.

Steve had lost the radiance of that night. His pallor and fatigued blotches — his overly white teeth, blond hair, yellow and gray stubble, and the meaty redness around his neck — gave him a motley look. He led me on a tour. Many of the rooms lacked furniture, and traces of the firefight remained only on a small area of wall where bullet holes were patterned like a star, clustered in the center, diffuse at the edges.

"Jackson Pollock couldn't have done it better," he said as I followed him into the safe room. We sat across from each other, on the couches where everyone had huddled, the trunk of guns between us. I'd expected a smell of sweat or at least a residue of smoke. A flat screen showed the security feeds.

"I wish I could tell you something," he said. "Clay's a guy I hired who didn't come to work one day. We sent someone over to his house. There were no clues. He owned nothing. He was a true mercenary."

"Did he ever say anything that might help explain what happened to Justin and Alexandra?"

Steve had his blue eyes on me. They were unexceptional, a little bloodshot, something faded in them, like scuffed glass. His was the gaze of a soldier exhausted from hypervigilance, scouring a landscape he could never master.

He cleared his throat. "Frank told you about the video feed, right?"

"He mentioned that you thought Clay might have died in the car bomb."

"That old meddler," he said and rubbed his knuckles against his chin in a simian motion, scratching his stubble. "Clay's dead. I wish I could tell you more. He's gone — maybe kidnapped, but I doubt it. I'd call this one dead. He was probably just in the wrong place when the Taliban went after his friends."

Still not swayed by the Taliban story, I asked, "So what about Idris?"

"Well, there's the mystery. Someone walked away. I'd place my bet on Idris having been radicalized."

"Do you know anything about him?"

"A little," he said. "During the attack, Idris was here — under the bed in my room, hiding."

"Why wasn't he in the safe room?"

"That's the question. Maybe he got scared, or he was digging around, robbing me, or he planned the whole thing. Clay and Justin vouched for him. Two days later they were all gone."

Steve walked me back out, through the gate, his hands in his pockets.

"I've decided to take that wall with me," he said. "I read it's sometimes done in Italy with ancient frescoes. I'm going home. I'll ship it out when I leave."

"Where's home?"

He sighed. "I don't quite know yet."

At the taxi, I thanked him for talking to me.

"Would you like to have dinner?" he asked.

"I have a flight tomorrow."

He shrugged and opened the taxi door for me.

"One more thing," he said.

I was halfway seated and twisted my neck to look up.

"Tell Frank to keep his mouth shut."

JUSTIN

FRIDAY HAD BEEN quiet. Justin's voice was still hoarse, but slightly better. That evening, he opened his notepad and entered the number in his cell, under *Clay Hervey*, making himself feel as if they'd seen each other recently. Then he went to the office to talk to Frank.

Frank turned from his laptop, swiveling in his chair. He threw one meager leg over the other, leaned back, pulled off his glasses, and picked up a tumbler of auburn liquid.

Come on in. You've caught me enjoying my Friday bourbon. My guts can't take it, but a man needs a holiday even if it hurts.

I wanted to talk to you about Idris. He told me he's worried he won't get a scholarship.

You pick one kid, Frank said, and it's favoritism. Then the others want to know why you didn't choose them.

But you pick kids all the time.

They pick themselves. I just do the paperwork.

What do you have against Idris?

Nothing, aside from his arrogance. He's not ready.

When will he be ready?

When he does the work without acting like he's owed something.

You're being unfair.

Nonsense. Idris has work to do before we can discuss

scholarships. Our school is for those who help themselves.
That's our motto. Leaders don't go asking for handouts. They
fight their way to the top. And — let me finish here, save your
voice — I've seen boys like Idris a hundred times. You get a thick
skin. When I first came here nine years ago —

I was reading online, Justin interrupted, about funding for
schools through the US and Afghan governments. If we set up
a certificate program, we can apply and —

And this place will be just another school churning out kids
who are going through the motions. I set out to build something different. I'm not going to throw that away.

This is a fiefdom, Justin said.

A what?

I mean —

I know what you mean. Hell, you sure know how to treat
a man on his night off. Thanks for reminding me why I got
divorced. At least I have that to feel good about.

Who are you evaluating for scholarships? Justin asked, his
voice raw again.

Most likely Sediqa.

Idris's English is perfect. He's taken every class here. And
he —

I'll tell you what he did. He told you his story. That he runs
all my errands and —

Are you educating people or training drivers?

We've got a tight budget. He's studying here for free —

So are the girls.

They're catching up from a lifetime of being held back.
Frank waved his battered glasses. The only way to change the
world is to find those who want to change themselves. You can
inspire people, but you can't fix them. Right now, my priority is

female role models. Inspiration for the girls. As for Idris, you'll see — it's not the men who are ready to change.

Justin pressed on, arguing that he was the academic director now and should have a say in who received the scholarship.

Fine then, Frank said, and he almost seemed to smile. I'll give you the list of scholarship candidates and their situations, and you can choose the most deserving person.

Justin was so startled by the sudden concession that it took him a moment to agree. Frank tipped his head forward, the way a king might, granting permission to leave.

Justin went downstairs, outside into the driveway where the Corolla was parked, and let himself out the metal door, into the street. The cold circled his wrists and throat. Here and there, the lights in compounds radiated up — luminous pedestals lifting the dull mass of the sky.

His exultation instilled him with courage. He took a step, the mud squelching. He paused, listened, took two steps, then three. He was moving the way a reptile or a rat might: stopping to take stock of danger. He reached the end of the lane. Far away, on the unfinished highway, passing vehicles lifted dust that rose in the breeze and fell like a slow surf. The bulk of the city lay beyond, its radiance amplified in the particulate air.

He'd known that a new beginning wouldn't be easy, but now he felt confident. It was time to make peace.

He held his phone, its LCD a dingy jewel. His thumb lingered over the call button. He composed a text instead.

Clay, this is Justin Falker. I'm in Kabul. Your mother gave me your number. Let me know if you're free to meet.

PART 3

LOUISIANA:

DECEMBER 1999–NOVEMBER 2001

JUSTIN

THE FIRST TIME he heard about the family, he had an impression of a story from his English class or something he'd seen on TV, about desperate, wandering people, and he was surprised that such characters might actually exist.

They've been living in a motel near the overpass, his father said. The brown one. Right after the exit ramp. They spent Christmas there. I told them they can move in on the first.

Justin was reading on the couch, and in the kitchen, his mother asked, Why not sooner? The carriage house is empty.

I've no inclination to rent to desperate people, his father replied. If they can't wait three days, they're not the right tenants.

That evening, Justin and his friends rollerbladed along the lakeshore's wide concrete path, racing, picking up speed, and then slowing to catch their breath. As they started back, Justin hesitated.

A white teenage boy stood on the shore with the black fishermen, watching where their lines disappeared against the water. His shoulder muscles ridged a threadbare T-shirt, his arms veined like a man's. His ratty clothes weren't jock or prep or even redneck. Justin's friends glanced over too — the girls a little longer.

On New Year's Eve, Justin went to a party, squeezing into

the packed car of Adam McCaskill, who'd just gotten his license. Though Justin didn't drink, most of his friends did, and not long after arriving at Douglas Breaux's house, they were wasted and hollering about the millennium. When a girl told Justin that her older brother was on a retreat in the woods, purifying himself for the Second Coming, he asked why she hadn't gone with him. She said she believed in Christ already and would be taken to heaven. Not tonight, she specified. The millennium is off by like a few months. The Rapture will probably happen in March.

He realized then that she'd never kiss him, and it was already too late to pair up with another girl, so he called his father for a ride home.

The next morning a small U-Haul truck and battered gray Ford sedan pulled into his driveway and past the garage, behind the hedges to the parking area next to the carriage house. Justin ate his cereal at the window as a lanky man unloaded the U-Haul, his face so full of harrowed lines that his forehead, cheeks, and mouth resembled a series of descending brackets.

A girl got out of the sedan. She looked young enough to go to his school, but like a TV star: dark bangs and shoulder-length hair, a black trench coat belted at the waist. The tall boy from the lakeside loped past her, his shoulders curved as if he might pounce.

Don't eat standing up, Justin's father said. He'd come downstairs in his golf clothes, his shirt tight across the chest, his big bones and residual muscle making his body seem lumpy.

Justin sat back down at the table, angled toward the window.

They won't be here long, his father said. People like that, they're running away from something.

Why did you rent to them?

It's hard to find a renter in the middle of the school year, and they didn't tell me they had a boy. But now I'm seeing the situation clearly, and I have no doubt they'll be gone before we know it. Just keep your distance. There's no point making friends.

His father normally rented to graduate students from McNeese State, but the girl who'd lived there had dropped out and moved home, leaving a rhyming handwritten note on the door. He'd ranted about the kind of person who absconds and apologizes with poetry.

He went into the garage. As the door mechanically rose and the Lincoln started up, Justin returned to the window, cradling his cereal bowl.

The carriage house was tiny, just a bathroom, an alcove kitchen, and a single room partially divided by shelves. His father was right. The family would soon be gone.

As the boy came out and walked down the driveway, Justin went to the living room and stood just inside the drapes. The boy stopped at the street. He was now visible in profile, and far bigger than he'd appeared leaning on the railing at the lake.

Justin didn't think he'd ever seen someone so still — the way he pictured the first woodsmen in America. His friends twitched with energy, rolling their ankles to stand on the edges of their feet or popping their knees in and out. This boy stood like an animal listening in a forest. He set off down the street.

Justin went to his room and read a chapter in a World War II memoir his father had given him for Christmas, his head propped on a pillow so he could look outside each time the screen door clapped.

The lanky man and the girl left with both vehicles and came back in a sedan. The man was so tall he had to stoop to go in the carriage house. The girl wasn't wearing her jacket, only a black tank top and jeans. Justin put his book down and crouched at the windowsill.

She had tattoos on her shoulders and on the inside of her wrist. There was a hint of another one near her cleavage. In her jeans, her hips were narrow, their curve just wider than her waist. She stood behind the car, opening the trunk, taking out groceries, moving almost dreamily, pausing before each action, as if she were underwater.

THE BOY DEPARTED first thing each morning and didn't come back until after Justin was in bed. Saturday evening, Justin read, staying up to see when he'd get home. He fell asleep and woke at dawn to the squeal of the sedan's engine. Ashen light filtered through the pecan tree, the mass of branches transformed into distinct shapes. At the wheel, the lanky man hunched like someone fearing a bullet from behind. The sedan lurched and then accelerated toward the street.

Justin couldn't get back to sleep. When the boy came out, Justin was watching from the dining room. The boy leveled a long glare in his direction and then walked down the driveway.

At church, Justin's father elbowed him awake.

I'll not have this kind of behavior, Justin George Falker.

The grogginess lasted through his chores. His father had long ago made the rule that his weekly tasks had to be completed before dark on Sunday. He quickly trimmed the hedges that ran the perimeter of the yard and had grown up densely on either side of a chain-link fence. He was moving along the hedge's inside, behind the carriage house, when he felt himself waking up, his peripheral vision expanding. The bathroom window was near his shoulder, the venetians so old and broken their gaps offered glimpses of the tub. The girl lay with her head against its edge, her nipples at the surface of the water.

Justin moved the electric clipper carefully now, catching every protruding leaf, slowing to tug at the extension cord, as if it were snagged on the cinder blocks that supported the corner of the carriage house. Each time he passed in front of the bathroom again, she was still there.

The sun hung low over the neighborhood trees as he gathered the fallen pecans into a bucket, raked leaves and clippings, filled a garbage bag, tied it, and put it by the trashcans.

The lanky man hadn't come back. A smaller hedge divided the carriage house parking area from the yard, and Justin trimmed it last, in the twilight, making sure the boy wasn't around.

He left the rake and a box of plastic garbage bags out, along with the bucket of pecans and the clipper. This way he'd appear to have good reason to be wandering around, picking things up. His parents were having dinner with friends.

With the lawn free of leaves, his step was silent. He neared the carriage house wall until his nose almost touched it. The siding's white paint scaled off. It smelled of decaying wood.

The bathroom window glowed at the crushed edges of the venetian blinds. He lifted his foot and quietly shifted to the right, moving one eye in front of a gap.

The crescents of her lashes lay against her cheeks. Her wet bangs were pushed back and her hair clung to her shoulders like weeds. Her collarbones spread just above the line of water. Her pale breasts floated slightly, the water rippling faintly around them.

A yellow lamp was lit on an end table in the corner. The bathwater had a greenish tinge and no suds. He couldn't understand why she'd stayed in it for so long.

Her waist narrowed and her hips spread, a faint dark patch where her thighs shadowed together. A Celtic design circled her belly button. On her shoulder, there was a heart in a cross of melting ice. Above her breast, a square of barbed wire opened on a colorless heart suspended like the moon in mist.

He touched his erection. That was crossing a line. He didn't want to become a pervert like the ones in the newspaper.

He steadied himself and moved away. He put the rake, the clippers, the bucket, and the plastic bags in the shed. He ran upstairs and grabbed a towel from the hamper and pulled off his shirt. He lay on his bed. He pushed down his pants and was gasping as soon as he started. He panted, seeing her in the bed, over him. The second time the pleasure was stronger.

He was hungry. He went downstairs and ate, and then put on his rollerblades.

The night was cool. He soared along the asphalt, the wheels swishing and skittering over dead leaves. He enjoyed hitting cracks, the instant, intuitive repositioning of his body. He raced through parking lots, jumping concrete dividers, and swept across empty streets. He reached the park along the lake and followed the path, picking up speed.

The boy was with the fishermen again, staring over the water toward the glow of the oil refineries on the far shore. One of the fishermen murmured to him, and the boy replied in a low voice. The men laughed.

Justin pivoted on his rollerblades and passed again, but by then the boy had turned, clearly realizing he was being watched — his face flushed, charged with anger.

Justin looked around as if he'd been deciding where to go, and skated off. The strength and angularity of the boy's bones lingered in his mind, like something he might have seen on a field trip — a savage fossil behind museum glass, a set of pre-historic jaws beneath a light.

JUSTIN LEARNED THE boy's name at school. Clay Hervey. No one knew anything about him, and Justin didn't divulge where he lived or that his father had left and never returned, abandoning him and his sister. Clay was in his homeroom, sitting in the back corner, his hands loose on the table, the skin scuffed off their knuckles. In place of his middle fingernail was clotted flesh.

The teacher introduced him and asked him if he wanted to say something about himself.

That's okay, he told her, his voice like a man's but soft, faintly hoarse.

Nothing? she asked.

Nah, he said, with the distant gaze of a soldier on parade.

How about where you're from?

Maine.

Thank you, Clay.

You're welcome.

Justin wondered if Clay knew, as Justin's father had asserted, that he wouldn't be here for long.

In the hall, Clay carried his books in one battered hand, his muscled arm slack. He kept his eyelids low, his focus somewhere between the floor and the horizon. Girls watched him. Boys edged away, trying to decide whether they could mock him. He was six foot two and had the hard, cooked-down muscle of a man, not the bloated bulk of young athletes.

After a week, kids started calling him *weirdo* behind his back. Girls who'd smiled at him and been ignored muttered *creep* or *psycho*.

In gym, the boys played basketball — shirts against skins. Justin scored two points. He and Clay were shirts. Clay intercepted passes, loping across the floor to feed the ball ahead. He probably didn't play often. Justin had seen other athletic kids who weren't good shots and didn't want to look bad work the defense like this.

The skins were rallying, and Dylan, their best player, kept blocking shots violently. He intercepted and threw a hard pass, and Clay lunged for the ball and caught it.

Dylan moved in to keep him from dribbling or passing. He was the largest boy in the grade, taller even than Clay, towheaded and so pale veins shone beneath his skin. He had a black belt and told stories about karate tournaments, and when he rammed his sweaty armpit into players' faces on the basketball court, they didn't retaliate. He tried this now, but Clay twisted away, the ball between his hands, his forearms parallel to the floor. Dylan closed the gap, and Clay swung back, his elbow catching Dylan's solar plexus — a hollow sound like a drum. Dylan's knees hit the floor. Justin felt the vibrations through the soles of his sneakers.

Between classes, kids talked about how Clay had braced with his foot, dipping his knee inward the way a boxer drives a punch. Dylan hadn't been able to stand up for ten minutes and was now announcing that he'd get revenge. In the hallway, as he was walking away from his girlfriend, Melody, Clay came up behind her.

Hey, he said. That was all the other kids heard. He leaned in and whispered something in her ear. Though she had the black hair and olive complexion of a Cajun, she turned red from her hairline down. She hurried to her next class, clutching her books to her chest.

Before lunch, Dylan found her at her locker, and as he lowered his head to speak to her, she backhanded him. Like he was a bitch, kids would later joke. He retreated, the imprint gathering in the stung, red skin.

Dylan found Clay in the cafeteria and squared off.

What did you tell her?

The truth. I heard what you said in the locker room. Why don't you own up?

Clay's words had the same low, gravelly restraint as when he'd spoken in class.

The lunch monitor was calling other teachers, not wanting to get between them by herself. Dylan made a fist and moved his shoulder back. Clay hadn't budged, hadn't even lifted his hands.

You're a liar, Dylan said, his voice suddenly whiny.

If I am, take me down. Prove it.

The lunch monitor was shouting, moving her arms as if directing traffic. Dylan walked away.

Over the next few days, everyone agreed that Dylan had bragged about what he'd done with Melody at the New Year's party in an upstairs bedroom, and one afternoon, in the lockers, a group of boys led by Melody's brother pushed him down, punching and kicking him.

Kids began gravitating to Clay, walking next to him between classes and sitting with him at lunch. He shared little about himself, keeping his answers simple: he was from Maine; neither the economy nor the weather was much up there, so his family came south. People repeated this. Justin told it to his father one evening, and his father sighed.

Son, Louisiana isn't exactly Silicon Valley. I wouldn't trust a word that boy says.

But Clay's reputation grew: his natural prowess in sports, his simultaneous competence and indifference in class, his modesty and adult disregard for most of what went on around him. Occasionally, he passed Justin in the hallway, and they nodded.

One afternoon Justin left his rollerblades in his locker and timed his departure with Clay's. Heading home? he asked.

Yeah, Clay said, and extended a hand. Hey, man. I'm Clay.

Justin.

They shook hands. Clay's irises were brown at the edges, green spreading raggedly from his pupils — small pale stars whose brightness eclipsed the rest.

I'll keep you company back. Most of the way at least.

I just wanted to say that what you did with Dylan was badass.

Clay shrugged, his stride loose and relaxed.

Dylan's soft, he said. You see the lunches his mother packs? Organic crackers and cookies. And his binders are all organized, with labels in a woman's handwriting. He's never kicked anyone's ass.

Justin said nothing. His mother helped him organize things and used to make his bed until his father called an end to it. His parents had fought for a week over her pampering — his father's word. That was just the previous summer.

Anyway, man, it was good to meet you, Clay said when they were a block from the house. He extended his hand. They shook, and he kept on past the driveway.

For the rest of the week, Justin walked home with Clay. He asked him questions — How long have you been practicing pull-ups? Did you run track at your old school? — but didn't mention team sports since it was clear Clay hadn't played them much.

Over dinner, Justin's parents speculated about whether

Clay's father would return, whether *that woman* — Justin's father didn't seem to know what to call her — would get a job.

She'll have to put her trench coat back on, he said. And the boy doesn't even live here. He comes at six in the morning, eats, I guess, and leaves.

Monday, a few kids gossiped that Clay had shown up at a party and that when Melody got drunk, he took her home in her car.

That afternoon, as he and Justin walked back from school, Clay said, Can I tell you something?

Justin nodded. He'd never felt this nervous around another kid and sometimes wished he'd taken his father's advice to leave Clay alone, but each casual disclosure seemed a step closer to an explanation for the mysteries of Clay's life.

You have to swear you'll never repeat it.

I won't. I promise.

It's just that, you know, we're neighbors and we're kind of becoming friends.

Justin moistened his lips with his tongue. They'd reached the shady street where they usually said goodbye. Clay asked if his parents were home, and when Justin said they weren't, he went up the walkway and sat on the brick porch. Justin joined him.

It's my father, Clay said. My real father, not the guy we came with. My father is dangerous. I'm here because we had to escape him.

You and your . . .

Yeah, me and my mother.

Justin closed his eyes, afraid they'd betray his shock, his sudden guilt that the woman he'd spied on wasn't Clay's sister.

My father went to prison when I was a baby. When he got

out, he tried to kidnap me and was put back in. Now he's out again, so we had to run away. My stepfather came down with us, but he was too scared to stay.

That's rough, Justin said, though he didn't believe it was possible to kidnap Clay.

Anyway, you can't tell anyone anything about me.

I won't. I swear.

Clay stood and Justin got up. They shook hands.

I'll see you later. I have to go to work.

Clay loped out past the hedges and down the street. Justin understood what he'd meant by *anything* — not his strange mother, not even the carriage house.

ONE AFTERNOON THEY talked about guns, and after Clay described the rifles he'd shot in Maine, Justin told him about an illustrated book on the history of the rifle he'd gotten for his last birthday. He invited Clay inside to see it, but when Justin opened the door to his room, Clay stopped and said, What in the hell do you need all this stuff for?

The room had a bed, a desk, and an exercise area with a bench press. Model airplanes hung from strings in an air battle that spanned the twentieth century: a Boeing P-26 Peashooter and a B-17 Flying Fortress positioned against the F-15 Eagle, the F-16 Fighting Falcon, and the F-117 Nighthawk. There were pennants, a rack of baseball caps, comics and graphic novels, *Narnia* and Tolkien. Fish glided through the aquarium.

Justin's cheeks burned. Clay hesitated, appearing startled by the intensity of his own reaction, but then he crossed the room and rapped his knuckles against an army recruitment poster: a soldier stalking through a forest and, beneath him, the words, *Be All You Can Be.*

But this, he said, this is fucking badass.

Justin's father had been in Vietnam, and his grandfather had told stories about Korea and about his own father and uncles in World War II — Salerno or Monte Cassino. A Falker had fought in every American war. Justin repeated all this, talking until the heat faded from his cheeks.

Let's join the Marines together, Clay said, as if there'd been no discomfort.

Justin nodded, his voice locked, a jammed mechanism.

You in? Clay asked.

Yeah, Justin said. Fuck yeah.

Clay laughed and extended his big palm, holding it up. They shook hands.

As soon as Clay left for work, Justin packed up his room: the pennants and books and balsa wood airplanes he'd made only a year before. He dug up family heirlooms from the army and positioned them on the shelves.

That Saturday, when his mother came in with his folded clothes, she stopped as abruptly as Clay had. She put the clothes on his chair, and minutes later her voice rose downstairs, soon overpowered as his father shouted that service was a family tradition — Just because Clinton starved the armed forces, he said, doesn't mean we don't need soldiers. You send a boy down a safe path, he won't come back a man.

All through the mild gulf winter and into the spring, Justin and Clay spent afternoons together. Justin forced himself not to think about Clay's mother, though, impulsively, he spied on her twice more — the times she was in the bathtub again as he did the yard.

With his allowance, Justin bought manuals on guns, fighter jets, and tanks. He and Clay hunched over them, contemplating the strengths and shortcomings of each weapon. They talked about little else. There were rumors at school that Clay was seeing Melody, but he rarely spoke to her in the hallway, and never mentioned her. He seemed contained, tightly wound, inspecting weapons in the manuals as if they were solutions.

At first, Clay left the house before Justin's parents came home — For work, he said, not disclosing where — but eventually Justin told his father that he and Clay planned to join the Marines together. His father warmed to the idea of their friendship, telling Justin's mother it reminded him of how boys used to be, that Justin and the military would set Clay on the straight and narrow. He explained to Justin that the army had made a coherent nation, joining men from different classes and cultures to forge an American identity. He showed them how to dismantle rifles and clean them, and shared stories about his tour in Vietnam and a stint in Okinawa managing supplies, after which he applied his skills to start a shipping company.

At a Friday night party, as Clay and Justin were talking about the best assault rifles, Willard, another junior, said he could outshoot both of them. Willard's father ran a boxing gym, and though Willard's height and build were average, he'd once dropped an older kid with a single punch. A round clump of scar tissue on his forehead made him look as if he'd been shot in the brain and left fearless.

You're dreaming on your feet, Clay told him, and Willard flushed, the knot of scar a white bead. Clay proposed a challenge: they'd separate into paintball teams of two and hunt each other. The boys paired off, and Willard punched Chuck in the shoulder. Chuck was an athlete and a hunter who wore army shirts to school, his sleeves rolled up on his biceps.

That Saturday, they met at a place Willard knew, an old

junkyard whose owner had arranged the defunct vehicles for tactical battles: an apocalyptic landscape of ruined buses, trucks, and cars, rusted-out husks sunken in weeds. The owner rented the area by the hour, supplying masks and guns, and sold only red paintballs. The scattered wrecks were splattered, paint mixing with shades of rust.

The boys had brought white undershirts, and with Sharpies they numbered each of the nine teams of two. It was May, the day hot and humid, and within minutes of spreading out to find a position, Justin was soaked with sweat. He kept licking his lips and had to pause to drink from the water bottle in his backpack.

A sign read: *Mowed grass sprayed monthly for chiggers and ticks, but enter trees at your own risk. Beware of snakes.*

Grass seed speckled Justin's arms as he and Clay crept past a collapsing farm machine and a wrecked UPS van shrouded in wisteria. Webbed windshields refracted the sunlight.

Clay led him to a four-car cluster on a slight rise where they had a vantage on the junkyard. Decades of vines and weeds had grown up through the chain link surrounding it, creating a living wall. He directed Justin's attention between two dense clumps of trees.

This is a bottleneck, he said. Three-fourths of the junkyard is on that side, and one-fourth is just past us. This clearing is the only alley between the trees. We'll stay here and pick them off. They'll drive each other toward us, and we'll drive them back into their enemies' fire.

The plan worked so well that, over the next two hours, they systematically picked off their opponents.

Watch for Willard, Clay told him. He's the only one who wants to win this bad enough.

Justin scanned the junkyard, though it was hard to draw his attention from Clay — the way he measured his energy, patiently taking out opponents but never exposing himself.

Running footsteps thudded as three boys sprinted between the scattered cars, each with a different number. Willard and Chuck followed — 2s on their sweat-soaked shirts — flushing the other boys into the bottleneck between the trees. Willard let Chuck outpace him, and when Clay shot Chuck in the forehead, red spraying into his hair and across his goggles, Willard veered off. He leapt into the undergrowth as Justin shot. Clay took out the three boys.

A gun clacked far off behind Justin, and the paintball struck a car inches away, spraying his cheek. Clay spun and shot their attacker, a seven.

Willard's almost to the other side, Justin said.

As the descending sun lit the trees, Willard stumbled through bands of light, his feet caught up in the trash and vines.

Come on, Clay said. They ran behind cars as Willard broke from the forest, a V of sweat from his shoulders to his crotch.

Go at him and keep firing, Clay whispered. Force him to head for the gap between the fence and that truck.

Justin sprinted, shooting as he came through the vehicles. Neither he nor Willard had a clear shot. Willard fired twice, the paintballs bursting into red splotches on the side of a car, and then he ran along the fence's gnarled growth toward a box truck. A gun fired three times, the shots hitting him in the chest. He put his elbows to his knees, panting, and peeled off his mask.

Justin was afraid Clay might lord the victory, but instead he offered his hand.

Hell of a good fight, brother.

Willard took it. It's fucking hot, he said.

You did all the work today. You took out most of them.

Thanks, man.

Silently, they met up with the others outside the junkyard. Willard said nothing as he got in his car.

Justin had inherited his father's Lincoln, and as he and Clay sat cooling themselves in the air conditioning, a sense of wariness grew in him the more he thought about how Clay seemed to plan every action. Maybe everything he did was premeditated.

To break the silence, he made himself speak. That was real, he said.

Clay barely smiled, his eyes inscrutable, almost contemptuous.

SUMMER CAME. CLAY explained that his job was at the docks, unloading bags of rice. Justin asked his father if he could work there too, but his father refused.

You're humping hundred-pound bags of rice all day. That's for people who have nothing else.

His father was finishing up his fried eggs, about to leave for work. He put his napkin on the table.

I'm impressed Clay has lasted. I knew a few men who came back from the docks with sprained hands and missing fingernails. I'd find something else for him, but nothing will pay as well. That's the thing about that place. No one will work there for minimum wage.

After the one week of vacation his father allotted him, Justin started at his company, checking orders or washing the delivery vehicles. His duties changed depending on which regulars had days off, and he cycled through their jobs. His father told him youth was a time to try everything and build a wide skillset, but Justin envied Clay the hard labor.

During weekday lunches, his father expounded on the importance of democracy for peace, how capitalism made people equal and allowed them to participate fully in society, and how the free market regulated itself, creating opportunity and rewarding ambition.

When Justin saw Clay, he repeated all this, Clay nodding, saying little, only, Go on.

That September, Justin played football and saw less of Clay, but on a long weekend in the fall, his father took them hunting. After waiting hours in the forest, they all aimed at a buck. His father shot, then Justin, then Clay. The buck fell, and Justin's father insisted on doing a ritual for a first kill that he'd done with Justin a year before.

Maybe you've killed up north, his father told Clay, but this is your first kill in the South.

As he moved his finger over Clay's cheekbones, Clay appeared absent, barely interested.

They finished dressing the carcass, carried it to camp, and hung it from a tree before going out again. Justin's father shot the next deer, and in the twilight, he walked out along the logging road to get the rental pickup. Clay and Justin waited with their kills, the moon new and the pine forest dark.

I could just stay out here, Clay said. Imagine that. Or imagine living on an island. There are uninhabited islands off the coast of America. They have everything you need to survive.

The gentleness in Clay's words surprised Justin, and he liked the idea of living in a pristine world too. The long, smooth stones of the forest floor shone in the diffuse glow of the stars. Absent the contrivances of man, divine presence seemed to permeate the earth.

Justin repeated the words of his pastor: Man chases the mystery of life and light. To his mind, only the first is real, yet he must turn toward the light.

Clay slowly cleared his throat — a faint rale.

It's still life. You have to get food. He paused briefly before continuing in a hushed voice. And war won't go away. We came out here knowing we were going to go home with a buck or empty-handed. But imagine if the question is whether you go home alive. Can you really become a man before you know what it's like to be hunted?

The perception made Justin uncomfortable. It indicated that Clay saw and thought far more than he shared — like those moments when his eyes divested themselves of restraint and dug into the people around him.

A week later, before a football game, Justin was walking the edge of the field, searching the bleachers for his parents. Clay was there. He never came to games. Melody sat next to him, her head down. As Justin ran up, she stood quickly and walked away, tears glowing on her cheeks in the radiance of the floodlights.

Is everything okay? Justin asked.

Clay shrugged. Nah. I made the mistake of sleeping with her.

Justin didn't know what to say. Boys never considered sex a mistake, though his pastor railed against it, and in health class, his teacher had talked about pregnancy and diseases. At the end of the bleachers, Melody joined a few girls, who huddled close.

Maybe I should try out for the team, Clay said. My old school didn't have football.

They were midway through the junior-year season, and Justin had never heard of anyone picking up football during senior year.

I have to get geared up before Coach sees me, Justin said, and ran down the bleachers.

He didn't play much that night. From the bench, he occasionally squinted through the floodlights to where Clay hunched, elbows on his knees, like one of those older men who showed up during games or practices and sat alone in the bleachers.

The next morning, in homeroom, Clay wasn't there, nor the day after. Justin was doing his homework when the doorbell rang. He went downstairs, but his father had already answered. Clay's mother stood on the porch in a black dress shirt with short sleeves.

I know Clay likes hanging out with your son, she said, but please tell him I miss him.

Clay's not here. His father turned to where Justin stood on the stairs. Is Clay here?

For the next two weeks, at home and school, speculation about Clay's disappearance dominated conversation. Police spoke to students. They met with Justin. He recounted Clay's words about the threat of kidnapping from his father, and about Melody. Students gossiped that she'd had an abortion, that Clay had run away because she was pregnant. Justin pictured him living in the wild, at peace with nature.

Over dinner, his parents talked about Clay's mother — they'd learned from Justin months before that she wasn't his sister.

She can't pay rent, his father said. Clay was supporting them. She's daft. It's like she's thirteen. But her boy went missing. It doesn't sit well with me to put her out.

So what are you thinking?

It crossed my mind, he said, his voice oddly tentative, that we could use a maid.

A maid?

A cleaning woman. She's very tidy. And she cooks. You've smelled her cooking. It would take the pressure off you.

What pressure? I'm not sure I want another woman in my home.

Well, think about it. It would be charity. We'd be doing her a kindness.

LEAVES WITHERED AND fell. Pecans plummeted, striking the metal roof of the carriage house with a sound like gunshots. Justin rarely saw Clay's mother, never spoke with her other than to say hello the few times they passed in the driveway. New Year's came, then spring. Milk cartons were printed with Clay's yearbook photo, nothing innocent about his face.

After school, Justin went to the carriage house and knocked. The smell of spices came from inside. The dwindling sun shone against the screen, barely revealing the spreading lines of her collarbone, the hollow of her throat, her breasts inside a black tank top. The inside of her elbow uncreased as she pushed open the door.

Bangs fringed her forehead, and there was a faint worried bite line on her bottom lip. Her skin was tight over narrow shoulders.

I'm Justin, Clay's friend. I wanted to ask how you're doing.

The color of her irises made him think of granite.

Have you heard from him?

No, ma'am.

Please don't call me ma'am. I'm still young.

He apologized. Yes, you are.

Would you like to come in?

She backed away, and he put his fingers on the coarse screen.

The dividing wall of shelves was packed with books, the floors scrubbed, the bed made, no cobwebs on the ceiling.

She·offered him orange juice and invited him to sit on the couch, and then brought him a glass, one hand lightly supporting the bottom in a strangely formal way. His fingers brushed against hers as he took it. She sat, the threadbare fibers of her jeans parting on the white skin of her knees. A Celtic mesh tattoo circled her wrist, with some illegible script below.

Are you worried about Clay? he asked.

No. I knew his father would take him. There are things you can't fight. Clay's grown up. I'm thinking about me. Imagine you were only thirty and could start over. What would you do?

Justin tried to hide his surprise, and she sighed, the corners of her mouth dropping.

I'm not old. I've had a lot of cavities, but I could begin a whole new life. I love to read. Every book is full of lives, and I'm waiting to find one that helps me know what I should do.

She spoke the way characters did in children's books, as if everything were possible.

I had my palm read, she told him. I found an ad in a magazine. For five dollars, I photocopied my palm and mailed it in.

What did it say?

That I'll live many lives. That I'm more logical than creative. A lot of things that have nothing to do with me. So I got a book on palm reading. Can I try to read yours?

Sure. His voice came out softly. His church judged things like this as Satanic. She took his hand and moved her fingertip over its lines. Instantly, he had an erection. He leaned forward, positioning his elbow on his crotch. She had short, unpainted nails and kept tracing the line from his wrist to the pad of his index finger.

I guess I have to look at that book again. She rolled his fingers closed, holding his hand in hers. It's nice to talk. If you ever want to, please come over. It matters that you're Clay's friend.

She drew her fingers from his hand.

Justin turned on the couch, careful to stand facing away from her, and pushed his penis up so his T-shirt hid it, its head just above his beltline, like a mouse peeking out from a pocket.

At the door, she kissed his cheek.

Thank you, she said.

You're welcome, he mumbled. Squinting into the slanting light, he crossed the yard and ran for the laundry hamper.

IN GRITTY ARMY memoirs and films, sexual adventure was part of a man's coming of age — prostitutes or crazy girlfriends, unrestrained lovemaking and heartbreak. Though the pastor called sex the devil's snare, a lot of the seniors had lost their virginity. Justin's father once said Justin hadn't needed many rules because he had an innate moral compass, but he was simply wary of shame. In books, men lost themselves with violence and whores, but the genuine love of a woman had the opposite effect. Clay's mother belonged in a soldier's memoir, already used up. If she was really thirty, she'd had Clay when she was thirteen.

His parents discussed her a few more times. His father no longer charged her rent, and finally his mother relented. Justin heard her speaking with Clay's mother downstairs.

What's your name again?

Elle.

Hello, Elle. I'm Karen.

The two of them sat at the table, his mother laying out the daily schedule. She must have been torn between wanting to supervise a stranger and not wanting to feel awkward as Elle cleaned. The second impulse won out. Elle would work until his mother got home.

The first afternoon Justin came back from school and was alone with her, he asked about her name. He'd seen it on the cover of a magazine in the convenience store.

It's French. It just means *her*.

I take Spanish. It's sort of similar.

She didn't pause from scrubbing the wall behind the stove, but later, she lingered at a bookshelf and asked him which books he'd read.

Those aren't mine. Mine are in my room. I'll show them to you.

He let her go upstairs first, watching the movement of her hips. At his shelf, she traced her finger along the spines, but he still couldn't make out the script inside her Celtic mesh.

It's all military, she said.

Yeah. There's history in there too. He considered adding that Clay had read a lot of the books, but he was trying to think of her as Elle, not as Clay's mother. He talked about the misunderstood purpose of the American armed forces abroad, how it prevented a power vacuum that would be occupied by illegitimate forces. He said active service should be a duty for all men, and the way she looked at him — seeming to admire his passion — made him feel like a man, except that he blushed.

Two weeks later, on the last day of school, Justin found a note in his locker — cursive handwriting faintly imprinted in pencil — from Andrea, a cheerleader in the grade below. *Ur cute and nice. Wanna come over some time?* She left her number. He went to throw it away but hesitated, conscious of summer's emptiness spreading out before him.

His father gave him the usual week off before starting work, and Justin read *Atlas Shrugged* and *Ideas Have Consequences*. While Elle cleaned, he described the books to her. She occasionally cooked for them now, food they ate only after she'd left.

That evening, he lay on his bed with Barry Goldwater's *The Conscience of a Conservative*. He could find no right or wrong in his desire. He'd soon be a senior and couldn't wait any longer. He struggled to focus and, later, to sleep. He woke impatient for his parents to leave.

Elle answered the door in a faded floral skirt, her white T-shirt stretched from having been slept in and her nipples showing through, as if she were used to him seeing her naked.

Do you need anything? she asked, glancing at the house, and he told her he'd been wondering how she was.

I'm fine, she said, and invited him to sit. He brought up palm reading, but she said she'd decided it was useless. She lifted her hand and put it against his cheek.

How long are you planning on staying? he whispered.

Until Clay comes back. Then maybe I'll go to college.

I guess I should leave.

He stood and hurried out. In his desk drawer, he found the scrap of paper and dialed.

Andrea?

Justin!

He made small talk for a few minutes, and by the end of the conversation she'd invited him over. He put on his rollerblades and skated to her house.

She was petite, strawberry blonde, and they were in her room listening to music when he asked if her hair was her natural color. She said yes. He touched it, and she brushed his with her fingertips and said, How about you? Then she kissed him.

Every thirty minutes or so they lost a piece of clothing. By the afternoon, they were in their underwear, their stomachs gurgling. Have you ever slept with anyone? she asked, breathing hard, patches of flushed skin on her breasts and belly. He admitted he hadn't. She seemed to waver and then said she hadn't either. I guess I'm not ready yet.

I am if it's the right person.

That's sweet, she said, and they kissed for another hour as she rubbed his penis through his underwear. Then she told him her parents would be home soon.

Tomorrow? she called behind him.

Yeah, he said, turning on his rollerblades, his balls aching.

In his driveway, he unlaced his rollerblades and went to Elle's door in his socks. His parents wouldn't be back for an hour. He knocked, and after a moment she answered in her bathrobe. She must have just come in from cleaning his house.

Are you okay? she asked. He searched for words, bothered that his feelings were so obvious. She held his wrist, drew him inside, and took the rollerblades off his shoulder. She put her hands on his biceps. Her mouth tasted sweet, of oranges, like marmalade.

She led him to the bed. The venetians were lowered, and the way she took off her bathrobe seemed the difference between a girl and a woman. There was a tattoo of flames he'd never noticed before on her thigh. She undressed him, kissing his body, knelt in front of him, and looked up. She asked if this was his first time. He nodded, afraid he might cry, but her lips were on him, and he came. He was still hard, and she got a condom from a drawer. She lay back and slid him inside her, and he followed the rhythm of her hands on his hips.

Across the yard, the garage door began to rumble.

She rolled onto her belly, propping herself on her elbows, and pulled his wrist so that he was close. She put his hand on her chest, her body so small his palm held both of her breasts.

Go slow, she told him and rubbed her cheek against his. It was a long time before he came, her fingers in his hair, his face against her throat.

They lay side by side, the sounds in his house surprisingly loud, the closing of a door, voices in the kitchen, the yammering of the TV. Outside, cars glided along the street. A squirrel rummaged in the gutter and scrambled over the metal roof.

I should go, he said. He raised the bathroom sash and slipped out. The dark was shrill with crickets, the air cool at last. He crossed the yard to the street, put on his rollerblades, and skated to the lake. The fishermen were there. He stopped, suddenly exhausted.

When he got home, he apologized to his parents for missing dinner. He ate leftovers — an Indian chicken curry with orange chutney she'd made — and climbed the stairs like a man returning from an expedition. He collapsed into bed and pulled up the covers.

HALFWAY THROUGH SUMMER, he lost count of how many times they'd slept together. They rarely talked. She said it felt good to be with a man after so long, and confessed that cleaning his house was her first job. He avoided any conversation that might lead to her past, and he didn't ask about the tattoos that had once fascinated him. He never answered Andrea's messages. He worked until mid-August, took a week off, and began his senior year.

The Tuesday the airliners flew into the World Trade Center, students gathered before the TVs in their homerooms. They cried or prayed. Some said this was the beginning of the Rapture, a sign of the End Times. When he got home, Elle was in the kitchen. Water pattered into the sink from the faucet, the elements ticking on the stove, heating up. She called his name as he ran upstairs, ignoring her. He knelt by his bed and prayed. The hinges on his door creaked.

Justin, his mother said. She knelt next to him and put her fingers in his hair, and he turned his face to her chest and cried.

Later, he and his parents went to an impromptu church service. His father invited Elle, but she declined, and as he drove, he briefly ruminated on her lack of gratitude. Attacking our country, he said through gritted teeth.

The pastor talked about choice, the freedom God gives man to determine his salvation. Justin used to think about the pastor's words the way he might an insight his English teacher made about a poem, but now he felt himself needing the pastor's clarity and saw that he wasn't alone. The air conditioning was off, and as the pastor paced, there were flecks of sweat on his cheeks. The future of America, he cried out, is your reward for faith. We are facing terrorists who believe they are right, but in the name of God, we must be the righteous ones.

Each day after school Justin worked out as he never had, impatient for the week of mourning to end and football practice to resume. He began coming home after his parents, and after Elle had gone back to the carriage house. He became part of the core team, scoring frequently, though he was resentful that boys a year older were enlisting.

That Friday night, his team won the home game, and the crowd surged onto the field, parents and friends patting each other, hugging or shaking hands. In the glare of floodlights, girls turned, smiling in his direction.

Andrea stopped him as he left the locker room, her palm on his shoulder.

Drive me home, she said. She wore a tank top, her midriff visible, a silver cross in her cleavage. She touched her lips to his chin and whispered, Please. He put his hands on her waist, her skin hot under his fingers. A passing boy hooted. Tear up that trim, Falker. You earned it!

Justin held her until the boy was out of earshot. I can't, he mumbled and hurried away, moving his shoulders as if striking, angling through the floodlight shadows between people. He got in his car and clutched the wheel. He'd renewed his vows each Sunday, praying for Christ to reveal his purpose since he was missing the most significant war of his lifetime.

He drove home, passed his driveway, parked on another street, and jogged back. Only Elle's bathroom was lit, and in the space next to the hedges, he knocked.

She stood, a thin weaving current shimmering over her abdomen. He raised the window, climbed in, and undressed. The bed was too loud, and he pulled her to the floor. They made love hard and fast until his parents' car pulled into the driveway.

After they finished, he dressed in the bathroom and climbed out the window. Leaves drifted to the sidewalk beneath the cooling trees, cracking under his sneakers.

Later, praying for forgiveness, he envisioned the islands off the coast and himself there with a woman as pure as the place.

That Saturday evening, when his parents went out, he crossed the yard to end it.

When the door opened, a man stood silhouetted, a short beard on the bone of his jaw, his black T-shirt torn at the collar. Clay was all angles, sunken eyes, crow's-feet. He caught Justin's shoulders and jerked him forward, hugging him.

CLAY SEEMED TO have returned from another era, with the jutting bones of a tramp, fibrous muscles, and cancroid bulges where he should have had biceps. Though the police spoke with him, he told Justin only that he'd been with his father.

Weeks passed, but they didn't see each other often. Justin spent time at football practice and Clay went back to work at the docks. Clay quickly put on weight, but the few boyish traits he'd had never returned. The school held him back a grade, and he was as standoffish with the other students as when he'd first shown up.

One morning, when Justin went out, Clay was on the carriage house porch and invited him on a run. Justin agreed. He took a carton of juice from the fridge and two bananas, and washed down mouthfuls as he hurried to his room and changed.

Right away, Clay set a hard pace. Justin wasn't warm and gulped air, having eaten too fast, and when Clay asked if he was okay, Justin said it was his recovery period.

Try the docks, Clay told him. Football training is nothing.

Justin kept quiet. The boy who'd disappeared had been quietly respectful, if calculating, but Clay now acted as if he'd been locked in a box. He ran, shooting quick, unfriendly glances like jabs. He hadn't said anything about Justin's visit to the carriage house, but maybe Elle had.

Justin asked what had happened with Melody, and Clay told him she'd had an abortion, that her parents were hardcore Christians but made her do it to protect their reputation.

When that whole thing went down with you and Dylan, Justin said, what did you whisper in her ear?

Just some stuff I made up. There's only so much a guy can do to a girl in high school.

They'd reached where the city limits abutted swampy forest, and Clay cut into it.

Fuck running in the street, he called back. It doesn't help us. It's not real.

We're going to get covered in ticks, Justin shouted, mud splashing his legs as Clay leapt between hummocks and roots with a desperate animal haste.

Justin forced himself to keep pace, his sneakers black, branches and thorns catching on his clothes and skin, but Clay charged ahead, oblivious to the blood on his arms.

When they reached another road, Clay said he'd wanted this — I want to break through, to wake up and really feel the world.

The disclosure surprised Justin. Like those islands? he asked, panting.

What? Oh yeah — Clay laughed — those fucking islands.

He kept running, his profile spare and angular, his wet hair bristling like a dog's hackles.

Anyway, he said, I'm going to enlist. There's no point waiting. We have a war to fight, and I've already fucked high school.

Justin's envy made it hard to speak.

When they reached their driveway, Justin told him that he was going to a prayer vigil for soldiers in Afghanistan. Clay declined his invitation.

As Justin showered, he considered the notion of breaking through — but spiritually. In war, Justin would be an officer, sustaining his men with faith. He found himself mixing the ideas of his pastor and father: that the wealth other countries envied America was the result of spiritual merit, that America had to create peace in the Middle East with democracy and the free market.

He toweled off at the window, watching the carriage house until Clay left. He dressed and went down, and knocked on the screen door.

She came slowly into the reflection of the sky, her face a sketch in blue light, her threadbare jeans and tank top just beyond the panel of screen. She pushed the door open.

He stepped inside, so close they almost touched.

Clay's back, he said. I think it's a bad idea for us to keep doing this.

She took a breath, her lips extended, full and suddenly pale, like the mouth of a fish. A tear gathered at the corner of each eye and descended, globular, as slow as beads of oil.

What's wrong?

I feel so stupid. She folded her arms over her stomach as if she'd been hit.

I'm just a kid, he told her, feeling frustrated. She didn't have a right to be upset. He was meant for more.

Then go home.

He reached for her shoulder. I'm sorry.

Go home, you fucking baby. Don't waste my time.

He hurried out. On its tired spring, the screen door bumped shut behind him.

Inside the kitchen, he placed his palm to his ribs and tried to breathe. She was trash, and he had nothing to feel bad about, but he couldn't ease his fear — it gripped the muscles of his chest — that Clay would find out.

The next morning, at school, the violence he'd foreseen in Clay was all anyone talked about. He'd crashed a party and taken on three football players. One had joked with a friend who'd been held back a grade, saying, within earshot of Clay, You get kidnapped too? Clay punched out his front teeth. It was so quick, everyone said, they hadn't even seen him swing. The others jumped on him, but they were drunk — too slow and clumsy. Clay broke an arm, scattered more teeth, and ended up in the pool, where he beat his final opponent unconscious. The boy was left floating in the water. Like he was drowned, a girl told Justin. No one pressed charges because it was three to one, though Clay had only a few bruises and split knuckles. When Justin showed up to practice, two members of the starting lineup were still in the hospital. The coach called it a holocaust.

We need to talk about Clay, Justin's father told him after school. Keep your distance. That boy isn't the same.

He's going to drop out and join the Marines.

He should have joined yesterday. Then he'd be killing Arabs and not hurting our boys.

A week passed and then another, but Clay no longer came around the carriage house. He never returned to school.

THE EVENING OF the team's final game, a gulf wind was blowing, drifting the lobbed football and making running feel like towing weight. Justin had gone to the Marines recruiting office that afternoon. He said he was graduating in seven months and wanted to join. He loved what he learned there — the merciless training, the unornamented uniforms. He wasn't applying to college. His parents no longer argued about it. His mother recognized a losing battle and had also been different since 9/11.

On the field, Justin dodged tackles and flattened a few oncoming players, driving them to the ground. He ran in for two touchdowns, and then a third — the last of the game.

In the locker room, a linebacker gave the location for the party, a construction site fifteen minutes outside town, where his father had poured a foundation. The players pooled money for a keg, and as they went through the crowd, they spread the word.

The loose convoy of cars and trucks exited the highway, followed a back road, and pulled onto a freshly graveled drive between rice fields, to a forested rise with a bulldozed lot. They parked in a circle around the concrete slab, leaving their low beams on. The concentrated luminance made the air around their legs palpable, as if they were walking through molten steel.

Justin had never been to a party this big before. There were more than a hundred people, and a second circle of cars around the first. Couples kissed in the dark or fucked in backseats. All around, the embers of cigarettes and joints flared like sparks from a fire.

Justin held a beer but didn't drink as kids patted his back or inflicted bear hugs. Then Andrea was there, her strawberry hair down.

Justin! She hugged his waist. I'm so proud of you. I was right there cheering.

She pushed him against a truck and stood on her toes to kiss him, a hint of alcohol on her breath and her tongue tasting of Pepsi. She slid a hand to his crotch.

Promise you'll never ditch me again.

Okay, he said, knowing he couldn't promise, but she was already unzipping his pants, and he had to get the exultation and impatience out of his body.

Nearby, in the circle, the talking grew louder until it became shouting and the music stopped.

Clay spoke loudly. You still itching from those chiggers you got hiding in the woods?

Willard replied, Get kidnapped, psycho.

People laughed nervously as Clay said something Justin couldn't hear.

Oh? You don't even know how to throw a pigskin, Willard told him.

Justin moved away from Andrea, toward the circle. The team had gathered behind Willard. Clay wore camo pants and a black long-sleeve T-shirt that held a sheen of sweat. A duffel hung from his shoulder, and when he put it on the concrete, metal clinked.

Your pigskin's not going to help us in Afghanistan, he said.

I thought the army wanted recruits with diplomas.

Boys guffawed, and a few girls covered their mouths.

Nah, Clay told him, they don't want recruits who can't back up their words.

There was more laughter, and Willard said, All right, Clay, what's the game this time?

Clay asked for the five best shots, and young men were pushed forward: Brandon and Aaron and Chuck.

Don't forget Justin, Clay said. He's the one who helped me bag Willard.

Hands prodded Justin forward, though he didn't want to compete against his teammates and said he wasn't that good.

You're one of the best, Clay told him. You'll make a better marine than anyone here.

Clay unzipped the duffel on six air rifles. No one appeared bothered. Most of the young men had had air rifles since they were boys.

Clay slid a silver CO_2 canister from a pack and plugged it into the forestock, just below the barrel. He told them that the air rifles were semi-automatic and fully loaded. He then took a white box from the duffel and opened it to reveal Christmas tree ornaments — rows of shiny bulbs, each pair a different color.

Justin, Clay said, and waved him over. He slid the wire of a white bulb through Justin's shirt, at the heart, and twisted it. He stepped behind him and did the same on his back.

If you're a marksman, he said, you take out the heart.

He handed Justin a rifle and then shoved a second rifle at Willard, the metal slapping his palms. He gave Willard two silver bulbs to put on his shirt and did the same for the others: green for Brandon, yellow for Aaron, orange for Chuck.

Go where you want, Clay said, but don't cross the paved road. If someone shoots you in the heart from either side, you're out. You shout your name and walk back into the circle with the gun over your head. If a bulb accidentally breaks, you come back and get another one at your own risk.

He attached a red bulb to his shirt and had Justin hook one to his back. Then he turned to take in the crowd, the seriousness of his gaze diminishing the absurdity of the ornaments.

There are no teams, he said. We walk in different directions. Everyone count to thirty. May the best man win.

Justin was stunned. The crowd's count rumbled in his ears like a chant during a game. Hands guided him beyond the circle, as if his touchdowns meant nothing. They aimed him along the gravel road between fields, and at twenty-five, he realized how exposed he was.

The moon was a few days from full, small clouds passing beneath, their shadows shuttling over the grass. At thirty, the crowd roared. He hid himself in a ditch of weeds.

The drained field compressed beneath his feet, insects ticking all around him. A cloud briefly blotted the moon, the gravel road glowing like a silver bridge. Beyond the trees, the incandescence of combined headlights spilled upward in a burning pillar.

Justin crawled toward the forest, his arms itching. If he waited for whoever survived to come for him, everyone would know he'd hidden until the end.

I'm out, someone shouted. It's me, Aaron!

Justin hadn't heard the shot, but the voice didn't sound far away. The crowd had been quiet — mutters, the occasional cough or cackle — and now cheered.

Willard got me, Aaron told them.

Justin scanned the forest edge. Clay would survive until the end. It would be far better for Justin to get shot by someone else.

The pop of the shattering bulb was clear this time.

It's me — Brandon. Clay got me.

Breeze-blown tassels of wild grass brushed Justin's cheeks, and briefly he saw the moon's radiance, stars brightest at its perimeter all along the horizon — the light of God as subtle as the truth of existence, invisible to those in the circle of human combustion. His desire to be in Afghanistan pulled at him, to behold for himself the images he'd seen on TV: helicopters crossing the pale, ragged crests of mountains set against a vast starlit dome.

Me, too — I'm out, Willard shouted. Chuck got me.

Justin snapped out of his reverie. The game was unrolling quickly. The others had probably put themselves in the line of fire. No one would leave the forest in favor of the field. He scuttled toward the trees, and as he reached them, a rifle clacked. At his shoulder, a chunk of bark flicked off one of the trunks. He scrambled behind a heap of brush.

Almost got you, Chuck called, sounding drunk. He laughed. I'm gonna get you!

Justin should have stayed exposed and let Chuck shoot him. He braced, taking a breath, and then put his face down and stepped back out.

The sound of the rifle was off to the right this time, and a bulb shattered.

Goddamn it, Chuck shouted. Coming out. Dead man walking!

Justin dropped down, sweating hard. An insect scurried over his hand. Treetops glowed, gauzy paths visible through the forest. He wanted to call to Clay. This ending made no sense.

The crowd was silent: the occasional beer crisply opened, bottles clinking. With his thumb to his cheekbone, his rifle leveled, Justin pivoted slowly, scanning the crosshatched forest, waiting for someone to shout in the circle of cars.

A cloud eclipsed the moon, and Willard yelled, Hurry up and kill each other!

With the laughter, Justin ran, dropped to a knee behind a tree, and spun. The static shapes of the forest dissolved against the dark earth. A rifle fired, and his gun hand convulsed, throbbing between his forefinger and thumb. A nerve flared along his arm. He steadied the rifle and swung it around.

Clay crouched between two trees, his black shirt merging with the night, the rifle to his shoulder, the red bulb on his chest invisible but for a glint — Justin's white and glowing. He aimed, closing his left eye.

The flash of light.

PART 4

KABUL: FEBRUARY/APRIL 2012

美智子

AFTER HIS DEATH, people talked about Justin, the story growing until he seemed more like a lesson about the compulsive madness of the occupation than someone who'd lived among us. He was remembered as the Mullah, though his Christianity was given so much importance everyone believed he'd been killed for proselytizing. A rumor also spread that he'd been fucking the Afghan girls he taught, and it thrived alongside a parallel rumor, that during his brief liaison with Alexandra, he'd refused to have sex — "With her of all people!" everyone agreed — because he didn't believe in intercourse before marriage.

Most of those who told stories about him had never spoken with him and didn't try to resolve the contradictions. In Afghanistan, telling conflicting stories about someone wasn't unusual. That was the nature of the war. Every project was successful. Every project was a failure. Everyone had done something amazing. Everyone was going nowhere.

Through stories, Justin finally belonged among the expats who gave the scene its color: not the legit correspondents and humanitarian workers so much as the errant visionaries — those who were unemployed and inserted themselves into the activities of others, showing up to events until someone hired them or they established, just by being here, the credentials to be the journalist, activist, or expert they'd dreamed of when they'd cobbled their funds together for a plane ticket.

Expats ran the gamut. Mackenzie Gray was a Wall Street bond trader who came with twenty grand in camera gear but no training and hired the best fixers to get him through police roadblocks so he could (lacking an agency to file with) post firefight images on social media. Rebecca Henley was a gasket tester in an Alabama Honda factory who, the day after she got her black belt, moved here with the dream of starting training camps that would teach girls how to gouge the eyes and break the arms of men — though, as Tam joked, her students would debilitate their aggressors only to be stoned by their communities. Sierra Light, née MacCarthy, intended to teach yoga to imprisoned Taliban and explained to us that crystals could cure them of fundamentalism, an energetic imbalance.

Alex Hilfar, a Kiwi, bragged about crossing Afghanistan on his motorcycle and getting shot at by Taliban when he ignored checkpoints. A broken body-armor plate that he claimed had saved his life hung in his room, painted with a skull by a Kabul street artist whose graffiti he'd seen on the Green Zone wall. We all knew his Facebook "saddle selfies" — riding in Paktia, Wardak, or some increasingly perilous area, the washed-out landscape unfurling beyond his leather jacket — matched with an apocryphal post: *Returning from having watched a Taliban explosives expert assemble* IEDs! *Unfortunately, he wouldn't let me film for fear of being recognized. What a great story it would have been!*

Whitney Weissbrot had written an Afghanistan novel based on interviews, without ever having been here. Her publisher suggested she visit for credibility's sake before the release, and she'd chartered an armored SUV whereas most foreigners got around in private taxis, ordinary Toyotas that cost five dollars per trip. She'd mortgaged her condo to afford a month here and hung out with the types of people she'd interviewed in the US — those who spent their stays locked in NGO or government compounds. She posted on Facebook hundreds of photos taken through bulletproof glass.

Pascal Boulay, a Belgian novelist, lived in a defunct kitchen behind a journo house and said he was writing about the American occupation. *Another day composing my great American novel*, he posted on Facebook. The comments that followed teased him, asking how a Belgian could do this. He let them pile up and responded with his standard pile driver: *Come on, guys, two words — Sergio Leone.*

Atul Green, an Indian-American, had a YouTube channel, *Atul in Kabul: yolo in the capital*, that featured interviews about cultural change with bearded men in shops or pretty university girls who worked as NGO secretaries (a detail we knew but he didn't divulge, giving the impression he courted them on the street), or that involved close-ups of him consuming Afghan dishes like *mantu* and *bolani*. At a party he missed, other expats mocked him and played the *bolani* webcast. Tam counted the seconds Atul allocated to speaking and to chewing potato-filled flatbread. The ratio was one to four. The video, everyone agreed, was of a guy chewing.

Anders Jameson was as swarthy as the average Afghan, since his mother was Balinese. He planned to journey overland with refugees to the Mediterranean, where they paid traffickers to strand them on rocky Greek isles so that, if they didn't die of dehydration, they'd be incarcerated by the coast guard, processed, and released into Europe. He studied Dari, claiming he'd pass as an Afghan — a popular assertion among expats, even the blond ones saying, "I could be Nuristani if I were a bit shorter or not so well-fed." For most of the expats, their only hope for anonymity was to pass as Nuristanis.

And there was Tam, with her poppy tattoos. Before we began dating, I heard people describe them, swearing they even framed her pubis. Expats debated what justified a poppy. "I mean, if she stumbles on a funeral in Balkh, does she add a poppy?" "What if she sees a bus fall into a raging river, but the dead are never recovered? Does she read the news and cover herself in poppies?" "And what if she sees dead bodies on TV? That doesn't happen often." The few times people teased her, she retorted with brutal stories: an embed on which ISAF soldiers mowed down five teenaged insurgents with rusted rifles; eight civilians torn apart when a bicycle IED detonated in a market; three US soldiers killed by a roadside bomb; and a man she'd dated, a photojournalist, shot in Oruzgan. He'd been there to document life-saving techniques the Afghan National Army was learning in order to decrease casualties. The soldiers used seek-and-destroy tactics, baiting the Taliban by driving around, and one of their Ford Rangers had been hit by an RPG. After a firefight, the insurgents escaped, leaving two of their dead. He videotaped all of it as well as the treatment of the wounded soldiers. He then slung his camera over his shoulder and had just texted her when a soldier shot him in the back of the neck. Tam rode her motorcycle to Oruzgan and composed a photo-essay showing the journey of his body through Afghanistan and back to his family in Delaware. In her absence, people questioned the size of his poppy, or said things like, "He'd only been here a week. He was just a fling." But they said it quietly since every expat who died here — even a neophyte — became a part of this place and its history.

There were so many characters living in rundown hotels with foreign mercenaries and businessmen, or in decrepit houses dating back to Kabul's heyday in the sixties — so many writers scraping by with online articles, dating transients in the NGO community, behaving like celebrities for their courage and rarity, even the most humble and hardworking of them radiating a sense of importance, careening like Gatsby's guests toward the next party.

And then there were the soldiers of fortune, military gone mercenary, mocked and avoided. One once approached me, a wiry, acne-scarred man with black stubble on his face and scalp. Proudly, he told me he'd been in the news for a video of a security crew partying — drugs and alcohol, in one case consumed while poured down an unidentified ass crack — that brought unwanted attention to his embassy employers. I asked if he'd had to leave the country, but he explained that the media had simply moved on. He had a new job, pretty much the same thing, but for an NGO. When he asked me back to his place, I declined.

All expats shared more than we liked to admit: a sense of addiction, an uncertainty about what we'd do if we went home, and a feeling of being awakened — our senses jolted into acuity each time we went outside, perceiving every detail in the street. We felt close to the world's brilliant core — not shielded, not squinting at screens. Our Facebook and Twitter feeds read like dispatches, and when we heard the resonant thud of a car bomb across the city, we knew we were minutes away from an event the rest of the planet would see on the news.

We were also fabricators, everyone caught in the freedom of invention, believing in the characters we saw emerging on our social media feeds. War is a collision of fictions, everyone involved — whether military or aid organization — declaring that their actions have profound impact and purpose. NATO tweets @ISAFmedia, @IJC_Press, and @ResoluteSupport described a stable Afghanistan with rock concerts and social service projects, and, in the years to come, as if by familiarity, their statements escalated into a Twitter war with the Taliban: *The outcome is inevitable. Question is how much longer will terrorists put innocent Afghans in harm's way?* A Taliban spokesman tweeted back: *I dnt knw.u hve bn pttng thm n 'harm's way' fr da pst 10 yrs. Razd whole vllgs n mrkts.n stil hv da nrve to talk bout 'harm's way.'* When Taliban spokesman @zabihmujahid accidentally activated his geo-location, he was mocked for being in Sindh province, in Pakistan, closer to India than to Afghanistan. Tweets asked if he was getting in some beach time, if the war was too hot for him. But the Taliban themselves used geo-location to their benefit, creating fake profiles of buxom, scantily clad women who befriended horny NATO soldiers so they could gather location information from their feeds to mount attacks.

When Justin and Alexandra died in the car bomb, @jihad_noorudin tweeted, *2 mr infdls elimntd by brv mujahid. Allah wl mk us vctorius.* NATO tweeted condolences for the families of humanitarian workers. We all read these, knowing how our deaths would sound on either side of this war of fabulation, and that we needed our own fictions — not just of all we'd accomplished but of everything we would achieve — to give us courage. We contrived public missions as covers for our own obsessions and narcissism, or to hide the wounds that drove us here.

I was no different. Dressing like a Hazara man and walking the streets was not a feat, but perceiving myself differently was — a labor illuminated by Justin's long, pontifical notes. It was better to enter the crucible and find a purpose — even if this meant becoming one of Kabul's mocked characters — than it would be to vanish from the pageant without leaving a myth.

As I wrote my tale about Justin and Clay, I let myself invent, fracturing the narrative, shifting the pieces, mixing them, inter-leafing my past and theirs, seeing myself through a prism. I felt as if all the books I'd loved had been incinerated in that car, as if American literature itself had come to an end. Its romantic, exaggerated stories of courage wandered into a place where they didn't belong, where they made no sense, only to burn away, to dissolve like smoke beneath the sun.

JUSTIN

JUSTIN WAS SURE to arrive first. To be the one waiting at the bar made him feel less like someone who'd just moved here. Johnny Cash strummed and proclaimed in the speakers. Three white men, bearded and tanned and wearing jeans, drank beer. He tested his voice, trying to hum, and his vocal cords gave a faint breathy rasp, like radio static.

As Westerners and a few Afghans came in, their expressions changed. They'd passed the guard booth, followed the driveway that wove between concrete blast walls, and now, inside the warm restaurant, with its wooden tables and polished bar, they paused. Some lost their vulnerability, inhaled and smiled. Others bustled in, dramatically brisk and nonchalant, demonstrating that living in a war zone had no effect on them.

Clay pressed open the door, neither entering tentatively nor hurrying through. He was darker than Justin remembered, his cheekbones running to a strong ridge below his temples. He was unshaved, and his hair, cut close, showed his squarish skull, its deep forehead and hard brow line. Faint scars on his cheeks, maybe from shrapnel or fistfights, lent him a warrior's demeanor, like African scarifications. His ease began to erode, as if he preferred the outside.

He turned to Justin and extended his hand.

Justin.

How are you, Clay?

I have no complaints.

Take a seat. Justin preferred to direct. Idris was at the end of the bar, a grammar workbook and a plate of spaghetti in front of him. Justin wanted time alone with Clay. They ordered steaks — listed on the menu as Nebraska beef.

So, your mother told me you quit the army to do security.

Clay's eyes were still, neutral maybe, but as Justin spoke, they grew colder, their stare making him feel as if they were an inch away, as if they could peel back his skin.

Security's a great gig. With the civilian surge, there's money in protecting expats. The company I work for provides armored SUVs and guards, and installs safe rooms. But I do the K&R.

K&R?

Kidnapping and ransom. Kidnappers almost always target rich Afghans. Foreigners are a headache. You take an expat, and you have American Special Ops storming your hideout, but they don't worry about Afghans. So I track down kidnapped people. It's extremely lucrative.

We've been working on a hard case — a businessman, guy named Ashraf Tarzi. He has a theological degree in Qu'ranic studies and runs his businesses along very strict lines. Very fair. Gives to the poor. People like him. He was expected to run for parliament. The family has been waiting weeks for word of ransom, but there's been nothing.

What will you do? Justin asked, his voice hoarse again.

For this one, I need to hire a hardworking young Afghan who has contacts.

Justin coughed. His throat had improved, but it constricted now. He steadied himself against the bar, his skin both warm and cold, night air seeming to linger in his clothes. Whatever weight-room muscle he'd put on felt like lead.

As a coughing fit doubled Justin over, Clay explained that nearly everyone who moved here got a respiratory infection, especially in the winter.

Justin cleared his throat, bringing up acrid phlegm.

Bathroom's that way. Clay pointed.

The waitress, a young blonde with lean Eastern European features, arrived with their ten-ounce sirloins and baked potatoes.

Justin locked the bathroom door and stood at the mirror. He'd learned to measure his moods by his reflection, the prosthetic eye a counterpoint to whatever he felt. He slowed his breathing. He'd been apprehensive because of what happened with Elle, and he also felt guilty whenever he spoke to soldiers and veterans. He knew he shouldn't: Clay was the reason Justin hadn't enlisted and Justin was serving nonetheless. He'd come tonight to forgive him.

When he returned to the table, Clay was starting in on a fresh beer. Idris was eating, angled away. There was something odd about how they sat, positioned like two people deliberately ignoring each other. Clay hadn't touched his steak.

Hanging in there? Clay asked, and lifted his beer for a toast.

Justin took his water and clinked it.

To old times, he said.

Clay's eyebrows shot up. Hell. Okay, man. To old times.

He drank and laughed, and then forked a chunk of meat into his mouth.

So why did you leave the military? Justin asked. You were perfect for it. That's all we ever talked about.

Clay's smile was already fading. He took another bite, breathing hard through his nose as he chewed.

That's all I knew about.

Is security or whatever — K&R — satisfying?

I can support my mother. That's been satisfying. She's finishing a master's degree in psychology. She doesn't have to waste her life scrubbing toilets for rich people.

Justin picked at the cooked edges of the steak. It was good, salted and grilled, but he had a hard time getting it down, his throat pulsing like a wound.

Anyway, what about you? Clay asked. What have you been up to?

Justin described his studies: undergraduate at Louisiana State, two master's degrees, and a nearly completed doctorate.

I never saw you as that type, Clay told him.

What else was I supposed to do? Get a job on the shrimp boats?

I figured you for the high life — a businessman, a stockbroker, a New York financier.

I was idealistic. Justin planted his elbows on either side of his plate. His anger toward Clay bothered him. He suddenly felt incapable of forgiving him without being certain that the shooting was about Elle. Maybe Clay hadn't known, and his violence had grown from his jealousy of Justin's place in the world.

So you enjoying this adventure? Clay asked. That's what a stint in Kabul is for most people. A way to prove something. Self-realization and bragging rights all on the same junket. There are tours and there is tourism.

Justin could no longer eat, his throat too raw. His anger and discomfort felt like fever, a visit to a place he'd never wanted to return to. I think I have to go, he said.

Kabul, Clay told him. It'll pass. You'll get used to being here.

Idris went to get the car. Clay and Justin walked out beneath the flat, smogged-up sky.

They shook hands.

Great to see you, man, Clay said. Maybe we'll cross paths again.

Maybe, Justin replied.

But then again, it's a big city, and everyone's busy.

Idris pulled up and Justin got in. As they neared the staggered concrete blast walls, he glanced back. Clay was staring, one eye slightly squinting, his nostrils pinched and his lips a firm line. He looked as if he were taking aim.

CLAY

FROM THE MOMENT Clay began speaking with Justin, he felt encumbered, the way he had in army training, treading water with clothes on. His brain worked best when he let it be: he knew things suddenly, or reacted, sensing a shift, a person about to appear, a deer crossing the forest, or out there, in the soundless sun-broken ranges, another man. By all standards, this made him lucky. It had saved his ass more times than he could count. Some men talked about angels or guardians, God and that stuff, but Clay's gut kept him safe. The truth was simple: he didn't spend much time thinking, so his head wasn't too busy to hear.

But as he sat next to Justin, all he did was think, the kind of thinking that got men killed. Justin had always had this effect on him.

When Justin hurried to the bathroom, Clay was relieved. His head calmed, and he took a drink. Then he caught the Afghan boy studying him.

What is it, kid?

The boy was tall and thin, with the fine features of someone who didn't see a square meal every day.

You have something to say?

No, I don't think so.

Don't bullshit me. What's your name?

Idris.

Nice to meet you, Idris.

Thank you, Mr. Clay.

Call me Clay. So, what's on your mind?

The waitress brought another beer and went back into the kitchen. A pan scraped and banged against the stovetop. A knife moved rapidly on a cutting board. The door swung closed.

This businessman you mentioned.

Ashraf Tarzi?

Yes, that one. I have a second cousin who was a police officer under the Taliban, and —

What? He's a Talib now?

No, not at all. It was just a job.

Story of my life. But he still knows people?

Yes. Maybe he can help.

I doubt it, but I'll give you my number. Maybe we can hire him from time to time.

Clay took out his cell, waiting to hear how Idris would present himself as the hardworking young Afghan Clay had mentioned needing. Idris's eyes were desperate, an expression more common than street signs in Kabul: hungry for a job, or frustrated, or angry, or all three. Clay couldn't save anyone, but taking something from Justin — even a driver or a student — might feel good.

There's something else, Idris said.

A sister in Al Qaeda?

No. There's a boy in our school. He goes to American University, but he takes English classes with me. His father is Kamal Rashidi.

The name rings a bell, Clay lied. In fact, he knew more about this man than he did about his own father.

He is very powerful, Idris said. He owns many businesses, and he and the other man you mentioned, Mr. Tarzi, they had a fight about construction contracts. It was in the papers. Tarzi accused Rashidi of bribing the government people so he could get contracts, even though he was overcharging.

That's common enough, isn't it?

There was going to be an investigation. But Tarzi disappeared. The journalist said Tarzi was threatening to investigate Rashidi.

Well, maybe we should track down that journalist. How about you give me your number?

Idris rattled the digits off, and Clay punched them in. He shoved the phone in his pocket. The bathroom door swung open, and Justin walked out, rubbing his throat as if someone had tried to strangle him in the shitter.

These had always been Clay's gifts — prescience and a sense of timing.

Justin seemed determined now to make the conversation tense, but Clay wasn't going to talk about his eye. The match was perfect, the prosthetic only a little sad.

There were basically two types of people: those who knew themselves from the outside in, and those from the inside out. Justin was the sort who stuck to a plan, gave practiced replies, and wondered later, when everything was going wrong, why his gut had been boiling. Clay lived with a visceral awareness, the tension in his solar plexus and his skin like an advance warning system. But now, after he and Justin said goodbye, as he rode his motorcycle over roads unlit but for the occasional lamp above a gate, his head remained busy.

He'd wrapped his face with a scarf, and to keep from standing out, he didn't wear a helmet. He veered onto his street, his mind snapping back to clarity as he made an obstacle course of the uneven surface, standing and kicking into the pedals to right himself.

Outside his gate, the earth, cut by motorcycle tracks, looked like gills. He drove in and parked under the overhang. The guard hurried out, always too late, and then returned to the guardhouse, its doorway glowing with the battered light of a cheap TV.

Clay's apartment was on the third and final floor, empty but for a bed and a desk, a few reading lamps and some weights. Outside his windows, neighboring compounds spread out like magnified skin cells he'd seen projected in an army classroom as a medic explained burns. His room offered the protection of anonymity. The little barbed wire on the walls was unconvincing, for show, like a Western girl in a headscarf.

In the dark, he started a fire. Flames writhed inside the open *bukhari*, shadows flickering along the walls, calling to mind people darting away from a searchlight. In the cold air, the fire's warmth caressed his face with the fleetingness of autumn sunshine.

He pulled off his boots and lay down. He knew meeting Justin would be unpleasant, but Clay had wanted to see what he'd created: a prisoner of conscience. It was no mystery that people like Justin were attracted to places like Kabul because they felt guilty that others were doing their country's dirty work.

Over the phone, Elle had told Clay that she'd briefly met Justin in the street and urged him to make peace. She'd asked Clay to do the same, but he hadn't been interested until she told him where Justin would be teaching: AOF — Academy of the Future. The absurdity of the name had struck him when he was doing his research. Luck like this didn't come often. The school was on a list of places people in Rashidi's family visited.

And yet, as Clay spoke to Justin, he was surprised by his urge to hurt him. His anger had always been there, making him quick to spot injustice, needing to be purged with exertion. At the bar, he became irritated by the very sight of Justin — his gym build and the precautionary beard that failed to hide his flushed cheeks and soft lips. Idris wasn't the kind of kid who belonged in a pretentiously named school. Clay had been that boy wanting out.

He sat up and put his elbows on his knees. Risen above the mountains, the moon lit the city: the slots of roads abandoned, the Afghans and expats asleep or watching pirated DVDs. Afghanistan taught people to live on the inside. That's why he was curious to find out what Idris could bring him. Hungry, fucked, or just fucked over by those who were supposed to teach him the way, Idris had no doubt learned that everything had a price if you weren't afraid.

Clay took his cell and typed a message.

Talk to Rashidi's son. Get to know him. Call me if you find anything, but don't tell anyone about this. I can't pay you if you do. Sound fair?

He hesitated between *Got it?* and *Sound fair?* He guessed the boy was hungrier for fairness than authority. And if he told Justin, it wouldn't matter. Clay wasn't breaking the law or even any code he himself ascribed to.

He lay back. He'd noticed how — when he stopped moving forward and stayed too long in one place, when the future's gravity lost its purchase — the past took hold. It was the sort of thing that would never have crossed his mind before his discharge.

JUSTIN

I DO NOT think it is me, Idris said as he drove through an empty roundabout.

It is I, Justin told him. That would be correct. Most people say *it is me*.

Thank you. Is it better to be formal?

That depends. *It is me* probably sounds more natural. What were you saying?

That I do not think it is I Frank dislikes. It is bigger than me.

Justin resisted correcting him again. He had vertigo, the city like swirling smoke around his head, his anger the only weight in his body.

What does Mr. Frank think will be Afghanistan's future? Idris asked. The women will not be choosing it. Even if we have a woman president, men will fight unless they are given education.

Justin had meant to buy food at the supermarket Frank had told him about. The school was on Kabul's outskirts, and Frank's cook came three times a day, making hard-boiled eggs for breakfast, or rice and potatoes that she thickened with vegetable oil. There was never meat or fruit or green vegetables. As Idris talked about his goal to study science in America, Justin interrupted to ask if they could stop at the store. He didn't feel like coming back into the city tomorrow.

Yes, Mr. Justin. The food at the school is not so good. I know.

Idris steered them onto another anonymous street and slowed to ease the tires in and out of ruts. Compound walls locked in the narrow lane, razor wire streaming against the sky.

After 9/11, Justin had understood that evil was real, and later that his own evil had come through his eye. He'd stood like King David lusting over Bathsheba, although Elle had not been innocent and he'd not acted brutally. But he had learned the stakes of spiritual warfare — that he would pay the consequences if he were weak before the devil's temptations. Since his arrival, he'd allowed himself to be irresolute.

He held his breath before each exhalation until his chest felt hard, the way a fasting body becomes taut, percussive in its awareness, a hint of rage in its focus. Military discipline had never lost its appeal: its minimalism carved determination into men, their muscles swift with perfected motions.

The supermarket, Finest, was a tall building with an armed guard. Idris waited in the car as Justin went to the entrance. The guard frisked him and sent him down a corridor to a metal door, where he was let inside.

Beneath the fluorescents, foreigners pushed shopping carts: an older, heavyset man with a gray crew cut, several women in their thirties and forties.

In the anemic light, the aisles looked like a narrow warehouse: frozen meats, spices, jars of artichoke hearts and pesto, everything labeled in both English and Arabic, and shipped out from the United Arab Emirates. Justin bought peel-top canned fruit, beef jerky, mixed nuts, apples and oranges. There were second, third, and fourth floors for electronics, appliances, and clothes, almost entirely from China.

A woman entered the aisle.

Justin? Alexandra smiled. He coughed into his fist and said nothing.

Are you okay? she asked, nearing him tentatively.

I'm fine, he said.

The air here is so bad. It must be hard to arrive sick. How is the school?

It has potential. How about where you're working?

Potential, she repeated, the word long in her accent, each syllable given equal attention. They stood before each other as if they hadn't walked together at night.

He angled himself away slightly, closing his eyes to cough. In Houston or even Lake Charles, he'd hardly notice her, but now she seemed like the only woman, shipwrecked here with him. Her amber irises had vanished again, her pupils mirroring his head — a tiny bearded icon. He pictured his own eyes, one small and bloodshot, the other limpid, impassive.

The school will require work, he said. It's what God wants.

God? All problems come from God. Religion is such an American thing. It has never made sense to me, for such a modern country.

Her cheekbones and the corners of her eyes tilted up. His own ran straight, but Clay's conferred a remorseless air on him. In college, Justin had read that in nineteenth-century Europe, people believed a downward slant to the eyes indicated a criminal nature.

Someone is waiting for me, he said. I need to go.

She nodded. Goodbye then.

He went downstairs. There was a brief final pull in his gut, the acknowledgment of his desire. A second later even that was gone. He paid for his groceries as foreigners went outside carrying white bags, winter air blowing past the metal door.

美智子

DOWNTOWN. AT SUNDOWN. throngs of people moved in silhouette through the packed traffic: turbaned heads and beards, the uniform shapes of *burqas*, men in Western clothes with *keffiyehs* at their throats, or on motorcycles creeping through the congestion, knees almost brushing fenders. Headlights came on here and there. Near the gutter, a legless beggar worked a crank with his arms, turning the wheels of the platform on which he traveled. At a checkpoint, I passed two police hunched over a smartphone laughing, their faces washed in pale light. Another smoked, pelvis and belly thrust out, his thumb hooked in the strap of his Kalashnikov.

This was nearly two months before the safe room, when Tam and I had been dating only a few weeks and I still grappled with fear, each excursion an act of bravery. The sky seemed to tilt, sloping into the eastward darkness above the rooftops. The branches of the trees on her street ran in spate against the west's dusty blue.

At Tam's house, I slipped through the metal door of the compound into relative quiet. The guard wished me *shab bekheir* before retreating into his room. I glimpsed the staticky pulsations of his TV, a flowery electric kettle on the floor, and orange *toshaks*, the cushions Afghans slept or rested on.

Tam's two dogs came from the terrace between the leafless

rosebushes and sniffed my shoes. I worked my fingers through the yellow fur beneath their ears, the city's dust puffing around my hands.

Inside, Tam was placing a bowl of shaved Parmesan on the table set for two, with green ziti and tomato sauce.

"When you walk in public, do people notice you?" she asked. She came over and kissed me. "I wish I could pass as an Afghan."

"There are redheaded Afghans."

"It's not my appearance. It's something else. The way we walk gives us away."

"It's also the way Westerners look around. Americans have forgotten the use of peripheral vision," I explained. "How you take in the world changes how others see you. Afghan women are cautious. A gaze isn't innocent. It's an invitation."

"How can you resist looking?"

"I don't, but it's a patient kind of looking. I let the information filter in from the corners, or I take it in when I check for traffic. Besides, I'm as tall as a man here."

"Is that why you cut your hair like that?"

"Yes. It's multifunctional." I tipped my head so that my hair fell from behind my ears. "Now I'm a woman." Then I pushed it back again.

She went into the kitchen and brought out charcuterie on a wooden cutting board, peppered salami alongside strips of Parmesan rubbed with raw honey. We sat, and as we ate, she told me about a journalist who had to repeatedly go through checkpoints to get his visa renewed. Though he was used to being groped during searches, today an officer had frisked him, whistled, and pinched his nipples. She laughed, touching my arm.

As she served the pasta, I asked her how many housemates

she had. She said Alexandra was the only one at the moment; the other bedrooms were vacant.

Even cooked, the tomatoes were firm, from the Pashtun south or Pakistan, the basil fragrant and a little woody, wild and seedy tasting. For dessert, there was a small block of Mexican chili chocolate that snapped and splintered under the knife, served alongside contraband cherry compote and dense rich cream.

Outside, the gate clanked. The guard had turned on the terrace light unnoticed while we were eating. A shadow passed across the curtains, the door opened, and Alexandra crouched, putting down her groceries to take off her boots. Tam called to her and asked if she'd like to join us for dessert.

"No thank you. I don't want to disturb you." Alexandra came to the table. She spoke precisely, as if she'd worked hard to chisel her consonants free of her birth language.

"You seem upset," Tam said. "Are you okay?"

I'd noticed Alexandra's slight discomfort but thought it was because she'd walked in on our dinner.

"I was offended," she told us, and then added quickly, "not by you, but . . ."

"Sit down," Tam told her.

Alexandra put her groceries on the counter. She came and sat, crossing her arms on the edge of the table, the way an expectant student or a chess player might.

"Justin," she said, "that idiot."

"I thought you liked him."

"I thought I did too."

In a brief aside, Tam filled me in on Justin and Alexandra, but just for show: after we'd watched them leave L'Atmos, Tam had dubbed him the Mullah and we'd wondered what war-zone grail he was seeking.

"The one time I saw him," Tam said to Alexandra now, "he seemed unfriendly."

"That's the way his face is. I'm pretty sure he's missing an eye. But there's so much going on under the surface."

She described the scene in the grocery store, him standing there, seeing her and saying nothing. She was sure he would have walked away if she hadn't addressed him.

"New people can be like that," Tam said as she went to get a third dessert plate. "They're in shock. Afghanistan stirs things up, and it takes them a while to figure out who they are here."

She brought Alexandra cream, compote, and chocolate.

"Michi changes her voice depending on what she's reading or who she's talking to," Tam explained. "I wasn't sure how to interpret her at first. I'd wait and listen, and then, after a while, she'd become familiar."

Her observation surprised me. I smiled to indicate it was true.

"Maybe she's just responding to your accent," Alexandra told Tam.

"I think there's more than that. I can see the chaos go away."

Alexandra hesitated before talking about Justin again, the care with which he moved, his cautious way of touching things. "He's less entitled than most," she said.

"Do you feel a real attraction to him or does he just seem safe?" Tam asked.

"I don't know yet."

Her interest hinted at an inner conflict that long preceded Justin, and even when I saw them together later, the distance between them was almost material, like an invisible body, a space painted on a canvas between two figures.

We picked at the remaining chocolate, pressing our

fingertips against the slivers to salvage every grain of taste. I asked Alexandra about her work, and she explained how men's crimes — not just in Afghanistan — often resulted in the punishment of the women who were the victims.

She sat straight in a gray *shalwar*, poised, archaic in her features, Latin in her way of proclaiming, almost regal. I pictured her body under her clothes, the strength and beauty that abnegation can give in youth. I sensed in her what I felt in Tam and knew in myself — the desire to have the courage to confront every fear.

After Alexandra said good night, Tam and I piled the dishes for the maid who came each morning. Not until we were in her room did I notice the distance between us. She seemed unlit; it was an impression I had sometimes, moving between people, between countries — even from one idea to the next — as if I'd looked into the sun and my eyes had to recalibrate.

We lay in bed and talked, and only in the dark did we find the momentum that had carried us through social events beyond an incipient friendship to this.

"It's true what I said," she told me. "About your voice."

"You haven't known me that long."

"But I hear it. Your voice gathers things, influences, stuff you pick up from your day."

As if my voice could, like a bee, gather the pollen of other voices, written or spoken.

"I find myself wondering about your real voice," she said, "and whether I actually know you."

Variations on that conversation took place over the weeks before the deaths of Alexandra and Justin, as I became far more inaccessible, absorbed in the lives of the dead, wanting solitude so I could reconstruct their stories. I told myself that I would expose a murderer and establish myself as a journalist — or, more often, that I would write a novel like those I loved.

So long as I was asking questions and writing, I felt safe. But whenever my investigations slowed, my fear returned — a sense of dread that whatever had led to the attacks wasn't over.

JUSTIN

IN THE BATHROOM, as he washed his face, the smell of sewage seemed a little stronger than usual. He went down to the kitchen, heated bottled water, and made mint tea. Holding the hot mug, he walked through the school and out the sliding glass door.

The bushes against the wall threw tangled shadows across the yard, their canes laden with thorns, like something to be harvested. His lungs drew more easily, and for once, the cold felt good.

In a sere blue sky, a small sun rose, its warmth barely perceptible on his skin: the same sun in every country, the same God present in everyone. He relaxed his eyelids, seeing a land of dim figures drifting from the looming dark of their inhospitable earth into the light.

Back at his desk, he held this feeling of promise as he developed grammar exercises that could edify by explaining democracy. *Compound-complex sentence: As citizens saw the successes of their democracy, they invested more in society, and national pride became more important than tribal allegiances.*

Someone knocked.

Come in, he called.

Sediqa let herself in and closed the door. Her headscarf hung back, her hair loose beneath, purple makeup heavy about her eyes.

I must speak with you, Mr. Justin.

Just Justin, please, he replied. Have a seat.

Sediqa took the wooden chair he'd brought in for meetings. She was one of the best students, writing concise sentences for each class exercise.

You've enrolled here to improve your English and you study Islamic law at Kabul University, is that right? Justin asked, holding his file on the students in a way that made him feel like a doctor glancing over a medical history before examining the patient.

I need a scholarship to America, she said.

But there are none, and Frank —

Mr. Frank said another one has just become available, but that you're in charge of it.

They stared at each other until it felt intimate.

The heels of pumps clattered on the stairs. A group of girls who didn't live in the basement was arriving; Idris had picked them up throughout the city.

Sediqa stood and, like a ballerina rising into a pirouette, opened the door in a single motion. She said something in Dari to the girls, smiled, closed it, and sat back down.

I need to discuss this with Frank, he told her.

Mr. Frank said you will be the one who chooses.

A lot of factors play into that —

I am going to be sold in marriage, she said quietly.

Oddly, she adjusted her chair so that it balanced on the rear legs, its back tapping the wall. She rocked it slightly, striking the wall more loudly, and then leaned forward so the front legs clacked against the tiles. There was a gap beneath the door, sounds passing easily, and the girls outside had hushed.

As Justin asked her to stop moving the chair, she put her hand to her mouth and made an odd sound somewhere between a sob and a gasp of pleasure. Holding her face, she brought the legs down. To anyone outside, it must sound as if they were having sex.

Whispering, she told him she gave her family what she earned typing for an NGO, how her father had died and her uncles were arranging to sell her for eight thousand dollars to a sixty-year-old farmer. She gasped as she described her future husband — ugly and uneducated — and convulsed, the chair legs tapping. She made breathy cries between her quiet words.

Please help me, she said, banging the chair forward and clutching his arm.

I have to talk to Frank, Justin repeated.

When she opened the door to leave, Sediqa adjusted her scarf and dress as the girls watched from the couches in the hallway. She smiled and shut the door behind her loudly, as if what was inside were her business alone.

All that day, students avoided speaking to Justin. Frank was either with the girls, on Skype, or sitting across from a student, having a conference. Each time Justin tried to talk to him, a sepulchral palm went up and Frank said, Later, Justin. Can't you see I'm busy?

Justin hated the lack of regulation in the classes, Frank's invitation being the only requirement for admission. Students attended one day, missed the next, or switched from morning Basic Grammar to afternoon Comp without knowing what had been done. He'd talked to Frank about how to chart their growth, and Frank had said, Discuss anything with them. Those who have ambition will make use of it. There's nothing we can do about the rest.

Some days, five students showed, other days, two dozen. Justin gave the same lessons over and over.

In his final class of the day, a young man came in fifteen minutes late and took a seat. His oily hair was pushed to the side, and he wore a pilot's jacket, the synthetic leather dull and rubbed through in places. He didn't bring a notebook or pen.

Justin had a list of names, and after class he asked for his. The boy slouched, lowered his chin, mumbled something in a husky voice, and left. The gate banged shut outside.

What did he say? Justin asked one of the girls.

He said, she told him — he said I'm somebody's cousin.

When Justin went upstairs, Frank had on a blazer and was leaving for dinner.

Why did you tell Sediqa about the scholarship?

I was in the office with the girls when I got the good news. Why wouldn't I share it?

Because it's going to create conflict.

They'd find out regardless. Look. This scholarship is yours. I told you that.

It's for Idris.

No, it's for you to decide. If you think Idris is most deserving, then choose him. Sediqa has been here as long — or almost as long. Her father's dead, and she's being sold.

Isn't there something else we can do for her?

No. The only option is getting her out of the country. Can you imagine a woman like her as a poppy farmer's third wife? Her father secretly educated her under the Taliban. After the US arrived, he sent her to the best schools. He was an interpreter for the voting commission, and during the last runoff he was at a polling station when a rocket hit. The shrapnel wounds in his abdomen got infected. He was the one who supported the whole family. So now they're forced to sell Sediqa.

There's always going to be a story like this, Justin said.

Doesn't mean it's not important. Frank neared his desk to see if he'd forgotten anything.

She came into my room and . . . and acted inappropriately.

Frank turned back, the lamp's glow in his glasses.

Half the time you're telling me what to do. The other half you're asking me what to do.

I haven't been here very long.

Then cool your heels. If someone's making your life difficult, it's usually because you like difficult situations.

Frank left the room, the soles of his shoes loud and jaunty on the floor. It sounded like the walk of someone relishing a victory. Justin went to his room and lay down, considering that the title of academic director held clout only on a ghostly future résumé.

美智子

THREE DAYS BEFORE my flight to New Orleans, I took a taxi through the darkening city. Tam's dogs greeted me and then lay on their bellies, forelegs parallel, like ancient Egyptian carvings. With their noses to the gap beneath the gate, they breathed the air outside the compound. Did they remember life as orphans, that early desperation, rooting through garbage, and still harbor loyalty to the street?

Tam had on a T-shirt, a bandana over her hair, and was packing away her room so she could sublet it. One housemate had moved in, a balding, handsomely bearded young man who visited incarcerated insurgents, recording their testimonies for evidence of torture. The other housemate would arrive in the morning, hours before she left: a photographer who'd been living near Fort Bragg in North Carolina and taking what she called "sexy pictures" of army wives to send to their husbands. "Service for my country, in my own way," she'd told Tam and me over drinks. She began doing embeds to document the husbands for a dual narrative photo-essay and got addicted to Afghanistan — "to the feeling," she'd said, "of being part of something bigger."

Tam showed me Alexandra's possessions boxed up in a closet and said she hadn't been able to find an address for her family, so she'd reached out to the Canadian embassy. She'd decided

to write about her death once she'd finished her embed with
the Special Forces.

She glanced at me. "What's wrong?"

"Can we talk?"

"Of course. Are you okay?"

I tried to find the words. My story was small, a few deaths
in a vast universe, in a measureless war, but Justin, Clay, and
Alexandra's lives held something I wanted.

Her eyes began to tear up. "You're breaking up with me,
aren't you?"

"No, that's not it."

"Then what is it?" She put her arms around me, wanting all
of me, all my mystery.

"I'm trying to write a novel about what happened," I confessed. It became the night's topic: I was going to take a much-
needed break from Kabul and travel to America for research.
I reassured her I would be gone only a few months. I didn't mention my investigation here — not Steve, or Alexandra's journal,
my visits to the school, or Clay's disappearance.

As we lay together, she told me that all the artists she knew
withdrew into themselves. Her description hardly captured the
greediness of my emotion, the compulsion to write the story,
how language converged on me from a lifetime of reading. I'd
grown up with American stories, their ideas of happiness and
success eclipsing my own. Even as a foreigner, I believed in
America's hopes, that I was part of its project. Now I wanted
some control over it. Maybe, in this way, I wasn't so different
from the photographer with her patriotic pornography.

The next morning, two dozen friends came by for breakfast,
and Tam partook in a little de rigueur bragging, asking, "How
many of us ever get out of Kabul?" She talked about the country,

its codes and wildness, the warmth and brutality of its traditions, and then got on her motorcycle to go meet the American documentary crew that had hired her, her gear bungeed to the back. She accelerated, throwing up a small but victorious rooster tail of mud, and sped away, swerving around potholes.

I gave myself over to my research. Online, there were mentions of Justin and Alexandra's deaths, and "a driver's." There was nothing about Clay, so I hired an Afghan fixer who charged a hundred and fifty a day and had a reputation for getting answers. He told me he'd have his contact in the Ministry of Foreign Affairs pull up a list of registered security contractors.

Clay, he said in perfect English, must be short for something.

He took out his phone and found a website for baby names. He suggested we search for Clay, Clayton, and Clement. Four hundred dollars later, he had a match to a visa application with a photo that, though stippled in the cheap ink of the photocopied form, was unquestionably the man I'd seen in the safe room. Clement Hervey.

Googling Clement Hervey brought up articles about a young Iraqi who'd approached a US Army encampment near his village's fields. Clay, startled and half-asleep and blinded by the rising sun, had shot him. It wasn't an unusual civilian casualty, one journalist remarked, and it made the news only because the village elders were organized and had connections in Baghdad. Clay had been acquitted and then discharged, and his story ended there.

When I visited the school a third time, Frank smiled intensely, his skin puckering up around his small eyes: a look somewhere between that of a door-to-door salesman and an evangelical, a hint of fanaticism in how it lingered. My determination must have impressed him, and I was fairly certain that, before I left, he would invite me to be a mentor.

I asked him again about Idris. This time, Frank sounded angry, as if arguments had been building in his head.

"Idris was a stranger to Justin," he told me. "He was the first person to ask for help and that got Justin excited. We hadn't clearly defined his role as academic director yet, and I knew the subject would come up. He'd paid for a ticket here and felt this was sacrifice enough for him to be calling the shots. But I created this place. I know the Afghans. I never said I was abdicating my position at the school."

Frank's fingers interlaced, knotting and releasing, the big knucklebones rubbing against each other, but he was smiling.

"Sometimes, the only way to teach a man is to give him the freedom to fall. So I put the scholarship in his hands. I told Sediqa, who wanted the scholarship as much as Idris, that she'd have to convince him. 'How badly do you want to go to America?' I asked. 'Badly,' she kept telling me, 'very, very badly.' 'Well, then you're going to have to use everything at your disposal and not be shy about it.' She blushed as bright as can be, but she understood, and I knew Justin was a goner. He'd be going home like the rest of them. My job is to teach these girls, and I'll do that any way I can."

"But did his death have anything to do with her?" I asked. "Or with the girls?"

Frank's smile dropped. "Oh no. No. Not at all. What goes on here doesn't leave these walls. I'm sure of that. It had something to do with Idris and Clay. They must have gotten themselves into trouble. Idris was working for Clay. I have no idea what he was doing."

I asked if he had any other information about Clay and how well he'd known him.

"I liked Clay," Frank said. "You could see he carried more than just the wars. It took me a long time to realize when I was younger that the worst thing for a person is too many choices. Choice fills the head with fantasies and unreal scenarios. But Clay had the stillness of someone who hadn't had much choice. He'd run up against some hard circumstances and had adapted. He was the sort of man you'd have a whiskey with and talk about your past.

"But the truth is I wish I'd never met him. I wish Justin had done what he'd come here to do and never found Clay or gotten Idris involved. If I'd known what was going to happen, I'd have thrown the first scholarship I could find at that boy, just to get him out of here."

"Do you know where Idris was taking Justin and Alexandra the day of the bomb?"

"I don't. He left with Justin. I thought it was an errand. I didn't even notice they were gone. I'm not sure why Alexandra was with them, or when Clay got in the car. Justin and Clay were at odds over Idris and over Alexandra too, I guess. It all makes no sense."

"What did Idris leave behind?"

"Nothing much. A laptop. Some grammar books. He liked to read spy novels, political thrillers, that sort of thing."

I asked if I could see what remained, and Frank told me he'd had the laptop reformatted since no one knew the password. Idris's books and clothes had been put back into circulation.

"The need is great," he added. "I'm not about to be sentimental over a kid who should have known better."

"What about his family?"

"I think he lost everyone during the war. He was basically an orphan."

He pointed to a sealed envelope on the edge of the desk.

"Anyway," he said, "there's the letter I wrote to Justin's parents. I put all of his stuff into one suitcase. The rest was only books, and his father told me to use them here."

He talked a bit more, not ready to give up his audience, circling back on the difference between himself and Justin, saying, "I've set the gold standard." He referenced his passion for teaching by again quoting Tennyson — *How dull it is to pause, to make an end, to rust unburnish'd* — before naming the girls he'd sent to study in the US: Sediqa, Sharefa, Najma, and Hasiba. At least one of them, he believed, would acquire the tools to take over the school, so he could retire once and for all.

As he walked me out, trailing the roller bag, he gestured about like a guide in a museum as he led up to his request.

He was the first old man I'd met who spoke like a boy, with no trace of self-consciousness, as if nothing could be denied. America seemed to confer authority and conviction on its people. Maybe by writing the dead into history, I could find those qualities for myself.

Frank's footsteps clapped along next to me, and at the gate, I turned to say goodbye. He was smiling, his face as raw and discolored as a skinned knee. He asked me to be a mentor.

CLAY

CLAY STOOD ON the third floor of the City Center Mall, at the railing above the food court, as women in headscarves walked past café tables below. Idris was supposed to meet him at Afghan Fried Chicken but had called to say he had to take a girl to the mall.

Clay hated the place. He'd parked his motorcycle outside the glitzy anomaly. A nine-storey, multi-million-dollar target. But Idris was compelling — a young man with resources and will who'd stopped believing in what he was taught just enough to contemplate another future. He'd come of age in the boom, the frenzied commerce in security, foreigners starting companies: fortifying homes, installing safe rooms and containment cages inside entrances, or establishing English academies, IT institutes, and private high schools. But the civilian surge and its bubble would end when the troops went home and the foreign aid flowed to a newly devastated land. Idris should profit from this sham while he could.

Idris arrived in a cheap leather jacket that hung on his bony shoulders. His black hair was getting long and would have made him resemble a gangly, overgrown child if it weren't for shadows beneath his eyes so dark he could be recovering from a boxing match.

What's with the girl? I've never heard of schools providing field trips to the mall.

I can't say no to my boss.

I thought you were a student.

I work for Mr. Frank too.

You need the money?

It's not about money. It's . . . all or nothing.

Idris seemed uncomfortable with the words: not a difficult colloquial expression but a greater implication, a servitude.

And what does Justin think of that?

Idris shrugged lamely. He wants to help, but . . . he must help everyone.

Bullshit, kid. You're not being straight. If you want to work for me, you have to be able to say hard things. That's how people trust you.

If I told other Americans the truth, they'd fire me.

I don't know about that, but the truth is going to get you the opposite with me.

Okay. Fine. Everyone in the school says Mr. Justin is making sex with this girl, Sediqa.

Jesus Christ. I didn't see that coming.

He said he would help me, but I don't think he'll stay long. The students don't like him.

Clay leaned against the railing. People ambled across the tiles, past shop windows, clearly in no rush, happy to be in the least dusty public spot the city could offer.

So you've talked to Rashidi's son?

Faisal. Yes. We've talked. He's sixteen but like a kid. You can tell he is very protected.

What do you mean?

I mean protected by his family. He does not come to the school with guards, just a driver and a regular car.

Clay hunched at the railing, feigning interest in the shoppers below.

So what do we do? Idris asked.

I'm thinking. You have any ideas?

I will try to become his friend. It's not easy. When someone offers you friendship, you wonder what the reason is. Nothing is innocent here.

Then be a good actor. I'll make it worth your while.

Clay took a folded hundred from his pocket and shook Idris's hand, the bill between their palms.

Do this your way. I trust you.

Clay let go and left. As he rode the elevator down, he neared the glass. Idris was still at the railing, head lowered, gazing into his palm.

At the mall entrance, a woman in a *burqa* ran up the stairs in high-heeled leather boots, her youth evident in the pliable lines of her body. Clay's pang of desire made him realize he'd been here too long. If only the Soviets and Americans hadn't waged their proxy war, she'd be wearing a skirt and blouse and looking him in the eye. Maybe, underneath it all, she was.

He started his motorcycle. A red sunset crowned the nearest range, light breaking between peaks.

Briefly, nostalgia for the army — for his friends, for immersion in that primal awareness so material in his body it felt like an element denser than his bones — ached in him. Few had liked being a soldier the way he had. He missed the camaraderie, even the boredom. But he'd hated seeing the enemy dead when they were hardly more than boys. A boy himself, he'd dreamed of mountains on the horizons and taking up his .22 to confront something so big its destruction would illuminate every facet of his life. Helping Idris felt good, though it didn't fix anything.

At home, Clay tried to read, but his mind drifted. He imagined an attack on his house, dealing himself worse hands and more insurgents with better weapons. And then he thought about an article he'd run across while perusing the online news. It described human habitations in South Africa dating back more than 70,000 years. Scientists had connected the cliff-side dwellings to a time when the human race almost went extinct, only a few thousand people remaining. The climate had been cold and dry, killing off most humans, and the survivors had retreated to the southern coast.

He pictured himself standing on cliffs above rocky shoals, in a world where everything was essential for survival: hunting, foraging, and reproduction — or killing whatever threatened the home. He could hardly fathom a life he could create now that would have that much purpose. The sky would be like it was in the desert — the spill of stars, the air so clear the atmosphere touched the outer dark of space.

JUSTIN

JUSTIN'S STUDENTS HAD become as unreadable as the Afghans in the street: their stares devoid of feeling, as if they were looking now only so they could remember. Because he, like the rest of the foreigners, would soon be gone.

As he worked on his curricula each morning, Sediqa timed her arrival before the rest of the girls. If he refused to let her in, she made things even worse — crying at his door and clutching his shirt with a conjugal intimacy. If he ushered her to the chair, the gasping and uncontrollable rocking began again. He hadn't expected an Afghan girl to be so bold. She'd thrown this country behind her, willing to destroy her reputation and his to get what she wanted. His frustration festered into anger, and only after he grabbed her arms, shook her, and commanded her to be quiet did she stop. In the days after, she still visited his room, at times bringing him tea, at others thanking him for saving her, even though his mind wasn't made up. In class, she smiled at him with complicity.

The girls, Idris told him one evening, are all talking about how you will pick who gets the new scholarship.

The school belongs to Frank, Justin said. I have to run everything by him.

So Sediqa will get it.

That's not decided. Besides, there are lots of scholarships for Afghan students —

For girls. Yes. The rest go to people who know people. I had a friend who got one. His cousin was in charge of the scholarship program. Otherwise, it's rich people bribing officials.

Idris's mouth trembled and then drew down, clamping his emotion in place.

Mr. Justin, I've done years of grammar classes. Is that all I'm ever going to do?

No. Justin sighed, searching for the right words, but before he could reply, Idris left. He went down through the school. The sound of the gate closing was barely audible.

In the days that followed, Idris rarely came to class, returning late to the pantry.

Unable to sleep one night, Justin prayed in the heater's radiance. As a teenager, he'd fantasized about being shipwrecked on an island where he'd meet an uncorrupted woman who would support his faith. Alexandra could not be more distant from this, but she might understand what he was living.

He took his Nokia, hesitated a moment, and called her.

Hello. Her voice came through thinly, her neat, foreign-sounding consonants. Faith dropped away. He was a body sitting on a thin mattress, holding a cheap plastic cell to his ear.

It's Justin. I wanted to say sorry. For how I was at the supermarket. It wasn't a good moment.

Oh. I guess that's how it is here.

He considered this. Beyond his window, a constellation of house lights along the mountainside pulsed with the uneven current of generators.

Are you there? she asked.

Yes. Sorry.

How is the school?

It's not much. Not yet at least.

Most offices and homes here are not much, she replied. But others are palaces.

Would you like to visit the school?

Just below the summit, a needle of light moved — the headlights of a car making its way over the steep dirt roads between the dwellings.

I would like that. Is tomorrow okay?

He said it was. Frank would be courting donors. He often had meetings with cell companies, Roshan or Etisalat, or local businessmen who profited from contracts with the US government. Frank both bragged about the status of the men he met and lamented that they were all talk and no action.

The next day his mind wandered from his lessons to how he should act with Alexandra and whether he should share his growing resentment. He'd expected Afghans to be grateful.

She arrived as the afternoon ended. The girls were at the mall, and he'd made tea and put chairs on the back porch. She asked about his goals and he described what he'd learned in university about stabilizing society with education. He explained how the curriculum he was developing would teach grammar simultaneously with democracy.

She smiled. It's like the Taliban textbooks that taught math with examples of how many infidels are killed if five bullets are shot and two miss.

He wasn't sure how to interpret her joke. The sun was going down, and she adjusted her scarf to shield her eyes.

Do you really believe so strongly in God? she asked.

How else can we understand this creation?

But what kind of God wants this world? The children who

walk on landmines. Girls splashed with acid. Women treated like cattle.

It's not for me to figure out. The mystery creates meaning and makes faith possible.

There are other ways to create meaning.

Like what? Pleasure? Personal satisfaction? How long can that sustain us?

Until we no longer exist. It's possible to be good without a divine judge. Fuck the God who wants to test us.

So why did you come to see me?

I can want to know you even if we don't agree. The missionary spirit isn't as common as it used to be. At least you care. At least sacrifice means something to you.

He wanted to talk about Job's suffering and the power of a higher purpose, but he'd read in books on conversion that the best way to change another was through example. The heart did not know reason: it felt and, in feeling truth, could be changed.

My brother died here, she said suddenly. He was a soldier.

Justin's thoughts lost their traction, struggling to place Canada in the war. Her brother must have been with NATO. The old guilt — that he himself had never served — was there again.

Are you okay?

Yes. I'm sorry about your brother.

She leaned forward and held his face, her fingers on the skin above his beard. He wasn't ready for this. She put her lips against his.

It's like I'm kissing a medieval king, she said. Or an ancient Christian hermit.

He tried to smile. You don't know any Christians in Canada?

In Quebec, yes, she replied. Canada's another story. In Quebec, there are grandmothers who believe. I don't personally know any young people who are serious about religion, but some exist.

She moved her fingers through the cropped hair above his ear.

This talk of belief is rather primitive, she said, but at least it's not predictable.

I'm sorry about your brother. Were you close?

He was my twin.

Her cell chimed, and she stood and told him next time she would invite him to her place since it was heated. She'd pre-ordered a taxi, and it was already outside, its headlights faint in the blue gloom of the dusk.

美智子

I READ FRANK'S letter on the plane. Nothing was written on the envelope and Justin's parents wouldn't know either way, so I tore it open. I would buy a new one after I landed.

His words were a medley of clichés, a rambling paean to the *warriors who carry no weapons.* It was as if Frank didn't just want to have the last say in his argument with Justin but to utter the final lines at his grave, give the verdict on the war itself — as if, when foreign armies withdrew and the president proclaimed America had done all it promised, Frank would take his place and declare: *Justin did more than give his life to our country. He made the ultimate sacrifice to do what war cannot — to change minds. He is not a memory but rather a part of all that he has met. I see him as he first walked through my door, embodying hope, a hope that has been breathed into every young Afghan.*

I resisted the urge to tear up the letter. His parents would picture a gleaming academy, not a crumbling school among many on the fringes of a city jerry-rigged with foreign aid.

But maybe Frank's language would make sense to Justin's parents — not those Americans I knew, who were educated and managed projects with clear goals, but those who believed in messiahs and empires, and confused the salvation of souls with that of nations.

The warmth of Louisiana startled me after Kabul's winter,

its ugliness more so. The buildings were ramshackle, much like in Kabul. Maybe there'd been a race for land here too — to put down anything and build with whatever was at hand.

I drove the rental car west from New Orleans, through hamlets of uneven clapboard and tin with a few characterless stores, and maybe a supermarket or gas station. The asphalt was fissured and warped, dissolving into the swamps the way mud dwellings erode back into the desert. Only the occasional cottage or plantation house behind immense mossy oaks seemed enduring.

Justin's home was itself vaguely plantation-style, curtailed for a suburban street and made on the cheap, with vinyl siding and no ornamentation. It was fortified with tall boxwood hedges that had grown up on either side of a chain-link fence.

I rang the doorbell with the roller bag at my side. Footsteps slowly approached.

Justin's mother was thin, with a face of rucked-up lines, and she began to cry when I told her I was a friend of Justin's from Kabul.

"Ed," she called. "Ed!" Justin's father came down the hall, stooped, his head jutting between the knobs of his shoulders. His sagging gut and the weight around his hips suggested grief more than excess. It wasn't until his hand was on his wife's back that she was able to wave me inside.

We sat facing each other over a coffee table. The mantle was a shrine to Justin, photos and flowers, football trophies and diplomas. He appeared as he had each time I saw him — like a soldier, his seriousness compelling, even if comical at those times when everyone else was laughing and having a drink.

Age and sadness had erased whatever resemblance his parents shared with him. Only his father's wide forehead and a few small faded scars held any memory of vitality.

He took the letter from me and began speaking. It was another version of that American voice, more sober and resigned than Frank's, but the rhythms echoed, as did the biblical undertones, the conviction behind the words that truth was within reach, if only he could devote himself to it.

"I've never seen anyone with such a sense of mission. You could take out his eye, but you couldn't kill his vision. I'd tell him to live a modest life and he'd look at me like I was the devil on the mount.

"So maybe he was better than us, but see where it landed him. We raised him to be humble. Pride is sin. I believe Jesus would have told you sure as he shows it in the Bible — you can't save the world if you're doing it for yourself."

His wife began to cry.

"It's my fault," he said. "I never should have agreed to let him go after he lost his chance to be a soldier. She didn't want him to be a soldier, but at least soldiers serve something greater than themselves. He cared about what mattered. But how can you care about what's right and still be led down the wrong path?"

As he spoke in searching cadenced tones, I sensed he believed Justin's death to be the result of his wife's victory somewhere along the way, or he simply needed to pin the blame on a person he could reach. His discourse was a vague philosophy, incomplete musings on weakness and the Fall, and I couldn't help but wonder if the sermon might be the impromptu oral form of this region, like ballads or *ghazals* in ancient lands. It might explain why Americans were given to rants and lectures, and were such bad conversationalists.

"I'm sorry," he said. "It's not easy for us. Thank you for coming all this way. You must have been close to him in the time he was over there."

As we sat, the smell, the sounds, the dry sterility of the air seemed typical of a suburban living room: a ticking clock, the faint odor of recently vacuumed carpets.

"Is there anything we can tell you?" he asked.

"Yes," I said. "I was wondering if you knew Clay."

"Clay?" He stared with such ferocity that I wondered if he had information about Justin's death that hadn't been made public. "How do you know Clay?"

"I'm sorry. He was with Justin in the car."

"The car? What car?"

"In Kabul. In the car that —"

"That's impossible."

I told them that Clay worked for a security company there, and suddenly Justin's mother shouted, "He's the one to blame. Not me. Not Justin's pride."

His father closed his eyes, in defense against his own rage cast back at him, and Justin's mother went on to tell me the story of their boyhoods. Anger eventually silenced her, and he took over, confessing he'd seen a future for Clay, but she interrupted, denouncing the boys' love of war. Only when she'd been silent a while did he finish by asking why the desire to save another so easily led to the destruction of the savior.

Just before we said goodbye, they asked me to come for dinner to tell them about the final months of Justin's life.

"Where are you from?" she asked.

"Japan," I told her.

"Oh my. My cousin Edith, she adopted an Asian girl."

"From Korea," he added.

"That's right," she told me. "You could meet her."

I said I'd be in town for a week or so. They invited me to

stay in their house, but I already had a hotel room. We planned for dinner in two days.

They'd mentioned Clay's mother, referring to her as Elle, and said they'd taken her into their lives, giving her work. "Elle Hervey?" I asked. "What kind of name is that?"

"Elle Moreau, actually," he replied. "Clay was a Hervey. They were French, down from Maine. They weren't Cajun. People here keep the original spelling. They say the *e*'s like the French but don't bother marking them up with accents."

When we stood to say goodbye, the room suddenly felt too still, like an abandoned house. The dark roller bag waited in the entrance, backlit by the fading light through the door's frosted window. It felt almost as if Justin had been there all along. His mother began to wail, and her husband held her as I quietly left.

Back at my hotel, I found Elle Moreau online and paid with my credit card to get her address history. She lived less than five minutes away.

After dinner, I drove to Elle's house. It was an odd structure, addition upon addition, each new layer built around the previous, like a temple after successive waves of religious conquest. It was set back from the street and didn't seem part of the city, landlocked by other fenced-in yards, a property parceled out from the gardens of a larger home. A path ran between two hedges into a jungle of rubber, banana, and avocado trees loud with the sounds of crickets, the house invisible until I was right in front of it.

The doorbell played the intro to "Stairway to Heaven."

Clay's mother peeked out the crack before removing the chain.

Her black hair was cut like a frame, and her tattoos made me expect a biker husband inside, but there were just books behind her, rooms of them. The house was otherwise empty and undecorated.

"So you're Clay's friend?" she said once we'd sat on thread-bare couches. The planks of the walls were wide and rustic. Dirty, leaf-covered skylights revealed a few specks of fading sky.

"I came to ask about him," I explained.

"I haven't heard from him in a while," she said. "He calls every week or two, but if he's on a job, he misses a few weeks."

I struggled to take a breath, realizing she didn't know. She kept talking. "He has my number memorized so he can call when he's on assignment and doesn't have his things."

She stopped. My throat was so dry it hurt to swallow.

"What? What's wrong?"

I shook my head and finally got the words out. "I shouldn't be the one telling you this. I thought you knew."

She lost her pallor, her face red and creased and swollen. She was grieving already, some part of her understanding. She held her hands out, her fingers crooked as if casting a hex, and she put her head back and wailed. Tears streamed into her ears and hair.

"Help me," she said. "Help me."

I moved close and put my arms around her. The expression of her emotion burned into me. I didn't know that people felt so loudly — not quietly, the way my mother did, when she called to ask when I'd come home, but demanding that the universe respond. As Elle cried, I wondered about my own lack of grief. I held her until long after the last daylight faded.

She spoke a little that night, then more each day when I visited, telling me Clay's story from childhood. He didn't have the desire to save others that Justin did, but he'd survived his family and the wilderness — his society's chaos and indifference — and given himself a life.

PART 5

MAINE AND LOUISIANA: 1976–2001

CLAY

ELLE ELIZABETH MOREAU, a Lewiston girl, disappeared when she was thirteen. The police learned that her kidnapper was Clement Hervey, a Biddeford bad boy five years her senior, a hulking shop rat who could build or fix anything and who spat through the student parking lot in a souped-up Yamaha.

A relative told the police his cousin had seen Clem in South Boston, but they unearthed no clues. Two years later, a tattooed Elle stepped off a Peter Pan bus in Lewiston with Clay in her arms. The police made it to the house just after dozens of family members. Clem, an expert in locks and hot-wiring and auto-body makeovers, had been arrested under another name for grand theft auto and resisting arrest.

Her parents welcomed her home. They'd had her late in life, their only child, and both were now in their mid-fifties. Her father was a high school janitor and her mother a clerk at Kmart. But Elle moved out again after her eighteenth birthday, when Fred Landry, the best friend of her cousin, Murray Leblanc, showed up at her door and proposed.

Fred had also stood out. When some of his classmates were nearing six feet, he reached his skinny sum inches from seven. The height from which his glasses fell ensured their destruction. The relay from his brain was slow to reach his feet, and on the basketball court he tripped into tortured arabesques and hit the floor like a load of two-by-fours.

Though the folding of his body into a desk made him look slouching and delinquent, he was actually scribbling notes, thinking up answers, too shy to tell others what he knew. Only once — when a teacher mentioned the national debt — did Fred raise his hand. He said that if the debt were in dollars and the bills were stood end-to-end, they'd reach the sun and back. The students found his enthusiasm hysterical; the teacher did too. Fred was swarthy — had the French coloring but not the spirit — and his cheeks resembled scrubbed iron.

At the University of Maine, he studied programming, and though he went on to work at a computer repair shop, he couldn't find a wife. His marriage to Elle surprised his friends and family, who discussed her like a car with too many miles and debated — often while waiting at the Shop 'n Save deli counter — whether Fred should change Clay's name.

The way Fred felt about her tattoos was no secret. He begged her to dress in long sleeves and jeans, but she watered the flower-beds in shorts, a ring of hellfire dancing up her thigh, burning — they imagined — her tender parts.

Winter was a blessing to him, but even then, with Elle covered up, her every gesture displayed the black writing on her wrist — the name Fred hated: Clem. Once, when he complained, she stretched the writing and veined flesh toward him and asked if he'd like her to cut it off. For her birthday, he bought her a gift certificate to a tattoo parlor and she returned with another Celtic circle, in the form of a bracelet.

That same year, at his company Christmas party, Elle took off her cardigan to dance, hiked up her skirt to move her knees. Fred's coworkers gawked, but he failed to recognize their envy.

Your wife's a great gal, they said. Life of the party. Sure can dance.

They'd have dropped cash for a second of her shimmy, but Fred feared they were discussing her markings among themselves as if she were a kind of trout.

ON A WARM October day when Clay was eight, he was walking the short distance from school when a pickup truck pulled onto the shoulder.

Clay, the man called. His forearm rested against the steering wheel, dwarfing it, his knuckles thick and square. He had on a half-unbuttoned red-and-black plaid shirt, and above his chest hair there was a tattoo of barbed wire strung across a clouded heart.

Come with me, his father told him and opened the door. Let's go for a drive.

Clay climbed in, and his father accelerated past the street where Clay lived.

I'm your dad.

I know. You've got Mom's tattoo.

His father squinted ahead. His dark hair was cut close to his skull, like the spines of a cactus. He had a thin mustache and goatee, the kind bad guys wore in movies, but his stubble was coming in around them.

Goddamn, he said, you're a smart kid.

The truck picked up speed, its engine knocking and the body rattling with each bump. The roadside trees made a tunnel, red leaves drifting down with gusts from passing cars.

I guess you don't remember me. That's normal. You were really little. But I used to play with you when we lived in Boston.

He slowed and entered the highway where the sign said

South. Clay had never called Fred Dad, and when he'd asked his mother why, she'd said that his real father had had to go away and that she'd explain when he was older.

A semi charged past, shaking the truck. His father told him he'd loved Elle, and that if she'd waited, Clay could have gotten to know him. He described his own childhood, how everyone in his family was big — Not tall like Fred, he said. I remember that guy. But big and tough, the way people used to be.

He talked until sunset, driving through the blazing striations surging between the hills. Rain-streaked dust glowed against the windshield.

He told Clay they were heading to the islands off the Georgia coast. He'd learned about them from an inmate. That's where slaves had escaped to over a hundred years ago, he said. He didn't mind black people and would scout out a small island, separate from the others, where he and Clay could live and fish.

You like clams? he asked. Lobster?

Clay's stomach ached. The taillights ahead rose and fell in slow undulations, as if the highway were shifting beneath them.

Damn, his father said as the knocking under the hood got louder. He exited onto a road through hilly forest and passed a gas station with a long yellow car parked in front of the pump. Inside, the clerk spoke and gesticulated to a bald man who leaned against the counter.

Clay's father made a U-turn, pulled onto the shoulder, and switched off the ignition. The engine ticked, the cooling metal creaking and popping, the way Clay's house did at night during winter's first hard cold. His father took a container of motor oil from under the seat. He lifted the hood and a few seconds later tossed the container in the ditch.

That'll buy us some time, but it ain't enough. Once we're on the island, we won't need money anymore. In a world without money, I'll be a model citizen, he said and laughed.

The gas station door swung open, and the bald man shuffled to the car and drove off.

You stay here, Clay's father told him. He went in, his right hand in his pocket.

Clay's bladder hurt. He yawned and his thoughts moved like feet through mud.

He lifted the door handle and climbed down, went to the glass door and pulled it open.

His father and the wide-bellied clerk — his nose a fat thumb and his mustache like a dead mouse — were staring at him. The clerk's right eyelid twitched as if to jump off his face. Clay's father was pointing a small pistol, and Clay suddenly knew his mother had no idea where he was.

What's up? his father asked.

I'm hungry.

His father reached down and peeled a bag of salt and vinegar chips off a metal clip.

Go eat these.

Clay returned to the truck. He undid his pants and peed against the tire. He got in, and as soon as he opened the bag, saliva flooded his mouth.

His father jogged back and swung open the door and jumped inside, throwing five containers of oil on the seat between them. He jammed the gearshift, and they sped off, the engine knocking with the sound of a hammer on stone.

Goddamn it. I knew I shouldn't of trusted this thing.

He swung onto the highway and accelerated.

This seems like a safe speed, he told Clay. Next major turn-off and we find a Greyhound station and get tickets to Atlanta.

Blue and red strobes lit up the night behind them.

Motherfucker, his father said and stomped on the gas. The knocking got so loud the truck shook.

Over the next rise, two police cars came into view, blocking the highway, officers waving other vehicles to the shoulder.

I'm sorry, son, his father said, slowing down. I'm so goddamn sorry. But you know me now. That's the reason I did this. No boy should grow up knowing nothing about his father.

The truck was barely moving. The officers stood, black guns aimed. The engine tapped, and the seat springs creaked as his father looked around.

Roll down your window, son.

The knob kept slipping from Clay's palm. The glass squeaked. His father had lowered his and put both hands on the wheel. They came to a stop.

My hands are on the wheel, he yelled. I ain't resisting.

The door opened, and he got out as men shouted. The lights surrounded him like hovering alien eyes. His arms were behind his back. Handcuffs clicked.

Not in front of my son, he shouted. Goddamn you.

A beam flashed over his strong, tear-streaked face.

CLAY BECAME MORE observant. What people did and did not say had consequences. Stories were building even when he didn't know it. Neighbors watched. Kids at school repeated their parents' gossip about his criminal father and the kidnapping. His mother never spoke of what happened. She just hugged him longer than usual and let him go.

As the years passed, he thought often of the islands off the coast of Georgia. He would never wear shoes. He would wade

in the shallow water, digging up clams or catching fish in his
hands. And then he'd remember the drive with his father. They
could have abandoned the truck on a back road and walked
through the forest. They didn't need to hold up the store.

At school, Clay realized that what he liked in books —
a simple life in the wild, the treks of Jack London — didn't
appeal to his peers, that his disregard for fashion, gossip, and
rivalries made him a liability. He studied them, their talk the
chirping of a different species, and they shied away. No one in
his home spoke more than to communicate basic needs. His
mother read all day, and he called her Elle because her parents
did. Occasionally, she sang, *Alouette, gentille alouette . . . alouette, je te plumerai*, and when he asked what the words meant,
she said she didn't know.

From his mother's second cousins — all at least ten years
older than Clay — he learned to shoot. They taught him with
a BB gun, setting up targets or playing war games in the forest,
once coming upon a Christmas tree dumped in the ditch, the
decorations still on it. They attached them to their shirts and
hid, hunting each other.

That fall, he killed his first buck, butchered it at their camp
in the shelter of a stony incline, and they cooked the pieces over
the fire, rubbing chunks with handfuls of Morton salt.

Billy, the oldest cousin — square built, his big jaw going
soft — was Clay's mother's age.

Even at thirteen, he said, your mother was the hottest thing
in town. I saw her. She was just like a woman. Everything. The
ass. The tits. It was wicked crazy. I swear only the thought of
jail kept men away. But your father knew if he waited until
she was legal, she'd belong to someone else. You ever hear of
a catch-22?

Yeah, Clay said, resenting his cousins. The four of them clutched their beers, grinning and shaking their heads as they remembered his mother's glory days.

That's what it was, Billy said. You break the law or you lose the woman. Nothing in between except vain hope.

He adjusted his chew with his tongue and spat into the fire.

In Boston, your father had to go underground. He'd have gone straight if she wasn't underage. You get me?

Billy glanced around, and the others nodded.

Your father was the best mechanic any of us ever seen. We thought he'd have his own shop or he'd be one of those Formula One hotshots. But because of your mother, he was a criminal. He did what he did to give you and Elle a good life. There ain't nobody in this town who was pulling in more or working harder or smarter. But somebody ratted him out, and ten years was more than she could wait. He got out on parole after seven for good behavior, but seven inside and all that heartbreak, it changes a man. The father you met wasn't the man we knew.

What about his family? Clay asked, bracing himself against more anger and humiliation.

Your father was in a foster home. His people are from the north, somewhere near Frenchville, up in Aroostook. We don't know a thing about them.

Clay glared at the fire, its light aching in the nerves of his eyes.

Each weekend, he hunted, packing the freezer with game meat that Fred gave away as quickly as he bought Styrofoam trays of chicken and sausage. Fred warned him to hunt with his cousins, but Clay went alone. He read the forest. Other hunters waited close to the road, cracking beer after beer. He prowled, gliding onto a rock where he knew the buck would pass below a ridge. He wasn't quick to shoot. The bucks died before they'd finished startling.

Often, he just lay beneath the trees as leaves fell.

Control, he decided, was the line an individual drew within himself to limit the pleasure of release. His father took a thirteen-year-old and ruined his life. Clay forgave him and would go now to those islands and live off the bounty of the ocean. But he didn't want to be his father. If Clem hadn't panicked at the knocking engine, they'd be on that unspoiled coast.

FRED WANTED TO move somewhere urban. The computer industry was booming, Boston the Silicon Valley of the east. He was ready to earn more, buy a bigger house, and have children of his own. He asked Elle to read less and consider their future. His voice filtered through the heating vents and reached Clay's bed. She said almost nothing.

The week after Clay's sixteenth birthday, the day he got his license, he came home just as the police were leaving. Fred wouldn't say why they'd been there. Through the wall, his voice frantically rationalized against Elle's silence: he would soon be forty and was tired of people laughing behind his back.

The sun was on the horizon when Clay left the house with his gun and walked through the forest. The leaves were damp and quiet underfoot, and he paused, watching the sky darken. He had no reason to be out. Deer season was over.

He went back to the house and crouched outside Fred and Elle's room. Fred's back was to the window as she lay in her bathrobe, a book in her hands.

Fred began to undress. The knobs of his spine ran in a long mongrel curve to his recessed buttocks and the bulge of scrotum. He took Elle's book and put it aside, opened her bathrobe and her legs. Her breasts shone briefly, the moonlike heart clear.

Clay put the rifle to his shoulder. Fred's hips were pumping — the pathetic, minute, selfish movement of a dog on a leg or an impatient masturbatory hand. Fred was staring down at Elle's body, and she turned her head to keep his hair out of her eyes. Clay sighted at his jaw. The bullet would pop its hinges so that it hung like a broken Halloween mask. Would his mother show horror or persist in her mysterious calm?

Snow began to flurry, a few flakes melting against the hot skin of Clay's neck. Resisting this violent urge, he felt powerful. His rage lived in his hand, in his finger, and then, like spilled gunpowder beneath a match, it flashed into energy and flowed back through his veins.

By the next morning, eight inches of snow had fallen, and Fred rushed around outside, staggering and slipping like a man lost in a blizzard, dumping their possessions in the yard. Family and neighbors came by to take things as he hurried about the house with the slack, rapid motion of a marionette.

He asked Clay to sit down.

Your father is getting out. He's been sending you letters for years. Now he's sent us a letter saying he knows we've been keeping his letters. It could be a threat.

Clay's mother sat, her arms loosely crossed. Clay had no idea what she believed or wanted, or whether she was happy.

Fred finished spilling their possessions into the yard. He packed what remained into a small U-Haul and sold the car for next to nothing at a nearby garage.

Clay loaded his backpack and walked through the house. There were tiny dents in the carpet where furniture had been: six round circles for the couch, four from most other objects,

and a faint blackening of the linoleum and carpet at the doorways where people had passed.

Elle's father dropped by to speak to Fred. He held a cane,
his hip broken the year before.

I have a baby brother in Louisiana, down in Lake Charles.
I called him. He said he'd put you up if you don't know where
to go.

Fred's eyes bulged, congealed with terror. He'd left Maine
only for a few seminars in Boston. Louisiana was warm and
far away, and had always been somewhere in his consciousness,
another French part of America with distant relatives. He wrote
down the address.

With each mile, the snow waned, thinning at the same rate
as Maine's forest. By the time they saw *New York Welcomes You*,
the gritty ice along the edge of the highway revealed the shred-
ded rinds of semi tires.

The father Clay barely knew had set the trajectory of his life.
He pictured that broad-shouldered man striding out of prison,
determined to hunt for his son across the continent.

That night, he and his mother and Fred slept in a cheap
motel, in beds hardly wider than their road atlas. They rose just
before dawn to begin driving again.

As they continued down Interstate 81 to 77, through the
leafless Virginia hills into North Carolina and then Georgia
on 85, the world forgot winter.

At a rest stop, Fred came out of the bathroom and froze.
Elle had changed into a T-shirt and shorts. In the South, there
would be no season without tattoos.

MINUTES FROM LAKE Charles, Elle spoke for the first time that
day.

I can't believe you of all people would want to stay with Uncle Demetrie. Pappy used to joke that his little brother lived in a henhouse down in old *Lac Charles*.

Fred didn't reply, the inside of his lip between his teeth. Often, after bad days at work, he'd complained about his stomach or mouth cankers.

Unlike the plantation-style buildings on the street, Demetrie's home was a composite structure inside an undergrowth of ferns and trees. The doorbell played the intro to "Stairway to Heaven." Demetrie answered, his face dark-complected and proportionate, like a wood carving with a bit of stubble.

He looked at each of them and then said to Elle, It's pretty much what your pappy described, huh? Come on in.

He led them down a corridor, part of an addition built around the wooden siding of what had clearly been the outside wall of a real henhouse. They came into a room with a few low plush couches and wall shelves of LPs. The only windows were four bubbled skylights overhung with trees. The space felt like the inner chamber of a pyramid.

Why were you living in a henhouse? Fred asked.

I had some questions, Demetrie said, chin to his neck as if suffering from whiplash, his movements stiff and deliberate. I can't say it was anything mighty, but I wanted to be alone. Then I won the lottery, and I had all the additions built.

If it's all right with you, Fred told him, maybe Clay can stay here for a few days. Elle and I will find a motel. Once we get our own place, Clay can move back with us.

Demetrie agreed, and as soon as Fred and Elle left, he showed Clay to his room. The ceiling was low, the vertical planks of the walls sanded and stained, reminding Clay of a manger — Part of the original structure, Demetrie said, and explained that the property had once been the gardens of a larger home. He'd renovated and expanded the henhouse, bought the land, fenced it, and planted the jungle.

Demetrie's life, though strange, seemed good. He was only thirty-eight, the youngest of thirteen children — Of my brood, he told Clay — and each morning, he climbed out of bed, put an album on the turntable, and blasted Motörhead or Iron Maiden as he fried eggs, nodding stiffly in rhythm.

A man, Demetrie said, has got to live by his standards, even if it means seeming crazy. If you don't, you end up hating yourself. People just do the same things and say the same things, and forget they said them yesterday. I woke up one day and was tired of listening to all that.

Why do you like this music? Clay asked.

It's angry. It's telling the truth. There will come a time when people will think it's obvious. But it wasn't. It isn't. Anyway, I don't need the message anymore. It just gives me comfort. That's all.

Because Clay had been raised by untalkative parents, Demetrie's stolid demeanor seemed normal. Together, long after the grungy sky had faded behind the leaf-strewn skylight, they stayed up, flopped on the couches inside the Stonehenge of speaker cabinets, reading heavy metal biographies to the hushed thunder of music.

One afternoon, Demetrie took Clay to a crawfish shack and, while waiting at a red light, got out of his pickup and stood in the street to take off his jean jacket. Behind him, a Mercedes-load of teenage girls pointed and laughed. Clay slid down in his seat.

Later, over the platter of crawfish, he asked Demetrie if he was happy.

I don't know exactly what to say. I do what I want. I've been asked why I left Maine and the family. I wasn't one of them, and they couldn't take it. They were waiting for me to change.

So what matters then?

I gave that question lots of thought. That's why I was in the coop. It's funny letting go. It ain't easy, but if you can do it, you can make a better life. I think your mother's like me. She doesn't want to be part of it all. She won't even talk about it. Imagine having everyone judge you for something that happened when you were a child. That was one hundred percent your father.

My father? You knew him?

We were in school together. Both of us dropped out about the same time. It ain't bad to strike out on your own. Only problem is there's this fragile thing in us, like an egg, and we all think it won't break. I don't know if he was bad the way people saw him. He was angry, and what he should have been protecting he destroyed. He probably thought he wanted it that way.

That evening, Clay wandered the flat boggy town, trying to exhaust the restlessness and anger that rose in him for no clear reason. Unsure of the person he'd be here, he walked street after street, some with large old homes overhung with immense trees, others with boxy houses, barred windows, small fenced-in yards, and barking dogs rushing the metal links. He spoke with the fishermen by the lake and listened to their stories, realizing that unfairness had no limits; it permeated all things, like decay.

When he decided to get a job, Demetrie told him he knew someone who hired for standby shifts at the docks. Demetrie made Clay the necessary fake ID, taking a small laminating machine from a drawer.

I once thought I'd be an artist, he admitted, but I discovered I didn't like artists.

The man who hired Clay was tall and rawboned with silver temples, and avoided eye contact as he spoke in a gravely whisper. He said that a lot of the union guys wanted time off for Christmas and New Year's.

The work, heaving hundred-pound bags of rice from trucks onto pallets, shocked Clay. His hands chafed through borrowed gloves, blisters forming and bursting.

The older men had gnarled arms that looked harder than muscle. They noticed Clay's determination and nodded when he didn't stop after tearing off a fingernail. The pain mirrored the pleasure he felt at overcoming weakness.

In the weeks that followed, he grew stronger, downing containers of potato salad and strawberry yogurt, grilled Cornish hens from oven bags, two at a sitting, and granola bars between pallets. His fingertips healed, a shiny blaze of scar on each one.

The morning that Fred and Elle picked up Clay and took him to visit the temporary place they'd found, they were driving a rattling Toyota sedan. Fred told Clay that once he had a job, they would move somewhere bigger and sign a lease.

When Clay saw the carriage house, he knew he'd be spending most of his time with Demetrie. Though his mother didn't appear concerned about the accommodations, Fred was tense and focused, his expression that of someone forcing himself through a choice he'd made.

THE BOY WAS more or less Clay's size and build, though the reflection of the sky and pecan tree on the window softened his traits, like a double exposure. Clay pretended he didn't notice he was being observed from the edge of the drapes. After a few days, he looked at the boy straight on, letting him know he'd been seen.

And then, at the lake with the fishermen, he caught the boy watching him, on his rollerblades with his friends, clearly confused, as if Clay's presence didn't make sense.

When school started, they were in the same homeroom, and the students had to stand and introduce themselves. The boy's name was Justin, and he was excessively polite with teachers, a little stern otherwise, and sat in the second row.

Demetrie was right. People were predictable, even controllable, but only if the puppet master — Demetrie told him — could control himself and pay attention. Though Clay had never been at ease in school, he decided he could master the situation.

So he took down Dylan on the basketball court, whispered inventions into Melody's ear, and cowed Dylan in the hallway, aware that Justin was watching. For all Justin's robotic discipline — his spine straight in class, his precision in sports — he wobbled when Clay passed. Then, as Clay expected, Justin began to walk home with him.

Clay chose his words carefully, calling Dylan soft, mocking the lunches his mother packed him, as Justin flinched. And later, after they'd become friends, Clay delivered his judgment on Justin's bedroom. He wanted it all — the model planes and comics and books — and his envy infuriated his voice.

Afraid he'd been too severe, he rapped his knuckles against the army recruitment poster — a soldier stalking through the forest, face painted in camouflage — and let Justin tell him about his family's war history. Alternating between harshness and praise gave better results than Clay could have planned. Feeling in control was addictive. At times, though, he wished they could have met as boys and shared Justin's innocence, his sense of belonging. He thought of his own father, the impression he had that his relatives weren't fully American and had yet to shed a trace of their French pasts.

When Fred left, Clay was happy to see him go, but he hated the idea of Justin watching his family fall apart and the words being spoken in that big house. Whenever Justin's parents passed Clay, they said hello but were slow to smile, clearly assessing a threat.

Only Melody mocked the moralism in Lake Charles. She'd slipped a note into his locker telling him to meet her thirty minutes after school, and so he walked a bit with Justin, ditched him, and found her on the street corner she'd named. As they wandered, she asked about his family, and when he gave brief, hesitant answers, she told him about how her parents hadn't let her be a cheerleader because it was prideful. She asked why, if God was love, there were so many rules. She said her parents were real estate agents who, when drawing no lines at making a sale, quoted Jesus: *Give unto Caesar* . . .

Clay and Melody met again the next day, and she took him to her favorite place, an old Buick in the woods overlooking a bayou. Its paint was flaking off, and she used the windshield's net of broken glass as a seatback, stretching her legs on the hood.

They sat side by side. A silver fish jumped three times, and dozens of long, tubular gars glided past, their small, prehistoric beaks skimming the surface.

Melody took Clay's big hand and traced its scars. She kissed him, pulling herself close. Her dark hair was unexpectedly fine, airy against his fingers, and her skin made him self-conscious about the roughness of his body.

In their pauses, she asked questions. Without planning to, he told her about the time he was kidnapped — that autumn afternoon in the battered truck, his father's desperation and lack of control — and he described the islands off the Georgia coast.

She kissed him again, and he held her breasts as she moved her tongue along his teeth and sucked on his bottom lip. Then she lay against him as he reclined on the windshield. The sun was low over the forest, illuminating the yellow water and the fish below.

Do you respect me? she asked. It's just — I know what you heard from Dylan.

No one has any business judging you, he said.

He didn't have the courage to tell her she was the first girl he'd kissed, that in his old school he'd been a loner.

CLAY RESENTED JUSTIN: the way he and his father tramped through the forest murmuring as if the deer wouldn't hear, or introduced him ceremoniously to the gun room next to their garage. His father taught them how to dismantle an M16, and they stood around the assault rifle with the demeanor of men conducting an autopsy. The bones of their hands seemed to click.

To get through school, he restrained himself daily, taming his impulses even as his frustration at his life — its constraints and the roles he had to play to be accepted — grew into rage. When he and Justin ran together, Clay craved obstacles, not the dutiful pounding of asphalt but the precise step through roots and stone.

He found release with Melody, at her house before her parents got home. All day, he thought about those thirty minutes on a blanket on the floor for silence, the window open so he could escape. Afterward, soaked in sweat, they lay watching the clock.

It was at the Buick that she told him she was two weeks late. She cried as he held her, his arms an enclosure in which she moved, testing its strength.

At the docks, Clay stood in for a half-shift, inexhaustible, his shoulders burning as he swung sacks of rice like pillows.

He finished at midnight and walked. High, thin clouds blew in, lit by the red flashing lights of radio towers and the distant sulfuric glow of the refineries. His gaze roved to find one thing at which to aim. He passed the cemetery. Across it, Broad Street glowed like a frontier. To the north, beyond Interstate 10, a train chugged, blaring its horn, coming out of Texas.

He made his way to the tracks. The moon was up, the wind steady from the gulf, and tatters of newspaper fluttered in the grass. He pictured himself crouching on the roof of the train, instantly an outlaw as he rushed into an unknown landscape. He'd have that kind of courage once he knew what he wanted.

When he got home, someone was playing guitar as Demetrie sang "Patience." By the entrance, a pair of tooled cowboy boots were toed in next to Demetrie's black ones. Fingers squeaked on strings.

In the living room, Demetrie sat next to a wiry man with a mustache shaved to a faint line and rings in both ears. He wore a sleeveless undershirt, a tattoo on each biceps: a yin-yang and the earth with the Americas showing. He stopped playing.

Hey, Clay, Demetrie said. This is Nash.

Nice duet.

Hi, Clay. Nash shook his hand.

Clay, Demetrie said, his tone grave. There's something I got to tell you.

Nash lit a cigarette, took a drag, and exhaled. He raised his eyebrows to say, Don't mind me.

Your father called. He's in Boston, but he wants to come here.

Clay interlaced his fingers behind his head and released them.

How did he sound?

About as you would expect after so long in prison. But he wants to know his only son. He asked me to arrange a meeting.

Yeah, Clay murmured. Yeah, I want to meet him.

He went to the door, intending to wander some more, but glanced back. Nash was looking off, legs crossed and one elbow propped on his knees as he smoked. For once, Demetrie had lost his impassivity, his face furrowed and sad.

THE FLEA MARKET tables held obsolete electronics and clothes, and the sellers wore outmoded dress, as if modeling their wares — a mix of plaid, paisley, bolo ties, and denim.

Clay stood before a heap of books edged or speckled with mildew, their spines cracking when he opened them. The seller had a blue jay feather in a mesh hat and a curved nose as spotted as a newt. He nudged a book in Clay's direction, saying, This one's good. See here. It's a national best-seller.

Clay had positioned himself to watch arriving cars. He instantly knew which one it was: a jade-green station wagon with no sign of make or model, riding low on its shocks like an alligator on a river of asphalt. The fenders were rusted above the wheel wells, the ragged edges resembling bloody teeth. The body had been repainted so often that scrapes and weathering revealed the multicolored striations of a sucked candy cane.

While the flea market regulars plodded among the heaped junk, the man who got out of the station wagon stalked between tables, swiveling at the hips with the poise of a boxer. He was taller than everyone else, slightly bowlegged, in a black T-shirt and new jeans. His forearms and biceps were veiny, his chest hollowed like that of a man trying to puff up his back, and his shoulders made Clay wince: their fronts dug in, eroded, his strength worked beyond its limits.

Clay walked toward him. His father kept lifting his head, squinting around, maybe losing his sight or no longer accustomed to seeing into the distance. Gray flecked his cropped black hair, but he had the same carved goatee and mustache.

Dad, Clay said.

His father stood before a booth of Elvis statues and clocks, and he turned, his arms raised as if to hug or make fists, but the hands stayed open.

Clay? His bloodshot eyes rolled down and back up. Goddamn, son. You've grown into a man. I was thinking about you all the way.

Clay couldn't speak, his throat tight, a line of pain at his sternum. His father took his shoulders in hands big enough to cover them and squeezed the way Clay, as a child, had imagined giants accidentally crushed humans — the grip that of someone who hadn't touched another person tenderly in over a decade.

Son, I'm sorry about that time.

It's okay. I wish we'd gotten away.

His father bit his bottom lip, his two front teeth yellower than the rest.

We were so close, he said..

You did a good job. I wanted to go with you.

Well, his father said, I have some work in Maine. I got permission to leave Boston and head up there. I was thinking maybe you'd want to come.

That could be okay, Clay said, needing to think this through. He stood at the table of Elvis paraphernalia. Its owner had lowered his head, showing only a puff of gray hair as he unscrewed the back of an Elvis clock on his knees.

If you want one of these, his father said, I'll work out a deal. I got a little money.

Nah. It's okay. I already have a clock.

Well, you're a man now. You can come with me if you want. I'd like to know you.

I got to think about it.

His father said nothing. The raised muscles and veins in his neck gave the impression he hadn't slept in years. He cleared his throat.

How's Elle? he asked hoarsely.

Same as always.

Always will be. That's what I loved about her. She was just this thing on her own. They all said I forced her. You could never force that woman to do nothing.

His father's gaze was distracted, aimed at the Elvis vendor, who glanced up nervously.

Anyway, he said, and seemed to come to. I have three days before I have to check in with parole up in Maine. I shouldn't be here.

He scanned the crowd with the look of someone expecting a problem, a setup maybe. No — this was in their blood: an almost predatory scrutiny of their surroundings.

You've never met my folks, he said. They're good people. They had some hard times when I was a kid, and I didn't live with them, but they've gotten clean and figured it out. We have a lot of history up there. That's something you should want to know about.

I do, Clay said.

Okay. You just give Demetrie the message.

They shook hands, palms meeting with the jarring of bones. His father walked off, checking out the tables of the flea market as if he'd come here to buy something. Or maybe everything was worth looking at after so many years in a cage.

CLAY BARELY SLEPT, and in the morning he walked through the drifting leaves along the quiet weekend streets, breathing the cool vestiges of the night.

Elle was asleep on the couch, in her faded jeans and black tank top, a book on her stomach. She woke as he came inside. She never startled. Even as a child, when he'd hidden behind doors to surprise her, she'd just smiled.

What are you reading?

A book about picking a future. I'm supposed to write who I want to become.

Oh. Why don't we sit outside? he said. Her place felt confining, humiliating, like having to go to school in too-short jeans or a T-shirt that showed his belly.

Sure. She stood and followed him out.

Here? she asked on the porch.

No. Over there.

At the concrete well cover, he sat, his knees to his chest, and she did the same.

Do I look old? she asked.

Of course not.

He scanned the yard and out the driveway beyond the hedges. The one time he'd joined Justin at church, the minister had said the pain of life could be washed away — *Sloughed off like the skin of a snake. We must shed our pleasure-craving skin and show our true selves.*

She sighed. Where do I connect my dreams to my life? Everything I read points to another way of living, but there's no place to change tracks.

She'd never said so much about herself. Maybe if he left, she'd have the freedom to become who she wanted to be.

Silently, they scratched their ankles where bugs bit them or the grass tickled their skin. They began picking up the closest pecans. They crumbled the piney husks and broke the shells with their heels against the concrete cover. The flesh inside was soft and faintly sweet.

When Clay said goodbye, it was as if they'd concluded a long deliberation. He walked off, past the hedges. In the heat radiating from the street, the pillared porches of the neighborhood loomed like a reflection in water.

I'll meet him tonight, he told Demetrie, who'd just come home, grease-stained bags of takeout on the table. Clay loaded his backpack. There wasn't much to put in it.

Demetrie walked him to the door, a small black bundle in his hands.

I want to give this to you. He handed him a T-shirt. Unlike those Demetrie liked, it had nothing printed on it. The material had been worn thin and felt as soft as silk.

I remember just where the words were. This is my first concert T-shirt.

Halfway through the jungle, Clay looked back. Demetrie lifted a fist, devil's horns. A few minutes later, Clay had to stop on the street, briefly doubled over, until he could dispel the feeling and keep on toward the school.

The whole city, it seemed, had arrived for the football game. He and Melody sat in the bleachers, hip to hip, her head against his shoulder as he traced his fingertips through her hair.

The player with the ball sprinted, dodged, and then dove to claim territory as an opponent caught his legs. Clay felt the motion in his body, a synaptic twitching in his limbs. He would never play football here, even though the school revolved around it, with pep rallies and the earnest encouragement of the principal for a good season.

The ball flew up, spinning beneath the field lights, the runners small and mechanical. Against the green, the player about to catch the soaring football called to mind an ancient Christian painting he'd seen in a book — a tiny figure with bent knees and lifted palms, its face to the sky.

At halftime, Clay pulled Melody close and kissed her.

I'll be back. I just have to do something.

His last words would become part of the story, making everyone believe his departure hadn't been his choice.

NORTH INTO THE scattered forests of the moon-rinsed land, the interstate ran wide and straight — a technological wonder, a skyscraper on the horizon or a spaceship blazing into ascent. Clay had always lived close to a highway without giving it much thought.

His father steered with his right hand, his left arm out the window, and Clay rolled up his own to hear him against the battering air: life in jail, how it became regular — confrontations and fights and rising in status — and then the move to low security and his mechanic's certificate.

When Clay woke at dawn, his father asked him to take the wheel. With his head back, his mouth open, he snored so loudly Clay could barely focus.

At a gas station, his father shouted at the cashier, accusing him of shortchanging. Their hollering grew in pitch until his father threatened to call the cops and the man handed him ten dollars, saying, Git the hell out. The next evening, at a remote one-pump station in rural Pennsylvania, his father did it again.

Everybody's afraid of the law, he said afterward. Everybody's guilty of something.

They reached their destination at sunrise: a stony hilltop in Aroostook County on the Canadian border; a one-room cabin without electricity or running water, surrounded by weeds and saplings. His father had been given use of the place so he could rebuild an old Dodge Power Wagon, a classic that had belonged to the grandfather of a rich man who'd moved out from Boston, back to where he'd grown up.

We're going to make it into a show car. A friend of mine from the pen lined this up for me. The guy's running his own garage now. You'll see, son. I have a gift.

His father pulled behind the cabin, next to the rusted, hulking vehicle, and told Clay about it: a 1958 WM-300 Carryall, the first with an extended cab for military and civilian use. It dwarfed any SUV Clay had seen.

The cabin held two folding metal cots and a wood-burning cookstove that they loaded with wood from a stack out front and fired up.

They slept through the day without eating and the next morning drove to the supermarket for bread, bacon, and eggs. They fried breakfast on the stove and then unloaded tarps, aluminum poles, a space heater, and a generator from the back of the Power Wagon. They rigged a hoop garage over it and inspected the engine.

Fucking rich people, his father said. First thing we're going to do is take this thing apart. Then we'll start from scratch.

Into the winter, through cold snaps and heavy snows, they

worked, ratcheting apart the Dodge. The rich man — chubby
with a celebrity haircut — had loaded it with tools. He visited
every few days, appearing too young to be retired.

Shouldn't you be in school? he asked Clay.

I'm eighteen. I already graduated.

I bet you did.

Clay hated him, the work, and the cabin. He was so lonely
that on grocery runs he gawped at the pimpled cashier, wanting to pull her into his arms. He refused to let himself think
of Melody or her pregnancy.

His father never entertained conversations, just worked and
spoke about people in prison and from his past: crooked cops
he'd known on the street and met again behind bars, inmates
who suffered as they followed lives on the outside, betrayals
and remarriages and children who forgot them. A furrow sank
between his eyebrows, flecks of spit on his lips, and with his face
to the antique engine, he talked about the life he'd deserved,
the money he should have earned with his gift for engineer-
ing — that's what he called it.

After a blizzard, he began to cough, and blaming his cold
on insufficient nutrients, he bought a shotgun. Clay used it to
hunt out of season, bringing back a turkey and doe that they
butchered and cooked on the stove. When their clothes were
falling apart, they raided the donation bin behind a thrift shop.
Clay found a heavy pleather jacket. He never wore the black
T-shirt Demetrie had given him but kept it in a plastic bag.

Helping his father for months, Clay said little, studying him. His father told him there'd never been a fair shake
for those who weren't Irish. He blamed his arrest on them.
Clay's grandfather had hated them too. The Irish had made
life in New England hard for the French, calling them scabs

for working during strikes, even though the French came from terrible poverty up north.

Clay finally understood the trace of foreignness in his family. He'd known they were French but hadn't thought of them as immigrants.

His father told the story of a long-dead relative — a great-great-uncle — who'd been killed by an Irish stone during a mill strike. He'd been hit in the temple, and his wife and eight children had to be sent back to relatives in Quebec.

Whenever he ranted, his father worked faster and harder, and then he'd do something strenuous — adjust the chassis or loosen a rusted rivet — and he'd stop to hold his chest.

Got in a bad fight one time, he said. Was hit hard in the heart. It's never felt the same, like I have this bruise or something, right here, right under my ribs.

He was peaceful only when he smoked, once an hour, for five minutes, a cigarette puffing dead center in his lips, sticking straight out and nearly touching the tip of his nose.

All that keeps me going these days, he said, is the feeling that a real life is just in reach, and if I don't give up, I'll get to achieve one meaningful thing.

Clay wanted him to explain what he meant, but his father started talking about prison again.

BY JUNE, with the trees blossoming, Clay often thought about Melody. Standing at the edge of the forest, he pulled open the collar of his shirt and, briefly, the warm wind against his throat was her breath.

Welding and rebuilding every part of the Dodge had taken months. The reassembly was so painstaking that they weren't quite finished, and the rich man came by too often now, just to admire the gleaming engine in the giant domed vehicle.

By the time the work was done and summer had bloomed, his father was the spitting image of a Wanted poster. He coughed constantly.

I don't want to be a grease monkey forever, he said. It's a hard life, you hear me?

He lowered his head and placed his hand against his chest as if in mourning.

Their earnings dwindled through the summer and took a dive when their station wagon died and his father bought an old Ford pickup. One night in September, he pulled away from the cabin, the sound of the motor waking Clay. Two hours later, as dawn lit the windows, his father came home and upended a garbage bag of pharmaceutical packets and containers across the floor.

Help me sort this, he said. I love pharmacies. One quick hit and we can sell for months. I'll drop you off at the closest college and you can unload it. I also know a guy who works the old folks crowd. A lot of people can't afford this stuff. We're helping them out.

We shouldn't have to do this, Clay told him. I had a real job in Lake Charles. I was paid well.

You think that because you don't know how the system works. I break my back for twelve hours a day and get a hundred bucks, while some other guy is making a thousand off my sweat.

Do you remember what you told me when I was a boy? Clay asked.

What's that?

About the islands off the coast of Georgia.

His father threw his head back and laughed, a short constricted burst of air that became a fit of coughing.

Yeah. I was crazy as hell back then, huh?

Two days later, Clay and his father learned about 9/11 getting groceries. The cashier's TV showed a replay of the airliners striking the Twin Towers. A woman's voice described bin Laden's intention to cripple the American economy and take down a symbol of its global power.

I'll be damned, his father said softly.

The fluorescents buzzed in the aisles as they bought potatoes and the cheapest meats. Clay felt disconnected — what they'd seen impossible here: a disaster from another country.

He couldn't keep living on the edge of America. Maybe all his life people had seen him the way he saw his father. Justin once said the military made men equal; merit and not money carried them through the ranks. Clay pictured himself as a soldier, undeniably American.

As his father steered the narrow forest roads back, he ranted. Those fucking animals. They should be thanking us for civilizing them. This is going to be war, son. It's going to be a hundred years of war.

That afternoon, an acquaintance dropped by and told his father there was a video feed outside the pharmacy and the police were searching for his truck. Clay's father moved it into the now-empty hoop garage and took off its rusty panels and license plates, the corroded skeleton like a muscled carcass stripped of skin. He popped pills as he worked.

The next day, when Clay came back from the forest with a turkey, he found his father sitting in the garage, his elbows on his knees.

You okay? Clay asked and sat across from him.

His father's expression had become gentle, confused and grandfatherly.

I was remembering when I first saw Elle, he said, a dreamy lag between his words. Me and my friends, we'd fixed up a car and were driving, and there she was in these short shorts on a picnic table reading. She had her knees together. She was the prettiest thing. I don't remember who made the bet. We were drunk on her beauty. You couldn't blame us.

I won. That's how come you're here. Her parents were older and not around much on account of work. She was always outside reading. She was French like me. I could see it in her. I brought her a box of books from a yard sale and a bag of candy. We talked. Then I asked if she wanted to go inside. It was beautiful, undressing her like that. She just watched as I did it.

He lifted his hands and looked into his palms as if they might glow.

I bragged to the other guys. I wasn't above that. I was nineteen. We were kids. It was a game. Edgar said he'd get her too, and I punched him out right there in the yard where we were rebuilding his Jeep. Then I went and picked her up and took her to Boston.

She agreed to that? Clay asked, with the feeling of having walked onto a frozen lake without realizing it, sensing the depth beneath him, the dizzying awareness of space and danger.

She didn't not agree. She was pregnant. She cried a lot, but I took good care of her. The police were after me, so we went underground. I got us new identities.

His father dropped his chin and then jerked his head up. The muggy air of the hoop garage smelled of grease and the dead turkey's thickening musk.

But Elle stayed sweet. I'd see the women other men had and hear the nagging. She never did that. She stayed a girl. I encouraged her to do the tattoos so I'd feel more like I was with a woman. I took her to the best parlor in Boston. She looked through the tattoos like a kid with a coloring book. It broke my heart. I felt maybe I'd done something wrong. Then she fell in love with the tattoo guy. Or that's how it seemed. He was just nice to her, and she was simple. I went back and beat him up. It wasn't his fault, but there are certain laws.

He lifted his hand again and rubbed his sternum. His eyes closed and his head hung and he began to snore. Clay took a stiff wool blanket and draped it over his shoulders. He then hung the gutted turkey from the eaves.

He put his few clothes and a blanket in a discolored duffel. His father slumped in the chair, his hands hanging toward his feet, a thinning patch on his crown. The muscular bulk of his back spread, the veins in his arms thick.

By dawn Clay was at a highway and got a lift until the early afternoon. He got two more rides and finally was driven well into the evening along Interstate 95 and left at an exit a half hour from Portsmouth. He slept in a stand of trees and woke with a tear in his jacket — he didn't know why and worried it would make getting a ride difficult.

On his fourth day, he was in a semi, riding through Tennessee, the landscape tilting against the line of the inter-state. His anger tasted metallic — unnatural, as if he'd taken medication on an empty stomach. It grew as he got closer to Lake Charles and considered how few options he had and how he would be seen upon his return.

The driver let him off, and the semi jerked forward, leaving a black slug of exhaust in the muggy air. Clay descended to the streets and crossed a bridge over a muddy arm of water onto a narrow island — crossed it, too, and stood on the bank of the ebbing Mississippi.

He threw his ruined jacket in, threw in everything but the cleanest pants and the black T-shirt from Demetrie. He'd arrive in Lake Charles as someone new, again.

He leaned his head back, his mouth open, the sunlight hot in his tears.

PART 6

UNITED STATES AND KABUL: FEBRUARY/APRIL-MAY 2012

美智子

ACROSS THE SULLEN water, the green of Arkansas glowed. I stood on the muddy shore, spring weeds already woody and faded, their tiny petals fallen.

After two weeks in Lake Charles, I'd traveled north by bus. In Kabul the dry earth had surprised me with its fertility — blossoming roses or pomegranate and mulberry harvests — whereas America's wilderness seemed persistent and slovenly: along ditches, train tracks, and highways, behind bypasses and strip malls, between subdivisions and farms, like corridors through which the country's imagined murderers wandered; nature's whorish ravines everywhere.

Despite the land's mythic danger, Americans rarely did more than talk. They asked where I was from, lectured me about what they knew of Japan from TV — love hotels, theme bars, and fast trains — and then spoke of themselves. While people in other countries had interests, Americans had missions: to own guns, eliminate taxes, guarantee privacy, spread the Gospel, or self-improve. In their stories, I sensed that all good required strife and they felt the need to be ready to confront every threat. When you had as much choice as they thought they did, maybe only extremes were meaningful. But I knew I wasn't likely to understand these people any better than I did the Afghans. Still, as the writerly expats in Kabul have demonstrated, there is a market for writing about places in ways their inhabitants wouldn't recognize.

In Aroostook, I spoke with the grandparents Clay never knew, ancient-looking though only in their sixties — hard-smoking and -drinking. They invited me to a game of horse-shoes during which they hashed out what they could about his father and how he'd gone into foster care when they were teen-agers. Like most, the little they knew was secondhand.

I met with Elle's parents. They said the family should never have left — that traditions and generations had put them there. They had relatives among the first French in Maine, families who'd fled Canada after the 1837 rebellions. The rest emigrated south to work in the mills when Lewiston built the railroad spur that connected it to the Portland–Montreal line in 1873. They invoked history as if it could prevent the accelerating dis-integration of their community.

I even spoke with Fred, calling him in Phoenix, where he'd married a young Mexican woman. His voice was soft and clipped with hesitation, so that he always sounded on the verge of stopping. In his words, I was startled to perceive Clay, his father, and even Elle as outsiders, part of a tribe whose French identity persisted but no longer referred to anything clear.

All spring, I traveled, keeping tabs on Tam through Facebook. She couldn't post her activities during the embed but kept her profile active with photos from previous trips. There was an image of her and her friends running across a de-mined field in Bamiyan — *the result of a drunken bet, though everyone knew (mostly knew) that the field was safe, just really muddy!* She posted a photo of a Panjshiri guard berating an Italian news crew for having a snowball fight near Masood's tomb, and mused on the expats' lack of respect for Afghan values, the Western inability to understand the gravity of the Panjshiris' sacrifice fighting the Soviets and the Taliban — how everything for us was tourism or gap-year self-enrichment, if we were lucky. She posted an overturned car burning on the road-side. Her friends didn't appear to realize it was all old material: *You're my hero! How did you get so brave? Wipe out the Taliban so you can come home, beautiful!*

Tam eventually broke up with me over Skype. I was grate-ful. This way it was all very casual. She said she didn't do long-distance well. The emotional intensity we'd shared had vanished. She sounded professional and matter-of-fact, and we eventually began talking about her embed and how long it was taking to wrap up edits.

After we said goodbye, I realized I was no longer so con-cerned that Tam would write about the car bomb and the school. My novel would be different: about the craving for war's transformative power and the way some people — needing to risk everything to validate what they believe — chase endlessly toward the frontiers of their lives. Behind this, there was some-thing else, harder to pin down — Americans trying to redeem, with repeated triumphant stories, the chaos and the violence on which their nation was built.

Since I'd been alone in the US, the peacefulness of being away from Afghanistan had calmed me. The muscles around my heart began to release a tension I hadn't perceived. Now, when I remembered the safe room, I experienced a growing sense of sadness and horror. I realized how little I'd slept in the past month, how often I got up to write manically until dawn. I began to fall into long, dreamless slumbers from which I woke with a sense of terror, sweating and shaking, feeling the bullet hurtle past my ear.

After the safe room, none of us had discussed the death of the house guard, or whether there had been only one. Now, even the slaughter of the insurgents there to kill us began to represent more than my survival. They gave meaning to the statistics I'd repeatedly read about poverty, unemployment, and the compromises Afghans made to support families and survive the winter. The Taliban recruited by capitalizing on the government's nepotism and graft — on the hopelessness of the teeming youth. The country's average age was eighteen, more than sixty percent of the population younger than twenty-five.

I was so ignorant of anything but my own experience that I didn't even know if any of the Afghan Special Forces trying to save us had been wounded or killed.

Memories haunted me: walking out from the safe room, into the odor of burnt flesh, bodies slumped and smoking; peering into the burning car as if into a blackened crèche; the hand on the asphalt, its palm turned up like that of a Muslim in personal prayer.

Gradually, it seemed to me that I, too, had been hunting trauma — death, loss, solitude, alienation — convinced it could teach me, or that I could master pain and understand the taxonomy or syntax of suffering.

Once we have lived through violence, are we drawn back to it, like insects wandering into a world of artificial lights, tiny proximate suns, our ancient sense of navigation confounded, so that we proceed in circles until we annihilate ourselves?

JUSTIN

JUSTIN WOKE GASPING. All he remembered was light. It wasn't mystical. It was the imprint of his injury, the flare, the splotched color: phosphenes and blood pulsing in the eye. It hadn't happened in years, but the nightmare used to be common, making him question his faith — that dreams didn't filter down from the divine but were memories of pain, the way injuries in muscle and bone leave traces.

The heater's elements lit the bed. He lay on its edge, as close to the warmth as possible, wearing his jacket, wrapped in blankets, hands between his thighs.

For a year after losing his eye, he wanted only to sleep. He delayed college, and when he forced himself outside, he stayed close to home, studying his surroundings, trying to remember where things were, stumbling often into all he failed to see. The pain of the phantom eye incited his rage that others were fighting his wars.

He'd often examined his remaining eye, seeing the trajectory of steel pellet through the clarity of the cornea and aqueous humor and lens, puncturing the vitreous body and retina. Herbivores had eyes on the sides of their heads, their field of vision nearly all around so they could detect predators, who had eyes in front, the overlapping binocular vision giving them a sense of depth and allowing them to close in on targets. Justin was no longer a hunter. He couldn't even bring himself to peer into the fleshy hole when he cleaned his prosthetic.

After his injury, the dream of light had come steadily for more than a year — and then sporadically, once or twice a month. One morning, he startled awake thinking of Judas and the power of betrayal to lay bare a truth: two boys in a forest, caught in a selfish contest, and through their sin, setting each other on their respective paths. He was in college then, and he went to the chapel and vowed to purify his injury with faith.

The dream left him after that. He excelled in his studies, working with eagerness and discipline. He ventured out more and more, gradually stripping his fear away.

Now the dream was back. From it, he had a recollection of Clay, aiming in the night, and somehow, it also seemed to be Idris.

The heater's meager glow warmed Justin's eyelids. A memory tugged at his mind, an impression he'd had at the restaurant. When he'd come out of the bathroom and seen Clay and Idris at the bar, the distance between them had seemed unnatural, as if they'd been forcing themselves to look away.

When he woke again, Sediqa was knocking on his door. Her makeup didn't hide her pallor.

My uncles are watching the school, she told him. They suspect something.

He took his teaching materials and went downstairs, too angry to eat. The only real pleasure he'd had in the past week was the emails he'd exchanged with Alexandra. She'd written that expats who'd been here longer said the city was changing dramatically and a generation of young people were growing up with Western values. Reading her words, he'd felt that transformation was possible, that every little action created a shift. She was finishing up a report for a deadline, so they'd planned to meet Thursday.

Classes were mostly empty. None of the students had done their homework, and by the time Conversational English rolled around, Justin was surly. The slack-jawed young man with the smudged face was there again. Toward the end of the lesson, someone began playing with a soccer ball in the driveway, repeatedly kicking it against the exterior of the school's wall.

After class, Justin went outside. Idris appeared to have just arrived and was standing there as Faisal and a girl competed for control of the ball. Frank had warned Justin never to reprimand Faisal since his father was one of the few people who donated to the school. Faisal was small, fifteen at most, with a clump of curly hair. He'd written an essay about how his father kept him in Afghanistan so he didn't lose sight of his roots. Though he attended a private high school during the day, he came here afterward to improve his English and get a broader view of Afghanistan. Three girls who'd been in class joined in the game. They called for Idris to play, but he refused.

Idris, did you finish those worksheets? Justin asked. He'd found them online — challenging grammar exercises to keep Idris motivated.

I am almost done with them. They are very good. I am sorry I am slow.

That's fine. Can I borrow your phone for a minute? Mine isn't working.

Sure, Mr. Justin. Idris handed him a blue Nokia. Justin went upstairs and scrolled through the cell's call log. The same number was there, over and over.

Idris, he said, when he returned the cell, I'm concerned you're not committed to getting a scholarship. You haven't been around much.

Sediqa will get it, Idris told him without emotion.

Justin struggled to make sense of why Idris and Clay would be in contact. An image from the dream came back to him: dim figures speaking, saying things he'd never know — the anxiety that there was so much he would never understand. And then the light flared and he woke.

Mr. Justin, are you okay?

Of course. I was thinking about the worksheets. We have to go over them. This is the level of grammar you'll need once you're in an American college.

The last volunteer teacher, Idris said, he told me that Americans hardly know grammar.

That's not true. Besides, the standards are higher for foreign students.

Okay then, Idris said, I will do the worksheets. But for now I must study with my friends.

He started toward the door.

Are you forgetting your books? Justin asked.

Idris stopped, not moving, not even seeming to breathe.

You are right. They are in my . . . my room.

Justin followed him to the pantry. Inside, Idris slipped some papers into a textbook.

Thank you for reminding me. This is so important.

There was nothing in Idris's voice: not mockery, nor anger. He quietly left.

As Justin stood, the footsteps of girls crossed the floor upstairs. He needed to think, maybe to sleep and find his way back to the dream, to understand where he'd erred — how his suffering and the faith that overcame it could have led him to failure.

CLAY

IN THE SAFE room, Steve slid the door closed and brought up the camera feeds, showing the empty yard and the street: two schoolboys walking home with matching black backpacks, a woman in a *burqa* hauling grocery bags, an old man bent double, his spine bulging above him as he reached ahead with his cane. Clay sat, and Steve poured the whiskey.

Nothing's recording in here? Clay asked.

Steve's girth had expanded since his bodybuilding equipment had arrived, his neck thick and sinewy.

Everything's off, he said.

I may have a lead, Clay told him — an Afghan who's friends with Rashidi's son. He can get close to the family.

Clay chose his words carefully. He talked in the established circular way about how saving Ashraf Tarzi might require a sacrifice. He didn't say the sacrificing of ethics.

I have a good feeling about Idris, he continued. He's hungry. He's willing to do what's necessary.

If we don't do something soon, Tarzi won't survive, if he's even still alive.

Each comment nudged the door open, neither of them outright saying how far they were willing to go. But Kabul was a place of conspiracies, so why not conspire? No matter what foreigners did, the Afghans would accuse them of dramatic and

underhanded plots. Most believed the Americans funded the
Taliban just to justify the occupation.

And what if Rashidi's not involved with Tarzi's disappearance? Steve asked.

It's the only plausible explanation. Any other kidnapper
would have announced a ransom. Rashidi was in direct competition. They were bidding against each other.

So then Tarzi's already dead.

People keep hostages for months — for years in this part
of the world. It's money in the bank. Killing a man like that
would be a waste. They're probably waiting for the right time.
Rashidi will make Tarzi disappear for a few major contracts
and then go for the ransom money. If we use Idris, we'll have a
quick answer. And if nothing comes of it, we wash our hands.

I doubt Tarzi's family will pay us much more without a
solid lead.

They sat in silence, like Quakers in congregation, awaiting
the next revelation. When none was forthcoming, Clay stood.

You should get out more, Steve told him as he opened the
safe room door. There's this thing I do when I crash the expat
parties. I spot the new female journalists, the independent ones
who think they're going to stumble onto a prize-winning corruption story their first week. I talk about all I know, the wrongdoing and double-handedness. Sometimes it works. There was
one Aussie girl who thought she was living in an Ian Fleming
novel while I was getting laid proper.

Clay made himself chuckle. I'll keep it in mind.

The traffic was slow, streets crammed as people got off
work, dust and exhaust gusting, wind lifting it so that it
resembled the darkness of an oncoming front. Clay dodged
cars on his motorcycle, following residential streets and

alleys, his shocks pulsing as he left the asphalt.

Two years earlier, he and Steve had been saying that Kabul would soon be the Baghdad of '07, but that hadn't happened. The civilian surge was dwindling, and security companies had begun going elsewhere. Billionaires and autocrats were hiring them to train elite guards or manage private armies. He'd once read that the Roman Empire's decline had been apparent in its increased dependence on mercenaries of dubious loyalty. But to make a comparison struck him as thin. The mercenaries pouring out of America might be the ronin of a decadent, warlike society, but they were less a sign of empire's decline than business as usual. Regardless, he would never be one of those guys with an exotic assault rifle walking government employees into guesthouses while Western journalists went about on their own, smoking and gossiping.

He and Steve had discussed K&R over drinks. Clay had been in charge of training the company's Nepalese guards, but he'd been bored. Establishing K&R, they agreed, would bring an influx of cash with little overhead. The operation had no offices, floating inside the parent company, and if it were to close, some permits wouldn't get renewed; that was all. Clay was its only employee on the books.

In its first months, he'd freed three kidnapped businessmen. He'd built a relationship with Afghan Special Forces, who'd arrested the kidnappers after the fact and recovered ransom moneys, taking their share, a reasonable one in Clay's view. But then something stalled. Kabul's aid bubble began imploding, and Afghans increasingly solved their own problems.

Clay's thoughts shifted, an impression like someone reaching for his shoulder in a crowd, and his anger was back, a memory of Justin's big ideas when they were in high school: evil's

axis and the imperatives of freedom. After repeating things his
father had told him about America's duty to spread democracy,
Justin would get a wistful look, as if realizing that the words
he'd spoken hadn't changed anything; the world was the same.

Clay reached the mountain and raced up the rain-gutted
road, the front wheel weightless as he dropped gears. The sun
had almost set, and he squinted against its brilliance, taking
the first hairpin turn and skidding. He climbed again, Kabul
spreading out at his shoulder beneath smog and dust that thickened with distance into a black line.

After the American invasion, the slopes had been largely
bare, but now mud-brick homes crowded them, migrants from
the provinces competing for every scrap of land, and Kabul was
the fifth-fastest-growing urban area on the planet. His house
guard had told him that the farther you ascended, the more the
ethnic groups changed. The top, being difficult to provision
with water, was for the poorest. But someday, Clay thought,
if Afghanistan calmed, Kabul would be the new Provence or
Tuscany. Tourists would flock here to buy up and renovate the
highest houses. With enough white paint, the mountainside
slums would look fine on a Greek postcard. A new breed of
expats could reminisce on history and romanticize the war,
writing memoirs as they enjoyed the view: the successive ridges
of the Hindu Kush running against the sky.

He rode faster, rushed into the next curve, barely staying
upright. His anger needed a target — it was always there in his
youth, in the military, aimed at those who hadn't earned their
status or who profited from the effort of others, from casualties they'd never see.

After he'd fled his father and crossed the continent, he'd
gone back to Lake Charles, to the familiarity of the swamp

town. No one answered at Demetrie's. Between cupped hands, he peered through the windows at empty rooms.

Later, his mother told him that Demetrie had hung himself. He'd left everything to Clay, but their family had descended upon Lake Charles and plundered the house, a tribal arrogation preceding written wills, a levy for having to mourn the body of the deceased.

Holding Clay, his mother cried as she told him about Demetrie. He'd never seen her tears before. They shone on her pale skin like beads, like an image from an old movie or a book, of ancient queens curtaining their faces with jewels.

Then she told him about Justin.

While I was in the bathtub, she'd said, I'd adjust my head real slow. I could see through my eyelashes. His eye was right at the edge of the window.

Before Clay's shock could explode into anger, she confessed that she'd liked it.

You know, with his life in there with that family — who wouldn't be lonely? I felt close to him. He was so desperate, and I knew he liked me.

But then she said that Justin changed his mind, as if she were a mistake — and her tears became those of a child.

Clay began the paperwork for his inheritance so that he and his mother could move into Demetrie's. Elle had been hesitant, saying she enjoyed living in the carriage house and had committed to cleaning for the Falkers, and he'd realized she was still hoping to be with Justin.

Now, climbing the mountain, Clay took each turn harder, the dim plate of the city tilting. He cranked the accelerator and went into a slide, his elbow scraping the road as the bike swung like a pendulum, ripping at loose dirt and rock. The muffler burned against his jeans. He heaved and kicked. The bike clattered down. The engine sputtered and then stalled.

Sunlight from a distant range struck the earth around him, dividing it between shadow and an ancient yellow radiance that seemed to emanate from the mud homes and naked stone.

In Lake Charles, he'd walked, trying to envision who he could become, as he had the first time he'd moved there. He followed roads through the swamps. At a yard sale, he opened a book of essays by Frederick Jackson Turner. In its musty pages, like a bookmarker, was a torn strip scrawled with, *An American hero is the lover of the spirit of the wilderness, and his acts of love and sacred affirmation are acts of violence against that spirit and her avatars.* He bought the book for a quarter, and though he'd read it twice, the line was written nowhere in its pages.

The night of the party, he'd tracked Justin easily. He aimed at his heart but followed the barrel up and in that instant, controlling his impulse, shot him in the hand.

Clay's body had gone silent, without breath or heartbeat. Justin swung his rifle toward him.

And then Clay had the thought, clear as if speaking it — My mother isn't your rite of passage, you privileged son of a bitch — and shot out his eye.

ALEXANDRA

A DRY WIND stripped Kabul's smog even as it stirred up a haze of dust that muted the sun. In front of Alexandra's taxi, a poorly repainted Toyota Hilux slowed, its bed heaped with handmade furniture, rugs between the pieces as padding. Dozens of cardboard boxes were tied on top, one torn, exposing a red soccer ball. As the truck jolted over potholes, a gust freed it.

She leaned close to the window as the ball bounced, ricocheted against the grill of a passing car, and soared across the street, veering as the wind pushed it off course. Pedestrians stopped, staring as it rolled, bumped a tire, skittered, and fell into a gutter. A man in a tan *shalwar kameez* scooped it up and walked down a street with it propped between his wrist and hip, looking as natural as someone who'd finished a game and was going home.

Alexandra exhaled. She'd been holding her breath. She felt as if something was going to happen. Since that morning, her frustration had been worse than usual. She'd been putting together a file on a girl incarcerated at fifteen for immorality: her uncle had raped her, and she'd had three children in prison in three years. Working in a place like this had been part of Alexandra's vision, but she could have done meaningful work in a number of countries — or, indeed, in Canada, where many women were also abused and unprotected, and the rapes and murders of Aboriginal women often went unpunished. But Afghanistan had seemed the greater challenge, and there was the appeal of the war itself: a chapter in history, generations of violence visible in people's lives. War had shaped the human race, and she wanted to experience a country depicted like a frontier, where she could test her will and courage.

The cold and pollution of Kabul, the rundown offices and houses and vehicles, the obvious corruption and ineffective foreign aid, the angry, discouraged, or manic expats, and the angrier, genuinely desperate Afghans weren't what she'd expected. Her job kept her in the office, and she had to argue with her employers so that she could live among other expats without armed guards. But she met few Afghans and wanted to work in the prisons. At the same time, she wanted to go home and have a drink with friends and take on less impossible cases. She accused herself of insincerity, worrying that she'd come here to satisfy guilt or prove something, so she pushed harder and each day woke more resentful. No one else knew how she felt, so self-absorbed that they took her silence for allure, not inner turmoil bordering on depression at her daily study of brutality.

There was no lack of men here who saw her as a seductive secret. Expat women had a saying: the odds are good, but the goods are odd. She'd smiled when she'd first heard it, but now it had become clichéd, repeated often in the same way that expats obliquely praised themselves for being here, making light of hardship to convey how superior they were for enduring it. In the past few years, the men she'd dated had been masculine, aggressive, on the verge of overcoming whatever was destroying them — drugs, rage at society, indifference to the future — but in the end, she walked away from all of them because change never took place.

Justin, though odd, also struggled with his purpose. Other men were more at ease here, but they tried so hard to convince her of their worth that she doubted it. Justin was big and muscled, yet cautious, a shyness that she imagined in recluses.

The taxi crossed the highway and pulled onto the school's street. She'd taken half the day off and arrived in time for lunch. As everyone ate oily rice mixed with raisins, Frank told a story about a day a few years ago when his car got caught in the middle of street protests.

There was a rumor, he said, that an American soldier out in the wilds somewhere had burned the Holy Qu'ran, and people were angry, though the protests never made the news in the US. I had no armed guards, no armored vehicle, and I got through. I live here without guns because the best defense is no defense. You can't be part of the people if you're locked in a fortress. I'll never live inside the wire. Everyone here knows this school is theirs. It's not separate. But it requires the bravery to fight evil. *Evil* is just *live* spelled backward. A great man wrote that. These girls are trying to live, and the people who want to prevent that are nothing less than evil.

Frank's bombast dominated the meal, but when he shut up and the girls spoke, Alexandra felt changed. She'd had contact with two Afghan women in her offices, both raised and educated abroad, and she'd expected local girls to be submissive and quiet. But these young women told her they intended to be journalists, doctors, and lawyers. Some lived in Kabul and commuted. Others were from the provinces. Frank found them through acquaintances. He listened for talk of strong-willed girls and invited them to live in the dormitory for free.

Sediqa told her story, how she'd convinced her father to let her go to school on her own.

Many men, she said, when they see you without a *burqa*, in the street, without a man, they are not kind. They think you are bad for leaving the house alone. So I did not look to the sides. I did not look at the men who were looking at me. I went to school. I got a job. I am still studying. Mr. Frank has helped me. But now my father is dead. My uncles will sell me. If they catch me trying to leave, they will beat me or kill me for dishonoring them.

Afterward, in Justin's room, Alexandra asked him if Sediqa would receive a scholarship. He closed the door and stopped, his back to her.

There is only one available, he said.

She put her hand on his shoulder and turned him, as if coaxing a child out of a corner.

Why wouldn't she get it? Her life is at stake.

He went to the bed and sat, his hands clasped beneath his chin, his elbows against his knees — his posture preacher-like and distinctly Southern. She sat next to him, and he explained how Frank had been using Idris, stringing him along with promises.

If he doesn't get a scholarship, what has he been working for all these years?

She had the sense he was talking through his decision and would come to the right conclusion. He mentioned Clay, an old friend who'd become a security contractor here and whom Idris had contacted, probably for work, and how Idris hadn't been showing up to class.

If he isn't attending class, she asked, why are you considering him for the scholarship? He's a man. He'll be fine. His life won't be destroyed.

Justin put his forehead to his knuckles.

She felt a twinge of disgust. Like the Afghans, he was caught between two cultures: progressive society and that contorted evangelical anachronism.

Sediqa is an amazing woman, she said. You have to save her.

He sighed and rubbed his face. I know you're right. I may as well do it now.

She followed him downstairs, where she was scheduled to give a talk to the class about her work and education.

Sediqa, Justin said.

She came from the girls clustered around the table and adjusted her headscarf as if his presence demanded modesty.

I'm pleased to announce that you will receive the scholarship to study in the United States.

Sediqa took two quick steps and wrapped her arms around him. Some girls smiled, and others blushed. Alexandra became aware of her heart as it gave a few sudden strong pulsations. Living here had so quickly accustomed her to distance.

Sediqa backed away, and for the sake of those who'd just arrived, Justin reintroduced Alexandra, describing her work as a lawyer.

When she began to speak the girls changed, an easing around their lips, the dispersal of wariness. She talked about the legal history of sex crimes in Canada, how even there, abused women had often been blamed. The girls asked questions, and she told them about her studies.

Frank came in and sat in the back of the room with the air of a general arriving unannounced to inspect his troops.

Afterward, in front of the class, he asked Alexandra to be a mentor. The girls clasped their hands and raised their eyebrows in expectation. Saying no wasn't an option — not that she would have — and yet who was she to mentor girls this courageous?

What you said in there, Frank told her and Justin later, as they waited outside for Idris — that can change a girl's life. He appeared deep in thought, chewing the earpiece of his glasses, and spoke like a man with a cigar in his teeth.

They stood just inside the gate, in the winter dusk that sapped the world of color. Justin's cell rang. It was Idris calling to say he would be late because traffic was bad and had been restricted from several roads due to security concerns. She and Justin had dinner reservations, and he'd planned on having Idris drive them. He suddenly appeared dejected, no doubt realizing he should have called a taxi now that Sediqa was getting the scholarship.

As they huddled in their jackets, Frank began to speak about scholarships, and how, unless instilled with national pride and hope, most young Afghans who went to America would cross the border to Canada as refugees.

Alexandra recalled Tam telling her about cowboy development workers who, drawn by the gold-rush aura of Obama's civilian surge, set up one-man shows whose apparent merits they preached in bars. She described a former National Guard from Missouri who told the Afghan security forces he was US Special Ops and, for a year before he was found out and arrested, kept a prison in his compound, interrogating Afghans so he could track down Mullah Omar.

The white Corolla splashed along the street and honked. Alexandra said good night to Frank, and he told her, Don't forget the girls. They need you.

Justin sat in the front, next to Idris, and she got into the back.

Idris, he said, this is Alexandra.

Pleased to meet you, Ms. Alexandra.

Pleased to meet you, Idris.

Idris drove fast, not along the main road but the side streets, dodging potholes and heaped stone, the tires swimming in the ruts. After ten minutes, he pulled onto a paved avenue, the rear window glowing with the condensed lights of the traffic jam he'd bypassed.

Kabul was largely unlit, and oncoming drivers jockeyed to pass each other, their headlights flashing into the windshield. The repeated acceleration and braking soon made Alexandra nauseous. Idris's focus seemed to justify their silence.

Closer to downtown, the traffic slowed, five cars side by side in two lanes, exhaust rising, and dust so thick that buildings became visible suddenly, materializing like mountains from behind clouds. Men who'd finished work edged between cars the way people squeeze behind chairs in a cramped dining room. They tapped on the windows to inquire after free space.

The car now inched along the river, next to a low stone wall. Forty-five minutes had gone by. Idris turned left, away from the river, and she pulled her headscarf down as men looked in, maybe hoping for a ride. She'd never seen traffic so congested, cars wedging in, six inches between doors.

Suddenly, a shrill sound — she couldn't tell from where — rose to a shriek. Ahead of them, across from the Serena Hotel, above a rooftop, a reddish flare traced a line before slanting down. From the far side of the hotel, pale light radiated like a camera flash, illuminating the street. Red embers leapt into the night and vanished. The detonation thudded in her bones, through the frame of the car.

The sound, the flare, the reverberation — the flash and embers — nothing connected. They hung in her mind, each impression separated by a sense of immeasurable time.

Rocket, Idris said flatly.

With a tidal pull, the traffic before their car vanished, pressing into streets and alleys beyond the hotel. In front of them appeared unlit asphalt like a dark plaza. Somewhere behind them, pedestrians shouted as they fled.

Idris accelerated and then struck the brakes almost immediately, and the car jolted in place. The street was open. A rocket had passed directly over it seconds ago. The only direction to go was through the line of fire.

Justin had his hands braced against the dash, his feet planted.

Idris hit the accelerator, his arms rigid.

The car lunged with the suddenness of a roller coaster after its first peak. Unlit buildings blurred past, broken asphalt streaking beneath the headlights. Another car raced at their side. Alexandra lay down and crammed herself behind the front seats.

The two or three seconds through that space seemed like minutes. In the attacks she'd read about — a few times against the Serena Hotel, where diplomats and foreigners stayed — there had been multiple rockets. Her mind worked methodically, evaluating the timing and probability of a second rocket. She felt suspended in thought, floating.

Then the car broke through to the other side and a glow of taillights reared up before them. Idris hit the brakes, jammed the wheel to one side and then the other, pulling as far as possible into the traffic.

Hide your faces! he shouted. Your faces — hide them!

Her mind kept measuring the distance to the rocket strike, fifty meters, maybe less. She looked back to assure herself that they were far from the hotel, but it was just behind them.

The car, caught in the brilliance of the traffic's light, seemed exposed. Dust swirled in updrafts of exhaust. A man walked through, pant legs flashing past headlights, his scarf over his mouth. Idris again told them to stay down.

The car just in front stopped while traffic advanced on either side. Idris threw open his door and ran out and beat on its roof, yelling. He returned and checked that the doors were locked. They began to move again.

Alexandra was still holding her cell and texted Tam. *Almost got hit by rocket.*

Fifteen seconds later, Tam answered, *You're joking.*

She tried to text back *No* but her thumb kept writing *On.*

She listened for her heart, felt the sensations surging through her body the way she had when she was a girl, after the first time she'd made herself come.

Sirens approached and police walked between cars, slapping fenders as if herding steer. They opened a channel, and several pickups, their beds loaded with men clutching rifles, moved in single file against the direction of the traffic. As the first truck pulled alongside the car, Alexandra realized that the only military in the area was inches away and could be a target.

A soldier with a short beard and full lips stared down at her, aiming his rifle just above the car's roof. The trucks passed, and the traffic closed the channel.

I should take you both home, Idris said.

She touched her solar plexus and slid her fingers to her stomach. The nausea was gone, and she was hungrier than she'd ever been.

I still want to go to the restaurant, she said.

Justin asked if she was sure. The misting cars made her think of close-packed cattle in a run, their breath and bodies steaming in the cold.

Only when the traffic was flowing did she and Justin begin to talk. As if recalling an event they'd experienced years ago, they pieced together their memories.

Have you seen anything like this before? he asked Idris.

During the civil war, he told them. There were many rockets and mortars.

Briefly, she felt guilty for her sense of bravery, for her growing pleasure at the adrenaline streaming through her.

Two hours after they'd left the school, they reached the checkpoints near the diplomatic area and were allowed inside. Idris pulled into the narrow drive to the restaurant, through two red-and-white striped gates and between staggered concrete blast walls.

I'll wait here, he said once he'd parked.

Justin told him to go home. We'll take a taxi. Please get some rest.

Idris insisted that he would study in the car. Otherwise, he explained, he'd spend the same amount of time in traffic. In an hour or two, the streets would be empty.

As Alexandra and Justin walked to the door, Idris got out of the car and spoke with a group of drivers, most likely about the attack. All the men were older, and when she glanced back, Idris stood out, their stern eyes evaluating him, a boy among men.

The guards passed a metal detector over Justin and Alexandra. Inside, dishes clinked as expats chattered and drank wine. It dawned on her that the attack might not make the news. She'd never felt so alive.

Justin sat across from her, flushed and seeming to glow. Danger had ignited a metabolic process that was making him incandescent.

Tell me about Clay, she said, her body so restless she felt

she was soothing an animal into place, coaxing it, petting it, gripping its collar.

He described Clay as one of those people who didn't understand what it meant to be part of society and took pleasure in the losses of others. An emotion stirred in her, a memory of her brother. Justin must not have joined the military because of his handicap, she realized. The thought of him as a born soldier forced to harness his violence and serve the world turned her on.

After dinner, Idris drove them to her house. When she invited Justin inside, he said he should head back to the school, but she reminded him that tomorrow was the holy day and insisted that he stay awhile. They said good night to Idris.

She led Justin inside, to her bedroom, and took fistfuls of his black *shalwar* in her hands. Stitches popped, and he whispered, Easy. They kissed as she pulled off his clothes and moved her fingers along the muscles of his chest. She pulled him onto the bed, bit his shoulder, and put his hand on her breast, squeezing his fingers with her own.

Fuck me, she said.

He moved away, onto his side.

What's wrong? she asked.

I've foresworn sexual intercourse until I'm married.

His palm pulsed against her nipple. His quick departure the evening he'd walked her home finally made sense.

Justin talked about his mission, how he had to give body, mind, and soul — how God made Himself known through a sense of purpose. She wanted to ask, Then why are you here with me? But having him here, their skin touching, was something she couldn't yet surrender.

He started talking about Clay again, and the years after losing his eye, and she understood that his determination was larger than the school or anything he could accomplish as a teacher.

Were you afraid tonight? she asked.

At times, I'm afraid of being killed before I've done something meaningful. But when my faith is strong, I know I won't be. I've been doubting a lot. Because of Idris and Sediqa, I've been questioning my purpose here. Tonight, that went away. Who am I to think I'm entitled to an easy path?

He laid a heavy arm against her ribs, its pressure on her diaphragm.

Let's sleep, he said.

She reached and shut off the lamp. Her brother had once written to her about life on the army base in Texas and bars where girls talked about Jesus and the Rapture, and fucked as if it was coming tomorrow. He described the erotic push-pull of desire and contrition, the guarded hymens, the generous blowjobs and anal sex to skirt the divine rules and share a little pleasure in the blind spot of the Lord. Why couldn't she have been so lucky?

Justin adjusted his body next to her and fell asleep.

美智子

THE MORNING AFTER the rocket attack, Tam and I ate a late breakfast and she warned me, cryptically, "Godfrey is here." Moments later, Justin followed Alexandra out of her room.

Tam invited them to a picnic. Two weeks earlier, an Afghan businessman she'd once interviewed had called to ask if she could find renters for a single-storey home that dated to the sixties. The Australian head of a surveillance company had renovated it, hanging numerous mirrors and transforming a bedroom into a pub. Between the house and the rear compound wall, he'd built a greenhouse, put a heater inside, and, not long after, returned home. When the businessman told Tam he was worried the plants would die, she asked him to keep the heater going. The bottom had dropped out of the housing market as foreigners left and the building boom continued — real estate being one of the few ways to invest earnings from the poppy fields that produced ninety percent of the world's heroin — so she convinced the owner to match the cost of rent at the much lesser building where some of her friends lived. They'd decided to celebrate with a picnic in the courtyard greenhouse, on the grass.

More than twenty people arrived, bearing bowls of chips, cheese plates, and kebabs. Bottles of wine were set along the wall, behind potted succulents whose neglected leaves had the texture of raisins.

Tam knew everyone at the picnic, and people were curious about who I was. I said only that I wrote for a Japanese magazine. One rule of expat ambition is that you don't voice your goals unless you've already made significant achievements; otherwise, people will mock you in your absence. Many great expat journalists emerged suddenly, after having published a feature in a notable American magazine, and then began waging cramped political debates on Twitter.

Word had gotten around that Alexandra was seeing Justin, and people gathered to speak to him. They wanted to understand her interest or draw him away so others could flirt with her.

Tam asked about his plans. "A lot of people come here with more than one," she said. "They teach a little while doing a bit of journalism or keeping a blog, and then end up working for an organization."

Justin said he was just volunteering, and Andrea, a Canadian administrator at the American University of Afganistan, told him she knew Frank.

"With a few exceptions, his kids aren't in the system. They don't get a sense of what is normal in education, of the levels and demands. We have tests, and if the kids don't work, they lose their scholarships. But Frank tells everyone he got fed up with us. The truth is he was fired for favoritism. He's proud of saying he's gone native, and in terms of nepotism, he was giving the Afghans a run for their money. Now he's chasing windmills."

Justin flushed a little but said nothing, maybe not willing to admit he'd come for a school built around one man's personality, whose mission wasn't even to let the best rise on their own vague merits, as claimed, but to ship his favorite girls to the States when money was available.

Paul, a handsome New Zealander with a red beard and receding hair, swirled his whiskey as he spoke with Alexandra. He oversaw historical preservation for UNESCO. Tam, who counted him among her conquests, pushed his shoulder and said, "Girl time, Paul. Scat!"

She walked Alexandra out of the greenhouse, and I followed, as did Holly, the busty Connecticut socialite who ran the dog shelter.

We walked down the hallway, into a bedroom where a mirror had been hung on the ceiling.

"So how was your sleepover with Mullah Omar?" Tam asked.

"It was . . ." Alexandra said, "terrible."

Tam flustered her with questions, and Alexandra explained his faith, his belief in waiting until marriage.

"What the fuck," Tam said. "That makes me so embarrassed to be American."

"But at least I discovered the school," Alexandra said. "It's another side to Afghanistan. I didn't know there were young women here who were so impressive."

"Just be careful," Tam told her. "Frank has asked me to be a mentor like a thousand times. He's a crazy old guy hanging out with a bunch of Afghan girls."

"There are boys too," Alexandra said.

"How many?"

"I don't know. They weren't there when I went."

"Exactly."

"But the girls are amazing." Then she talked about the scholarship, about Sediqa and Idris, and how Justin had called him that morning and planned to take him to lunch and tell him.

"The kid just needs to escape that school," Tam said. "Frank will promise anything to get what he wants. As for Justin, you're living the quintessential Kabul experience. Expats bond quickly. You have the impression of sharing so much. You're both brave. You're exceptional. You're all alone. And then you wake up one day and realize you're in bed with a whack-job."

Alexandra hesitated. "At least he's trying to help the girls. If he doesn't, who will?"

Tam shrugged. "Anyway," she said, "you rarely get bonding like that back home, and there's no downside, because the disappointment isn't much different. Well, maybe the Mullah is a special case."

She tilted her head back to the mirror, and we did too, standing where the bed must have been, staring up at our four faces as they floated above us, as if in a sunlit well.

As we explored the house, Holly talked about her frequent Kabul romances, how she'd had her heart broken by one she'd thought was different — Luis, a former army dog trainer from Florida who'd come back to Afghanistan to work for her organization as a civilian. Alexandra asked about her work, and Tam grimaced in my direction, showing her teeth as Holly talked about the shelter and her favorite dog, Hank, who pushed on things with his paw to make sure they were safe before eating them.

Tam opened a storage room that hadn't been renovated, its ceiling water-stained and old hand-carved furniture crowding it. We moved through, touching headboards, dressers, and a rolltop desk, and then worked the dust off our fingertips as if crumbling salt. Piled against the walls were dozens of full-to-bursting roller bags, eight padlocked aluminum trunks, numerous taped-up cardboard boxes, two plastic Christmas trees, a bike with flat tires, and a few Kabul street signs — the ultimate souvenirs, stolen during binges of drunken partying. Tam said that expats often abandoned everything they owned in other people's houses when they left, promising they'd return for some not-yet-funded project.

"But this furniture is really old," Alexandra said. She opened a cabinet, rows of pigeonholes crammed with fusty yellow papers. We began pulling them out, looking at news clippings from the late seventies and eighties, from the Soviet period and the civil war.

"I should write a piece about this cabinet," Tam said.

Holly reached to one of the upper pigeonholes. A roll of what might be receipts was stuffed in like a cork. She removed them, felt around inside, and brought out a dusty sphere whose rugged surface resembled chunky tire treads.

"Oh my God," she said. "Oh fuck. Oh my God. What do I do?"

"Don't move," Tam told her and cupped her hands. "Just slowly tip it into my hands."

Holly did as she was told. She backed away and then ran into the house, shouting, "We found a grenade! We found a grenade!"

People lined the hallway as Tam marched through with the pomp of one bearing a Fabergé egg. In the greenhouse's winter light, she placed the grenade in the grass.

Holly was talking quickly to Paul. "I just kind of grabbed it. I had no idea. I mean, the pin could have fallen out."

Expats often did this — seeing danger constantly, heightening encounters with the police by speaking loudly, waving their hands, getting flustered. If a ministry was attacked, they talked about every time they'd been there. In the expat bubble, living in a war zone was less dramatic than they'd expected, and they were compensating.

Justin stood by the doorway alone, his jacket on, his cell to his ear.

"Idris," he said. "Come inside. Maybe you can help us."

Everyone was crouched, as if the grenade had fallen from one of the potted trees — a cubist avocado.

Idris came inside wearing a snug new leather jacket. The cold had left two pink thumbprints on his cheeks. He walked to the center of the small crowd.

"It is a Russian grenade, an old one. These are known for being very fair weapons."

"You mean because they're effective?" Paul asked.

"No, because sometimes they blow up your enemy — sometimes, when you pull the pin, they blow you up. They do not pick sides."

People laughed and sat back on their heels or cross-legged in the grass. The mood had shifted. Expats loved a humorist who could make light of the war.

"How do you know this?" Paul asked. "You're too young to have been in the army."

"Actually," Idris said, "I am too old. They like their recruits fresh and tender."

Everyone laughed again. Most of the wine was gone, and sensing he had an audience, Idris stood a little straighter, his smile bringing out his youth and easing his angular features.

"Afghans know grenades the way Americans know cars," he told them.

Tam interrupted to say she'd read that Soviet grenades had different fuse systems. The average delay was 3.5 to 4 seconds, but some exploded immediately for use in booby traps.

Idris cocked his head in Holly's direction.

"Yes, it was a thirty-year-old booby trap. The string tied to the pin must have rotted off."

"Oh my God," Holly said and held up her palms as if she'd touched filth.

After the laughter subsided, Idris reassured her this wasn't true. "It's not a booby trap. These used to be as common as pomegranates. During the civil war, when it was very bad here, I lived with my uncle in Laghman Province, and he taught me how to fish with them."

"How bucolic," Paul said.

"We would build a dam with rocks," Idris told them, "to stop the fish. Then we'd throw in the grenade or shoot in an RPG, and we'd all hide. We got sometimes a hundred fish, enough for the whole village, but we had to be careful of pieces of metal in the fish, the *chara* . . ."

"The shrapnel," Tam said.

"Yes. Thank you. The shrapnel." Idris flushed a little and glanced at Holly. "Dynamite is much better and easier and cheaper now that Afghanistan has used up most of its grenades."

"Where do you get dynamite?" Holly asked.

"Everywhere. In any bazaar. A stick is maybe one dollar. People make it with fertilizer."

"How comforting," Paul chimed in.

"You do not have to hide as much from dynamite, so many Afghans use it, or electricity."

"Electricity?" several people said at once.

"Yes, you take a generator and put the wires in the river. But fishing like this is illegal now. Too many people were electrocuting their neighbors. One man would be taking a bath, and his neighbor would put the wires in."

"He didn't look first?" Paul asked.

"People get very hungry," Idris told him.

After another burst of laughter, the conversation shifted away from Idris, expats talking among themselves. He moved closer to Holly. I heard him ask what she did, and she described her NGO, the street dogs they took in, nurtured, and flew to the United States for adoption.

"Oh," he said, the color draining from his cheeks.

"And what do you do?" she asked, cocking her head, trying to interpret his reaction.

"I am a . . ." — he faltered — "a jack-of-all-trades, but I am trying to be a student. *Inshallah*, I will someday join your dogs in America."

She laughed, touching his arm, and his color returned. No longer focusing on Alexandra and Justin, the expats now talked while keeping track of Idris and Holly. Though a number of the men had dipped a toe in her water and found it far too electric, others awaited their chance. They began to encroach on the conversation.

"Idris," Justin interrupted, "we need to head out."

Everyone shifted their attention to see how he would bid farewell to Alexandra. He lifted his hand in a vague gesture. If there was any emotion on his lips, his beard hid it.

Paul thanked Idris for his stories, stepped between him and Holly, and escorted him to the door.

When men presented themselves to a woman as protectors, I wondered, did they know they were simply making her more available to their own advances? It was an old simian ruse, yet I suspected few of them saw into the biology behind it.

"Thanks for the stories," Paul told Idris. "*Hoda hafez*, mate."

Holly stood on her toes. She waved, but Idris was gone.

CLAY

THE JEANS CLAY had worn on the motorcycle were torn along the thigh. He sat on his bed, holding them, and then went to the closet: his entire wardrobe was threadbare, as if everything had conspired to deteriorate at once.

He pulled on his least worn-out jeans, buttoned up a flannel shirt, and put his jacket on. He'd come out of an existence of mechanical efficiency into a rage he no longer thought possible. He had a burn on his calf, and bruises all along his leg. The only drama in his life was that which he created.

The day was brisk. A light predawn snow had melted. He rode to Wazir Akbar Khan and parked. At a checkpoint, the police lifted the gate, and he walked down a dirt road. He knocked at a metal door. The slot opened and then the deadbolt clanked. The guard frisked him and banged on a second door. Just inside, there was an ornately carved Nuristani doorway and, beyond it, a courtyard.

He sat at a wooden table in an empty room with a domed brick ceiling like a kiln. Low heartless trance throbbed in the speakers. Idris walked through the courtyard, and as he passed the window, Clay called. Idris stopped, backlit by the sun, his gangly silhouette cartoonish.

The steak kebabs are good, Clay said as Idris joined him.

The menu was pricey even by American standards, and

Idris's eyebrows shot up as Clay ordered fresh carrot juice, two bowls of potage, and three plates of steak kebabs and fries.

So have you become best friends with the kid?

Yes. I have been inviting him to see movies. A guy I know made his house into a cinema.

Did you get a sense of whether he has information about what his father does?

He's a kid. He plays video games and does his homework. He doesn't think like a man. He doesn't even talk about girls.

That's a shame.

Idris smiled. He thinks his life is hard because his father won't let him go to university in America. He tells me how bad living here is, as if I do not know. I was in Kabul during the civil war, but he was in Pakistan. His father thinks he's too soft and would stay soft in America. He wouldn't know how life worked in Afghanistan. So Faisal must do his university degree here and then he will be allowed to do the master's in America.

Poor kid, Clay said.

Yes. I do not feel sorry. Every Afghan would want his problems.

Clay took his time, speaking the way he had with Steve, letting the conversation lull and eddy, creating space for Idris to consider the paths to the success he craved.

I don't know what to do, Clay told him. I'll pay you for your work, but I'm not sure there's anywhere to go with this case.

Maybe you can take him for questioning, Idris suggested.

Quiet. That's serious.

I mean —

I know what you mean. I have to think about that. Maybe if his father talks, if he feels some pressure, we can save Tarzi.

Yes, Idris said and enunciated carefully: That would be good.

Clay shook his head. It's a shame Rashidi has put us in this position.

I know. Ashraf Tarzi is a good man. He is liked by many people for creating jobs and running his businesses well, and for helping the poor.

Clay knew this situation was happening all over the earth — the desperation, the sense of going nowhere — and then a glimmer, barely even hope, just a small change, the thought that if you nudged the world, it might, when the dust settled, be a place where you could belong.

I don't want to call this off, Clay told him. I know you've invested a lot of time and hard work, and I respect that. But what can we do?

The question had a rhetorical edge that gave it the finality of surrender. He changed the subject and asked what was happening with Justin these days. Is he still banging the girl?

Idris smiled faintly. Banging? Yes, he is.

And the scholarship?

Idris's smile vanished. He has given it to the girl he is banging.

That's rough, man.

I heard it from a girl at school. Justin will talk to me very seriously about it and tell me lies.

I'm really sorry, Clay said, grateful for the timing of the betrayal.

I think you should speak with him.

Who?

Faisal. He and I are going to see a movie this evening. Maybe I will get stuck on the road, and you can take him and talk to him.

Clay let furrows gather in his brow. Idris must know this was theatre, but it was honest theatre that laid bare the mechanisms of deliberation, the peeling away of options.

It is the only way to save Tarzi, Idris told him. Faisal has enjoyed the money of corruption. He is Rashidi's son. I will not be sad for him.

Clay unfolded a hundred-dollar bill. Listen. I really can't say how much I appreciate your help, but you can't talk about this because people wouldn't understand. You get that, right?

Of course.

But what you're doing is good. When all this is finished, a lot of people are going to be thanking you. And I'll make sure you're paid very well. Eight hundred dollars if you get Tarzi. Fuck. How about a thousand? You're doing all the work.

The food arrived, the carrot juice sweet and clean-tasting, steam rising from the potage and beef. Clay glanced at the waiter and said, Whiskey? He got a nod and ordered a triple.

He asked Idris where he'd grown up, and when he replied, Kabul, Clay said it must have been rough.

Idris put a piece of beef in his mouth and shrugged. I saw worse things after the Americans came.

The waiter brought the whiskey, and its heat eased the tension in Clay's body.

Idris paused, his fork daintily held in his thin fingers.

Once, after the Americans came, my uncle, my cousin, and I were walking in the street, and we passed two men who were sitting on some cement. They were sweating and shaking. My uncle thought they must be on drugs, so we crossed the street. An American convoy came through, and the men ran at it and blew themselves up. I was on my knees. I couldn't breathe. There was so much smoke and dust everyone's faces were black. I remember all the white eyes. On the road, there was a jawbone.

No shit, Clay said and took a long drink. Idris chewed slowly, taking his time with the meat, sipping his juice. He appeared unaccustomed to food. Clay had to pace himself.

Idris's cell rang.

Yes, Mr. Justin, he said. Yes. I will pick you up. I will be there soon.

Justin is at a picnic, he told Clay. He needs a ride to the school. You'd think he'd call a taxi.

I suppose so. How do you know Justin?

We went to high school together and then lost track of each other. Anyway, tonight, we need to be careful. It has to be clear that you have nothing to do with this. It would be smart if you at least got bruised.

Then bruise me, Idris said.

It won't be badly. Just a punch. When we take the boy.

Idris drew a map, marking a section of road where there were few buildings. He wrote down 8:30 p.m., and they went over the details of the plan.

They left the restaurant, out past guards in gray fatigues, through the metal detector and past the police with Kalashnikovs at the checkpoint. From the booth, an officer lifted his hand, to wave or to motion them through — the gesture loose, unfamiliar, more like a curse. A helicopter thudded out above the city. All across the mountains, lights were coming on.

Clay was suddenly breathing hard. The air felt thin, not cold enough to resist the heat of his skin.

You're being straight with me, right?

Of course I am.

Of course, he repeated. Of course. He'd begun to sweat, angry that this was his life, wondering if he'd end up in an

Afghan prison. I can take care of things if they get out of hand, he said. I've done it before. I've killed boys like you.

You can trust me, Idris told him. I promise.

They said goodbye without shaking hands or even looking at each other.

At home, Clay called Steve. It's on. Tonight. Have the room ready. Then he lay down.

In Maine, his father had talked about finding a meaningful moment when he could feel satisfied with life, if only briefly. Clay had come closest to that in the army: the brotherhood venturing into alien landscapes, the bracing of muscle, the raw clamoring of heart and lungs.

On his last Dubai trip, he'd stopped in a mall bookstore and perused a collection of Persian poetry — Rumi and Hafez — their words giving him a sense of an enduring culture, as if Afghanistan were a restless ocean under which its history lay like Atlantis. It made him wonder what he didn't know. A poem exhorted him not to believe in his wrath, nor to be satisfied with the veil of this world. Lines like those should be accompanied with an instruction manual.

His alarm chimed. He sent a confirmation text and rode to Steve's house.

A drink? Steve asked.

Nah. Not now.

Crossing over to the dark side comes easily for you, I see.

There aren't any sides.

They took a company Corolla. One of the armored suvs would attract attention, and the Corolla had a space in the trunk for a spare tire that Steve had expanded into a compartment large enough to hold weapons — or a person. He had a map of the most common places for checkpoints, but the police rarely did more than glance through the windows. Steve sipped bourbon as he drove.

They parked on the roadside and waited, the lights off, hot air in the vents. Clay took his balaclava out of his pocket, draped it on his knee, and prepared the chloroform.

Another Corolla neared. As planned, Idris had removed the bulb from inside his left headlamp. The car crept past, and they followed.

You hit the kid, Clay said. But go easy.

Idris's car wobbled and slid, the front tire dropping into a rut. The brake lights flared and dimmed. The doors opened, and two figures emerged.

Steve pulled close and flicked on the high beams. He and Clay put on their balaclavas and got out.

Faisal squinted as Clay approached at an angle so that his body didn't shield the boy from the high beams and allow him to see in along the shadow. Steve was coming from the other side, toward Idris, his breath swirling past his shoulder.

Clay grabbed Faisal and pinned him to his chest, the heat of panic radiating from the boy's back as Clay held the rag to his nose and mouth.

Idris stood next to the car, arms slack.

"Sorry, kid," Steve told him. He punched him in the face, and Idris spun convincingly to the ground.

Clay popped the trunk and placed Faisal into the compartment, locked it, and got in the passenger seat. Steve turned the car around. Idris remained on his knees, leaning against the fender, one hand on the metal, the other on his forehead.

How's that for a little adventure? Steve asked.

If you find yourself chloroforming a fifteen-year-old, Clay told him, you know your days of adventure are over.

JUSTIN

A RUSSIAN SEDAN idled in the street outside the school. It was
small and square, its grill gone and the body patched and hammered into shape. Two men sat in the front, three in the back,
all sporting beards. The front passenger was older, grizzled, a
scar passing over his cheekbone from his temple to his prominent nose. He stared as Justin closed the gate.

Justin had been looking for Idris. He hadn't seen him since
he'd told him about the scholarship. Appearing unbothered,
Idris had said, I knew that would be the case. He'd even refused
Justin's lunch invitation, saying he had plans. In the day since,
he hadn't answered his phone or come to class. Justin had grown
so restless that when he'd heard the car outside, he'd gone down
to the street. Sediqa had warned him that her uncles might
come by. She'd said one of them had fought in the civil war
and had a scarred face.

Justin walked back to the guard's quarters.

Shafiq reclined on *toshaks*, in a tank top, and squeezed hand-
grips from which the padding had worn off, the metal squeak-
ing as his forearm flexed, wormlike veins all along it. His hand
was as red as a tomato.

Mahmoud, a boy who sometimes came to class, was sitting
with him, watching TV as President Karzai spoke at a podium.

Shafiq, Justin asked, do you have a gun?

The boy translated the question and Shafiq's response: Five months ago, during a farewell party for a visiting teacher, someone stole it from under his bed.

Why don't we get a new one?

Shafiq listened to the boy and shrugged.

Frank has no money.

Justin knew that to be true. Frank had asked him to call around to his friends back home to help raise funds. The previous night, Justin had heard him through his door, Skyping to the US, asking for donations — Yes, that's what I'm explaining to you, Frank had been saying. We can barely keep our lights on here . . . No, we aren't a 501c3, but I'm going to register as a nonprofit . . . Well, even if it's not much, it will make a difference. Every day, we're creating a future for Afghanistan. Not a penny gets wasted . . .

After the rocket attack, Justin had told Frank about it, pleased to see the old man's envy. He'd found an article in the local English paper. Four Afghans had been wounded: a businessman, a police officer, and two women. The target was the Serena Hotel or perhaps a police truck outside. Justin cut out the article, still thrilled by the experience — the streaking red light, the open space in front of the car before Idris hit the accelerator.

In his room, he phoned Clay.

What are you doing with Idris?

Hey, Justin. No hello? No how are you?

I asked you a question.

And it's any of your business?

He's my student.

I hired him to run errands. Isn't that what you use him for? Oh, and hey, Idris told me about the rocket attack. I was in bed with an NGO chick one time, and right when we came, the house shook. Car bomb. In Iraq, every other time I jerked off, a mortar was hitting, but in Kabul every little explosion feels special.

Anyway, Clay continued, I just want to help Idris too. How about we talk this through in person? The traffic's awful right now, but one of the guys I work with is having a party tonight. We can find a quiet space to sit down. I'll text you the address.

Okay, Justin said and hung up.

He lay on his bed, suddenly exhausted, the chill penetrating his jacket and fleece as he fell asleep. When someone began knocking on his door, he jerked awake, panting and enraged, his hands in fists. A red glow hung on the wall, melting to brown. The sun had finished setting.

He opened the door. Idris was there, unshaven, with bruises on his forehead, the purple spots of two knuckles near his hairline, one dark with coagulated blood just beneath the skin.

What happened?

I got mugged. And then I got sick. Maybe it was the shock.

Are you all right?

Yes. I am better now.

Good. I need you to drive me. You know Clay, right? It's to see him.

Idris blinked, as if trying to decide how to react.

What kind of work are you doing for Clay? Justin asked and tried to inhale.

Idris looked off, out the dusty second-storey window and into the street.

Justin didn't realize how angry he was until he was already grabbing Idris by the collar, spinning, and slamming him against the wall. The back of Idris's head struck the concrete.

His body had felt airy, like Styrofoam. Idris was wincing, but his hands were slack.

Just errands, he whispered, his head lowered.

Did Clay start this?

I did. I asked if he had work.

Justin grabbed his jaw and lifted his face.

Why would you do that?

I don't see why I can't have a job. I am not paid here. And I am not getting a scholarship.

Justin let go.

Idris's shirt had come untucked, stretched around the collar, and he moved his hands to fix it, but they shook and he let them drop. When he raised his eyes again, they were different, distant, vaguely relaxed, maybe even peaceful.

I will drive you. I am sorry. I did not realize this situation would upset you.

Idris bent his knees and picked up his backpack. He went downstairs slowly, looking cautious and off balance.

Justin sat at his desk, his hands on the wood laminate. The school suddenly seemed like an existence in which everything was coming undone: the cheapest Chinese-made power strips and surge protectors smoking suddenly, the plumbing leaking days after being installed, the internet repeatedly going down, electrical cords breaking, faucets dripping, toilets running, desks wobbling, pens spilling ink. The school was ruining him, but his violence could not be excused. He would pray for forgiveness.

He changed into jeans and a shirt. He'd begun to dress normally more often and attended the church where the embassy workers went, comforted to be around others like himself.

As Justin was leaving, Frank called from his office, asking where he was off to.

A party, Justin told him.

Glad to see you getting out, Frank said.

During the drive, neither Justin nor Idris spoke. They came to the address: walls with floodlights and razor wire, a red metal gate with an open door in it. Clay was standing outside, wearing only a shirt, its sleeves rolled up, showing not just muscle but poise, the way he didn't settle into his joints but lifted out of them. As Justin walked toward him, Clay pointed to the car.

Is that Idris? Invite him in. Don't make him sit out here like a driver.

Justin called back, and Idris got out and told Clay he was supposed to meet some friends.

Clay's eyes narrowed, as if seeing something in the street behind Idris.

Come on. You can be late. This is going to be one hell of a party.

Idris tried to refuse again, but Clay walked into the muddy street and put his arm around him and said, Good to see you, buddy. Let me introduce you to my friends.

More than a dozen people were drinking on the second floor, in a living room with a wall of windows and a sliding glass door to a balcony where a few expats smoked.

Idris went to a table with bowls of nuts, chips, and salsa as Clay led Justin into an empty lounge with couches and a flat-screen TV.

So how are the Afghan girls in bed? Clay asked. I've always wondered.

Whatever you've heard isn't true.

Hey, I'm not judging. I know how hard up a guy can get here.

Clay, Justin said. What are you doing with Idris?

I'm giving him a job.

There's no future in what you're doing. You're distracting him from a real education.

It's true there's no future in security. The American money is on its way out, so this is his last chance. If he doesn't take his opportunities now, he's going to be scraping for the rest of his life. At least this way, he won't have to beg. Regardless, I got Frank's permission. He and I had a good sit-down and talked this through. I agreed to pay Idris a real wage that will cover some translating and errands for me plus whatever he does for the school.

When did you see Frank? Justin asked.

I think you were at church.

If Clay hadn't mentioned Frank's permission earlier, it was to humiliate Justin in person. And Frank must not have told Justin for the same reason.

As Justin turned to leave, Alexandra came into the doorway. She saw Clay first and smiled. Then she saw Justin.

You two know each other? Justin asked.

We met at the school, she said.

You were there without me?

I wanted some time with the girls, she said sternly, her pupils gleaming like gun barrels.

Clay patted his back. I invited her and her friends over. It's a party. You invite people.

Hey, Clay! An excessively tanned man with a bald, saurian head shook his hand and, in a Jersey accent, began describing how he'd been ripped off, his tone angry and yet oddly gleeful.

So me and these guys, we decided to ship Afghan rugs to the States. We worked it out. The profit was high. Real high. We rented a shipping container, had it weighed and sealed. Then we sent it to Pakistan and from there to the US. When it arrived, the seal was in perfect condition — date, place, and weight, all correct. But inside there was just dirt. Somewhere along the way, someone replaced the rugs with dirt to the exact ounce and put an identical seal on it.

The man, whom Clay introduced as Mike, cursed and laughed, oblivious to the tension. Justin wanted to warn Alexandra that Clay was using her and Idris to get revenge.

Suddenly, Mike hunkered down, one hand on the floor, like a quarterback. Air boomed into the lounge, clapping against the walls, more palpable than the shaking of the house. Justin's ears ached. People were rushing into the lounge from the living room, shards popping beneath their feet against the tiles. Clay told Alexandra to stay there.

Outside, rifles fired rapidly. Another detonation battered the air, and a man with a crew cut closed an iron door as thick as a wall.

In the sudden silence, the ringing didn't let up. On the flat-screen TV's video feed, the insurgents blew open the house's front security door.

Justin realized this was the life he'd prayed for. All he'd braved in Kabul — desperation, manipulation, filth, cold, and now violence — was the unlit path of faith.

This was the war he had been denied.

美智子

THE FIRST TIME I saw Clay was through Alexandra's words, two days after the picnic. I'd been at her house, waiting for Tam, taking a pause from reading to brainstorm an article that wouldn't feel like a burden to write. Tam had texted me: *Traffic is terrible. Make yourself at home!* A moment later, Alexandra arrived. She kissed my cheeks and sat across from me.

"I don't think I've ever seen you without a book," she told me.

Dos Passos's *The 42nd Parallel* was on my knees, salvaged from a storage room, its moldy smell making my eyes itch if I held it too close.

"I wish," I said, "that every person in my life were an author. I don't know if people like these characters really exist, but I do know that some authors have so much life in them they need to create worlds to contain it."

Alexandra was studying me. Most people's faces opened toward others, but she normally contained herself, organizing what was within her. Her expression shifted, and I had the sense she was making a little space for me.

"You're right. A world of authors might be fun," she said. "Books showed me the boundaries that society creates and how to cross them."

"And now you're here," I concluded.

She tilted her head, as if taking time to interpret my words. "Yes," she said. "But maybe it's futile. Maybe authors create meaning because they are desperate to exist, so they keep pushing back the boundaries, like dictators trying to conquer territory."

We spoke in this vein for a few minutes, discussing whether art was a response to being subjugated by another's meaning, or if we simply wish to be more than we are — a private desire, not conquest but liberation.

Alexandra then asked if she could share something in confidence. She explained that she'd met Clay that afternoon. She'd gone to the school while Justin was at church, her desire to work with the girls outweighing her growing aversion to him and Frank. The guard had let her in, and from the stairs she'd heard Frank and Clay laughing, unaware that she was there. Frank had been talking about Justin, saying he lacked an understanding of men — words I could easily imagine him speaking. Alexandra described the scene to me, and, later, she detailed it in her journal.

Men know walls exist, Frank had explained as she reached the second floor, because we've walked into them. Girls don't need to do that. Idris is young. He has to be tamed.

Slow grumbling laughter followed.

I'll give him some work, the other voice — Clay's — said. I'll get him in line.

Frank described the situation with Sediqa. You know, I've spent a decade in Afghanistan, but Idris told me I don't understand how things work here. He actually said, Maybe her uncles are going to sell her, or maybe not. Afghans know how stupid foreigners are. If she gets the scholarship, the entire family benefits.

Why do you keep Idris around? Clay asked.

I have to work with Afghanistan the way it is. This is how Afghan men are. They were raised to be aggressive and manipulative.

Clay and Frank laughed about the nature of men, an all-knowing understanding in their words, a vague, affected compassion, though Clay's voice sounded perfunctory.

Hello, she said.

As she came to the door, Clay glanced up.

Sitting on the couches, as we waited for Tam, Alexandra told me she couldn't deny her immediate attraction to him.

"As for Justin, I feel protective toward him," she said. "I worry about him and admire how much he cares. But I'm wary of his fanaticism. There's something cold and ideological about him. If he'd succeeded in refusing his need for comfort, he'd never have called me."

Frank stood, excitedly shook her hand, and introduced her to Clay. She said she felt like she was entering a cage, an old lion trainer displaying his beast: the big man in the folding metal chair, with his hands on his thighs.

"Why is it," Alexandra asked me, "that we desire those who are bad for us?"

"But it doesn't hurt you to want him."

"It does. Because women want men like him, they exist."

I have a proposition for you, Frank had told her. Pardon me, Clay. I haven't lost track of our conversation, but I've been looking forward to speaking with this remarkable woman all day.

Clay said he had a few calls to make and would step into the backyard so she and Frank could have their meeting. Frank asked if she'd be interested in taking over the school — not right away, but gradually working in that direction, since it needed a woman's leadership. She knew he was offering her Justin's job, and she said she couldn't think that far ahead but agreed to be a mentor for the girls.

While Frank and Clay resumed speaking, she met with Sediqa, who'd been sitting with four girls in the other office, all on their laptops, using Facebook. She and Sediqa went downstairs. They discussed her plans for study in the US. Only at the end of the conversation did Alexandra ask her to tell the other girls that nothing had happened with Justin.

They will never believe, Sediqa said. In our culture, the only power of women is to undercut each other. If we leave the group, if we do anything out of the ordinary, we need men to give us permission and defend our decisions.

But don't destroy Justin in the process.

No matter what I say or do, no one will believe. The way things are now, they can accept that I got the scholarship. The injustice is acceptable, since I am no more deserving than they are.

But you're in danger.

We are all in danger.

Sediqa just stared from across the table.

Involuntarily, Alexandra thought of Clay again and how he'd come when Justin was away. This couldn't be a coincidence. Justin almost never left. Idris must have told Clay.

As she was saying goodbye to Sediqa, Clay came down the stairs and offered her a ride. She accepted, and Frank walked them out. He said he was counting on her. His bones suggested the man he'd once been. After the loss of such strength, he must have sought out new ways to have agency.

As Clay rode his motorcycle out the gate, she waved. In the unlit driveway, Frank's fossilized head appeared suspended, grinning like a warning on a stick.

Alexandra tightened her headscarf and held the motorcycle with her legs, the vibrations pleasant in her muscles. Despite the jolts against the ruts, she was slow to put her hands on Clay's back.

The street was darker than the sky, compound lights casting the road in the shadow of walls. Clay read the terrain ahead, weaving through the mud with tiny adjustments or following the gritty tracks of cars over ice. His driving was so steady she didn't have to hold on tightly. Most men she'd ridden on motorcycles with had taken risks only to oblige her to clutch them.

She wondered how military contractors saw themselves — certainly not as members of a parasitic subculture barely welcome in the very expat circles they guarded. NGO workers and diplomats went about like the cavaliers of Kabul society, having knighted themselves by their very decision to come here. But maybe soldiers of fortune considered themselves the elect.

Arriving at her house, Alexandra loosened her headscarf. Clay was flush from the cold. He didn't appear hurried, like many expats when they went outside.

She got off the motorcycle. The guard of a house five compounds down stood outside his gate, dressed in white, his hands behind his back in that dignified Afghan way, one hand holding the other's wrist. He was out of earshot but no doubt noticed every detail.

In her diary later that night, she would write about her brother, Samuel, and the familiar impression she had seeing Clay. Sam had been killed by an IED in Kandahar. *Why can I not help but love the vitality of violent men?*

Standing outside her gate, she asked Clay what he thought of Frank, and they agreed he was typical.

Typical in type, Clay said, but extreme in nature. Most people are here to make a quick buck or to prove they're not cowards even though they never served, or to escape a long list of fuck-ups back home, or to fight some private war in a place where it feels like it counts.

But the girls are amazing.

That's the mystery of this place. What's good and bad are hard for us to tell apart . . .

She hadn't expected him to speak this way, his locutions clear and unselfconscious — *like someone who so rarely voices his thoughts that when he does, it's not in the register of common language. He chooses his words evenly, with a hint of resignation. He told me Frank was trying to build the Afghanistan he wanted, an Afghanistan many Afghans would hate. If Frank had his way, every man in this country would unite — even if they are as diverse as we are — and they'd take up arms against us, and we'd finally have a clear target.*

Clay told her that wanting an easy solution to war made people crazy.

We have to be careful, he said. I don't pretend to save anyone. I've never saved anyone.

With Justin, she felt herself walking through a winter desert. She'd been blindsided by Kabul, vulnerable and drawn to his vulnerability. But in his quiet way he was a braggart with his piety, unlike Clay, who was just here for himself, who inhabited his body as if it were the only thing he owned.

He told her about the party and said, Please come. Bring your friends.

"Come with me," Alexandra implored me. "You and Tam."

Sometimes Justin seemed youthful, his skin radiant, and at first Alexandra had thought of him, with all his faith, as a sort of noble savage; only later had she realized that he shone brightest in the moments when he tamed the chaos within himself.

She'd once seen a TV interview with three bearded Taliban commanders. They'd glowed too. Their teeth flashed in their beards as they laughed. Their joy had been that of superiority, of righteousness — the certainty of those who organized life into one clear story and knew their heroic roles in it. They had seemed devoid of life to her, like something that ignites, blazes, and burns out quickly.

I can't refuse Clay. Justin will be an anecdote, but Clay is code; blueprints; peeled back to the animal circuitry.

That night, Tam and I went with Alexandra. She walked into the lounge we didn't know was a safe room, one of her rare smiles transformed from a sign of joy to — as Justin must have seen it — one of betrayal.

After the explosion, I fled to the safe room where twenty-one people sweated and cried, and the TV screen showed Afghans fighting the insurgents to save us.

Months later, as I wrote my novel in interstate motels near swamp forest or rocky pine, crickets sawed in weeds and the moon drifted against ebbing clouds. I traveled from Clay's relatives toward their origins in Quebec. Maine seemed the frontier of an infinite wilderness — rocky, forested, gouged by the southward descent of two and a half million years of glaciers, long lakes like footprints.

Across the Appalachians, in Quebec, I found tamed land, straight roads between farms, villages clustered around gothic Catholic spires — a culture largely unknown to Americans. I learned new myths, about a people who crossed the ocean and copied the ways of the Aboriginals, hunting and fishing and trapping, wandering from Gaspé to Manitoba, to south of the Great Lakes, Ohio and Missouri, down the Mississippi to Louisiana. I realized what I should have in Kabul: America was not the only colonial power in love with stories of frontiers. It had simply written history as if it were the inventor of everything daring and new.

I met Alexandra's mother in Montreal. She was gaunt: leathery skin on bones, a bulbous nose, and broken veins on her cheeks. Smoke had stained the peeling wallpaper in her apartment, the air stale and dry, smelling of marijuana and cigarettes. A man watched TV, not bothering to get up, his back to me, a seam of the recliner torn, batting hanging like entrails. The screen shone through the sparse clumps of his hair. There were sounds of trumpets and the hooves of horses pounding the earth.

Alexandra's mother clutched her reddened, scaly hands.

That fucking country stealed my babies, she said in a heavy accent.

It made sense that Alexandra had come from her. It took me a moment to see this. She'd needed to be the savior she hadn't had.

I drove along the Saint Lawrence afterward, further north.

On my phone, I received an email from my mother, who wrote that she was marrying a wealthy man she'd known for years from the hostess bar. She thought I was still in Kabul, and asked if I'd bought body armor yet and if I would come home soon. She'd tried to protect me, a futile gesture for one woman in a society that had the limited ambition of preventing only the most obvious forms of violence.

On a northern coast, where the May sun flashed against bits of ice in the crevices and the horizon didn't seem to touch the gulf, I reread parts of Alexandra's diary.

When I first learned English, I tried to make sense of the words *person* and *persona*. The etymology was the same: *per sona*, that through which the sound passes, a word for an actor's mask in ancient Etruscan. It came to mean *character* or *function* in Roman theater and, later, law. It embodied the knowledge that many individuals could assume one role, as well as its duties and powers. Maybe a mask was reassuring — a coherent part to play in the middle of so much chaos — like these masks of world-savers in war zones.

I wanted to hold Alexandra's face in my hands, wash it in spring water, and lift it into the light.

PART 7

QUEBEC: 1998–2006

ALEXANDRA

CAREFUL. HE SAID. It was their game. To never touch. He might have started it. She was no longer sure. They'd been born together, and now, if they touched, would become one again. They neared in a game of chicken: simultaneous lunges for a plate of cookies or the TV remote. They cackled at the proximity of annihilation. When they brushed each other, they jumped away, pretending they'd almost touched. She pictured a spaceship escaping the pull of a black hole.

Some days the ideas were hers: to create ninja weapons with nails and wires in the trash of a construction site; to rig up primitive telephones with tin cans and strings so they could talk while guarding both entrances to their house. Then the ideas would be his: to hone their slingshot skills with targets swinging from branches; to scatter bang-snaps on the back porch like landmines.

They were twelve when they split and their ideas became their own, no longer a shared spirit of insurrection, a genie that moved between them. They'd begun spying on the houses in their neighborhood, keeping a journal of what people did. So much was uninteresting. Dinners at 225 Verchères where the family lit candles and the four girls resembled mice. In 366 Rouville, the wife walked between the kitchen and the living room, raising and shaking her hands and shouting as the fat husband sprawled before the hockey game.

But there were revelations. The fat man alone watching naked people on TV as he banged his fist between his thighs. The oldest mouse girl in her bedroom with a shaggy boy, taking turns sucking smoke from a glass tube before he lowered his pants and lay back as if at the doctor's, and his pale mushroom sprouted. In 410 Bourget, the grotesquely muscled husband often had sex with his tiny wife who wore a fluffy yellow nightgown like a marshmallow Peep.

Sometimes they spied on an elderly invalid. His yard was an infiltrator's heaven, crowded with trees and bushes, banks of lanky weeds bursting through flowerbeds. Parked in his wheelchair on the back porch, he slouched, half asleep.

They dared each other to get close, crabbing and wriggling on the ground, burrs and hard seeds embedded in their clothes. Jowly, glowering, his belly bulging, the invalid didn't move. A tube ran to his nose from metal tanks on his wheelchair. They'd thought he was a vegetable until they saw him finger the switches on his armrest and drive his whirring seat into the house.

Alexandra had been at a birthday party the day the split with Samuel happened. A new girl had invited her, not realizing Alexandra wasn't popular, or maybe obliged by her mother to ask all the girls in her class. Alexandra tried to ignore the invitation, but at the last minute the thought of cake overwhelmed her, and she ran out the door, shouting to Sam that she had to go, the way their mother did when picking up a last-minute shift at the bar.

She entered the house unnoticed, all the girls surrounding Alpha, the only boy there, as if he were the birthday present. Alpha was tall, from Ivory Coast, and each time he played pin the tail on the donkey, he won. They made him do it over and over, adjusting his blindfold, spinning him, and reluctantly letting him go. He wandered, bumping into them playfully, but always found his way to the donkey.

Les nègres, the birthday girl's father told them from the back porch doorway where he stood with his beer, they're more physical than us. It's like throwing a cat from a window.

The girls rushed Alpha upstairs, still blindfolded, to a bedroom, and as one opened the window, the others took turns kissing him on the mouth or cheeks. They leaned him against the sill as Alexandra hung back, wanting to rush in and kiss him too. Alpha began to tip and pulled off the blindfold, laughing. Seeing his eyes, they calmed and returned downstairs. They ate cake, and when it was time to open presents, Alexandra slipped out. She hadn't brought one.

When he'd found himself alone, Sam had left their house to prowl. Though he was angry at Alexandra, he later told her what had happened, his excitement overriding his resentment. He'd been crouching in the weeds at the invalid's house when the old man spoke.

Boy, he called from the wheelchair. It was the first time Sam had heard his voice. I'm going to pay you a lot of money to do something for me.

Sam had half risen from his crouch, ready to bolt. He'd schemed for nothing so hard as money: the key to sugar, the savagery of films, the superpowers in comic books.

I asked him what I had to do for the money, he told Alexandra. They lay in their beds across the room from each other. She closed her eyes, imagining him standing up from the weeds.

You any good with that slingshot? the old man asked.

Yeah. I'm good.

Ten dollars. I'll give you ten dollars for every squirrel you kill. Here?

Anywhere. They don't respect whose property is whose. They come from all over and eat and shit and have babies. They chew through the eaves and make nests in the walls and attic. They're rats with fluffy tails.

The neighborhood was full of squirrels. Sam counted them: in a tree; on a fence, an electric wire, and a gutter. He ran to the driveway and back with a fistful of gravel. The old man's expression remained saurian, the skin of his throat loose. Sam aimed and shot. The chunk of gravel struck the squirrel in the hips. It almost fell off the branch, extending its legs for better purchase. With his head back, Sam stepped, trees and telephone poles pivoting against the sky. He hit near the squirrel's nose, and it ran. He shot its flank, and it fell but caught the top of the fence and was gone.

You'll need something better, the old man said. There's a cage in the garage. It's a trap.

Sam described to Alexandra the cluttered garage: work-benches heaped with tools, dusty boxes to the ceiling. He took a cage with spring-powered doors and carried it to Mr. Leclerc, whose name he learned from the mail on the kitchen counter when he was sent to get peanut butter.

At the bottom of the oak tree, among the husks of acorns, he smeared the trap's trigger plate.

The wait was short. A squirrel trotted across the yard, paused, and stood on its hind legs to sniff. It made quick for the trap, nosed around, and went inside. The doors snapped shut.

We got the fucker, Mr. Leclerc said. Pick up the cage with-out putting your fingers in there, and don't let its doors come unlocked. Those monsters bite.

The squirrel thrashed, making a throaty growl with intermittent chirps. Sam slid his hands beneath the cage. Inches
from his face, the squirrel threw its body against the wires.

Bring it inside, Mr. Leclerc said. He touched the controls
on his chair and it whirred, carrying him through the kitchen
into the bathroom. He lifted a plastic stool with metal legs
out of the tub and told Sam to set the cage where it had been.

The squirrel was clutching the wires, staring.

Do you think hot or cold water is better? Mr. Leclerc asked.
It gets really hot.

When Sam reached for the knob with the red circle, Mr.
Leclerc chuckled. Do cold. I like your spirit, but the water will
be too hot to get the cage out, and we can kill one more today.

The squirrel thrashed again, soaking itself before the water
was an inch deep. Its fur spiked, standing in daggers, its tail
narrow and feral, ratlike at last. It grabbed the cage's ceiling
and hoisted itself there until the water was too high.

Alexandra didn't understand why the man had chosen
Sam. He'd earned thirty dollars. She'd played in the yard just
as much. She could see and hear everything she'd missed. The
way the squirrel lashed the cage with its body, a blur of movement, and then went still, only its legs twitching. The line of
dwindling bubbles that rose like beads from its mouth. The old
man smoking afterward, the way lovers do in movies.

The next day, Mr. Leclerc refused her. *T'es une fille* —
You're a girl. Only Sam could do his bidding. He kept using
the trap, drowning squirrels, but Mr. Leclerc also taught him
to make his slingshot lethal with used ball bearings from auto
repair shops. Sam shot squirrels out of trees and off power
lines, and then dispatched them with a club. The old man
watched, sometimes tolerating Alexandra as she stood on the

edge of the porch. More often than not, though, he shooed her home.

Sam, she called. *Viens!*

Va-t-en, he replied. Go away. I'm working. He spoke the way their mother did when they called the bar, music blaring in the background, to get her to arbitrate a fight.

Evenings, Sam returned to Alexandra, flush with cash but reluctant to let her see it.

Come on, she said. Let's go spy. I've been waiting all day.

He followed her onto the back porch, where the wind gusted, pushed by distant clouds. The maple beyond their yard shook in the yellow radiance of the streetlamp. They plodded along the sidewalk. They weren't furtive. There was no joyous scrabbling and prowling. She walked behind as if goading him. They passed the mouse family's dining room and the kitchen of the angry wife, and let themselves into the garden inside the fence.

From their vantage, they could see into the bathroom. In the mirror, the muscular man and his little wife were brushing their teeth and spitting. The man came out and flopped onto the bed, his forearm across his eyes. The woman followed, pushed off the shoulder straps of her thin blue gown, and flicked it with her foot over the lampshade, filling the room with the watery glow of an aquarium.

Facing the bed, she made a ta-da motion with her hands. He peeked from under his forearm and shook his head. She crossed her arms beneath her breasts, her voice warbling behind the glass. He shook his head again. She crawled onto the bed and did what the mouse girl had done to the shaggy boy. Soon the big man was on his knees and they were having sex.

The sound of Sam's breathing vanished. The man banged

his hips and flipped the woman onto her back. Heat spread through Alexandra's chest.

Sam drew back the slingshot's elastic and shut the eye closest to her, his face going dark. She moved behind him, sighting along his arm. The metal crook moved from the man to the glinting ring in her belly button, and finally to the place where he plunged in and out.

Sam let off a shot and the window thudded, cracks jabbing out from an icy hole. The lamp in the corner shattered, the bulb briefly tumbling within the shade before it died.

Alexandra sprinted behind Sam to their house and through the back door. They stood against the wall panting, and she took his hand. His fingers didn't grip hers back. He just breathed. She pressed her nails into his palm. His skin was cool. She let go.

THERE WAS MILK and a plate of toast with jam on the table. The cereal was piled higher than the bowls. Their mother was cutting sandwiches and putting them in lunch bags. A macaroni casserole cooled on the stove for their dinner. The air smelled of burnt cheese.

There was a shooting last night, she told them. That's what people are saying. But one of the police who dropped by the bar told me it was someone with a slingshot.

Alexandra held down the mound of cereal and poured the milk between two of her fingers, and then passed it to Sam.

Their mother studied them, her hand on the counter, the hem of her skirt against her thick calves. Sam shoveled cereal into his mouth.

At school, kids talked about the shooting. They said there'd been a silencer on the gun. No one was supposed to walk in front of windows anymore.

Sam sat across the classroom from Alexandra with a few of the popular boys. He was wearing new running shoes. It was the first time he hadn't picked a desk near hers. Normally, they kept to themselves, navigating the dangers of unpopularity, avoiding attention to keep the bullies from commenting on how they were dressed. They often argued with their mother, asking her to spend more on their clothing, but she said her priority was rent, heating, water, food. They didn't mind being cold and would stop taking showers, they told her. Only when their clothes were far too small would she replace them.

Sam must have changed into the shoes in the school bathroom, Alexandra thought. At lunch, he sat with the popular boys again, who were considered delinquents. He shared candy bars with them and leaned forward, speaking, and they all laughed.

Let's do it again, she told him after school.

He said nothing, just got his slingshot and bag of ball bearings, put them in his backpack, and went out.

She stayed home and, in the days that followed, gave up trying to go with him. She read until the sunset condensed against the horizon and faded from the cluttered rooftops, the streetlights coming on, the fading glow in the western sky merging with the city's amber night.

She'd once had a tiny grandmother, pale skin, the bones of her face like pieces of broken teacups, her eyes as blue as the sky above the water crashing on rocks, the Baie des Chaleurs visible from her creaking wooden porch. Alexandra and Sam and their mother had visited her each summer, a day in the car just to get there. She had an old black Lab, and after her funeral, Alexandra lay with it on the floor, hugging it as it twitched in its dreams, its feet in a quivering run, its heart thudding.

She listened to the squelch of its intestines, throaty growls and whimpers. She stroked through the coarse fur, searching for the soft spots. Then her mother drove the dog somewhere, though Alexandra had begged to keep it.

There was the story of their father from that same town on the bay. He left them or maybe died — depending on which evening their mother told it. Her mom hated talking about him. I'm doing my job, she said. I'm raising you. You can't ask for more than that.

As the weeks passed, Sam came home later and less often. He no longer showed interest in the books. He slept over with his new friends or walked to school before she was ready.

Alexandra wandered from yard to yard alone. Before, the world had been laid out for her, windows like the frames in comics. Now she feared the people would stare back, that she would be discovered, the gardens flooded with police lights and sirens.

THEY WERE ALMOST fourteen when Mr. Leclerc died. Sam told Alexandra the house had been emptied and put up for sale. She'd never known the extent of the agreement between her brother and the old man, only that he killed squirrels and kept him company at times, or ran chores. He told her he'd met Leclerc's daughter, who was well past fifty and suffered from back pains that made her visits rare. Sam never saw her again after the death.

La crisse de bitch, he told Alexandra. He must have left me some money. What am I going to do?

Now, every day after school, he went to the weight room with his friends. He'd become broad through the shoulders, his movements swift and defiant. He stood or turned as if to throw a punch. At home, he was always reluctant to go inside, pacing the yard or sitting on the porch.

He hung out with dropouts and older kids, got in fights, stole from stores and cars, and sold drugs. He told their mother he did odd jobs so he could buy clothes. Alexandra heard rumors from her classmates about a brawl: one of his friends beat up for selling hash at a metro station on a local gang's turf, and Sam among the group that took revenge, leaving one teenager with a broken collarbone and another with a concussion.

Alexandra spent more time at the library, where Mrs. Ducharme, the librarian, often recommended her favorite books. Alexandra read them quickly, and when she returned them, Mrs. Ducharme asked her questions — casual oral quizzes — her mouth quivering with a contained smile. Her daughter, Julie, was in Alexandra's grade. She was a skinny, flat-chested girl who chewed the tips of her hair and rarely spoke, vanishing between classes, as if she'd learned to dematerialize to pass through the gaggles of popular girls who'd tormented her since kindergarten.

At Alexandra's house, there was only one bedroom for her and Sam, and sometimes, when he did come home to sleep or get clothes, he stared at her in her threadbare pajamas, his eyes so deep-set his skull seemed like a helmet.

Walking back from school on the first warm day of spring, she passed a police car in front of Mr. Leclerc's house. Two officers walked around it, hands on their belts. The yard was mowed, the weeds gone, the trees pruned back, and all the windows broken.

At home, in her room, she lifted the sash, dead bugs falling from the wood. She sat against the wall and read with her head near the sill, the fresh air at her cheek keeping her awake.

A car engine grew louder and stopped just outside. Its doors creaked open, and voices spoke in the backyard, four or five of them — nasal and adolescent. One sounded older.

The boys tramped disjointedly through the downstairs hallway. The house echoed, giving her vertigo, the sounds rising like waves, her room seeming to sway with the motion of the sea.

It was too dark to read anymore. The boys laughed below her, bottles clinking.

She stood up, her knees cracking, eased her door open, and crept down the stairs, putting her foot on the side of each step so that it wouldn't creak. At the bottom, she peeked past the edge of the kitchen door.

Sam and his friends were sitting around the table and on the counter, since there weren't enough chairs. They wore jean and leather jackets, dirty sneakers, and scuffed boots. An older boy was at the table, his blond hair swept behind his ears and his beard shaved except for a patch beneath his bottom lip. He jerked his head in her direction.

Hey! he said. Who's that?

Alexandra darted upstairs and got into bed. The lights were off, and she pretended to be asleep.

The boys were shouting, angry that she'd been spying. She couldn't make out what they were saying, but she hoped she hadn't embarrassed Sam. The voices dropped in tone, their words broken by long pauses and then a longer silence.

The footsteps that began coming up the stairs were heavier than Sam's. The door creaked, and someone sat on the edge of her bed.

Hey, he said, his words less a whisper than a sound like steam escaping from a radiator. He smelled of cigarette smoke and beer. I'm Sam's friend.

She didn't move. Downstairs, the boys were laughing again.

He was doing something near the floor. She cracked an eye. He was taking off his shoes.

You can't sleep here, she told him.

What? He chuckled. I'm not going to sleep.

Then why are you taking off your shoes?

He popped the button on his jeans, slid them down his hips, and hesitated, looking unsure as to whether he should take them off.

Don't undress, she said. She tried to push him off the bed with her foot, but he was big. If you want to sleep here, go to Sam's bed.

He pulled back the covers.

I'm just going to lie with you. Sam said it was okay.

No he didn't.

He did. I'm Gérard. We're friends. Just relax. This will be fun.

No, it won't. Get out of my bed.

She shoved at his chest as he pulled her against him, grabbing her breast.

That hurts. Stop it!

Sam said I could. He slid his hand inside her pajamas, between her legs. She thrashed, trying to kick him.

You stop it, he told her. I paid for this.

What?

I paid Sam. We made a deal.

Get off me.

He had an arm around her neck, pinning her against him, and as he pushed down her pajamas, she bit his wrist, the skin coming away under her teeth, her mouth salty.

He jerked back and punched her, her head digging into the

pillow, lights flashing in her eyes, her cheekbone aching.

I didn't want to do that, he said. I paid him forty fucking dollars. Now lie still.

Her body was tugged at, rearranged, and then he began to tear her in half. She knew the word for it, had been taught about it at school, but could remember nothing. His hand clamped her throat, and each time she tried to move, he squeezed and her temples throbbed.

He shuddered and gasped, and pushed himself off her, leaning into her throat. He pulled on his pants and shoes, and looked at his wrist as if checking the time. *Crisse de bitch*, he said before going downstairs.

Footsteps stomped outside. The car engine fired up and then faded into silence.

She slid her legs off the bed, put schoolbooks into her backpack, and picked up her clothes from the floor. She dressed and went quietly downstairs. Everyone was gone, but they could come back. In the bathroom, she found a sanitary pad for the blood. She washed herself, trying not to cry.

Three blocks away, she crawled through a willow tree's overhang, into the hut-like space where she often hid to read. She lay down. As her eyes adjusted, the sky seemed to brighten through the branches, becoming golden. The leaves rustled near the ground, and a black and white cat she often petted peeked in. It rubbed against her, purring, and then lay, preening itself.

She woke shivering. The air had cooled, her body ached, and she forced herself up.

Before each cross street, she crouched and listened. Leading into the distance was a line of staggered lampposts: bright stitches against the dark.

At the library, she sat against the door and fell back asleep.

She awoke to a pressure on her cheekbone and jerked her head away. Mrs. Ducharme stood above her, her fingers extended.

What happened?

Alexandra shook her head. Her bottom lip trembled.

Mrs. Ducharme led her inside, sat her in a chair, and spoke to someone on the phone. The police arrived. Coaxed by Mrs. Ducharme, Alexandra told them about the slingshot, the ball bearings, the attack against the couple in bed, the squirrels, Mr. Leclerc, the broken windows, the drug dealing, and then, as if the least important, the rape Sam had been paid for.

The day became a blur, and Alexandra dozed as people talked around her. She was taken to the police station and to a hospital. She met with a social worker. A nurse held her hand and explained what a rape kit was, and why it was necessary.

You can stay with Julie and me for as long as you want, Mrs. Ducharme told Alexandra after they met with a social worker. From now on, I want you to call me Colette.

Her brick rambler had white shutters and a front door with glass filigreed in the shape of vines. Blue crushed gravel surrounded the path's round flagstones. There was no father here either.

When Julie arrived home, Mrs. Ducharme took her aside to speak with her privately. Julie came back and asked Alexandra if she wanted to share her room. Alexandra feared Julie would be jealous and resent the intrusion, so when they were alone, she said, You're so pretty. If you had contacts and let your hair down, you'd be the prettiest girl in school.

Me? Julie said. I don't have breasts. Then she giggled. Do you want me to put makeup on your cheek? I have a little. For pimples, you know.

Alexandra sat in front of the mirror. The bruise ran from

her temple to her cheekbone, not quite a black eye as much as a crescent, like the night around the halo of the moon.

As Julie gently touched makeup onto her skin, the slight pressure of her fingers, the tickling caresses, made Alexandra sleepy again.

Later, while they were eating dinner, Alexandra's mother arrived in her red skirt and heels, tripped on the flagstones, and shouted.

You little bitch! You ruined our family!

Mrs. Ducharme told her to go home, but Alexandra's mother pushed at the door, one hand thrusting inside. Mrs. Ducharme slammed it on her wrist. There was a cry, and when the hand jerked back, she closed the door and snapped the lock.

The next day, Alexandra and Mrs. Ducharme went back to the police station, and she identified the older boy who had raped her. The police told her he couldn't see through the one-way glass. Sam was in the lineup too, and appeared bored, cracking his knuckles. When the police asked which one was her brother, she pointed at him and turned away.

OVER THE MONTHS and the years that followed, Alexandra disciplined herself. She got straight As, did chores and anything else that she thought would please Mrs. Ducharme and Julie. Though Sam had been sent away to reform school and her rapist had gone to jail, she bought a jackknife and Mace. She wore clothes that hid her body. She studied her emotions, predicting their outcomes. She went to the gym, ran, exercised, and convinced Mrs. Ducharme to let her and Julie take self-defense classes. When a girl made fun of Julie at school, Alexandra put her in a headlock and held her until she apologized. Her newfound strength was intoxicating but also scared her. She never realized she could find so much pleasure in having power over another.

She didn't see her mother again, and she returned home only once, a week after the rape, with the social worker to get her belongings. Her heart raced as she searched her mother's drawers on impulse, hoping for a hint of her father's identity. She found and kept only a blocky ruby-red plastic ring in a faded black box. A few months later, the social worker told her that her mother had moved in with a boyfriend and had signed papers making Alexandra a ward of the state.

At school, the counselor and nurse gave an assembly for the girls on how to protect themselves from rape. They told the students to stay in groups and dress modestly when walking alone. Hélène Lapierre, tall and blonde and the best student in the grade, raised her hand.

Why should we have to change our behavior and live in fear? Why aren't you teaching boys not to behave like dogs? I shouldn't be punished for how I dress.

The counselor stammered through an explanation about living in the world as it was and not how we wanted it to be. Hélène spoke over her, saying, The world changes. None of us are carrying rosaries.

After the assembly, Alexandra approached her and said she agreed. Hélène told her if she was interested in being more than an object, she had some work to do. Her parents taught at the university, and she loaned Alexandra battered copies of Friedan, Woolf, and de Beauvoir. Alexandra felt less alone in her fear and anger. With Hélène, she went to rallies against sexual violence and for women's equity.

In the bathroom, Alexandra undressed before the mirror. She had muscles along her torso and over her ribs, thin, tight biceps, and lines in her shoulders. She had yet to go on a single date. While Hélène chose men who were boyish and often effeminately beautiful, those who caught Alexandra's attention had nothing gentle about them. She ignored her desire, worrying that she'd become a feminist as another means of self-protection, and she wondered who she would be without her fear.

A few years later, she began university in Quebec City, at Laval, and studied law. She got an apartment with Hélène and two other girls. Julie went to the University of Quebec at Montreal with her boyfriend. She and Alexandra emailed, but their exchanges hardly extended beyond Julie's talk of her relationship.

One snowy evening, after drinks at a party, Hélène and Alexandra stumbled against each other as they took off their boots. The warm woolen smell of Hélène's open jacket filled Alexandra's nostrils. Alexandra put her arms around her. Hélène laughed and said, *Pauvre Alex, t'es vraiment soule —* you're really drunk.

Their faces were enclosed in their hair, and Alexandra moved her cheek against Hélène's, an electric gradation of feeling until the edges of their lips touched. She kissed her, just a soft pressing, mouth to mouth, breathing each other's air.

Hélène pulled back, stroking Alexandra's cheek with her thumb.

Alex, she said quietly, you like men. I like men. We don't have to sleep with each other just because we can't stand how they behave.

Over Thanksgiving, Alexandra went to Montreal to visit Julie and Mrs. Ducharme. She was in the Berri–UQAM metro station, on her way to visit a friend, when she saw the group of five young men. The saliva in her mouth thickened as if she'd inhaled dust.

Sam stood at their center. They were staring at something he was holding. He lifted his hand, and she flinched. He held up a playing card, his fingertips framing its edges as he showed the others its suit and symbol: a king in black, spades or clubs. The young men laughed. His sleeves were rolled up, a cross tattooed on the meat of his forearm.

The lines of the metro hall — white pillars and gleaming turnstiles — seemed to join with the nerves in her eyes. She hurried down to the platform as the blue train was gliding in.

Her ribs squeezed her lungs, a suffocating band beneath her breasts, a corset of bloodless muscle. Her brain was a nest of brambles.

THE SUMMER AFTER her first year of classes, Alexandra stayed in Quebec City, waitressing in a restaurant on Rue Saint-Jean, practicing her English so she could serve tourists. She often walked the narrow cobbled streets of the walled old city, looking up at the apartments owned by the foreign rich who rarely resided there. In the late afternoons, she read on the Plains of Abraham or jogged along the grassy ramparts, sneaking glances at men as the river below fell into the shadow of the tor on which Quebec stood.

Hélène had left to travel in Europe, and when she came back, she told Alexandra stories about her hookups with Swedish, French, and Italian men. She bragged that she'd lost two weeks from her itinerary because she couldn't bring herself to leave a lover in Madrid.

Alexandra never discussed how she loathed the men she was drawn to. Portrayals of violent men turned her on — soldiers, adventurers, fighters, frontiersmen. Once, after meeting friends at a bar, she'd almost gone home with a stranger in his late thirties, a former professional boxer whose stubble felt like sandpaper when they kissed. At a street corner, she bolted, not even saying goodbye. She ignored his calls, the small, frantic echoing of her footsteps enraging her.

She continued to excel at university and added courses in English. The more she learned about injustice — the de facto slavery of women in many countries, culturally sanctioned rape and genital mutilation — the more she focused on women's rights globally. She felt reassured by the sense that there was something concrete to fix — countries where women couldn't vote or drive — and that she could apply her ideas and save them. Her old love of exploration and adventure stirred in her. She began to crave movement, feeling restless at her desk and at home.

One night, after descending from the yellow glow of the bus, she found a letter in her mailbox. She'd never seen her name in his handwriting.

Chère Alexandra.

She considered that. *Chère.* Did he have the right to that word? How had he found her address? She felt as if he'd been spying on her. The return address was a base in Afghanistan.

I think of you often. It's strange to dream of being children, playing, exploring, testing the limits of danger. I dream often here. I relive every detail of that pathetic little room, our tiny beds, the steep stairs with their wood worn so smooth we often slipped. In detention, I never thought about it. When I enlisted, it never crossed my mind. I wanted something I have no word for, that I can describe only as distance — danger, adventure, the unknown — but I wanted it so badly I didn't understand what it was. I was just motion, like water running down a mountain. When I started training, in Canada and later at Fort Bliss, in Texas, I knew I'd made a mistake. I didn't realize I'd have to obey others. I had no idea that discipline outweighed fierceness in the military, that chaos would be something I'd be trained to resist. If they'd told me, run in the forest, hunt each other, kill if you want, I'd have been content. If I didn't do what they commanded, they weren't going to kick me out — they were just going to punish me. And then I got it. I guess it's like breaking a horse or training a dog. I realized that for all those years I was just an animal running free. I read books because books were a greater distance in which to run. If I didn't like one, I found another. Through them, I was inhabiting stronger bodies, waiting for mine to be ready to take on the world. There were no consequences, just experience.

Samuel

Every few days, a new letter arrived, sometimes two at once, so that she had to order them by their postmarks. He described his boredom — hours in the desert, standing guard during meetings with village elders, riding in armored convoys, watching over a water project where it was so hot he struggled to keep the sweat out of his eyes and stay alert — but also the attacks, mortars coming into their camp, or RPGs fired down from the hills. The firefights sounded nothing like in films, he said. Incoming bullets snapped or whirred. He missed life in Texas, the clubs where the military men took off their wedding rings and went crazy with local girls. He thought constantly about a young Southern Baptist he'd dated and had anal sex and oral sex with night after night. She kept asking him to marry her before he deployed.

Americans are insane. As if God judges between the anus and the vagina, one Golgotha, the other Gethsemane. Who could believe in such a ridiculous divine anatomist? But if she'd cut off

*all pleasure, I'd have married her. I should throw this letter away,
but I promised myself I'd write whatever comes to mind. I guess
I'm saying that our desire doesn't care how we go about getting
what we want. There's a part of our brain that judges how desire
does its business, but it's not as powerful. The guys here, they go
crazy. When nothing's happening, when we're waiting and there's
too much downtime, they go after each other. Two or three guys
will hold another guy down and pretend to rape him. They don't
actually rape him, but it's not so different. It's our desire trying to
find a release, and we're barely in control.*

   Samuel

She read and reread his letters. She could hear his apology
in every line. A friend wept over a dead soldier Sam hadn't
liked, and yet Sam himself cried at night, his fingers pushed
into his mouth, for the grief of the friend. He tried not to hate
the Afghans, their hennaed beards and hair, their toothless
mouths, the women in *burqas* like ambulant socks, the ragged
barefoot youths who fought and died too easily and the ones he
never saw or thought he never saw and wished he did, who left
the bombs in the road that blew their vehicles into the fields,
turning them into shrapnel and incinerating limbs.

She never wrote back, unsure of what she should say. The
stories she read in class about the brutalities inflicted on women
made her feel that her own suffering was insignificant, that she
still had to experience so much more to understand life.

The next summer, she took a job near Blanc Sablon, on the
north coast of the Saint Lawrence, where the river opened into
the gulf, just below Labrador and seventeen hundred kilometers
north of Montreal. She'd seen the area on a satellite photo:
thousands of square kilometers of stone pocked with lakes,
scored with long striations from repeated cycles of glaciation.

As she flew in on a Cessna, the plane bouncing through the sky against surging winds off the gulf, she studied the shield of scoured stone and found herself thinking about Sam's letters gathering in her mailbox, how her subtenant was collecting them in a grocery bag.

She was one of ten university students hired by the government to record the wildlife they saw. They were each given a station, hers on a rise overlooking the desolate coast, the planet so curved this far north that, wherever she stood, she felt she was at its highest point. The horizons ran in long descending sweeps, land and sea broken only by the occasional jut of stone.

The project's goal was to compose a biodiversity map that showed the fluctuation of species due to climate change. She had a clipboard with a checklist: weasels, minks, otters, martens, fishers, wolverines, beavers, muskrats, voles, lemmings, rats, mice, shrews, moles, hares, porcupines, caribou, moose, muskoxen, lynx, coyotes, wolves, black bears, polar bears, and several types of foxes. She used her guidebook and binoculars, and put marks down whenever she saw geese or puffins, seals or falcons. She also had a canister of bear spray, an emergency whistle, sealed army rations, a large water bottle, and a walkie-talkie.

Each night, two dozen young spotters gathered at the bunkhouse to smoke pot and drink beer, but she preferred to sit alone on the shore. Some of the group slept in the dormitory, and others fell asleep on the rocks as they waited for the sky to darken enough for the faint green blur of the aurora borealis to become visible. If the bear alarm rang, they ran inside or stood in the doorways with their spray. Alexandra wore earplugs and slept better than she had in years.

Each morning at 6 a.m., she returned to her station. Michel, a young man with straw-colored hair and an olive complexion, was at the next one along the coast. Evenings, he joined her where the ATV driver picked them up. They said little to each other. He dressed like a scarecrow: loose corduroy pants belted around his narrow waist, threadbare shirts. He seemed fragile, his body a sign of pacifism and weakness. But one morning he came out of the showers in just a towel, his torso and arms thin but finely muscled.

Every few hours, during the long, bright days, the walkie-talkies crackled in harmony as everyone checked in with their group leader. Michel had brought with him a yellowed anthology of French poetry, and when he found a verse about the sea, he read it to them at their stations along the coast.

Valéry, he said.

The sea, the sea, always resumed,
Oh, such a reward after a thought
To gaze so long on the calm of the gods!

The hiss of the wind behind his voice echoed in the static and made her scalp tingle.

On another afternoon, he read Mallarmé.

The flesh is sad, alas! and I have read all the books.
Flee! Flee to that place! I sense that the birds are drunk
Between the immeasurable waves and the skies!

He never read poetry more than once a day, and not every day. The rarity of his reading pleased her. His recitations felt meditative, a reflection of his spirit rather than a need for attention.

Rimbaud, he murmured late one morning, after a night when a storm had hammered the coast, rain and wind sieving through their dormitory. Now, the waves were quiet and their crashing did not mask the grinding of the small stones and shells moved by the tide.

At times, martyr weary of poles and zones,
The ocean whose sob was my gentle roll
Lifted flowers of shadow with yellow suckers,
And I stayed, like a woman on her knees . . .

Later that afternoon, he pressed the walkie-talkie button to speak again. It wasn't time for a check-in, and she was surprised to hear his voice twice in the same day.

Alexandra, a friend of yours just dropped by.

Did he say his name?

No. I have no idea how he got here. He's a handsome guy. I sent him your way.

All right.

Let me know if you need anything.

She scanned the coast, where a few wiry bushes trembled in the wind. She put her bear spray in her pocket, drew her knees up, and waited.

His silhouette was immediately familiar, shimmering in the heat lines. He still walked with his entire body, tipping his shoulders, a rangy determination in his stride, like a man crossing a desert.

She stayed sitting on the ridge above the coast. He stopped below her, lifted his hands and showed her his palms, a gesture of reassurance that she imagined he'd picked up while deployed. He had four small purple scars on the right side of his face.

Hesitantly, he neared and sat a few feet from her, on the stone, looking out. The tide was low, breaking far away and gliding in, meshing with the sand so that, briefly, the ocean was edged with a band of silver and the sunlight flashed in the air.

I'm sorry, he said.

She shot a sidelong glance his way.

I know, she told him.

He took a short, sharp breath as a wave glided in and dissolved.

What's this job?

I keep a record of wildlife.

He almost smiled.

It's not so different from what we used to do. Watching. It's what I mostly do too.

A falcon rode the breeze far above, adjusting its wings as it scanned the coast.

Thank you for the letters, she said. They helped.

I guess I wrote some strange stuff in them.

It was honest.

The way they sat reminded her of how they'd most often been: in silence, reading or observing the world. She had no idea what to say and was grateful when he spoke.

On my way here, he told her, I saw an old boat washed up just across that point.

Show me. She shouldered her knapsack. She wasn't afraid. Whatever he'd been — roving and untamed — had found an anchor. His body conveyed discipline in how he moved, the feral boy reappearing only in glimpses. The hissing of wind-blown sand against coastal weeds muted their footsteps, making them sound far away.

At a promontory, they climbed the stone carved from the landscape by the last glacier and worn smooth by the ocean. The watery horizon spread out, fuller than a half circle, curving away in all directions. Seabirds planed, and the sun was so low in the northwest that even this slight increase in altitude gave the impression that its light shone up at them, grazing the sea.

Down the coast, against a sandbar thirty feet out, the iron hulk of a ship was lodged almost upright, the remains of its collapsed cabin on top.

Maybe the storm last night blew it in, she told him. It wasn't there a few days ago.

They climbed down the other side of the rock and walked closer. The rusted hull had lost its paint and any trace of a name or insignia.

It's some kind of fishing trawler, he said. We should swim out to it.

With the day's mild wind, the sun felt warmer than usual, but her team had been warned that even in the height of summer, swimming could bring on hypothermia within minutes. The exceptions were a few shallow areas where wide sandbars shut out the currents and allowed the sun to warm the water. Her team had visited one such area near the camp, and even there, the cold had left her breathless. Here, the water was deeper, almost black where a current ran through.

She tilted her head, still not ready to look directly at him.

We can do it, he said. He shrugged off his motorcycle jacket and pulled his gray hoodie over his head and then a pale olive T-shirt with *Infidel* printed on it — the Arabic script for the word below. There were more purple scars on his shoulder. He had two tattoos: the cross on his forearm and a rifle with a key instead of a muzzle, over his heart.

She undressed to her T-shirt, and then, reluctantly, when he removed his shoes and pants and stepped into the water in his underwear, to her black sports bra. He went in up to his ankles and called back, Hurry up. It's fucking freezing.

She didn't know why they were doing this, but seeing him like a little muscular boy and the pattern of vulnerability in his scars made her feel safe. She entered the water, and her feet were instantly numb.

Go! he shouted. They ran, a line of cold in her shinbones, and then lunged and paddled. The green water became black, and she struggled to draw a full breath. Her arms felt wooden, and her muscles burned. The gloom beneath them turned to green, then yellow, and they half-crawled, half-ran onto the sandbar. He began doing jumping jacks, and she did the same, facing away. She wrung out her hair and used her hands to skim the water off her arms and legs.

He turned, grabbed the edge of the hull, and pulled himself up. Barnacles covered the metal. Above her, it curved, faintly ragged against the sky.

There's not much up here, he said. The boat's been underwater a long time.

Gingerly now, he lowered himself. He had scrapes on his knees, blood between his fingers. He crossed his arms, his hands in fists, as if to hide his cuts. The sun was too weak to warm them against the minor wind. There was gooseflesh on his arms, and he began to shiver, careful even now to preserve the distance between them.

Let's swim back, she said.

He inhaled a few times, expanding his lungs against the inevitable contractions. They ran, splashing onto their bellies. She took short, frantic breaths, biting the air. At the dark interval between the sandbar and the beach, the heat of her body drew toward her core. Her limbs flailed, and she clambered onto the sand, gasping.

There were faint blue lines on his knees and palms where his skin was too cold to bleed. He did jumping jacks again, and she picked up her clothes and walked toward the promontory. On the other side, she took off her underwear, dressed, and pulled her fleece hat over her wet hair. She went up to the rocks and sat. He climbed up next to her, and they warmed their palms against the stone.

How did you find me? she asked.

I googled you. You were on a list of volunteers up here, so I bought a motorcycle. I took the highway from the south and then the ferries. That was the shortest route. It felt good to ride and not worry about anything. I was missing open spaces.

The sun drifted toward the north, gradually descending. Silently, they took in the landscape purged by the intensity of its winters.

I should head back, he told her. My leave is almost over.

They got up and briefly — turning her shoulder in, the world adjusting around her like a compass — she finally looked into his eyes. They seemed metallic, steady, resigned.

He walked away, fading back into the familiar silhouette. She bit her lip and tasted salt.

SUMMER PASSED SLOWLY in the white silence of the beach. The calm was broken only by the storms that blew in more frequently toward the end of the season. Beaches melted away, leaving shelves of stone, and new spits of sand appeared. The ship vanished.

One morning in her last week, after the ATV driver dropped off her and Michel, they began to speak. She asked him about his book of poems, whether he'd finished it, and he told her he'd read it several times and knew the poems he loved by heart. She asked him to recite his favorites, and they sat in the sand as he did: Baudelaire's "Albatross," Rimbaud's "Sleeper in the Valley," Nerval's "El Desdichado." *Dans la nuit du Tombeau, Toi qui m'as consolé — In the night of the Tomb, you who consoled me.* He wondered if Baudelaire, in his visions of distant indolent tropical islands, had envisioned a place like this one, so perfect and yet inhospitable.

The sea is your mirror; you contemplate your soul
In the infinite unrolling of its swell,
And your spirit is not an abyss less bitter.

As he recited the poem, she kissed him. She grabbed his jacket and pulled him against her, and then pushed the jacket back off his shoulders. They kissed and yanked at each other's clothes.

They made love, and afterward they lay together under their jackets, not talking. A scrim of clouds crossed the sky like a raft. She put her head on his shoulder and thought of the land around them, grateful for the isolation. They made love again, longer this time. Before meeting the ATV driver, they jotted on their checklists so that the pages were consistent with the days before.

She awoke the next morning, ran to the ATV, and got on behind Michel. As soon as they were alone, they found a large smooth rock and undressed. In breaks between lovemaking, they called out the names of the species they saw. Michel told her about Eastern mystics who didn't orgasm during intercourse so they could retain the strength and desire necessary to achieve enlightenment — who cultivated desire with detachment so they could direct their desire to the path of enlightenment without craving enlightenment.

That's the paradox of liberation, he explained. You need to have the strength to achieve it, and that requires desire, but if you desire with attachment, you trap yourself in suffering.

He told her that those who died with attachment became hungry ghosts who roamed the earth but, because they lacked bodies, couldn't experience the objects of their desire.

In one of his letters, Sam had written that he'd read Buddhist and Hindu scriptures, curious about the limits and powers of the mind, about individuals who could understand the universe without science: *I concluded that the wisest holy people were seeing only patterns like those created by wind on water, and knew nothing — knowing they knew nothing — about the dark ocean below.*

Her last day, she and Michel made love slowly, touching, exploring.

Later, at the camp, they lay in their separate bunks. She couldn't sleep, wanting the summer to continue. She knew that once they were back in the city her attraction to him would fade. In the emptiness of this landscape, she could forget that he wasn't what she craved.

Suddenly, she felt sick with anger, hardly able to contain it — her resentment at poverty and neglect, that she and Sam had been alone, that he'd become so desperate for acceptance he'd sold her for forty fucking dollars, the price of four squirrels. She'd built a life that would protect her and had judged herself for it. She'd chosen a career that gave her the courage she'd been born with and lost. She'd denied herself so much.

Maybe Sam had suggested they swim to the boat because it would be easier than speaking — or because it was a reminder of the childhood they'd shared.

Tears gathered and ran down her cheeks to the corners of her mouth. Nature had scoured her body, left it hard and lean, her lungs purified, her skin tanned and tight. She felt sad and enraged and desperate for life. She touched her tongue to her lips, expecting the taste of salt, of the ocean's brine, not this cleanness, this feeling of youth.

PART 8

KABUL: FEBRUARY/JUNE 2012

美智子

I WAS IN a taxi from the airport, back from my trip to the US, and on my way to see Frank. Two days before, Tam had emailed to say she'd finished her embed and had begun researching Justin and Alexandra for an article about the deaths of expats during the civilian surge. The piece would ask why those serving in various roles during the surge — funded as part of the American strategy — were not viewed as a kind of soldier. Her angle was provocative, sure to offend and spark debate.

I didn't answer her, and a day later she wrote to say that Frank had told her I'd been doing my own story and had taken a letter to Justin's family. *Are you the one who messed with Alexandra's computer?* She wanted to know what I'd been working on. *I thought you were writing a novel.* I was no longer sure what I'd call the form into which I'd written all that I'd learned. But the story was incomplete. I had to try one more time to ask Frank about Idris.

I rang the buzzer until the taxi driver got out and banged on the door for me. Frank finally opened it, his eyebrows rising when he saw me.

"Sorry," he said, "I was already going deaf when I got out of the military. Artillery did that to me."

I thought he'd be interested to hear about Justin's family, but he simply complained about finances. The car bomb had cursed the school, turning it into a dicey venture for donors. He asked if I knew any rich people in Japan.

"I need to rebrand," he said. "All the money's going to girls' schools. I don't know why I didn't start one to begin with. The problem with boys is they want respect without earning it. They've grown up seeing people cheat the system . . ."

Ignoring his rant, I lifted my hand, palm facing forward, feeling like a student myself. I asked if he could recall any details about Idris he might not have mentioned.

"There's nothing," he told me. "He had no real friends. The signs were there, that he was involved in something bad. He went through a period when he became someone else. It was the difference between a feral creature and one raised on the love of people. Toward the end, he got this dead stare. It was menacing. All he needed was patience and humility."

He sat, elbows on the armrests of his weathered office chair, hands slack on his knees, the veins sinking in the backs of them, as if his pulse were fading.

"You know," he said, "I saw what was left of the car they were in. I'd been envious of them. They'd stepped off a plane and not long after had gotten to watch a rocket hit Kabul's premier hotel. I remember thinking, 'A decade, and I haven't seen a thing.' I'm not here to rubberneck, but I know the Afghans so well, and it would be good to experience what they've been up against. So when I heard the car bomb, I had a taxi take me there. I looked at the blasted Corolla without even realizing it was mine."

Frank hesitated. This was as vulnerable as I'd ever seen him, and the moment didn't last long.

Only Clay, I would later learn, had gotten under his skin. He'd visited twice, the first time alone, when Justin was out with Alexandra. The second when Alexandra was there, when he'd cemented his agreement with Frank concerning Idris.

The first time, Clay had called and asked to see the school. He told Frank he'd met Idris and wanted to hire him, with Frank's permission, of course. He showed up with a fifth of Wild Turkey and poured it into coffee mugs, but after five minutes of Frank's pontification, Clay's face went sour.

Whoa now. Just because you're old doesn't mean you were always old.

Frank's eyes stopped like two marbles rolled into sand.

That's a brilliant observation, son.

I mean, quit preaching. You used to chase them and fuck them as good as the next guy.

Frank didn't smile. I'm not denying it.

You were in the army.

I was.

So you know. That's the thing I hate about old men. They speak like they weren't their dick's henchmen for forty years.

No, it's true. I have stories to back it up.

Tell me one.

I'm going to lower my voice.

That's fine. I'm not the one who's hard of hearing.

This was the thing about Frank: he was a man who'd grown up in the company of men and longed to please them. People who spent time with Clay said they could feel the regrets he harbored, and maybe this quality encouraged Frank to talk.

As if telling a bar joke, he began a story from his childhood about a daft farm girl. She was one of five daughters on the neighboring property, her family too poor to pay attention to her or help her through school.

She wasn't an idiot, Frank said. She could speak, but did

so quietly. She was pretty enough, well built. The rumor was that she had some brain problem that made reading and doing sums impossible, but she worked the farm and would make a fine wife.

He described how local boys began paying her for sex with chocolate. If she'd understood math, she'd have realized she was giving it up for pennies. She was thirteen, Frank fifteen, the first time he'd fucked her. A boy at school had told him to tell her to come by the barn at night, that it was that simple, and it was.

Frank admitted he'd told the story of the daft girl only once before, in the army. His buddies laughed and asked him to tell it again, and he'd promised himself he'd never breathe another word of it. The farm girl got pregnant. Frank denied responsibility to his parents, other boys denied it, and the girl disappeared, sent away to live with relatives.

This is how it is, Frank said. By the time a man can no longer get it up, he's done so much wrong that not even with every second of his last years can he pay the tender sex back.

After Vietnam, he courted and married a woman with academic ambitions, and each time she struggled, he reminded her that academia was fusty and uninspired. She became careful not to complain, but what person can live without admitting to difficulty?

You're not really happy, he told her, until she finally gave up on her PhD, stayed home, and birthed four daughters. He'd have been evil, he admitted, if he hadn't been so common.

As his daughters grew, he made himself scarce, finding new ambitions, starting businesses, running for mayor. The girls chased into his absence, trying to win his pride. He watched the oldest creep into a woman's body, like a child moving along a dark hallway, one step at a time, to see the presents below a

Christmas tree. He saw his daughters transforming from slender, too-intelligent girls into women as they explored outside the home, until hurt made them stupid and maybe, finally, if they were lucky, thoughtful.

Frank adjusted his bones in the chair as Clay reclined and sipped bourbon.

It wasn't easy to leave my wife, Frank told him, but Afghanistan was every man's dream: a country razed, where, as Tennyson wrote, *some work of noble note may yet be done*. In a society's beginnings, men can be giants. The first of us here were practically founding fathers. But coming here wasn't simple. I was a soldier in Nam. I did and saw the usual terrible things. We didn't bring our memories home. We closed them off. The world changed, and what our power could give us became wrong. I've read novels and seen myself in the good guys and the bad guys, and I guess I've come here as much to make the world a better place as because the part of me that stayed in Vietnam needed to do penance. Besides, a bored man is a dead one. Sometimes, when I wake up, before I take stock of this goddamned thing of a body and realize how old I am, I think, briefly, I'll admit it, that I'm just beginning.

He and Clay drank, neither speaking, Clay with his head slightly lowered, as if in deference, and Frank in thought, his fingers cupping his chin, pulling at the loose skin of his jaw.

In the *Aeneid*, Frank said, breaking the silence, there's a sibyl. Aeneas wants answers, and she writes words on oak leaves that she organizes into prophecies just as the wind blows them away. Men have always wanted a quest, a purpose in life.

Clay nodded. For a moment, he couldn't remember why he'd come here. His desire to establish a rapport hadn't been innocent.

You know, Frank said, I had a dream one time, about this girl in Nam — a prostitute one of the guys brought into camp for all of us. When I woke up, Idris was downstairs. He had the ugliest look I'd ever seen, his eyes red and swollen like he was on drugs. He said he was sick and maybe he was, but I told him to get out. I hated that the girls saw me do that. They needed Idris. More than a few of them may have had a crush. When I finally called him, I didn't know what to say. I told him the office needed a new lightbulb.

I can give him work, Clay said, refocusing.

In the emails Justin wrote to Alexandra, he described how Frank frequently suspected Idris of wrongdoing, fearing that he stole from the school or lusted after the girls or would sell them all out with his insider's knowledge. When Frank told Justin he'd picked the wrong person to save, Justin replied: But who are we to judge who deserves to be saved?

On that last visit to the school, as I pulled up my headscarf to leave, Frank appeared unsettled, perhaps realizing I'd no longer be courting him for information.

"You know, you're not the only one working on this story. Steve has dropped in a few times to learn more about Idris. And Tam, she's come by, but I haven't told her about Steve or Clay. I'm keeping that to myself. I shouldn't have told you. Steve wasn't happy about that."

I was surprised: I'd expected Steve to have left Kabul by now.

Frank sat a moment longer and sighed. "Strangers have been coming around. I've seen cars parked outside. A few of the girls, the ones who have means, they won't attend classes anymore."

I asked to see the room Idris had slept in.

We went downstairs, to the kitchen that smelled of propane and mold. He opened the pantry. As I had with Justin's room on my first visit, I asked for a little time alone inside — "Just so I know what it feels like. For the story."

He shrugged and went out the hallway, onto the back porch, maybe to stand and admire the yard as it recovered from the frost, before the summer scorched it dry.

The room held nothing. I shut the door, and a blade of diffuse kitchen light glowed beneath it. Even for me, the pantry was small. I took a step, and it sounded closed in and loud. I lay on the floor and couldn't extend my arms above my head. Idris must have slept at an angle. Or curled on his side. I did just that, and the cold pressed from the concrete into my ribs, my knee, and the bone of my hip. I knew that anyone who'd had the determination and resilience to live here was still alive.

The door was at my back, the light drifting past me. As my eyes adjusted, I discerned my shadow on the wall, low and blunt, like that of a stone.

IDRIS

IN THE SCHOOL, at night, the silence hummed — maybe the sound of his blood or the collective rumble of the city vibrating deep within the earth. The pantry was the length of his body, corner to corner, from his head to his extended toes: a pleasure, but not as great as that of the solitude it afforded him.

At his uncle's house, Idris slept in a room with Farzad, his fourteen-year-old cousin. Idris gave him English lessons, but Farzad drifted off, and Uncle Osman blamed Idris for the lack of progress. The young man had difficulty focusing since the attack on the American convoy, when Idris, his uncle, and cousin had fallen, gasping in the reeking smoke of incinerated bodies. At Farzad's knee lay the jawbone, sheared and stripped of flesh with the upward blast of the suicide vest. He picked it up. His father, his two white eyes in a sooty demonic face, struck the bone from his hand and slapped him for touching the dead in a forbidden way. Farzad had told Idris that he'd just reached for the first object he could make out. Asleep, he thrashed.

You're dreaming, Idris would tell him, but his cousin didn't wake up. He calmed for a while before the flailing began again. They'd all seen horrible things. Idris had his own nightmares.

In the pantry, his body heated the air. During the winter, he was careful; if he touched the concrete walls, the chill invaded him like an electric current, upsetting the warmth he'd kindled inside his clothes. He sat cross-legged in blankets, hunched over his computer. The earbuds were cold when he put them in. Aisha had sent a message on Skype that she was online. *I'm here now. Let there be a good connection, inshallah.*

He moved the mouse onto video call, anticipating her appearance on the screen: the way her white headscarf accentuated her freckles, the fullness of her lips, the blue in her eyes. He loved that first moment, before they began talking. Suddenly, he shut the computer, the pantry now fully dark. He lay back. With the earbuds still in, his heartbeat thudded.

She was the only American girl he'd been able to find online. She'd converted to Islam with a friend, taken the name Aisha, and joined a chat site for young American Muslims. Not many of them wanted to help Afghan boys practice English, but her parents were professors at the University of Ohio. She'd called them bleeding-heart liberals and told him they'd educated her to defend the underdogs. At the dinner table, she'd learned how the Palestinians were being driven from their land just as the Native Americans had been. She'd grown up hearing expressions like "Western imperialism" and "American extremism." Her parents referred to America's right wing as little better than the Taliban in their militant views and attitudes toward women's bodies. But her parents were hypocrites, she'd said. They worried she would compromise herself as a woman by converting. They'd asked her to see a therapist.

They aren't bad people, she'd told him, but they're not as different as they think.

In his last conversation with her, he'd described the novels he was reading to perfect his English: Tom Clancy, John le Carré, Ian Fleming, Robert Ludlum — foxed paperbacks Frank brought to the school from his trips to the US. She'd asked him why he read such trash when the holy book held all the wisdom necessary for a lifetime. But the battered novels had revealed to him an existence in which individual wile and commitment to the details of a plan created change. Vision was crucial, and a certain impassivity: victory over desire, self-abnegation.

When he'd gone onto the chat site, he'd wanted to meet someone like Holly. With her, he wouldn't have to worry about global injustice or hear advice like that of the mullahs. He could live in that awkward joy of American TV shows, where the youth were protected and rich with faith in the kindness of life, defying the bad people and stumbling toward joy. But Idris had to give that up for now. He had to sharpen his mind, to discipline himself. He'd been childish and trusting, and it had gotten him nowhere.

He would deny himself Aisha. He would never beg again. He would earn what he wanted. Everyone had a plan, and in each plan, others were pawns. The trick to success was making sure each pawn thought he was serving himself, when in fact he was serving you. This is what the American novels taught. It was America's success. Idris had read the few history books in the school. America made countries believe they were pursuing their own goals when they were actually serving America. He would not reject the power that came with this knowledge. It had won the world.

He'd begun analyzing his role as a pawn in the plans of each American he knew. With Frank, it was obvious. Frank could be friends with an Afghan man in a way he couldn't with the girls. He needed the company of another man to feel like a man himself, and to feel he had a place among the Afghans. Frank also needed help. No foreigner could understand the workings of Kabul, and Idris brokered his existence. Tasks that were casual for him would have been almost impossible for Frank. Idris bought items at the market for the school that would have cost five times as much in one of the stores catering to foreigners.

As for Justin, his plan was also clear, no more or less deluded than Frank's. Americans came here to be brave, to be Americans who did something good for Afghanistan. Idris would be Justin's messenger back to America, the perfect student whose success showcased Justin's courage in coming here. Justin had pretended their friendship could be real, almost equal. But pawns were expendable. Justin had saved the person he wanted to be known for saving.

And while Clay gave money and expected results, it became clear he was motivated by an underlying rivalry. Disdain came into his expression whenever he mentioned Justin, and the night the two men met in the restaurant, their conversation had been tense. Justin might have given Idris the scholarship if not for Clay.

Now all that mattered was Idris's own plan. The novels were right. Most people couldn't make a plan, much less perceive another's. Success depended on controlling desire. He could resist the urge to open the computer and chat with Aisha. It was a difficult decision but became easier when he thought of it as an exercise. He had to give up how he felt when she looked at him — as if he were the only true person who existed.

I like you, she'd told him. You're my street cred.

Human desire — simple needs — ruined plans. Seen coldly, kidnapping Faisal was easy. Nearly all plans contained elements that could be construed as wrong. Most human weakness grew from fear of being judged. Plans worked when you raised them above all else.

Clay had played him perfectly, waiting with the illusion of

deference for Idris to propose the only way to get Tarzi back. Idris had done so, giving voice to, and taking responsibility for, what Clay already intended. Rashidi's corruption had made this easier for Idris. He'd enriched himself by impoverishing people. A journalist had written an article describing how foreign aid vanished into his pockets, how projects meant to create jobs hardly materialized, if at all. The poor, unable to find work, suffered through winter after winter.

Faisal demonstrated no signs of this corruption, but corruption made possible his almost American childlike ease. In class, when students shared writing so that Justin could critique the grammar, Faisal read an essay about how no one in Afghanistan could be trusted. He described his years in Pakistan and how much better life was there. He didn't realize what he was saying. There was a divide between those who grew up under the Taliban and those who spent their childhoods in the safety of Iran or Pakistan or Tajikistan. Returning Afghans could not fathom the suffering of those who'd stayed. People had been forced to survive any way they could. *No one likes you for who you are here*, Faisal had written, *but for what they can get from you*. Justin had corrected him that *no one* was singular and *they* was plural. *No one* should be followed by *he* or *she*. Americans always taught rules that they themselves failed to follow.

Faisal had been easy to befriend. Idris knew of a house on Kabul's outskirts. The owner had bought a projector at the bush bazaar and transformed his living room into a cinema, showing bootleg American new releases the day they came out and charging ten afghani. Idris had invited Faisal, and they'd exchanged numbers, shoulder to shoulder, heads lowered solemnly as if Faisal were doing his duty in agreeing to take part in the Afghanistan outside his home.

Once, at Faisal's four-storey home downtown, Idris met Rashidi. He was a short, stern man with an angular nose like a rectangle stuck to his face. He asked Idris a few terse questions: who his family was, how he and Faisal knew each other. Rashidi seemed satisfied with the answers. Maybe he thought Idris was a tough local boy who would finally help his son integrate into this new Afghanistan. Idris told himself it was true: there were few more authentic Afghan experiences than getting kidnapped. Faisal would be able to head to America with his credentials in order.

In his room, Faisal taught Idris to play Xbox. They sat on cushions in front of an electric heater larger than the grill of a truck. He had the newest video games from Dubai, but not even he could get bootleg movies the day of release.

Idris took him to the makeshift cinema twice before the kidnapping. That night, swerving to avoid a rock, Idris drove the car into an icy rut and pretended to be stuck. When he and Faisal got out, the doors of the car behind them opened. One of the men caught Faisal and held a rag to his mouth. The other approached Idris. He had on a balaclava. His eyes weren't Clay's.

Sorry, kid.

The punch spun Idris. His knees hit the ground, burning and wet. His forehead throbbed. He heard the car trunk slam and the doors shut.

He found the police at a checkpoint and told them what had happened. The bruise on his forehead was swelling. They took him to Rashidi's house. A detective verified that Idris and Faisal had been to the cinema before. Idris played the part: bewildered and repentant.

He couldn't have learned any of this at American University. Society told people that everything beyond the obvious was impossible. When he'd begun to think about plans, he'd believed himself incapable of creating one. He walked across the city and through the market stalls, seeing how little most Afghans possessed in comparison to him, how each one made currency of their life: for some, the skills they'd learned from a father or an uncle; for others, a friendship with a successful merchant or the son of a businessman.

In the pantry, Idris set his laptop aside. He put on his boots and the stocking cap he'd used to hide the bruises on his forehead. He'd been coming in late and hadn't seen Justin in a few days.

He left his room, pausing in the hallway. Faint giggling and tinny music came from the girls' basement. As a small child, he'd watched his mother and a group of her friends dance one evening. She'd put a cassette in a black recorder, and they'd moved their hands and shoulders. The curtains were drawn, a tasseled lamp was lit, and the women's bare feet brushed over the rug, past the cushions where he and his sister sat. A few years later, his mother and sister would be dead. What could Faisal know about those who'd stayed here and their reasons?

Idris left the school and walked a few blocks to an empty lot. He had a vague recollection of this neighborhood from the civil war, when all that stood here were hundreds of crumbling walls, their roofs destroyed by mortars fired from the mountain. The dust of blasted stone had turned everything white under the sun. Now, marking off a future construction project, yellow ribbons fluttered on metal wires stuck into the ground. Someone would steal them soon.

Clay and whoever he was working with had to keep the circle small. They needed an Afghan to negotiate with Rashidi, so

Clay had coached him. Idris crossed an arm against his chest to keep the warm air inside his jacket. He called Rashidi.

The response was quick. Rashidi had been waiting. *Bale . . .*

It's me. It's Idris, Faisal's friend.

Idris *jan*, what is it?

These people, they came to see me.

Which people?

The ones who took Faisal.

Who are they?

I don't know. I was leaving the school tonight, going to the taxi, and they picked me up. They had guns. They told me they didn't want any contact with you. They said I had to be the one to speak to you for them.

Silence. The sound of a TV grew distant. He heard footsteps, then the closing of a door.

Rashidi's voice now rasped. Idris, are you part of this?

I'm not. I swear I'm not.

I don't believe you.

They told me they know you are involved in Tarzi's abduction.

Silence again and then a slow, uneven exhalation.

I don't know Tarzi, Idris said. I don't know what they're talking about. They said I have to deliver messages to you. If you try to do anything, they'll kill Faisal. If Tarzi never comes back, Faisal will be killed. They said that if you or I call the NDS, they'll strangle Faisal.

Idris felt the steadiness of his hand, his fingers numb but the cell not shaking at his ear. The worst thought for him was the NDS, the National Directorate of Security, who were rumored to torture people.

Okay, Rashidi said, his voice quiet and raw. It's okay.

I believe you. Tell me what they want. Maybe we've been for-tunate after all.

They told me that when Tarzi is released, Faisal will be let go. I don't know their names. They said they'd call me. They didn't say when.

So far, the plan didn't belong to Idris. He was still a pawn, but there would be a moment when that could change. Until now, his own plan was to study, to itemize what he could use, to find opportunities.

The situation is complicated, Rashidi said. It wasn't my choice. There are others involved in this who find Tarzi dif-ficult. Please believe that.

I believe you.

We just had to make him disappear during the bidding on a government construction contract, for a very short time. He would never have been hurt.

Idris believed none of this. Rashidi's earlier admission that they were fortunate — a statement as involuntary as an exclamation, as giving thanks — suggested Tarzi was alive but shouldn't be.

Here's the problem, Rashidi told him. Tarzi is in a village whose mullah won't let him leave. Tarzi is an Islamic scholar. He studied in Saudi Arabia, and this mullah found out and is making Tarzi give him lessons. The kidnappers told me that Tarzi is no longer in their control.

Idris said nothing, not surprised to hear a situation almost comical — a barely literate village mullah wanting to expand his knowledge of the Qu'ran and finding himself with a kidnapped man who could give him daily lessons. The story said much about Afghanistan — its faith and desperation and disparity.

But this mullah, Rashidi continued, he works between the true Taliban who come in from Pakistan and the criminals here we sometimes call Taliban, the men who hire themselves out for profit. They were paid to do this job, but the mullah's friends from Pakistan know what Tarzi is worth. They've told us they will keep him until they are properly compensated. They'll approach the family for the ransom only once the mullah is satisfied with his lessons.

Rashidi told Idris to wait a moment while he called them.

The line disconnected, and Idris began walking quickly back to the school. He'd always been thin — putting on weight was difficult — and the cold gouged at his body. He hurried across the lot, breathing into his collar.

He did a lap around the block, heat building at his ribs, his knees sliding against his jeans, their fabric stiffening as it froze. He was nearing the edge of the lot when his cell vibrated.

Rashidi was so hoarse he could hardly speak. They said no. They won't return him.

Why? Idris was commanding himself to think, to find some way to take control.

That idiot mullah refuses.

What did he say?

He asked why he should have mercy on me. He told me I'm a man who betrays Islam and gets fat from American money. Why should he care about my son when the true believers are starving? But it's the fault of those idiots. They can't change their ways and benefit. Why are they blaming me?

Idris was thinking quickly, methodically. Human currency was spent daily here — probably everywhere — and always had been.

Sir, Idris said, testing phrases in his mind and hearing how precarious his proposition would be. Sir, Faisal is my friend. One does not have many friends in Afghanistan now.

Yes. I know. Faisal would agree.

Please, then, let me help. I have an idea. It's extreme, but it may work.

Tell me. It will be okay, Idris. We must consider all possibilities for Faisal.

What if we exchange foreigners for Tarzi?

Why would they want foreigners?

We will give them knowledge to strike the occupiers and bring victory to the Taliban.

Rashidi didn't speak. Idris's heart moved like a flame inside his chest.

Idris *jan*, explain to me very carefully what you mean. What would we be giving?

I know the foreigners' lives, where they go and when they're unprotected. Let's give the Taliban an easy strike. Idris drove anger into his voice. I can send the mullah's people to a place where they can eliminate the infidels who come here to drink and sleep with Afghan girls.

A long silence. Rashidi was himself a maker of plans. He would see this proposition from every angle and try to fathom who else Idris might be serving.

So we offer foreigners in exchange for Tarzi. And you'll help?

I'll do it for Faisal.

Then I'll make sure you're safe.

But we must go to them. We have to make them realize we're on their side.

Rashidi again hesitated. You're a valuable young man. After this, after Faisal is back, you'll work for me. Come here tonight. Early tomorrow, we'll go and do this negotiation. Tonight we'll plan.

The line cut off. Idris pressed the back of the cell until it clicked. He removed the rear cover and slid the SIM card out with his thumb. He inserted his old SIM and called Clay.

Yes, Clay murmured, sounding sleepy. What's the news?

Idris told him the story, about the mullah, Tarzi giving lessons.

Clay laughed. Fucking Afghanistan. He cleared his throat. So that's why they never asked for a ransom.

I will know more tomorrow. Rashidi is the one who had him kidnapped, but now he must pay a ransom to get him back.

My God, Clay said, that's unbelievable. What a story.

After they hung up, Idris switched the cards again. He slipped the SIM into the pocket of his jeans. Then he just stood, the cold against his eyelids. Rashidi, Tarzi — all great men — they planned. They did not live day to day waiting to be helped. This knowledge grew inside Idris, and he let it, so that when he opened his eyes, he would see the world in its light.

CLAY

AFTER THE ATTACK on the safe room, Clay rode home to meet with Alexandra, his mind silent the way it had been his first years as a soldier, when he reacted in battle before he fully grasped the threat. He hadn't needed the constant coffee and energy drinks others depended on. But by his third tour, his reactions were unstable, like an alarm system that triggers for no reason.

He didn't understand why he gave himself over to a course of action — a feeling of being caught in a river, rushed forward — when he knew it would end poorly. The sky seemed wider when he gave himself over. He was closer to nature, free of the delusion of a reasoning self. He'd seen a rifle lifted, the shot that took out a distant man. He'd become a sacrifice, another soldier thrown into the media's volcano as requital for the wars' endless mistakes.

After leaving Iraq in 2008, he traveled America with his savings, only twenty-four, not sure who his people were. In cafés and bars, he eavesdropped, disgusted by the empty talk. These self-absorbed idiots weren't capable of what he'd done. They should look at him with admiration and fear.

He ate and drank his savings, stayed in hotels, took buses and trains, or walked, everything he owned in a small backpack. Sometimes, in the afternoon, when the sky was empty, the sun at a late angle, the air cooling and leaves falling, he heard the truck pulling up, its tires against the asphalt, the knocking in its engine, and he turned, seeing the blunt, caring face of his father.

His only release from anger was sex. He went home with women he barely knew, going at them so hard he didn't remember pleasure, only the sound of his pelvis hitting theirs — until one day something burned out in him. He'd seduce a woman, get her in his hands, and then he'd start to go soft. The chase was already over, and he was staring into the time in between.

A quiet set in. He lived in hotels and ate out and read all day. He spent a year in Lafayette, down the highway from Lake Charles, and never told his mother he was there.

He ran out of money and stayed in a flophouse, clipping his beard and hair with rusty scissors he found in a drawer next to a burnt spoon he used for meals. He took a job caretaking for an old man, Mr. Dupre, going each day to his third-floor apartment of mismatched furniture, where bottles lined the windowsills and the fridge was empty except for grape jam and Wonder Bread. Clay carried him onto the landing so Dupre could get air. The old man sat, wearing a straw hat as he read a *World Book* encyclopedia with a cover like a worn-out saddle. Clay reread the novels of Jack London that he'd loved as a boy.

Often, Mr. Dupre told stories, his head copper in the late light as he described his first visits to brothels in the oil towns of Beaumont and Port Arthur, or the way his elementary teacher had made the boys lie under the schoolhouse for speaking French.

We could hear the lessons well enough through the floor, he said, but these are swamplands and there's reasons houses don't sit on the ground. When you couldn't speak the language no more, there was only one French thing left to do and that was wander. It's in the blood. Every Englishman who discovered something had a Frenchman to paddle him there.

Then he laughed, a strung-out cackle that ended in a smoker's cough.

Terrestrial shelf life is limited, and only Jesus knows your expiration date. That's what my preacher used to say. Something popped in his brain and he dropped dead with a hot dog in his hand. You never know if you've got a thing on the brain.

Mr. Dupre told stories of the war in the Pacific, VD and whores, Great Depression America. His skin was like paper from the trash, so crumpled he had to point out his mended harelip.

One morning Dupre said, I'm blind. It happened in my sleep. Just like that.

Clay carried him down the zigzagging stairs like a princess, the old man's breath reeking of tobacco, his bony shoulders folded to his chin, as fragile as a bird's wings.

Don't cry, Dupre said.

I'm not, Clay told him as tears flooded his beard.

I don't want to depart the earth wearing diapers, Dupre said. Good Lord, I do not.

Clay kept working his throat to make himself swallow.

Stop, Dupre told him. I just remembered I hate hospitals.

Clay stood on the fractured sidewalk, the old man insubstantial in his arms.

How about we drink one last good time, Dupre said. I have a few stories left. Then I'll go in my sleep like a civilized man.

They sat up all night, Dupre's eyes half-lidded or wide and aimed at nothing as he described the phases of a life that shone before Clay more briefly than the sun flashing between clouds:

a stint as a boxer, a manager of a sporting goods store, a UPS driver, a forklift driver, an inventory manager, a tire salesman, a quality checker for extension cords. Dawn came up over the swamps, and in the hazy, humid air it ballooned into an immense pearl before the light released and washed into the sky. Dupre was asleep. Clay carried him to his bed.

Late that afternoon, hangover like a wind in the back of his head, he got up off the couch and went into the bedroom and drew the sheet up over Dupre's head.

Baptism by firefight, one of his friends had said. What can we go back to after that?

Clay sat alone in the house and cried harder than he had in years.

After the funeral, he found himself a job as a security contractor in Kabul. He was promoted from guarding to training and managing other men, but he grew restless. He'd be almost asleep and become aware of the beating of his heart. Repeated thuds. Like footsteps in an empty house. Had he heard or thought something, or just slipped past thought into the systolic rhythm of his blood? Nothing calmed him, not drink or masturbation or reading.

At first, Alexandra had seemed like a much-needed adventure, but in the safe room, she'd become more than a long-overdue fuck or a means of revenge. She neither cried nor withdrew into herself, and her eyes didn't become empty. She gazed at the screen like someone who'd been broken and needed to face destruction again — if not to master it, then to master herself in its place.

Justin's expression could have been mistaken for hers, but his was the delusion of a mystic: the refusal to realize that only men killing each other — and nothing divine — would save

him. After 9/11, in Lake Charles, Justin and his parents had
changed, their faith and militancy fused. On Clay's only visit to
their church, the pastor described their battle against the devil
and lowered his voice to incite them to redeem their country
through spiritual warfare. But Alexandra had come here aware
of the reality, and now that something had happened, she was
determined not to turn away.

Clay had been tense but confident. He knew that if the door
was blasted open and the insurgents fired, he would be among
the survivors. Other foreigners might die, but he wouldn't. He
felt the uplift of adrenaline, the familiar bracing; that was all.

Only after the last attacker fell and the trembling expats
drank their gin did desire flood his body. They all filed out,
blood and burnt flesh squelching under their shoes, some of
them gagging, until they were outside, walking in the frozen
mud. Alexandra was leaving with her friends, and there was no
way to talk to her alone.

The street blazed, a circus of army and police trucks, milling
with soldiers, neighbors, photojournalists, cameramen, and the
rabble of expat war tourists who'd yet to find a regular gig that
legitimized voyeurism. Afghan Special Forces led Idris outside.
Clay had eventually noticed his absence in the safe room. He
hurried over to say Idris was his employee.

Justin joined them. Idris was soaked in sweat. He'd hidden
in the bedroom, too terrified to come out after the blast.

The NDS agent who spoke with him seemed doubtful, but
that was his job. Justin vouched for Idris. The agent took Idris's
cell, searched him, and left.

As Idris was leaving with Justin, he looked back at Clay, pale
and terrified, as if the danger hadn't ended. Clay's gut clenched.
Kidnapping Rashidi's son — Steve had him in the basement, its

entrance hidden, virtually impossible for the police to find —
and the negotiations had gone too well. He wondered if the
attack was more than a random targeting of foreigners.

He texted Alexandra.

Meet me at my place.

He scanned the crowd. His phone buzzed.

Why?

I want you.

He put the cell in his pocket and was climbing onto his
motorcycle when it buzzed again.

*I'll text when I'm in the taxi. In about an hour. What's your
address?*

He sent it and rode home. Involuntarily, he considered
Idris's fear. He'd been cautious and obedient during the negotiations, and he'd been good under pressure. He should have
known better than to hide in the bedroom.

Clay climbed his stairs. He stopped on his terrace, too
impatient to go inside. The clouds had blown past and to the
north a military surveillance blimp glinted in its usual place.

The night before he'd shot Justin, his mother had gotten the
news from her family in Maine that his father was dead. Clem
had fallen asleep in the hoop garage with his truck running.
He and his mother kept quiet, alone with their thoughts. The
next day Clay bought the air rifles and the Christmas tree bulbs,
spending everything he had. He hardly remembered making
the plan. He wasn't even sure he'd carry it out.

When the police arrived, Clay claimed he'd blinded Justin
by accident. The officers were so busy rounding up drunk,
underage kids and getting them home that they accepted his
answer. Justin's father said he wouldn't press charges but gave
Clay and his mother until dawn to be out of the carriage house.

They packed and moved into Demetrie's. The power was off and the rooms were musty. Later, unable to sleep, he went outside, through the weeds and bladelike grass and vines of the jungle. He walked to Justin's house, where he climbed the pecan tree.

The aquarium illuminated the bedroom. Justin lay bundled, his shoulders and head on pillows. A bandage covered his eye, artfully arranged, the way doctors and nurses did it, and this, too, seemed a mark of privilege — a beret jauntily worn, or a blazon. The uncovered part of his face appeared waxy in the blue light. Clay felt that if Justin opened his eye, everything from that night would be erased.

The next day Clay enlisted. It was the beginning he'd been attempting for so long.

A car passed somewhere, sounding too decrepit to be bringing Alexandra, its muffler's heat shield rattling.

Blood pulsed at the junctures of his limbs and behind his solar plexus, his abdomen as tight as a drum.

Even as a boy, aiming a weapon had been automatic, as if every act of violence were inherited — a gesture repeated across centuries.

Destroying his own life had felt like the only way out of it.

ALEXANDRA

ALEXANDRA'S HOUSE WAS crowded, the impromptu gathering point for survivors and friends and journalists who'd followed the attack on Twitter. People were crying, holding each other, stroking each other's backs and hair. Holly had suddenly begun bawling, going such long stretches that she ran out of breath and began gasping and choking.

Justin lingered, his back to the wall, Idris shivering next to him, his jacket pulled close. The guard was stoking the *bukhari*, and people sat on the floor around it, talking and holding hands.

The room had quieted, only Holly still crying. Idris watched her from his corner, likely the only person in the house who actually wanted to comfort her. Alexandra had tried and lost patience.

Can I talk to you? Justin asked when she broke from a cluster of people.

She motioned him into the empty dining room. During the attack, he hadn't touched or reassured her, just leveled his fanatic stare at the screen, so certain of his survival.

What's going on with you and Clay?

Nothing. He came to the school. I met him there.

I saw how you looked at him.

Does it matter?

Just be careful. Nothing Clay does is innocent.

You don't need to save me, she said, but she wondered why Clay hadn't warned her that Justin would be at the party. Maybe he didn't think she would care.

She was about to turn away, but there was something broken and familiar in Justin's face that she might have recognized in the mirror years ago. A sudden tenderness like nostalgia overcame her, and she kissed his cheekbone.

Justin called to Idris, and the two of them left.

Alexandra went into her room, changed, and requested a taxi. She rubbed a body wipe along her arms and legs. She took a second, then third, scouring away the smell of sweat and fear. She dressed and wrapped her head and shoulders in a scarf.

She walked down the hall, past the conversations and chiming cells in the living room, to the taxi already waiting outside. She texted, *On my way*.

In the safe room, Clay had seemed at ease. She had no illusions about what she was about to do. She wanted what hadn't happened the night of the rocket attack. She knew the pop-psychology diagnoses, the way people acted on wounds, believing—deluded—that the past could be healed. She didn't particularly care. Clay was an experience she wanted. The violence in him lay just beneath the surface, not cocooned as it was in Justin.

When the taxi dropped her off, the driver didn't leave until Clay opened the gate. He led her up two flights of external concrete stairs to a top landing heaped with firewood. Inside, windows lined the small apartment. Maybe the view made up for the lack of furnishing, she thought. There was a lamp on a stool near the bed and some books on the floor.

Clay turned to her, flushed, his chest lifting. His neck was hot beneath her palm, his hands on her waist, the skin of his lips cold and then suddenly hot. They undressed and fucked against the wall, but in the moment before he came, when he looked at her, she realized she'd been wrong. Everyone in that room had been afraid.

She took his hand and led him to the bed. She lay next to him and moved her fingertips over his skin. The room was hot, both of them sweating. She explored the lines of his muscles, pausing at small scars not unlike those on Sam's body. She'd have spent a hundred years with him, exploring the coast — two hunter-gatherers discovering their place in the world. As a child, she wanted to kill the squirrel, to see it thrashing underwater like a fish. In dreams, she stood in the crescent of shadow beneath the hull as he climbed the rusted edge against the sky.

Clay jerked and opened his eyes, and when he saw her, he flinched.

What is it between you and Justin? she asked.

That's not easy to explain.

Tell me.

He described his family and fleeing his father. In Lake Charles, he wanted to make space for himself. His first year there he'd been in control and entered the community with dignity, not fully on his terms — no one did anything fully on his own terms — but close enough. When he returned, he was raging, unable to restrain himself, seeing in those around him the negation of all that had created him.

She hadn't expected his rush of words. She kept moving her fingers over his muscles as he told her about the game with the air rifles and Christmas ornaments. He'd intended to humiliate Justin, but once they were in the forest, he realized how petty that would look. He was trapped in his own game. The ending had to be dramatic and final, and now, years later, he hated Justin no less.

And why Idris? Why me? she asked.

Idris deserves more. He's a smart kid, and there's nothing for him in that school. Why does he need to be a servant because he's poor?

And me?

Isn't that fucking obvious?

He switched off the lamp and set his arm at his side with a deliberate movement, like a man putting down a weapon, and his breathing was instantly deep. She'd thought she'd be satisfied and would be able to sleep, but the tension from the safe room hadn't left her body.

The sky began to lighten. The room was cooling, and she got up and fed the *bukhari*. When she lay back down, his eyes were open, his face gentle with fatigue, its angles softened.

IDRIS

IDRIS LAY IN Faisal's bed, facing the electric heater. He didn't want to fall asleep, to lose consciousness of its warmth on his skin, but he couldn't resist his fatigue. It seemed only seconds later that someone was tapping at the door. He dressed and went out to the Land Cruiser and sat next to Rashidi. The driver and a guard in front had Kalashnikovs.

They sped through empty roundabouts and intersections, and soon were on the Kabul–Jalalabad road. The highway descended along the canyon above the river, passing through small Soviet tunnels.

By the time the landscape opened and the road straightened and leveled, the sun was up. A line of Pakistani jingle trucks painted in green, blue, and red passed in the opposite direction. The driver circumvented the outskirts of Jalalabad, and continued into the arid mountains before veering onto a dirt road. An hour later, they stopped in a village, near the mosque.

Bearded men came to the doorways of houses. They showed no guns, but their postures suggested readiness. A compound gate opened, and a tall guard motioned for them to leave their vehicle and come inside.

Let's get out, Rashidi told Idris — just the two of us.

They pushed their doors open. The air was warm, and a generator thrummed somewhere inside the compound.

The guard led them through the gate, past a Toyota pickup and a Corolla, to a doorway where two men sat cross-legged on cushions near a tarnished samovar. They were dressed similarly, in white *shalwar kameez*, brown vests, and black turbans. One was squat, with jowls that made his beard seem unusually wide, though his hands were small and pale. He introduced himself as Mullah Akhund. The other, Noorudin, an envoy from Peshawar, was tall and elegant, prayer beads in his fingers, his skin gleaming, as if rubbed with oil, and his mustache neatly trimmed above his full lips. Idris understood immediately that he was the Taliban representative.

They sat around the samovar. It rested on a square of rubber neatly cut from an inner tube, and an electric cord ran into its top to boil the water. The guard carefully removed the cord, its two strands bent apart at the end to keep their exposed copper from touching. He unplugged it from a power strip loaded up with cell chargers, put it aside, and poured them tea. He went out, and a moment later the generator sputtered and was silent.

The mullah said that he hoped their journey had been good. Then he spoke about life in the village, the challenges of winter, the lack of jobs, and the government benefits that were promised but never arrived. He talked about the young men, and Idris realized he meant the kidnappers who had taken Tarzi.

These young men, he said, they got permission from me to do this work. We needed to repair the mosque, after it was damaged by fighting. Tarzi is comfortable among us. He can't be here today because we have to trust you first.

Idris sensed that Mullah Akhund was coming to the point of contention and tried to anticipate how the demands would be justified.

The mullah turned to the Talib. Our friend here lost one of

his brothers in a drone strike. When one of the believers dies
in the war, we must ask what those of you who benefit from
America can do for us. Do you understand?

How much do you want? Rashidi asked.

Noorudin remained silent, his expression reposed and
dignified.

It's for the jihad, Mullah Akhund said. For you, half a million dollars is nothing.

That's not true. It's more than I have.

Idris sensed Rashidi looking over and felt strange to have a
powerful man needing him.

May I ask a question? Idris said.

Of course. The mullah nodded, and Noorudin's gaze shifted
now, quizzical, curious to see what a beardless youth had to say.

If the purpose of this money, Idris told him, is to continue
the fight against the infidels, then it would be simpler to strike
the heart of the foreign occupation.

Rashidi gestured to Idris. This is a very resourceful young
man, very intelligent. He's an orphan and from a poor family,
but he has studied the foreigners for years.

Idris had never received such attention from elders before.
Fortunately, the mullah and Noorudin's shared ideology would
force them to accept his plan. The code of honor — of blood for
blood — would compel them, and if foreigners died, the mullah and Noorudin would get cash rewards from the Taliban
leadership.

What if I can get revenge? Foreigners in exchange for Tarzi's
release?

The mullah glanced at Noorudin, who took a moment to
consider Idris.

Why should we believe you? Noorudin asked.

We're all Afghan. We're tired of the occupiers. They come. They sleep with our girls. They drink alcohol. They consume drugs. And they become rich from our suffering. So I will give you a group of barely defended foreigners.

How many?

It will depend on the occasion. How many do you want?

At least three. We have lost so many to their drones while they live in wealth.

Three is easy. I'll try to get more.

I have men in Kabul who are ready to give their lives, Noorudin told him. They can detonate doors, but too many armed guards would be a problem.

This is the secret about foreigners, Idris said. Many of them have no protection. There's often just a gate and one man with a gun.

Noorudin stroked his beard. Can we trust these men? he asked the mullah.

Rashidi cleared his throat. Of course you can. I will lose my son if we fail.

This is true, the mullah admitted. And if anything goes wrong or the NDS comes for us, I'll tell them you hired our young men to do the kidnapping and we have been protecting Tarzi. They'll see that we've treated him with respect and didn't kill him as you asked. And we didn't send him back because we feared for the safety of such a devout man.

In the Land Cruiser, after bidding farewell, Rashidi and Idris didn't speak until they reached the asphalt of the Kabul–Jalalabad road.

Their lies are distasteful, Rashidi said. Who believes they fight for more than money?

Idris agreed but felt there was no sense in voicing obvious

hypocrisies. Idris had no love for the Taliban, but everyone knew the Americans had empowered certain tribes who abused others and made the poor so desperate they had no choice but to side with the extremists.

Idris was aware that he needed to find foreigners fast enough to make Clay believe Tarzi was being released in exchange for money and not lives. He had to stay focused. He had to anticipate every plan Rashidi, Noorudin, and Clay could fabricate.

After leaving Rashidi, Idris returned to the empty lot near the school and changed his SIM card. He called Clay.

They won't let Tarzi go for less than seven hundred thousand, he said. Rashidi does not have as much as I thought. He has only two hundred thousand now and is trying to get more.

Seven hundred, huh? Clay said. The mullah's a greenhorn. We can get more than that from Tarzi's family. Rich Afghans are loaded.

Idris hadn't foreseen this. He should have named a higher amount. Clay would ask Tarzi's family for more and keep the difference. The profitability of his business was suddenly clear. *Greenhorn* — Idris didn't know the word but sensed its meaning. Regardless, he would make half a million, if his plan succeeded. Not all that bad for a greenhorn.

Meet me tonight, Clay said. I'll get the money and give it to you, but we have to trust you. This is a lot of cash. You could run.

I won't.

You say that, but Faisal is nothing to you, and we can't turn you in because we're all guilty. So I need to tell you that the person I work for is dangerous. If you run, he will make sure you are killed.

I believe you.

We will pay you better than promised. Twenty-five thousand. You'll walk away able to start your own business or get an education or whatever you want.

Thank you, Mr. Clay.

Clay.

Thank you, Clay.

Clay gave him the instructions for meeting and said goodbye.

Idris had to get the timing right and decide whose lives he would choose. He couldn't be sentimental. Foreigners were his capital. Reaching the world he desired would require sacrificing those who inhabited it. Frank often brought expats to fawn over the girls, but though Idris would rather the victims be people he didn't know, he had to act quickly.

Idris took a battered taxi to Afghan Fried Chicken, went inside, texted Clay, and ate while he waited. When he received a reply, he walked around the block and, a few minutes later, a car stopped. Clay told him to get in the back. They drove a bit and pulled over far from any doorways or gates where security cameras would likely be installed.

There's a backpack on the floor. Take a taxi straight to Rashidi, give the backpack to him, and tell him his son will be released as soon as Tarzi is home.

The bag holding the bundled cash was lighter than Idris had expected.

And listen, Clay added, Justin called me. He saw my number in your phone and knows you're working for me. So be careful from now on. Once you've dropped off the money, go to the school and act normal. I got Frank's permission to hire you, and Justin doesn't have much say. I'll be seeing him tonight at a party a friend is having. You can drive him in two hours. As far as he's concerned, you're running errands for me, translating, doing odd jobs. Got it?

Yes, Idris told him, barely hearing the words. This would be easy, but he wanted to target a party where Clay and Justin wouldn't be. He just had to wait. In Kabul, there was a party of foreigners somewhere almost every evening. Frank talked daily about this or that gathering.

Idris got out and went to the cross street. Clay had circled the block and watched Idris on the main road as he hailed a taxi with tassels along the top of the split windshield.

Idris asked to be let out near Rashidi's house. He knocked and went inside. Surely, Clay and whoever he worked with had the house under surveillance and Idris would need to be seen paying a visit. But Rashidi wasn't home. Had he been, Idris would have simply told him that the plan was ready. He left and caught another taxi to the school.

Though Idris wanted to lock the backpack in the pantry, Justin heard him come in and called down. Idris took off his stocking cap and went upstairs. He explained to Justin that he'd been mugged and had gotten sick.

Justin's hands were in his *kameez* pockets, his shoulders back with authority.

There's a party tonight, he said. I need you to take me. I'm going to see Clay.

Idris tried to focus, but the weight of his decision made it difficult.

What kind of work are you doing for Clay? Justin asked. He was suddenly breathing hard, opening and closing his hands. One of his eyes focused in, glaring, the other abstracted, a prisoner in the contracting muscles.

As Idris began to speak, Justin grabbed his collar and swung him against the wall. The strength, the intensity of the torque seemed impossible coming from another person. The backpack slid across the floor, and Idris's teeth clacked together. Green circles flashed before him. The back of his head stung. He doubled over, trying to get air into his lungs, but his arms hung loose as if broken. He couldn't feel his hands. He didn't let himself check on the backpack. He didn't want to betray that he cared about it more than his pain.

Just errands. He could barely speak.

Did Clay start this?

I did. I asked if he had work.

Justin's fingers dug into the muscles of his jaw, pinching the insides of his cheeks against his teeth. Idris tasted warm, metallic blood. Justin's glass eye seemed empty, refusing to witness this humiliation.

Why would you do that?

I don't see why I can't have a job. I am not paid here. And I am not getting a scholarship.

Justin let go. He was panting. He drew his hand soothingly over his own face.

Idris tried to straighten his jacket and tuck his shirt in. Sensation was coming back to his hands, but his fingers would not obey him.

I will drive you to the party, he said. I am sorry. I did not realize this situation would bother you.

The back of his skull hurt, and a headache was beginning. He was suddenly sure of himself, like the first time he really gave himself to prayer, before his doubt that the divine could create a world of such violence had stripped him of that comfort. Maybe some things were truly God's will and he shouldn't question his own victory.

Justin was flushed, staring at the floor like a little boy. Idris said nothing, picked up his backpack, and went downstairs.

Inside the pantry, Idris began to cry, sobbing so hard his throat ached. He found some tissue and cleared his nose. He reached into the backpack and felt the thick paper of the banded one-hundred-dollar bills. The bundles were small and would be easy to hide separately. He stashed the money in a bag of clothes, locked the pantry door, and walked back over to the lot. He called Clay and said that Rashidi had the money. Then he called the mullah and told him to ready his men near the expat neighborhoods, either Taimani or Wazir Akbar Khan.

As Idris walked back through the school's door, he heard Frank asking where Justin was going. Had Frank been there all along? Had he heard what had happened, or did he even care?

A party, Justin said.

Glad to see you getting out more.

The drive was silent. Idris steered effortlessly. He'd spent years navigating this traffic. Even now, surrendered to his plan, he negotiated the melee of cars. But the images hardly reached his brain. He was counting down to the text message he would send. He parked outside the compound and observed it: its lights and security cameras and concertina wire, and the large metal gate with an inset door.

Clay came out in a shirt, his sleeves rolled with the modest authority of a general who removes his jacket and turns up his cuffs. He called to Idris as if he hadn't seen him in days.

Some of my friends are expecting me, Idris said.

Come on. You can be late. This is going to be one hell of a party.

When Idris refused again, Clay crossed the mud and put an arm around him.

Good to see you, buddy. Let me introduce you to my friends.

Idris realized his lie had rung false, especially now with the ransom. Clay likely didn't suspect anything, but he was a keen observer. Idris commanded himself to relax.

They moved through the party toward the bar. Next to them, a young German man was talking to two women about his ropes.

Ya, you see, I have five-fifty paracord. A thin strand holds five hundred and fifty pounds. I keep a hundred feet in my jacket and two carabiners. I can escape from any place.

As he manically described knots and his tiny titanium grappling hooks, the women laughed.

Ropes can't save you from every situation, one said.

Yes, they can. This is a city of walls and flat roofs. As long as I can get on a roof and get off the next wall, and do it fast, I will survive.

Clay and Justin were talking, and Idris stepped away, pretending to make for the food. He listened to the foreigners' chatter, edging past each group so he could hear them over the music.

A woman ranted about a *Rolling Stone* journalist who'd mocked her on Twitter. A boyish man bragged that during an embed he'd joined a few marines for their morning run and kept up effortlessly. A woman with pouched eyes said she hated Kabul and was counting the days on her contract until she could live someplace where the air was clean and the food didn't liquefy her intestines.

Idris wandered until he found the bathroom. He sent a text, describing the location and that there was a single armed guard. He deleted it and any questionable numbers from the log, removed the SIM, and flushed it.

Back in the living room, Holly's blonde corkscrews bounced as she laughed. Regret spooled inside him. No, fuck her and the dogs she sent to America. Her friends had laughed at his jokes and stories, and then shouldered him aside.

He went down the hall and found the bedroom. He shut himself in but left the door unlocked. The closet was empty, with nothing to give him cover. Under the bed there was just enough space. The box spring pressed on his chest. At last he'd discovered a benefit to years of hunger. The tender spot on the back of his head stung as he rested it against the tile floor.

The explosion came as fast as he'd expected. A man began shouting for people to follow him, and a second explosion thudded through the building. Kalashnikovs rattled. The door creaked open, and someone said, If anyone's hiding, come out. We have a safe room.

The man's voice belonged to the kidnapper who'd punched Idris in the street.

Idris commanded his heart to slow, but it was beating too hard and he couldn't breathe deeply enough to calm it.

Another detonation shook the floor. Then the firing started up again, louder and more constant. Had security forces arrived already? Idris hadn't expected the house to be so fortified. If the insurgents failed, he would be held accountable.

There was yet another explosion, and the firing got closer but more intermittent. Then it intensified — the high notes of bullets ricocheting along the halls, the violent telegraphic sound of the guns like a conversation across the distance — until there was a final burst.

Sweat soaked him. He wanted to push the box spring off. Footsteps moved through the house. Afghans were speaking, clearing the rooms. When someone came into the bedroom, he called for help. Two soldiers lifted the bed. He could hardly stand, and they held him under his arms and walked him out, their boots grinding against broken glass and bullet casings. Holes pocked the walls in uneven lines and clusters, and two insurgents lay dead, their blood congealing.

The foreigners were coming out of the safe room, most of them covering their faces. Justin and Alexandra passed, their eyes bright, staring at the dead. The assailants had known this was a suicide mission — almost all attacks in Kabul were — but they'd expected something in exchange for their lives. One had been partially dismembered by his own explosives.

Outside, vehicles packed the street, foreign and Afghan cameramen pressing in.

Clay arrived and put an arm around Idris. He's with us, he told the security forces. The night washed over them, blue lights eddying along walls, headlamps shining on mud. There was an etheric quality to the air — the fumes of a city ready to burst into flame.

An NDS agent in a suit approached Idris.

You are the Afghan who hid under the bed?

Yes.

Please give me your phone.

Idris handed it over.

Clay vouched for him, and the agent checked Idris's call record and shrugged.

Okay. Maybe he is sheep. Maybe he is wolf. Go, you take him.

Then the agent walked away.

It'll be okay, Clay said, a hand on Idris's shoulder, but he was looking around, the muscles of his neck taut.

Idris crossed his arms. His sweat had gone cold. Rashidi,

the mullah, Noorudin — what would they do? He hugged his jacket against himself, his wet shirt making him shiver.

Private taxis and NGO drivers began pulling up, and among the foreigners he heard weeping and a strange hysterical laughter, an animal sound, like dogs yipping far away.

People hurried through the churned mud in no semblance of order, to and from points he couldn't perceive, and all of them, Afghan or foreigner, searched his face as if they knew.

美智子

AS MY TAXI pulled away from the school, I called Steve. I was fantasizing about my success while imagining how people might speak of me if all this went wrong: expats concocting conspiracies in which I was a threat to those in power, and old classmates in Tokyo calling each other to say, Did you hear about Michiko Kimura? — Yes, on the news, dead in Afghanistan.

"Michiko," Steve said, "how's your investigation coming along?" He must have programmed my name into his phone.

"My investigation?"

"I wish you'd told me that you're a journalist. There's a lot more I would have shared."

I asked what that would be, and he said, "Why don't you come over? I'm here now. It won't take long."

I directed the taxi driver to Steve's house and told him to wait for me. I rang the buzzer and the guard let me into the familiar courtyard.

The muscles in Steve's arms and shoulders were larger than I remembered, and a stress rash covered the side of his neck to his hairline.

"Come on in." He shook my hand, a little hard.

The house remained empty, as if he'd planned to leave, but it now had monitors in each room, with images sectioned into four feeds, showing the street, the inside of the gate, the front yard, and the side walkway. We went upstairs, to the safe room, which had since been converted to his bedroom and office. A laptop was on an otherwise bare desk.

From the street came the bleating tune of an ice cream cart passing, an irritating electronic rendition of "Happy Birthday," and Steve muttered, "That fucking ice cream man's been hanging around all day." Then he took a breath and turned his attention on me. "I know you've been investigating the deaths last winter. It's been what, three months?"

"Yes, but I'm not really interested in answers."

"Go again?" The hostility in his voice couldn't have been clearer.

"I've been researching their lives, who they were, what brought them here. It's more of a human interest story."

"Uh huh. So you haven't found anything?"

"In what way?"

"Regarding Clay or Idris . . . or anything else?"

"No. It's all a dead end."

He just stared, the veins in his eyes forking out from his irises like lightning.

A buzzer sounded.

"Goddamn it," he said. In one square of the monitor, two police trucks had stopped and a man who was almost certainly a plainclothes agent in a leather jacket — they were usually the ones to speak to foreigners — had reached up to the buzzer.

"Come with me." Steve hurried me downstairs, but at the door, he appeared uncertain.

"Wait here. I'll just be a minute."

He went out, paused to look back while crossing the yard and then again at the gate before saying something to the guard. The hall monitor showed him enter the street and speak to the agent, gesturing to the house, most likely to say he couldn't invite them in. The agent reluctantly led Steve to the truck. He opened a briefcase on the hood and took out some papers. The police leaned against the fenders, Kalashnikovs hanging from their shoulders.

I walked through the first floor. The rooms were empty. In one, a bookshelf had been slid back. There was an iron door behind it, with a key in the lock. Having heard so many rumors of contractor conspiracies, I wasn't surprised he'd have a secret passage, only that he'd leave it exposed. I pushed, and the door opened soundlessly onto a narrow staircase.

I glanced back at the monitors. Steve was still examining the papers, photographs now, and shaking his head.

The stairs led into a different climate, coolness emanating from the walls. I descended into a hallway whose only light was yet another monitor. Steve examined the documents, listening to the agent, who looked often at the compound gate and street camera, as if right at me. Maybe he'd been here before and had been invited inside, and was now dragging this meeting out, suspicious of Steve's reluctance to let him in. Though Steve had been the victim of an attack, security contractors were often in trouble with the government for taxes or permits, as well as with the police, who viewed them as competition for work they could be paid for themselves.

The unlit corridor led to an open door with two locks on it. A windowless concrete chamber held a small table on wheels with a TV and DVD player, and a metal folding chair with a box of Kleenex next to it on the floor. I turned on the TV and played the DVD. Two people were having sex against a wall, the woman with her elbows over the man's shoulders, her breasts in his face. It wasn't commercial porn but rather a poorly lit video feed. I moved closer. It was Alexandra, her fingers in Clay's short hair.

Steve must not have trusted Clay. I shut off the TV, ran into the hall, and checked the monitor. Steve was still outside. The agent was gesturing toward the house. Evenings, when I rode in taxis with other foreigners — on those occasions when I dressed as a woman — the police often checked my passport, since they thought I was Hazara and suspected me of being a prostitute. But Steve could easily explain that I was a foreigner.

There was another door at the end of the corridor, also open, and I ran to check it quickly. The thin mattress of a cot lay next to a bucket, a loaf of bread in a plastic bag, and a jar of water. Had the cell been prepared to contain someone else, or did Steve think I had knowledge that could hurt him? In the middle of the ceiling was a small metal plate with a circle of glass. A camera. I rushed back into the room with the folding chair. The same fixture was there.

On the monitor, Steve was putting the documents and photos back in the briefcase.

I tried to breathe, my heart working so fast and hard that my ears buzzed, and then I was back in the clarity I'd experienced in the safe room — my entire life a prelude to this moment.

I ran upstairs. I had only minutes to guarantee my safety, but once I left, I wouldn't be able to find out what Steve was up to. I sprinted to the safe room, took his laptop, and shoved it into my backpack. On the screen, Steve closed the briefcase, pushed it away on the hood, and threw up his hands. I raced downstairs. He argued with the police, edging closer to the door.

October sunlight raked my eyes as I hurried to the gate. The guard scrambled out and held up his palm. He was a small man in stonewashed jeans and a leather jacket, his hair cut in a mullet and a gold hoop in his ear. He said something in Dari I couldn't make out.

"What?" I asked. "I am not Hazara."

"Ah. I did not know. Mr. Steve said no matter what, you stay inside. It is not safe for you to go out."

I was suddenly convinced the small room in the basement had been prepared for me. My hands shook as I fumbled in my bag. I pushed close to him and took out a hundred dollars.

"The cameras can't see this," I told him. "I'm too close to you. Take it. Tell Steve I lied to you. Tell him I threatened to call the police."

The money was quickly in his hand and hidden from the camera. The police were just across the wall, and if he refused, I would scream. He must have seen this in my eyes. He went into the guard house. I pulled the latch on the door and let myself out. The police leaning on the truck fenders began to laugh.

"So this is why you do not want us inside," the agent told Steve, who'd flushed, his rash visibly larger along his neck. "But we do not mind. She is a pretty one."

I walked off. They'd never remember me as anything other than a Hazara prostitute. If I spoke, I would have an insurance policy against Steve, but I would also be on their radar if he reported the theft of the laptop.

My taxi was gone. Steve must have had the guard pay the driver and tell him to leave. I walked, conscious of the laptop's weight in my backpack. I pulled my headscarf close, and at the cross street, I turned. Two blocks farther down, the security guards at the Finest Supermarket let me inside. I went up several floors to the section selling household items. I sat in a chair wrapped in plastic and called a taxi in case Steve was searching the streets.

I'd heard that the Afghan government not only was trying to rein in the expats' sense of entitlement but was becoming more protective of its image. The NDS was increasingly investigating claims published in the foreign media. It must have suspected something. Steve had to be in trouble. What other reason could there be for the mattress, the bucket, the jar of water, and the loaf of bread at the end of that basement hallway?

The tiny cell suddenly seemed the destination for this journey, as if everything I'd done was to confront a fear of being closed away and made powerless, or at least to write it into a story bigger than my life.

Before I ever read of America, I knew the novels and history of my nation, its exceptionalism and colonial spirit, the way it forged a single identity — inflicted upon us — before it was forced on others. Then Japan was finally dominated, colonized by America, until it assimilated even that re-education into its pride, rebuilding the pieces into the unflinching image of empire's rising sun.

In school, the girls sensed how I admired them, and their groups refused to let me join in even though I attempted to ingratiate myself. When I told my mother about the meanness, she said they were trying to teach me to fit in. The boys observed my orbiting and smirked, but I saw how others aligned themselves, and I believed that dressing and speaking and laughing the right way would help me overcome my difference.

On a day that I stayed late, working in the lab to finish an assignment, four boys were talking in the hallway and watched me pass with drifting eyes. They followed in a row, their stride arrogant and symmetric, so much like something from a music video it seemed harmless. They were suddenly behind me and one had his hand over my mouth. I didn't notice the janitor's closet until I was inside it. They held me to the floor. One stood with his back to the door.

There is nothing special in these details. I have lived with them for too long. Their rotation in the hurried silent satisfaction of needs. They'd done this before and didn't have to speak to direct the routine, or had simply been synchronized by the precision of their culture.

At the end, a punch, unnecessary, anticlimactic: not hard, though it did flash stars in my vision. It seemed more an assertion of agency than a desire to inflict pain.

Or maybe sourceless anger needed release, that anger that doesn't begin in our lives but somewhere millions of years ago in the gap between desire and reality, the awareness of — and rage at — what isn't.

Or it could have simply been a correction, punishment for what I was not.

They hurried out, and I spent the night on the concrete, in that small room. Briefly, after hours of lying there, I experienced a state that resembled lucid sleep. I went outside before dawn, when I was least likely to be caught. I pushed through the school's door that locked behind me.

My mother was waiting in a chair, too afraid to call the police in case I'd been the one who'd done something wrong.

She took off my clothes and put me in the shower, dressed me in pajamas and tucked me in. The next day was her day off. The two of us sat on the couch and enacted our weekly ritual of watching TV and eating a week's worth of chocolates from her suitors.

At night, for years, I was afraid to walk alone. Narrow streets I once loved I raced through. At school, I feared groups of teenagers and the spaces between them. I lived with the people in books and built myself with their words. But as I advanced in biology and genetics, I learned to see myself as a creature whose fears might not have begun that day. I studied the *we* of groups, of our species: genomic truths and the science of fear, our predictability and the limited paths of our lives. Maybe there are no first actions, and our pains, emotions, and aspirations precede our births, there in our biology and culture, cohering to form a personality, and we set about confirming them with story so that the mysteries of existence seem to emerge from our lives.

But whereas the science I learned pried at the mysteries of the self, literature inhabited them, and novels led me on journeys whose experiences gave a different sense of inevitability: the accretion of detail endowing character with gravity whose consequence becomes destiny.

The crystalline emptiness of space collapsed back into a dark node of animal panic. My hands shook as I held myself. Sitting among chairs and rugs in Kabul's Finest Supermarket, I wished for Tam, for lovers scattered around the earth, for my mother.

JUSTIN

ONE NIGHT, WELL before the dawn call to prayer, Justin awakened. Sitting up, he noticed a pale spot in the backyard. Cold radiated from the window as he neared his face to the glass. Shafiq stood in only his pants, his naked muscles bulging, breath misting around his head.

In the morning, Justin asked Frank about what he'd seen. Frank said that Shafiq used the freezing air to tone his muscles as part of his preparation for the Mr. Kabul competition. Almost proudly, Frank described how Shafiq had lived through the civil war and hated the Taliban and the *mujahedeen* — even those who remained heroes to the people, if they'd fought over Kabul. He had no interest in English, probably hated America too. He worked in exchange for a place to stay, and his only ambition was weightlifting.

Nightly, Shafiq tested himself in the yard. Seeing the small man tempering his gnarled muscle, his chest lifted to confront the winter, Justin realized how unexceptional his own asceticism had been. His pain suddenly seemed insignificant.

The day after the safe room attack, Sediqa didn't show up to class, and her absence was palpable. The students glared at him. One complained that his exercises were obvious; they knew about democracy and didn't want to be distracted from their grammar lessons.

Afterward, Justin went onto the back porch. He'd been spending his days in his room, pacing in front of his desk, trying to find solutions for the school, to repair all the damage that had been done — or praying.

She's gone.

Frank was sitting in a chair as the sun went down, the mountains edged in gold. Justin hadn't noticed him.

To America?

A thick cream scarf was wrapped under Frank's chin. He sipped coffee, his scrawny legs crossed, the ratty hiking boots with their torn laces looking too big on his feet.

She left this morning, he said. I already had her passport made and the visa ready. She didn't know it. This isn't the first time I've had to do this sort of thing. There is serious jealousy in this country. Once the word got around about the scholarship, she didn't have much time. This is the sort of thing you do to save people. They might not understand when it's happening, but they'll thank you later. Decades, I tell myself every day, think in decades.

And what about her uncles? Won't they figure out we were involved?

I can't be worried about that, Frank told him. God, it feels good to do something meaningful, to really make things happen.

Justin excused himself. He went outside the gate, his boots growing heavy with mud. By the time he reached the poorly lit edge of the neighborhood, the sun's glow had withdrawn. He was startled by the sudden appearance of stars behind the city's light pollution.

He knew so little of this place and had no sense of the reasons for all that was happening around him — the millions of people overwhelming the city with desperation, building and destroying because they had no choice. In his mind, endings were followed by clear rebirths, but his fear was gone, and nothing had changed.

美智子

I TOOK THE taxi from the supermarket to Tam's house. I'd had time enough to formulate a plan. I would have to leave Kabul for a good long while. Steve wouldn't give up now. The theft of the laptop would confirm his fears.

Tam's house was under construction. Afghan workmen were drilling and welding, installing iron security doors and bars on the windows. White drop cloths covered the furniture.

On my way to find Tam, I glanced into the room that had been Alexandra's. I thought of her writing in her journal after that first night with Clay, recording and contemplating every detail of their encounter, before she went back to his place the next evening. No one was in the room now, though a new tenant was renting it: a recently divorced Californian woman who was establishing a women's artisanal cooperative, flooding the already saturated market.

Tam wasn't in her room, and I checked the rest of the house before pulling open the new iron door to the narrow walkway along the compound's rear wall. She was sitting in a folding chair, an olive scarf on her shoulders and earbuds in as she read a biography of Robert Capa. The sun reflected off the white walls, but the mountain air was already cooling.

When she saw me, she jumped up and hugged me, her earbuds swinging on their wires. Her book fell, splayed open, its pages fanning and swaying like the fronds of an aquatic plant.

I'd expected her to be reticent or angry, but when she pulled back, she smiled and said, "So, Brutus, what are you writing?"

"That's a long story."

"Ah, your voice has changed again."

I suddenly realized that, to her mind, we were simply journalists hunting a story. She might have cared more when we were together, but so much had happened since. Violence was increasing across the country. She'd had harrowing encounters and was frequently insulted in the street. The Afghans wanted the occupation to end. Whereas they once invited foreigners to their homes and their weddings, they were now offended if we came anywhere near their events, and insisted we go away.

I began telling her my story. At one point, Tam locked the iron doors to the kitchen and to the side of the house so no one would walk in on us. She said that the fortifications would make it easier to rent rooms, since organizations were requiring employees to live in places that passed a security code.

A few clouds moved past the sun, but it kept reappearing, sustaining us.

"You're more ambitious than I thought," she said. "I wouldn't have told you either. In fact, you missed a pile of letters from Alexandra's brother when you searched her room. Do you want to swap what we have?"

I agreed to give her the journal, the emails, and other files. I'd been mulling over telling her about Steve, but I wanted to peruse his laptop first.

"I'll be curious to read what you write," she said.

"It might take some time."

"All the better." She smiled. "Do you want to dance?" She lifted her earbuds and put one in my right ear and the other in her left. "I just found this," she said and tapped her phone.

As she slid her arms around me, the music began — strumming, raw drums, and a man's low soulful vocals. It was a cover of a Lana Del Rey song, and I thought of the safe room and how everything since then had unfolded in the shadow of that experience. In the US, in Southern diners and Brooklyn bars, I'd heard her voice with a shudder. I'd seen her image in magazines — a carefully fashioned icon with an anthem for everyone — and considered that Americans were masters of not only nostalgia but also forgetting. The country they loved was a mirage from the past, a stylized memory bereft of history itself.

After a moment, I gave myself over to the music and began stepping in slow circles. Tam pulled herself against me, her face to my shoulder to hide tears. I wished I could tell her something about this journey — about purpose and transformation, and how if what breaks us has no place in our daily life, we will travel far to find it. But unlike Frank, I knew I was fabricating. I saw the dangers of his revisions.

Maybe the attraction to war is simpler than so many expats claim. Just by setting foot in Afghanistan, we have the authority we crave back home. Our journey is a story of the greatest human strength: leaving one's domain and crossing the frontier into the territory of the other.

There is an Afghan joke I have heard many times.

An Afghan meets an American and asks how long he will be staying. The American says, "A week, but I leave tomorrow. I just came to write a book."

The Afghan asks what the subject of the book is, and the American says, "Afghanistan: Past, Present, and Future."

The first time an Afghan told me this — I have since heard the joke many times — he added, "I will someday go to America and do the same, *inshallah*."

PART 9

AFGHANISTAN: 1993-2012

IDRIS

THE TWO MINDS lived in his head, successive — day and night — but asymmetric, as if the sun could shine months unbroken before dropping into weeks of night. He had no place of origin except his memories of a large house in Wazir Akbar Khan. War had eroded it like a hillside beneath rain. Bullets pocked the compound wall and the exposed second floor. A mortar had punched through the dining room roof and splintered the table into the kindling they then fed their *bukhari*. His brother bought a sheet of plastic in the market and draped it over the hole, pinning the edges with chunks of cement he collected in the street. But the plastic was cheap, and gouts of water penetrated, slapping into a bucket like a hand on a drum.

From his bed, Idris stared out the window where the glass had been shattered by shrapnel. If the street was quiet, he could hear the *tock tock* of drops striking into the bucket, echoing in the empty rooms. He pictured an immense clock with a human arm moving in increments, its pointed finger accusing the world before indicting the mystery of the sky. When looters came, they took the pots and pans, the scant food, the bedding, clothes, and shoes, even the bucket.

One mind woke excited to kick a ball, run in the street, watch people passing: the boys gathering trash, the stooped men with creases around their eyes, bowed beneath bundles of sticks or sisal sacks or rickety wooden boxes of produce. He wanted to read the books his mother kept on the tops of cabinets where no one could find them, stories of springtime and the New Year, of children gathering pomegranates or wandering too far from home.

His other mind could not get up. It turned his arms and legs to concrete, his skin to dust. Night was a giant black cat, carrying something dead and heavy in its mouth, dropping it on him, a breathless weight that made his body rank. He lay in bed, numb to the prodding of his family, until one night the hunter came again and lifted from him what it had left behind. His mind was as mysterious as the war that lulled and raged, that battered the city the way a woman beats a rug with a broom. Sometimes his mind fell silent, a barking dog called away with a bone.

There was an evening when his mother stroked the hair from his forehead as he lay in a fever, his chest bandaged, and told him that if he'd been born two years earlier, he might have a memory of life without war. Maybe she'd told him what month he was born, or the year, whether it was before the chaos or as it was beginning. Being a child, he'd trusted that he would be able to ask again, but by the time he was six, his entire family was gone.

His father had always been gone. Idris had no memory of him other than a photograph of a man standing with other men beneath a flag with three horizontal bands of color — black, red, and green — and a seal on its left containing a book, a rising sun, and a red star. His mother said he'd been an engineer, a scientist who joined the military, and Idris decided he wanted to study science too. His mother burned the photograph, telling them it was for their safety.

Miriam, his sister, disappeared next. She was the eldest, a second mother. She was taking him and his older brother, Reza, to the park when uniformed men stopped them at a checkpoint. Two of them grabbed her arms and led her into the nearest house. Idris and Reza waited. A soldier came over and considered Reza. The men argued, and there was some pushing, but then Reza was taken inside too. Idris waited. A soldier with pockmarks on his cheeks crouched before him. He reached into the front pocket of his green jacket and pulled out a candy. He unwrapped it and put it on his palm and held it before Idris. It tasted faintly of honey. The man told him to be careful not to choke.

Put it in your cheek, he said, like this, and pushed his own cheek out from the inside with his tongue. He touched Idris on the shoulder and stood, observing the street.

Reza came back. He was blushing, his fists clenched like pale rocks. Two men hauled Miriam out by the arms. She sagged between them, and they lowered her to the curb. One of her hands groped at her headscarf and pulled it over her face. Her lip was bleeding. The soldiers argued until an old man with a handcart arrived. The soldier with the pocked skin gave him something from his pocket. Two soldiers, different from the ones who'd brought her out, loaded her into the handcart. She pulled her knees up and curled onto her side.

The old man wheeled her home. At their house, he helped her inside, to the corner of the room where the family now slept on pieces of cardboard with blankets on top. She didn't move. Their mother returned later with a small bag of rice and sent Idris and his brother into the compound yard to play. The spring air had chilled, the sky packed with stars. The breeze brought odors of wood smoke and burning plastic and diesel.

When she called them back in, she fed them salted rice drizzled with oil and put them to bed. Idris slept. He awoke to his mother's sobbing. Around his sister was a pool of gummy blood. His mother picked up her arm and squeezed her wrist, clamping it with her white fingers.

Idris almost died next. Two months of calm had drawn the children outside. They kicked a ball between the raw walls of the compounds on either side of the street. The sidewalk trees had been cut down for firewood, and so few working cars and so little gasoline remained in Kabul that the residential lane might as well have been a schoolyard.

When Reza played soccer now, he kicked the ball violently. The other kids held back as he raced for it. Idris was too small to keep up. He edged close to the action or drew away when it neared him, content to admire Reza's lanky stride, the way he lunged and slid in the grit on the soles of his old shoes.

A whistling sound resonated between the walls long enough for Idris to lift his hands to his ears. One of the boys pushed into him, and Idris hit the wall, his skull jarring. His chest felt wet. Had he fallen into water? Reza's face was gray, with the lines of an old man's. He lifted Idris's arm and draped it over his shoulder. The street spun, and spots from the sun flared in Idris's eyes.

Once, years before, he'd asked his mother what war was — the booms and rumbling, the sudden nearby crashes, the repeated echoing in the night sky like ice cracking, the tracers that rose as if falling stars swarmed up from the earth. She'd tried to explain it. A gun was a stick that shot stones. A bomb was a bowl that fell from the sky filled with fire. Men used these things to win wars the way boys kicked balls toward goals to beat each other's teams.

The war must have been over because he could no longer hear it outside. His mother lay next to him, her body warm as she sang and brushed her fingertips through his hair and soothed his forehead with wet cloths. When she left, Reza took care of him, his eyes as deep as echoing wells, dark as the other mind.

As Idris dozed, Miriam came to tell him about a land where the sun didn't rise all winter and how their father traveled there so he could learn to make their lives better. That must be the land of the other mind. His body felt hot, like metal in the sun. She whispered to him to go inside. Her fingertips slid through his fingers.

An old man appeared above him, moving his hands to remove the weight from Idris's chest. He must be the old man with the handcart. Everyone had become an old man with a beard, with brusque hands as hard as wood.

His mother showed Idris his chest. He lay beneath the weight of the other mind, but it was not so heavy. He could lift his head. Two purple notches marked his ribs.

You are partly made of steel now, she told him. She moved his hand with her own and traced it over the glossy skin. You have iron protecting your heart.

She was the next to disappear. She'd begun dressing differently, going out in a blue *burqa* he'd never seen before. A week later she didn't come back. He was alone in the house for days. Reza dropped by briefly to give him a crust of bread and an overripe orange. Idris waited, peering out the gate. The explosions had ended. The old men looked older. Many passed with crutches.

During the worst part of the war, when attacks had started suddenly, mortars shrieking down from the mountains, he and

Reza had run home from playing. Dead people lay in the streets. Handcarts ferried bodies home — women, children, or old men pushing them. An ashen neighbor was wheeled home, his leg missing below the calf. Idris had believed the looters were taking hands and feet since everything else had been stolen. So many people were without limbs. But since his mother's disappearance, the looting had stopped, as if she'd taken the war with her.

Reza hated everyone — the *mujahedeen* leaders who'd fought over Kabul and failed to make a government and keep the Taliban out, and the Taliban itself. He'd heard that their mother had angered a Talib and been arrested. There were only rumors.

She would panic, he said.

Panic? Idris asked, not understanding the word.

Scared. She'd get upset easily. She had fits. It's because of the rocket attack that almost killed her.

What rocket attack?

You were too little to remember. The Talibs must have thought she was ignoring them or fighting back. But she can't help herself. She gets anxious. She begins to shout.

Idris had no idea what Reza was talking about. Reza said he would leave Kabul and join Dostum's army in the northwest because it would be easier to reach than Massoud's in Panjshir.

He bundled their remaining blankets and clothes, and tied them with a string, and then he locked the front gate of the house. He led Idris across Kabul, along dusty streets lined with broken or shattered buildings to a neighborhood connected to the city by a single lane. A rut carved the middle of it, veering off at times — maybe created by rain and helped by shovels to drain the spring floodwaters. This seemed a sign of the place's poverty: the road unable to afford a gutter on both sides.

Reza knocked at a rusted gate. A slot snapped open, and a large eye appeared. Black hairs sprouted almost to the cheekbone.

The slot shut, and the gate swung out.

The man was tall and thin and seemed less old than others despite his profuse beard. Two other men were inside, similarly dressed in dusty white, bearded and with short hair. They had the hood up on an old Soviet Moskvich. Its panels were powder blue, dented and scratched, a bullet hole in one fender and cracks bisecting the windshield.

Hello, Idris, the thin man said.

Idris searched his mind, but the man was just another bearded stranger.

Reza took his hand and led him closer.

Don't be afraid, he said. This is Osman, your uncle. He'll take you to stay with his family in the countryside.

Where are you going? Idris asked.

To fight.

How old are you now, Reza? Osman put his hand on his shoulder.

Old enough to fight.

Do you know how old?

At least twelve.

And your brother?

Reza shrugged. He reached into his pocket and took out the keys to the house and gave them to Osman.

You're not old enough to fight, Osman told him.

And what will you do? Force me to go with you? I'll leave. I'll just run away. I know what I want to do.

Children should not kill.

I haven't been a child for a long time.

Reza stepped back as the men at the car watched.

Goodbye, Reza said. Please take care of Idris.

IF IT WEREN'T for the two minds, Idris would have fit himself into the lives of Osman's children. But days came when he couldn't get up, when the weight pressed him to the floor. Osman tried to talk to him. The children encouraged him to play, but the best he could do was sit in a chair, dozing off, his face to the sun so it would burn through the colorless haze in his head.

When Husnia, Osman's wife, got angry at him, Osman told her to leave him alone. He confided in Idris that he'd lost his first wife and newborn when a mortar fell on their home in the Karteh Seh district of Kabul. He'd moved to the family land in Laghman and remarried, but his sadness had taken years to go away.

It will get better, he said and pressed Idris's shoulder. This was the only moment of physical affection Idris would recall in the years after his mother's disappearance.

Osman grew pomegranates, melons, and other fruits and vegetables that he loaded into the back seat and trunk of the Moskvich and drove into Kabul to sell, before bringing back knives, pots, pans, and medicine to use for barter in the villages. With food scarce and prices high, Osman had his children and Idris in the fields each dawn, though at night he made them read old books he hid in the floor. He reminded them that their family had once been rich and educated and would be again, but that they must never talk about this or their reading. When Idris asked if he could become a scientist, Osman said that under the Taliban science was not allowed, that he must wait and keep his dream a secret.

Once or twice a year, Idris accompanied Osman to Kabul. The city came into view, resembling a tilled field washed out by the spring rains: the destroyed and abandoned neighborhoods at its edges fading into colorless swaths.

Osman checked the family houses for which he held the deeds. On one trip, he and Idris went to Ghazi stadium for a soccer game. Before it started, Talibs drove two white Toyota Hiluxes inside, men with Kalashnikovs in the backs.

A man read from the Qu'ran over the speakers, and the Talibs took a bound thief from a pickup and laid him in the grass. A Talib stooped at his side and when he stood again, he was holding a severed hand.

The Talib with the loudspeaker declared that they would next stone a woman for adultery. They took her from the truck and made her kneel on the playing field. When the first rock struck her head, a woman a few rows before Idris shrieked, and he knew that she must be a sister or mother or daughter. Both wore blue *burqas*. The *burqa* of the woman being stoned was quickly darkening. In the stands, boys and men backed away from the screaming woman. Urine puddled around her feet.

Osman and Idris never went back to the stadium, and their trips to Kabul were brief, to collect rent or deliver produce. Sometimes they stopped at the house where Idris once lived but only long enough to knock and take money from the guard. They stayed the night with one of Osman's friends and returned to Laghman the next morning.

Two years after Idris moved onto the farm, a limping fig- ure approached along the dusty road. Every so often it stooped, holding its knees. Idris and the other children went to the edge of the melon field. In the afternoon's glare, the silhouette was like a burnt post stuck crookedly into the earth, with heat waves all around.

Just below a curve in the driveway, the boy came into focus. He was older than Osman's children, with wisps of beard, and thin as a sick child. He wore a T-shirt the color of dirt, his skin visible through the holes, and his pants were tattered below the knees. Large flies clustered around a black sore on his calf.

Idris, he said as he hobbled close. It's me, Reza.

His eyes were still, as if thought didn't follow sight, as if two of the black flies had gone inside his head and died.

After dinner, the doctor came and drained the puss from the sore and removed shrapnel. Reza told them he'd been with the Taliban hunting down Hazara rebels in the mountains.

I fought for Dostum, he said. But why? He shelled Kabul. His men ran those checkpoints. He has fled Afghanistan now. One of his commanders made a deal with the Taliban, so we soldiers became Taliban soldiers, just like that, because a stupid man said so. I could join Massoud, but they all had their checkpoints. Kabul was their *buzkashi* goat, torn piece from piece. The Taliban are just the most recent. Now it's a job. Maybe someday there will be other jobs.

Osman told Reza he could stay, get healthy, work on the farm, but Reza had the same look as the day he'd left. His leg healed, and he gained weight, but in the fields, his motions were never economical enough to maintain a pace that could be sustained in the heat. In everything he did — weeding, digging, picking fruit — his movements jarred. He'd been recoiling, flinching, retreating for so long the memory of violence had gotten lodged in him. He had to stop and pant, his forehead streaming with sweat. He stared off as if men might be watching from the eroded hills. Maybe the only harvest he could fathom was a soldier's.

One morning, Reza was no longer there. He wasn't in his bed. The family ate, heads lowered, their hands moving quickly. The walls glowed as the sun's radiance infused the room. Idris went back to his blanket, lay down, and drew it up to his eyes.

ON THE FARM, a washboard of plowed earth surrounded by scarped and bleached hills, the American invasion was nothing more than a story. Rumors spread that the Americans were bombing training camps and then the front lines where the Taliban had been fighting the Northern Alliance. Idris heard no bombs, no gunshots, just the words of a cousin who visited to say that the Taliban were fleeing Kabul and who contemplated whether it was too soon to cut his beard — whether the Taliban could come back.

Osman began shouting to his children to load the car with whatever produce was ready. He went inside and reappeared with a pistol that he checked before putting it in his pocket.

Idris, come with me.

The backseat was only partially loaded, and Osman drove at a speed Idris had never experienced. The country had always crawled, vehicles so patched together and fragile that a bump might undo years of jerry-rigging. There had been no benefit to hurrying, nothing more interesting than the slow scrolling of the landscape.

Where are we going? Idris asked.

To the family houses. They'll be empty. The people renting them will be running away. We have to make sure that no one tries to take them. I have the papers.

Osman knew the road well and rarely braked, letting the car coast until they came upon trenches from spring rains, huge potholes, or bomb craters. Dozens of cars passed going the other way, plumes of dust rising behind them. On the road-side were the burning husks of vehicles, torn-apart bodies smoking around them.

They're all heading to Pakistan, Osman said. Let's pray the American bombers will see we're going west.

When they arrived, a few solitary pillars of smoke hung above the city. Trucks full of Tajik fighters rumbled in from the north, their new black weapons at the ready.

The first house Osman stopped at was the one where Idris had grown up. After Osman hammered at the door, the guard told him that the Arab tenants had fled that morning. One by one, Osman checked on his properties and discovered all of his renters gone. He swapped their locks and hired men he knew to stay in the homes as guards until he found new renters.

That night, he and Idris slept on *toshaks* in one of the houses. They'd gathered up the possessions of those who'd left, and itemized them to make sure their guards didn't steal them. Over the next week, Osman began moving his family back into the city. Foreigners were already arriving and needed places to stay, and by the end of December, all of his houses were rented. He told Idris that farming was no match for real estate and went out daily to find new properties.

All through that long winter into the spring, as snow or hail fell and rains flooded the streets — the floating filth so thick it resembled solid ground — Idris waited for Reza.

At intersections, in the shade of walls, his scrawny brother would appear to him, a glimpse of starved limbs and hollowed eyes filled with ash. Idris would stare with such intensity that the beggar would hold out his hand.

KABUL THRIVED, NEW compounds built as foreign aid workers and civilian contractors arrived, and thousands of refugees who had lived in Pakistan, Tajikistan, and Iran during the civil war and Taliban era flooded back. The capital was transformed from a cluster of buildings in a broad valley to a sprawl of unfinished highways and crowded neighborhoods. Rows of homes were built up the mountainsides, their foundations cut from the stone of steep inclines, and children carried buckets of water and supplies up the paths all day.

When America invaded Iraq, the growth faltered, and the presence of foreigners and American soldiers in Kabul was reduced, but as the insurgency gained traction, the foreigners rushed back en masse.

This is the time to become rich, Osman told Idris. Tomorrow we could all be refugees.

His uncle lived simply in a small compound. He owned six houses and had one torn down and rebuilt, and then rented it to a Dutch NGO. He now had eight children and sent them to the best private schools. He explained to Idris that with so many responsibilities — so many buildings to maintain and rebuild, bribes to pay, not to mention relatives who needed schooling and medical treatment — he couldn't offer him as much as he would like. Idris attended a free school run by an Afghan woman who had lived in the United States. Many of her students were from a nearby orphanage and had spent years on the street.

His kindest classmate was also the toughest, a muscular boy named Abdullah, whose shaved scalp was nicked with white scars: a lifetime of fights and thrown rocks. But those who were just below him in the hierarchy were bullies craving to be leaders, fearing Abdullah and trying to propel themselves to the top by beating up everyone beneath them.

When Idris refused to play ball with them after school, one of the boys pushed him down. Abdullah stepped up and held the back of his hand in front of the boy. He had scars on his forearm, too, on his palm.

Leave him alone. He looked down. What's your name?

Idris.

You don't like football?

Idris stood and brushed dust from his pants. I hate it.

What do you like?

Idris hesitated. All day he'd been mulling Osman's words from the previous evening, a nebulous comment: Americans do not know the meaning of suffering.

America, Idris said. I'll go to America, and I'll be a scientist there.

America's the home of sinners. I've seen it on a TV.

In America, the people have good lives without suffering.

Abdullah rubbed one of his big, dark hands over his battered scalp.

In America, he said, on hot days, people go outside in their underwear. They walk down the street. They go to the store. Men and women just stand around in their underwear.

The other boys laughed, but Idris realized that he knew far more than they did about foreigners. He'd gone with Osman to visit the houses the foreigners rented, when water pipes burst or wires shorted. He'd seen the wine bottles clustered on the tables and windowsills, the crammed ashtrays. A young woman in a dress had once taken them from room to room, pointing up at the brown stains of water damage on the ceiling tiles, the inside of her arm pale.

I can tell you about Americans, he said. Come with me and I'll show you Americans.

The boys crowded close, but Abdullah warned them off and agreed.

Though Idris didn't end up showing Abdullah much that afternoon — only a house he knew was occupied by foreigners — he fabricated stories from those Osman had told him about the constant partying and drugs, the endless money to buy electronics and computers, and the variety of expensive foods that stocked their kitchens. He also told him about the female renter who let out the extra rooms in the house to foreign men. Impressed, Abdullah asked where the foreigners got their money, and Idris gave vague answers.

Later, to Osman, Idris repeated the questions and listened, trying to make sense of politics: oil, religion, war. By the time he went to bed he had more stories for Abdullah and a growing desire to do what he'd so spontaneously declared.

Over the weeks that followed, he imagined the foreigners' lives of luxury, picturing the parties and wealth in the house where he'd grown up. His former home was Osman's best property — located near the embassies — and ever since he'd rented it out, Idris had been only just inside the gate with him a few times to collect payments. Grapevines now grew on an arbor along the walkway, and roses lined the yard. At times, the sound of foreign voices — along with clinking dishes and, once, a strumming, mumbling music Idris did not recognize — came from inside.

Idris excelled in school, studying with Abdullah and helping him with homework. Winter was still hard, but since he'd relocated to Kabul, the seesawing of his minds had eased. When the other mind came, it wasn't as bad as it had been before, and the knowledge that it would pass quickly made it easier to endure. As the days lengthened, the sun burned the cold out of his bones, his muscles pliable, his mind fast.

Idris's interest in America was no longer to please Abdullah or sustain his alliance that had solidified into friendship. Osman became wary of his questions, telling him many Afghans traveled to the West and found only menial jobs — educated people who now dug holes like the poor in Afghanistan. He'd insisted Idris put an end to his questions and focus on his studies. When Idris asked to go to school in English, Osman told him it was too expensive.

The truth is bitter, his uncle said — an adage he'd uttered often in Laghman but hadn't used in years. After the fall of the Taliban, shaving his beard had revealed him to be a handsome, youthful man who presented well in a suit.

Idris's questions continued to multiply, and one in particular began to trouble him. He counted the years back to his earliest memories but was unable to determine his age. Osman didn't know, guessing that Idris must be thirteen or fourteen.

Your mother had documents. She was a nurse. She kept track of those things. But who knows where they are now?

The revelation that she'd been a nurse stunned Idris. He hadn't known she'd had an occupation before the Taliban came. He remembered how she fed him and cared for him, and how she hid possessions throughout the house. The documents must have been hidden there as well.

After school, he told Abdullah he had to go home and help his uncle, but he walked alone to the house and banged on the gate.

The guard recognized him and slid back the bolt.

I must speak to the people who live here, Idris told him.

Come, the guard said. He couldn't refuse him, since Idris was Osman's nephew, but he would mention the visit the next time Osman came by. He led Idris to the terrace and knocked on the door frame. A woman called out in Dari for him to enter.

Two women came from the living room, one larger than any man Idris knew, with short red hair and flushed, jowly cheeks, and the other of average height, shorter than Idris, with her brown curly hair uncovered. Though she wore a *shalwar*, her bosom seemed more pronounced because of her posture. He pinned his gaze on the floor.

The guard told the second woman that Idris was the owner's nephew, and she evaluated him, looking up at him through her glasses, her dark eyes large and birdlike.

What do you need? she asked in slow Dari.

I'm trying to find some documents.

Documents? We have a rental contract.

No, I'm sorry — personal documents, he told her. They say how old I am.

She nodded to the guard and said she'd like to speak with Idris alone. The big woman shrugged nervously, repeatedly squinting as if she had a twitch. They exchanged a few words, and she went into the living room, sat, poured coffee from a press, and picked up a magazine.

The smaller woman considered Idris. How old are you?

I don't know. I was born here. I grew up here during the war. But everyone is gone — my mother, my father, my sister, my brother.

Well then, let's find those documents, she told him and led him upstairs to the bedroom where he'd once slept with his family. He blushed at the sight of the bed piled with pillows. A desk cluttered with papers and books sat against the wall. The flowery pattern of the carved wooden armoire was as familiar as the skin of his hands.

This was here, he told her.

She reached to the top of the frame and turned the piece of wood that held the door in place. Clothes hung inside: so many colors. She opened the drawer in the bottom, even took it out. They continued this ritual throughout the house. He watched as she searched inside cabinets or behind the drawers of a warped buffet built into the concrete wall.

I'm sorry, she told him when they found nothing. They stood in the dining room, where the mortar had fallen and smashed the table his mother had wiped down daily until it shined, where the bucket had tocked all night, sleeplessness a meaningless procession of time.

A furrow scored her brow. She observed him the way Abdullah had when Idris first told him about Americans. Sunlight filled Idris's mind, and he felt that he was looking down into it from the mountains above Kabul, his thoughts as clear as the cars flitting or following in lines.

May I ask you one more favor? he said.

Of course.

I want to learn English so much, but my uncle won't send me to a school that teaches it.

What is your phone number? I may be able to help find something for you.

He had a cheap cell Osman had given him to coordinate errands, and she put its number into a phone with a screen almost the size of its body.

I'll call you, she said as she continued to study him.

He thanked her, and they walked onto the terrace.

My name is Sarah.

Thank you, Sarah. I'm Idris.

When he glanced back from the gate, she was still there, her interest in him strange and clear even at a distance.

FRANK STILL HAD enough meat on him back then that a smile made handsome lines around his mouth. In Kabul, beards were disappearing, cleanly razored Pashto, Tajik, Uzbek, and Hazara youths wearing slim, embroidered jeans and leather jackets, their hair styled with gel and trimmed on the sides. As these young men flooded in from the provinces, hunting jobs, driving taxis, establishing businesses, Frank aged exponentially. He became older than the bearded laborers; he was a foreign elder, the grandfather of America come to save Afghanistan, or — Idris sometimes mused — the grandfather of the war itself.

Sarah had called Idris and told him that she'd arranged for him to attend an academy after his normal school hours, or whenever his uncle would allow. It would be free, but students were required to participate in the upkeep, to make it their own. Idris's uncle accepted that he attend, saying that the free education would enrich the family, and that Idris could do fewer errands now if he contributed more later, once he was educated and employed.

Never had Idris wanted to make himself more useful than at the school. The building was clean and spacious with large new tables and silver-gray folding metal chairs. Books were displayed openly, stacks of textbooks filled with graphs and equations he didn't understand.

Here, English would offer him a path to science. His first day, he knew so few words he felt he could hold them in his fists: *hello, how are you.* But they soon exceeded the points of his knuckles, spreading from his wrists to his neck, encasing him, his arms less slack, buoyed, a density about his shoulders, until finally, after months of matching English's few sounds to its endless combination of letters, they filled him and he no longer echoed with the city's rumble.

The heft of a new language brought with it the confidence required to gather more of it into himself, and in that calm he studied the school, fixing broken objects, replacing blown bulbs or cracked electrical wires. Frank praised the simple skills that the Afghans used to preserve what little they owned; he denounced the lost savvy of America.

Necessity is the mother of invention, and there isn't much we need back home anymore.

Idris was beginning to make sense of complex sentences, and Frank had gone from a grinning grandfather to an orator who spoke the strangest things Idris had ever heard.

He gave the statement some thought and said, Maybe needing to win this war will make America invent again.

Maybe, Frank conceded, his small blue eyes studying Idris crosswise before darting away. Idris later heard Frank repeat the idea to another student, but by then Idris had moved on to consider that a war like this one could make all sides more inventive.

Now that Idris could follow stories, Frank told them constantly. One was about a girl who was going to be married to a man she hated when she was in love with a boy her own age, and how Frank planned their escape. The boy was angry that an American was involved until he met Frank and realized he would put his own life in danger to drive them to Pakistan.

The moment of my death does not bother me, Frank said. I am not afraid. Men's ends are dictated at their birth and they . . . How does it go again? . . . they will seek their deaths in the face of every obstacle. I forget the rest, but in any case, it says that men don't meet death in strange or obscure places that they might have avoided. No, they find it there because they have sought it.

Why did you decide to move to Afghanistan? Idris asked him.

I owe a debt to the world. We men have done much harm, and most of the suffering we create falls on women. So naturally it's our responsibility to remedy it.

One morning, when Idris woke in his uncle's house, the weight of the other mind pinned him to the bed. He knew all he would lose if he neglected the school, if he wasn't there to reset or replace fuses. Power surges came often. Adapters and bulbs blew.

He commanded himself to get up but couldn't. He feared for his place at the school, knowing that Frank would never treat him the way he did the girls. He bought them clothes, books, even laptops and plane tickets. With the boys, Frank made it clear that they could survive on their own. Few lasted long, having to find jobs, bowing to the demands of their families. When Frank smiled at Idris, his eyes remained stern. He looked at the girls the way Sarah had looked at Idris, with an air of need that made no sense.

After five days, Idris got out of bed. His hands trembled. His ankles and knees hurt. He tore off a piece of bread and chewed. His stomach felt as small and tight as the pocket of his jeans. He ate bread with jam, a small wedge of cheese, and two eggs. With each bite, he wanted to throw up. He drank water to wash the painful mass of food into his muscles.

At the school, Frank saw him from the stairs. His gauntness had yet to reduce his anger to the single slack expression he could make other than his smile.

Where have you been? You have responsibilities.

I was sick.

Being sick is a luxury.

Idris swept the floor, organized the books, and inspected

the adapters for computers and laptops. He checked the fuses, checked the bulbs, removing those that had blown.

In his readings, he'd run across *crucial* and had checked the dictionary — an echo of the cross to suggest importance, though he struggled to understand the origin: an indicator at a crossroad or an evocation of Christ? Wanting to be something of the cross might make him an infidel, so he found synonyms: *vital, essential, pivotal, key.*

A light fixture on the living room ceiling had never worked, so he shut off the breaker and removed it. He found door hinges that creaked. He went to the market and bought a new fixture and oil and a small can of paint for metal. He bought kebabs and ate fast on the roadside, his knees trembling, cars rushing past, leaving delirious tracers.

At the school, he replaced the fixture, oiled the hinges, and then carefully, with a small plastic brush, painted the rust-pitted surface of the kitchen fridge. The brush left faint striations that settled and smoothed into a glossy finish.

What do I owe you for the material? Frank asked when Idris showed him all he'd done.

Nothing. This is my school too.

Frank tilted his head, swiveling on invisible hips somewhere in the folds of his clothes.

Have I not done a good job? Idris asked.

Be modest, Frank said. Look up *modesty*. Look up *humility*. Let me appreciate your work without you having to tell me.

He climbed halfway up the stairs and then turned, as if he wanted a platform from which to deliver his moral.

Sometimes, even when you're sick, it's good to get up. You'll feel better once you're working. You don't really know if you're sick until you try not to be.

WINTER BEGAN, AND Idris feared the distancing of the sun that burned away the other mind. Frank continued to offer him lessons but never kindness.

Idris knew Afghans who ingratiated themselves with foreigners only to use them. They talked about the naiveté of Westerners, their lack of strength, how easy it was to lie to them and to steal from them when they were out. Other Afghans were loyal to those they worked for and refused to speak of disparity. Idris knew the day would come when Frank would acknowledge his value, but he thought less about this when American volunteers began to arrive.

The first was Michael, a young man who'd been in the Marines and come back on a three-month visa to teach conversational English. A string of academics followed, interested in women's rights or learning Dari or firsthand experience with the people they were tasked with writing about, as if teaching grammar or moderating classroom debates between teenagers would help them with their dissertations on the history of foreign involvement and the rise of militancy from the *mujahedeen* to the Taliban.

Once, when Michael had been helping Idris practice English, James came to the door. James was a paper-white blond New Yorker doing a PhD on governance in Afghanistan.

Did I hear you guys talking about the war?

I'm just getting Idris to describe things for practice.

You saw the civil war? James asked him.

Idris shrugged.

Did you ever see any battles?

Not really, Idris told him.

There was a lot of fighting here. You must have heard things.

Yes.

Bombs?

Yes.

Anyway, Michael said, we were focusing on politics, not the war itself. We were discussing warlords who become politicians and how to integrate those guys but keep them from ruining the democratic process.

What's your position on Dostum? James asked them. Do you think he should be in the Afghan government or prosecuted in the International Criminal Court?

Sorry, man, Michael told him, you might have to fill me in. To be honest, Idris was the one explaining the politics to me. I'm still learning the whole warlord thing.

You don't know about the Convoys of Death?

Nah, I don't.

James described how, after the American invasion, Dostum, an Uzbek general in the Northern Alliance, was accused of loading men who'd been fighting for the Taliban into box trucks and driving them across the desert, under the full sun, to a prison. The captives suffocated in the heat, and when the doors were opened, according to a few testimonies, the asphyxiated, sweat-soaked bodies poured out like fish.

That's horrible, Michael told him. Yes, I'd say that's criminal.

But do we expect angels to emerge from decades of war? James asked. If Dostum were a nice guy, he wouldn't have survived, and he wouldn't have been our ally. If there'd been no 9/11, the Taliban, with Saudi funding and Pakistani support, would have conquered the rest of Afghanistan. Dostum had been fighting for so long he probably didn't believe the war would end. America had abandoned him once before, after the Soviet withdrawal. Why should he trust that the Americans' ouster of the Taliban would be anything but temporary? He was eliminating his enemies before they regrouped. I bet he figured he was going to kill them sooner or later.

Idris stood, said good night, and went down to the basement to sleep. With the other mind — the one that felt the proximity of death — he could understand James's words, but he didn't want to. Though Reza had gone to fight for Dostum, he'd ended up with the Taliban to survive.

Over the years, most volunteers, especially the women, came for the girls. They talked to them and touched their arms and hands, and made the sounds of mothers cooing over babies. They painted and photographed them. They told them about the history of the women's liberation movement in America and the West. They brought them gifts and paid for them to study in America or contacted people they knew to find them scholarships.

But these volunteers also asked insistently about the war. Once, Idris had seen one of the girls trying to answer, her expression frozen, her voice barely a whisper: We saw people . . .

With the fingertips of one hand she touched her other arm.

People with no . . . members, no . . .

She was searching for the right word, unable to say it. Foreigners didn't realize that telling the story meant remembering.

For five years, Idris tried to make sense of the volunteers. There was guilt in their words — guilt that their country had armed the *mujahedeen* who'd defeated the Soviets and gone on to destroy Kabul. Were they trying to correct a historical wrong or their country's present actions? Were they trying to correct the Afghans' impression of America by showing they cared? Or to correct Afghanistan, by doing the work of soldiers in the daily lives of Afghans, as James once claimed?

Though the school took up most of his time, Idris stayed close to Abdullah and Aziz, another boy who'd fallen under Abdullah's protection. Having taught himself programming on an old laptop he'd bought in the bazaar, Aziz had given up on high school. He wore his hair flopped to the side, as he'd once seen in a movie, to hide a shrapnel scar on his left temple. He'd opened what he called his shop-of-all-things, selling code-broken software from Pakistan and making ID cards that the illiterate police couldn't discern from official ones. He'd helped so many government officials repair their computers or get documents that he spoke of his capital as the people who owed him favors rather than the secondhand electronics that crowded the walls of his alley shop. It was the width of a closet — so many young Afghans forced to aspire in spaces as narrow as coffins. Idris, Abdullah, and Aziz watched movies there, crammed hip to hip. The ritual ended only when Abdullah joined the army.

As Idris excelled at English, his other mind came less frequently, and the few times it did, he managed to go to the school. But after he graduated high school, as the summer burned the city, his mind came alive, wanting more. He had conversations in English with himself, debating both sides, arguing with Frank over how he deserved to be rewarded, or seducing foreign women in fantasies of New York and Los Angeles.

In the course of his readings, he looked up *philosophy*, surprised a word existed for lovers of wisdom: people devout before knowledge as if before God — as if the two could be disconnected or a person might find a cavern burning with the sun's glow, divine radiance existing separate from its source. One of the volunteers told him that the great Persian poets — Jalal al-din Rumi and Hafez — were best-sellers in America. He spoke

of them in a way that called to mind philosophers: their attention to how people understand themselves and find peace with
each other. Idris hadn't known that Persian literature was so
popular in the West. He read their mystical lines, stopping on
one: *Every desire is holy.*

He observed his mind's natural expansion toward all that
he wanted, but when the ways into the world refused to open
to his desires, when he found no space into which to expand,
his energy fell back in on itself. The impasse at which he found
himself was hard to deny as winter invaded and the fumes of
poverty dulled the sky.

He'd been able to push himself for years to learn so much,
to do chores because he'd envisioned a door that would open
one day on a life filled with light. But delay after delay, Idris
struggled to keep ahead of the other mind. As he lay down
in exhaustion, the cold pinned him to his mattress. He saw it
clearly at last, how the other mind rose around the collapse of
the first, like suffocating smoke, like dark water.

By the end of 2011, Afghans were talking about the changes to come, warning that the money was leaving with the foreigners, that America and NATO were leaving, and the time
to become rich was passing. New buildings were still lifting
Kabul's skyline, but everyone understood that this was how
drug lords invested the heroin money they couldn't smuggle
out. Wealth was condensing around the rich, disappearing into
their fortified palatial homes. The rest of the city scrambled for
the crumbs. Even Frank was frantic, telling Idris to buy only
the essentials at the market.

Vital, essential, pivotal, key. He tried to be the source of the
school's life, the essence: the fulcrum on which events turned,
the key to all he wanted.

When boys complained about the girls' opportunities, Frank told them to leave, but most left on their own. He seemed to bait them, primed to discard them, lining up their errands while simultaneously spoiling the girls. When he could no longer pay rent for the girls' dorm, he told the boys that financing had gotten thin and the girls would be moving into the basement. In the weeks that followed, a few boys tried to make it back for classes but their families lived far away, and the cost of travel and the time required were too much. Only those who'd never lived in the basement, like Faisal, continued to attend classes, oblivious to the upheaval. To Idris, Frank offered the pantry.

You've been a real asset. The space isn't much, but you'll have privacy.

One night Idris came out in wool socks a volunteer had given him and sat on the stairs, listening to one of Frank's Skype conversations.

I have two options, he heard him say. Make this school self-sustaining and guide one of the girls into running it, or close it down as soon as every last girl has a scholarship in America.

The next day, Idris was at the market for masonry screws so he could install a new whiteboard on the classroom wall, when he heard his name.

Abdullah hadn't grown much since he'd been a boy at the orphanage. He wore army pants, a black T-shirt, and a leather jacket. His hand, when he shook Idris's, was as coarse as concrete but stony in its density.

They fell into stride, walking as they used to.

So you do know Americans now, Abdullah said.

Idris described the American obsession with Afghan girls and repeated a story he'd heard from his cousin who studied at American University, about foreign professors who made female students sleep with them for better grades.

This is exactly the problem, Abdullah told him. If they come to our country, they should follow our rules. What will we do if America takes our women or makes them like theirs?

Idris agreed. He wanted a country where his mother and sister would have survived, but he didn't want to be treated like a Talib and left behind.

As if synced to his thoughts, Abdullah said, I've never cared for the Taliban, but is America any better? I joined the army because we need Muslim soldiers to defend a Muslim land. The Americans can't lead us when they hide behind walls in our cities. They say they'll do great things, but the Taliban are the ones talking to the people. They hear their suffering. They know that the rich who serve America aren't suffering like this.

Abdullah and Idris passed rows of vendors — carts of oranges, apricots, strawberries. Their shoes scuffed the uneven roadway, over grit, gum and candy wrappers, and gray bits of tire-shredded refuse. Idris nodded, but he would never see any good in the Taliban.

Most of us, Abdullah said, we were children when the Taliban was here. Do you know what the older people remember? The stealing ended. One man told me you could have left a bar of gold in the street and it would have been there the next day. People want to know if we'll protect them like that. The police and army have robbed people. When the poor tribes fight the corruption, the ruling tribes call them Taliban and send Americans to kill them. The Americans get to brag that they fought evil men when they were just shooting down farmers.

So you'll go back to the army? Idris asked.

No. I'm finished with the army. Do you know how we found the Taliban? We drove around and made ourselves targets so they'd attack. But we didn't have the American vehicles with their armor. We were in little Ford trucks. Mine was blown up. I woke up on the grass. Only two of us survived. So I left. This isn't a way to defend a country. Let the Taliban come back. They'll be no worse than what we have now. What is this war? If you ask me, it's America on both sides. America funds Pakistan, and Pakistan funds the Taliban. America wants our country. It's about China. It's about Iran. It's their way of controlling the earth.

Idris had heard Afghans repeat such things. Many of them believed America fabricated an endless war. He'd read about this online but also knew that the situation was far more complex.

So what will you do now? Idris asked.

I have become a thief, Abdullah told him and laughed.

Idris stopped. Abdullah took a few more steps, turned on his heel, and walked back, his shoulders level, his legs swinging confidently.

It's not so bad, my friend. We are ruled by thieves. Should we not partake in the banquet?

He looked down, just in front of his scuffed army boots. His black hair was still cut short, and the dozens of white notches in his scalp remained visible. He seemed to be lowering his head to show Idris the lifetime of abuse he'd endured, a map of lines leading nowhere.

I tried, he said, to be a true believer. I went to mosque. I prayed. But why does Allah make us suffer when we have given him only love?

With his head lowered, Abdullah lifted his eyes, like an actor who bows to the audience while glancing up to see if someone has felt his story.

Over the weeks that followed, he and Idris met a few times, Abdullah always paying their meals, revealing his success at his new vocation. They visited Aziz, ate large dinners and watched movies. And then one evening Abdullah failed to arrive. Idris stood in the street, outside the kebab shop, the smoke of burning mutton rising from the doorway, his stomach in a knot.

He visited Aziz, who told him Abdullah had been arrested. He'd been caught in someone's home and had killed the guard in self-defense.

When you're a thief who kills a guard who attacks you, Aziz said, you're a murderer, and you'll be hanged. We must forget him. He's dead.

Idris knew he should eat to calm his constricting body, but the bright doors in his mind were closing. The next morning he lay beneath his other mind. Three days passed before he forced himself up. The weight wasn't so heavy. He realized he had to change his life soon. This country would swallow everyone.

He'd been driving the girls by then. He called Frank to apologize for his absence.

You're fired, Frank told him.

I was sick, Idris croaked. It was very bad, Mr. Frank.

You're no longer welcome here.

The line beeped and went dead.

Idris dressed. His numb feet bumped the floor. In the kitchen, he forced himself to eat before going outside, blinking in the painful light, his tears streaming.

He took a taxi to the school and begged for his job back.

Frank tilted his head and gestured him inside.

Never again, he said. Never again.

Idris had tried to be perfect, but his desire to please others was fading. The men who'd hurt his sister and mother hadn't been born cruel. They'd changed as Reza had, broken beneath the weight of something dead. If you were broken, could you only be further broken, crushed until you had no shape of your own, like dust pushed with each gust of wind?

Daily, he drove the girls to the mall, to their jobs and appointments. Small pleasures sustained him. A volunteer gave him an old laptop when he left. The hard drive was filled with episodes from TV shows, and Idris studied the exuberance and innocence of America. But there were also shows about desperation, men and women who rejected their old way of living, their beliefs even, and chose a violence they could justify. To Idris, it seemed less criminal than liberating.

JUSTIN WAS UNLIKE any previous volunteer. He had the posture of devotion, a straight spine, and the moral certitude that subdued the body's joggle and twitch, and put it to a higher service. He sized up Idris the way a man might survey a plain where a city was to be built. Maybe his seriousness was due to his handicap — the artificial eye immediately evident to Idris, a Western luxury: a man could walk the street and work and feed his family without a glass eye.

Justin demanded that Idris meet the goals he set, and this made Idris believe that, unlike other volunteers, Justin wasn't here to experience the war through him but to help.

At first, Idris thought that Justin's cold — the rusty sound from his vocal cords — made him reticent to speak, but even after he'd recovered, he remained quiet. Idris saw the questions in him, the way he stared at things or people and didn't ask but made up his mind as if he'd deduced the answer.

Sometimes, Idris intuited Justin's inner dialogue and tried to address it. Once, as they waited in traffic, a pale redheaded man was scrounging in the trash alongside the street, and Idris said, He could be European, Irish maybe, if he wasn't picking bottles out of the gutter, but maybe that is his disguise.

His disguise? Justin asked.

Maybe he is an American, and he gets around Kabul as a trash collector so he won't be noticed. Who would suspect him?

Hmm, Justin said, nothing more. He didn't seem to have a sense of humor. Maybe it was because he was so Christian. None of the other volunteers had kept a bible next to their bed.

Once, after a class when Justin flushed upon learning that no one had done the homework, Idris explained to him that in Afghanistan homework was often seen as being for children.

People, he said, they will think you are talking down to them.

Maybe we need to have a discussion about self-realization, Justin replied. Transformation happens on people's own time. Class is never enough.

One evening, as Idris drove Frank to Le Jardin, Frank ranted: Justin will get things sooner or later . . . He might be good with grammar, but he couldn't pull off a comeback to save his life . . . And he's definitely a hard read — should give up education and hit the poker tables.

The conflict between the two men provided Idris with protection, and for the first time, he argued with Frank, asking, When am I going to get a scholarship?

I've already had two earfuls from Justin. Cut me some slack. I'm going to show up to dinner with no appetite.

But, Mr. Frank, Idris said, measuring his words, you care more about me fixing the toilets than my education. I didn't know I was attending the Plumbing Academy of the Future.

Plumbers make good money in the States.

I want to be a scientist and go to a good university in the US.

I'm not training young people so they can run away to America. We have enough slackers there already. I want students who will come back here and fix the problems in Afghanistan. You should give some thought to politics.

Politics, yes, maybe someday. But science first.

A lot of good you'll do anyone cramped up in a lab.

In the weeks after Justin's arrival, Idris challenged Frank more often, and when he'd gone too far and angered him, he returned quickly to his helpful, subservient self.

If Frank thought Idris stood a chance in politics, he was deluded. Idris had an average education, no significant family connections, no wealth. He'd tried to read his future in Afghanistan's and seen only hardship. When volunteers left books, many of them about Afghanistan, he read them, learning that his country was likely named by foreign powers — that his people were historically fierce warriors, repelling invading empires. He must deserve better than becoming a plumber.

Idris focused on the life he wanted, on getting a scholarship, but when Sediqa began appearing from Justin's room early each morning, he realized what was happening. And the few times she cried to Frank, Idris had to drive her to the mall. In the car, they hardly spoke as she cleaned up her running makeup. She was already a university student. Maybe if Idris's parents had lived, he would have had the status to ask for her hand. His uncle had told him that once he had a career, they would discuss marriage.

Now, when Justin came into the classroom, the students quieted. Smiles faded. Then, as he wrote grammar lessons on the whiteboard, the murmuring started up in Dari.

Is everything okay? he asked.

None of the gazes were friendly — wary at best.

Yes, Mr. Justin, Idris said in a faintly dismissive voice. Please continue.

As Justin faced back to the board, someone snickered, but he did nothing.

Day after day, Justin seemed less assured. He began moving like a man with an injury, afraid to be jostled. After a snow-storm, when no students came, he told Idris he needed a break from the school. Idris drove him to a café. Justin flinched when the guard with the Kalashnikov opened the metal door. Inside, Bollywood videos played on a flat-screen TV. Expat women had pulled chairs into a circle and were having a meeting of some sort. Windows let in a gray light. Justin flinched again when a stout man in Afghan dress and a solid beard came in to stoke the *bukhari*.

Justin hardly touched his French fries and kebabs, his immorality no doubt weighing on him, Idris thought.

Snow began to fall, and after leaving, as they crossed the white street, Justin stopped before a single boot print.

What is it? Idris asked.

This . . . this print . . . There's only one.

The treads of a boot were marked in the snow, no footprints before or after it.

Who knows? Idris said, but Justin was glancing around, appearing to search for the source of the mystery above the walls or in the blotted sky.

On the way back to the school, Justin told him that he'd once gone to a fair where a palm reader said he would choose his destiny in war.

But fortune-tellers serve the devil. That's what we believe in my church.

Idris nodded. Ahead of them, a car skidded on worn tires. Winter would end soon. The sun would return. His body wanted that warmth.

After Faisal's kidnapping and the meeting with Rashidi, Idris hadn't been able to decide whom he could sacrifice — the word itself another foreign idea, this time pagan: making something holy by giving it up. For whom or what would those he chose become holy?

Asking questions of this sort kept him from having to admit his choice was already made, until Justin threw him against the wall and vengeance at last became one of the few lights Idris could see through the dark of that encroaching mind.

Clay had been harder to betray. When they met at the restaurant, Clay drank his whiskey, and his eyes became somber and empty. As they left — out past the guards and into the night — Idris felt electric with the fear of kidnapping Faisal.

You're being straight with me, right? Clay asked.

Of course, Clay.

Of course, Clay repeated. Of course. Sweat gleamed on his forehead and neck. I can take care of things if they get out of hand. I've done it before. I've killed boys like you.

When Idris returned to the school, Shafiq was in the backyard, in the dark. He had on only his pants, the muscles of his arms corded, his skin like a film over them.

What are you doing?

I must compete soon. The cold will take away the fat. It will give me strength.

Small scars marked his body.

Shrapnel? Idris asked.

Yes. The *mujahedeen* sent mortars into the street when I was a boy.

Because of his bloodless skin or the moon infusing the low
·clouds, Shafiq appeared a statue, a memorial to the endurance
of damaged bodies.

THE NIGHT OF the party, after the foreigners locked themselves in
the safe room, as Noorudin's men died one by one and Idris lay
under the bed — the box spring against his chest, sweat pooling
around his eyelids, in his navel, in the hollow of his throat — he
fully understood that the cost of failure was his life.

Back at the school, he changed into dry clothes and then
took a taxi to the market. He bought a new phone and several
SIM cards. He returned to the lot.

This is a disaster, Rashidi said. It's all over the news. You're
· an idiot.

I'll set this right.

How is that possible?

I'll kill the foreigners myself.

Idris heard his footsteps — not walking to a private place,
but pacing: quick steps in one direction, a lull, quick steps in
the other.

Did the NDS talk to you?

They did.

Then I can never meet with you again.

You won't have to. I need just one thing. A passport with
my photograph in it.

That's easy. With your name?

No. Pick any name. Can it be ready by tomorrow?

I can make that possible, but how do I know you won't just
escape with the passport?

The deaths of the foreigners will be in the news. If I'm alive,
I'll pick up the passport.

Rashidi's breathing was faintly audible. You're not so innocent. I don't know what part of all this you're to blame for. I'll never know. Just get Faisal back.

Faisal will be released, Idris told him, and you'll never see me again.

He hung up and took a taxi to the market. Aziz was alone, watching *Alien*. He pushed his hair into position over his temple.

On the screen, men shouted and fired weapons into passageways as Idris asked for a favor. He needed a passport, with his photo and the name Jalal Hafiz. He needed it within a day. Aziz told him it would be expensive. He broke down the costs on a scrap of paper.

Four thousand dollars, he said. We might be able to do it for less. But it'll be hard. Everyone along the chain will need to be paid.

And how do we make sure no one reports it after he's paid?

They'll receive a bonus once the passport has been proven to work.

Idris counted out eight thousand dollars. Can you have it by tomorrow night?

With this much, yes.

Idris thanked him and stood, but paused in the doorway.

The birthday, he said, make it Nawruz. Let Jalal Hafiz be a child of the New Year.

He then went to the Serena Hotel, took a room, and locked his money in the safe. Idris texted Frank to say that the car was burning oil badly and he would have it fixed in the morning, at his cousin's repair shop. He received a quick *OK*.

Though he'd never been in a bed so luxurious, Idris barely slept. His mind obsessively evaluated his plan. He twisted in his blankets, sweating and then shivering. He changed shirts three times before dawn.

In the morning, he drove out along the Kabul–Jalalabad highway, down through the winding canyon, the traffic heavy in a haze of diesel emissions.

Out of the mountains, he passed an Afghan National Army checkpoint, where a few men crouched next to a tan Ford Ranger, beneath camouflage netting on poles to diffuse the sun.

Sweat soaked his shirt again. If he showed up without warning, the mullah and Noorudin might have him killed. His fingers shook as he punched in the numbers. He knew the words, the rhetoric, the way he had to speak. He hadn't shaven. *I will give you my life. All I need is a bomb. In the name of Allah, I will set this right for Afghanistan.*

He called.

I can give you what you want, he said as soon as the ringing stopped.

You've betrayed us.

I'll kill the foreigners myself. I'll do it today or tomorrow.

Why would you?

He described the girls' school, the men there who slept with the female students, how Idris had seen the corruption of their wealth. I'll kill at least two.

The poor boy always sees the truth, the mullah said.

I need a bomb, one I can hide in the car.

Come. We'll give that to you.

Idris hung up. The mullah and Noorudin could claim victory — an attack against a girls' school — and, with the Taliban reward for foreign deaths, have financing to better their lives.

The possibility that Idris would die in the next twenty-four hours was undeniable. Having seen every eventuality in his mind, he began to empty it, to leave space for nothing else, so that he could race through this crucial period.

Only one brief fantasy haunted him, an image of Tarzi as he imagined him, with an inch-long silver beard from his time with the mullah. He had his reputation for fairness, a true Muslim who studied the holy book and lived his duties. Idris saw himself talking with him in the mullah's compound, discussing a way to resolve all this. Tarzi would see Idris for who he was and offer him a better life.

But Idris dispelled this. He'd learned that being saved — even by the person you were saving — wasn't freedom. There were simple acts of help — pushing someone out of the way of a car or a mother shielding her child from shrapnel — but the kind of saving foreigners came to do resembled what Idris was now doing: using others to attain his own salvation.

Far beyond Jalalabad, at the village compound, there was no meeting with the mullah or Noorudin. A man Idris had never seen walked out with a canvas bag. Idris lowered the window.

It's powerful, the man said and opened the bag to show several bricks attached by wires. I'll fit it inside one of the back seats so that when you go through Kabul's checkpoints, the police will see nothing.

He opened the car's rear door and took out a knife and shears. He lifted the seat cushion and cut into it until he'd made space for the bomb. He returned the seat to its normal position and inspected it. He took a cell from his pocket. He opened the contacts. There was only one.

This is the number. When you call it, the bomb will detonate. Choose a place with many infidels. The explosion will be great.

He returned through the gate without looking back.

The road tunneled into Idris's head. He passed checkpoints

and drove to Aziz's shop and picked up the passport. He said goodbye as if he and Aziz would see each other soon, but Aziz glanced away.

In Wazir Akbar Khan, Idris bought a suit and shoes, a leather briefcase, and travel luggage. He stood at the mirror. With his faint beard, he could be a devout businessman, a moderate believer who found a compromise between his faith and modernity.

He purchased a laptop and a case, and went back to his hotel. He tested where to stash money in his jacket and luggage. This was a formality, since everyone knew that well-dressed men carried suitcases of cash into the Emirates daily, spending Afghanistan's drug wealth in malls, hotels, and resorts. Dubai had no interest in impeding them.

He called Clay and told him Rashidi planned to deliver the ransom the next day. Then he left everything he'd just bought in the room and drove to the school, going slowly, taking in Kabul. It had been utterly transformed during his short life — new constructions jammed in every available space, with, here and there, the occasional prewar concrete ruins, crumbling and white, like fossils embedded in the generational layers of the city.

He was ready to break free of it.

In the pantry, he lay down to think.

Rashidi would be left with the unclaimed fake passport, thinking Idris dead. Tarzi would gain his freedom, and Faisal would be released.

Only a simple calculation remained. He pushed the heels of his hands against his eyelids. Though Frank had let him live in the school and learn an English superior to that of almost any other Afghan Idris knew, Idris had to pick someone. He would wait and see if Justin needed a ride to meet other foreigners. If not, Idris would put the bomb in Frank's desk, wait until Justin was in the room, and then walk outside and call. But the car would be better: the explosion would destroy the steering wheel — if the police even bothered to check which side it was on — and if anything remained from the bodies, the one in front would look like the driver.

He lowered his hands. He would leave everything he'd owned in the pantry, with the door locked, as if he planned to return. There would be nothing to say to his uncle and cousins. His family had been disappearing for years.

PART 10

KABUL–DUBAI: MARCH/JUNE 2012

美智子

FROM OUTSIDE MY hotel room came the unfamiliar croaking of a bird. I'd barely slept, but I went to the window. In a tree, a small silhouette hunched against the dawn. In old Afghan stories, maybe its cry was an omen, but I would never feel the resonance of this land's myths.

The previous day, after saying goodbye to Tam, I'd met with the fixer who helped me find Clay's visa records. He took me to a shop in the market where a young man hacked Steve's laptop. He removed its hard drive and set it up so I could access it externally with my computer. I let him keep the rest of the laptop along with two hundred dollars.

The fixer then made some calls for me and found out that Steve was a suspect in a criminal case. One of the cars registered to his business had passed security cameras, making a quick trip to the point of a kidnapping and back. The NDS had a travel restriction on him and weren't letting him leave the country until the case was resolved. I'd commented that all the rumors about contractors being corrupt must be true, but the fixer just shrugged and said that everyone with power had a hand in something.

Outside the hotel, I got into the taxi idling in the street. I didn't often see the dawn. Over the past year, my days had passed so quickly Kabul seemed a calendar of sunsets, as if trying to come to an end once and for all, though the earth itself refused, its mountains holding back the flames.

By the time we reached the airport, the sun was beginning its ascent. I'd never had a plan for leaving. When I'd arrived in the spring — the airplane jostling down through clouds — I'd been more terrified and certain of my actions than ever before.

Now, as the plane lifted, Kabul was a thatch of streets far below, a raft on a sea of geologic waves. Tam and I had discussed the degrading security, robberies and attacks, and all the foreigners going home. I told myself I'd have had to leave eventually.

As the plane rumbled through the sky, I connected Steve's hard drive to my laptop and reopened the folder I'd found the evening before: photos of Idris, the files organized by date and place, three days ago in Dubai. Steve had a private investigator tracking him. Maybe he hadn't wanted me to tell anyone that Idris might still be alive, or he was afraid that I'd found Idris already and had information about the kidnapping. An email contained Idris's address and information about his daily activities — a technological institute where he studied, and a woman he was dating.

In the photos, Idris was well dressed, in a modest but expensive suit, leaning against the railing near the fountains below the Burj Khalifa, the tallest skyscraper ever built. He stood next to a dark young woman with braided hair who was smiling at him.

Among the files, there were video feeds from Clay's house. Maybe Steve was right to be cautious. Duplicity, I had seen in myself, arises easily to serve one's self-interest.

The hard drive would join the material I continued to gather long after Tam published her article, the most intellectual piece

I'd seen from her and one in which I recognized my own ideas from our conversations — at least, I thought they were mine.

Whereas, in most cases, soldiers serve, many expats come imbued with a messianic sense of their role globally, compelled not just by the desire to help but by a sort of reverence for the power of their culture.

Even if her critique of Americans — and of herself — were true, I'd cherished the closeness of that small community, the way expats relished the character flaws that had brought them to Afghanistan. They perverted their weaknesses into bigger and better stories for late-night drinks, sometimes just to give themselves the courage to head back out and do something more daring. Tam wasn't wrong: we acted like a sort of chosen people, better than our countrymen who stayed home, though we hungered for their admiration, and Afghanistan was our stage.

Are we any different from the British Empire, Tam wrote, *surviving in their colonies by the grace of foreign servants, creating a class of Afghans who may someday have to choose between their countrymen and their foreign sponsors?* She wrote of the Afghans' anger, our surprise when they became hostile to us. *Our belief in our superiority is so great that we hate our victims for not loving us.*

By the time I arrived in Dubai, there was an email in my inbox from Tam, with an audio file and large Word document. At my hotel, I listened to the mp3 she'd stealthily made at the school. It began with Tam telling Frank that her friends in the army were letting her use their postal boxes on the base. She'd gotten chocolates from home and had come to share. She also had a bottle of Johnnie Walker from a friend who'd just flown in from Istanbul. He seemed hesitant and must have pointed to his gut because she asked if he had stomach problems.

"It's my own personal insurgency," he told her.

"The ghost of Mullah Omar."

"If only he were dead. Whoever's in there built his Tora Bora years ago and never left. Bin Laden, I suspect."

"In Iraq, dysentery is called Saddam's revenge."

"We've killed enough bad guys for the entire world to have the runs until judgment day." He hesitated. "But what the hell. It won't be the first time I've pissed off my enemies."

They ate the chocolates and talked, and she told him about her embed with Special Forces. She mentioned a magazine writer she'd been dating. "A renegade," she said.

"I can't see you with anything less than an outlaw," he replied.

She cracked the whiskey, and their glasses clinked — she must have brought those along as well. Their talk rambled on in a similar vein, and then she described Afghan women teachers she'd photographed in Oruzgan the year before. He told her she should be a mentor.

"If all our girls turned out like you," he said, "this country wouldn't need an army."

"Well, I'd be interested in doing a photo-essay about the effect of the tragedy on the students here — the loss of someone who'd sacrificed everything to teach them."

"Nice angle," he told her flatly, no doubt wanting his sacrifice acknowledged instead. "You'll have to excuse me. I need to make a pit stop."

His footsteps clomped out. She moved around. There were a few clicks and then silence. When he came back, he talked about Sediqa, and Tam asked if he was afraid.

"Not at all. So what if Sediqa's uncles drive past in their beat-to-shit car? They don't want to be hunted down by the

NDS. And what's the worst they'll do to a man five years shy of being an octogenarian?"

Then he didn't speak for a long time, and I was impressed that Tam allowed him to sit within that silence.

"But you know, last night I came out to use the bathroom, and standing there, at the top of the stairs, was this grimy boy in a pilot jacket. 'What are you doing here, son?' I said. I'd never seen him before. He just stared, breathing through his mouth. Then he walked downstairs and out of the building. That did worry me a little, but he looked more confused than danger-ous. Maybe he's someone's friend come to see what all the fuss about education is.

"In truth, I've been so busy calling State-side for donors, try-ing to keep this machine oiled, that I can't think about much else. And yet, when I saw that boy, I had to curse Justin. The students say he was involved with Sediqa. I did see her coming out of his room unreasonably early. He said she'd been begging for the scholarship, visiting him, but no Afghan girl would do that. It's not believable. So I'm not sure that a photo-essay about Justin is going to elicit much sympathy here.

"There's a story I should have told him. My first year in Kabul, a man I knew was involved with an Afghan girl, a Pashto. He was the spitting image of that Scottish actor. What's his name? They shot him while he was walking out of a res-taurant. They shot her in the market. They were setting exam-ples. When you get right down to it, everything is basically just education."

After a bit of small talk, their steps pattered. Her motor-cycle revved. A few minutes later, Tam spoke into the recorder, saying, "I copied his personal files onto a zip drive," and then shut it off.

This was the other Tam, the mercenary people talked about. She was showing me just how good her game was.

The document attached to the email was Frank's, shared only because it added nothing to her article. I would read it the next day. It was an attempt at a memoir about his redemption, his vaguely flawed youth in Middle America, his experiences in Vietnam, his all-American career as a businessman, and his transformation into an activist. He touched on the borders of what pained him — allusions to mistreating women, to the pursuit of ambition and the neglect of his family — confessions that dissolved into vague lessons: moralizing as a form of denial.

I preferred his first chapters. He described the Afghanistan that I, like most expats come late, wished I'd seen. He'd arrived after the US invasion and driven cross-country. He evoked the dramatic vistas of the Salang Pass, green fields, or mountainsides painted in wildflowers, all absent of people. But then, the writing felt like a history book of which he was author and subject — the war's chronology interleaved with personal experience and tirades.

Now, the Afghans build without believing, and homes fall apart before they are finished. A handyman told me there'd always be some kind of war, that everyone knows the house will be destroyed. No one spoke with such fatalism when I first came. A group of them are still learning our ways, and it is not too late for us "by slow prudence to make mild a rugged people, and thro' soft degrees subdue them to the useful and the good."

That winter, in an email, Tam would write to me that Frank had gotten sick and asked her to help at the school. Few students remained. Even the guard was gone, having won the Mr. Kabul title and opened a bodybuilding gym. In a fever,

Frank told her that since the Taliban had declared war on civilian expats, vowing to eliminate the foreign contamination, he'd begun seeing the ghosts of old acquaintances wandering the rooms of the school. He woke soaked in sweat, not knowing where he was, lost in his past.

The soul is doing this work, he said. It's like my body no longer lives in these rooms.

He told her about his health issues: sinus infections and rashes and a turbulent gut.

The part of me that feels has gone somewhere else.

He talked about the men in the Russian car who occasionally stopped in the street.

I know they're out there. I'm not afraid of what's coming. I won't be running home.

Tam wrote that one of the girls he'd sent to America did come back with her degree and took over, as he always said would happen. Money then began trickling in again. After months of illness, Frank recovered and lived on in an apartment and visited the school as his protégée rebuilt it. He told Tam his job was to make himself obsolete, but he wasn't ready to die. He wouldn't vanish in a ball of fire because that wasn't his game. He hadn't lived by the sword.

I have my wits, he told her. I have my vision. But unlike Odysseus, I'm not going home. All these girls will sail off, and only then will I climb on the pyre.

I didn't know what Tam's future would be — she had more transformations in front of her — but as for Frank, he'd become a name in Kabul, and I couldn't imagine him surviving a return to America. Under his flapping clothes, I pictured a body less emaciated than fibrous, knotted, and enduring. His strength as he neared eighty seemed the product of conflicting

pressures, the constant contrariness, the war a dense, obstin-
ate element in which he thrived. He would never leave. He'd
have to be pulled, a mandrake, naked and screaming, from
that mutinous earth.

CLAY

IN THE LULL between sleep and full consciousness, questions moved through him: whether he was blinded by Alexandra when he should've been most vigilant — whether Idris could be trusted and the mullah would honor the agreement, and Steve would let this play out without taking it in hand and putting their identities at risk. A memory resurfaced: Justin the evening they'd met in the restaurant. There had been something new in him, a new voice, conviction or passion. Clay hadn't wanted to admit that. Maybe he'd resented him having anything less than failure.

Sleet had blown through on his second night with Alexandra, pattering on the roof and windows and terrace. Whatever they'd been twenty-four hours before was largely gone. They made love and then just lay, the rain a vibration in the air, a sense of stillness across the city.

The dawn filtered through his eyelids. He never slept past first light, but he lay for a while, enjoying her warmth. She'd burrowed deeper into the comforter, the fire long since gone out. The chill held his face like a mask.

He slipped away from her, air coursing over him. Quietly, he started a fire, piling tinder and gnarled chunks of wood he'd had delivered: trees far from maturity, hacked-up undergrowth, scant remainders in a country deforested from three decades of wartime winters.

Flames rose, heat emanating from the metal cylinder. He pulled on his pants and went onto the terrace, the cold so intense now that he had to breathe powerfully.

Sunrise climbed the far slopes of the mountains, revealing the gleaming arch of the atmosphere. He liked this time, when heaters and generators were off, and the combustion of sawdust, trash, kerosene, diesel, and gas had ended, when breezes erased the ceiling of smog and dust that the hot urban air lifted and trapped against the alpine sky. Now, the only smell was of his own *bukhari*'s stovepipe, the nostalgic fragrance of wood smoke.

Something had changed. Idris was different. He had a taint of betrayal around him — another of Kabul's odors. But there was so much betrayal here it was hard to know its target.

He tried to conjure back how he'd felt with Alexandra. He should have told her about the killing in Iraq, explained how he'd come to this life. He saw her trying to understand.

He went inside. She was in the kitchen in her underwear, looking at the empty counter. The air was hot now. He stood behind her, placed his hands on her arms, and breathed the fragrance of her hair.

She turned and kissed him. She led him back to the bed, drawing him down so that his head was against her chest. He'd never been with a woman like this before.

Is this how you've always lived?

What do you mean? he asked though he knew, just wanted to hear how she saw it.

Like . . . like a monk.

He wasn't used to being touched.

She began to speak again, but there was a catch in her breath, and he jerked up.

Justin stood at the window, touching it to steady himself.

Clay was on his feet instantly, lunging for the door. He opened it, caught Justin's collar, and swung him inside. He drove his elbow into his solar plexus and, in the same motion, kicked his legs out and slammed him against the floor.

Alexandra was reaching toward them, lunging, fingers extended. Clay straddled Justin and punched him three times in the head. Alexandra grabbed his shoulder, pulling him back, and Clay stumbled to his feet, struggling against rage as if against an incline.

Justin lay with one eye closed, the other knocked from the socket, upside-down on the floor.

ALEXANDRA

DEFEATED, ALEXANDRA WROTE in her journal the morning after her first visit to Clay's house. *I don't know that I've met another person with so much history and so little future. He doesn't appear aware of all that's behind him. If I ever believed my presence here could create lasting change I would see, being with him reminded me of how many others have preceded me.*

Before I came here, the war was confusion, impersonal contradictory reports. I'd read and heard explanations from Afghans and expats, and had a sense of an immense puzzle whose pieces came together in islands that could almost be bridged. But Clay told me to give up.

"You'd have to understand not just centuries of powers clashing and more than three decades of civil war, but millions of resilient individuals and their personal motivations, the tribal traditions and pashtunwali, *and the ways the brain reacts when you're hungry and scared and angry and traumatized. Half the country is under eighteen and sexually frustrated, and there's not much on the horizon. They go to war the way we play paintball."*

"So what are we doing here?" I asked, skeptical of his statements.

He laughed. "Building résumés, making a buck, sweating out guilt. As for America" — he said it as if no other country had fought here — "Afghanistan is giving us new rules for war.

*Our future soldiers will be the de facto officers who lead foreign
armies into battle."*

*Hearing him speak, I realized that for America, this war would
matter only if it almost failed, only if the insurgency rose and challenged them, and America was changed, its soldiers becoming like
frontiersmen in the Western wilds, learning the skills of natives —
only then would this story deserve to be told, about an enemy worthy
of America's transformation. This was the myth that Clay had
brought to the war, and without it, as he lived now, he had nothing.*

But maybe this was also true of those who weren't soldiers.

When Alexandra saw Clay the second time, she had no
questions. There would be no answers unless she asked in
the way that a journalist or lawyer led a subject. She'd never
make sense of how a man so brutal could speak in such paced,
thoughtful lines.

His punches had the sound of an axe hitting wood.

A minute before, as he stood outside, she'd gone to the window. The lines of his back had reminded her of a sculpture,
the evidence of his strength excessive in the way that art could
evoke an abundance of life.

Justin's breath rumbled when he exhaled, and she shook
him. Idris was outside now. He must have watched from the
stairs. Clay had spun toward the wall, clutching his face. Blood
was puddling from a gash in the back of Justin's scalp, where
he'd hit the floor. She got a towel from the bathroom and
wrapped his head.

He's unconscious, she told Idris, who was now standing in
the doorway. We need to take him to the hospital.

I have the car outside.

Let me, Clay said. He was pale and haggard as he put on his
shirt and jacket, and his boots without socks.

She dressed, startled at how little Idris paid mind to her exposed skin. He held the door as Clay lifted Justin, and she followed them to the car. The guard tried to explain something to Clay about the downstairs neighbor letting Justin in because Justin said he was a friend.

Alexandra sat in the back, and as Clay slid Justin inside, she took his head in her hands. Clay sat in the passenger seat. No one spoke. Idris seemed to know where he was taking them.

Clay stared ahead, the vein on the side of his neck gorged, his body suddenly an object she couldn't imagine touching.

What was there for her to conclude or redeem here? Her brother's last letter had reached her after his death. *I didn't have the courage to talk about what happened to you in person, but I wanted to . . . After I left, I lied to myself that it might not be necessary, but I realized that if I died, you would need it.*

Though she believed in nothing more than this inexplicable accidental life, Sam's prescience seemed a mystical force aligned with something far greater than human knowledge.

There is no justification, only explanations of the realities I grew up in — how boys taught each other how to see girls and how we acted upon that to prove ourselves. I didn't know how hungry I was to belong, not to be the poor kid. Since it was like you were part of me, it only made sense that you would do what was necessary for me to have what I wanted. I would have fucked for money — would have done anything for it. It's not until you were gone that I began to understand. I became more violent. I broke more laws. I wanted proof of something. Order maybe. Or maybe I was trying to hurt the world enough to make it show its true face.

Idris swerved to the side of the road and shut off the ignition. Clay snapped to, seeming to wake from reverie. He didn't look back at her and Justin, only at Idris.

There is a problem the motor has been having. One minute. I can fix it.

Idris glanced back as he got out. Briefly, he was familiar to her, both resolve and resignation in his eyes.

JUSTIN

THAT MORNING, JUSTIN had lain in bed considering that he'd seen Sediqa wrong. Frank hadn't saved her. She'd saved herself and used them to do it. If she was the protagonist in her story, who was he? Not evil, not even her enemy. At best, a fool.

When he got up and went downstairs, Idris was at the pantry door, with the tired expression of a night-shift worker. Justin asked to talk, and Idris sighed. Yes, Mr. Justin. What is it? Justin gave him some printouts and described his plan to help him apply to colleges directly for scholarships. Idris scanned the list of college websites he should read, the application essays he had to prepare.

Thank you, he said softly, almost reverentially.

Idris, why are you so tired?

Because — because I am working for Mr. Clay.

That was your decision.

Yes. I regret it. He leaves no time to study. Mr. Clay makes me work constantly. It is not what Mr. Frank agreed with him. I have done many hours of work, but Mr. Clay will not pay me. I was just at his home. He refused.

Just now?

Yes. Will you please come and tell him how important my studies are?

Justin put on his jacket, and they went to the car. It was the wrong hour for a confrontation: the air clean, the city peaceful.

They arrived at the gate as the downstairs neighbor was leaving, the redheaded Australian Justin had met at the picnic, and he waved them in.

After climbing the stairs, Justin stood at the window — Clay inside with his face to her chest, her fingers in his hair.

Clay came at him. Justin woke in the car, and now her fingers were stroking his face, as if he'd gone in and lain where Clay had been.

She smiled. Clay was in the front. Justin prayed silently for all of them, wanting Clay to turn — to look away from the sun blazing over the mountains, infusing the world with light.

CLAY

CLAY WISHED LIFE could be a series of junctions, quiet intersections where he could stop and contemplate each future to
decide in which direction lay peace. Every action seemed locked
to another, as indistinguishable as the currents in a river. The
shifts that might have changed it all were tiny. The adjusting of
his rifle to sight past the bright speck of the eye. Or a moment
when he could have reached over and nudged a rifle barrel aside.

Just before the airstrike in Iraq, someone had put on
Metallica, and he'd been jolted into thinking of his days in
Lake Charles, wondering if the music had made its audience
more open to passions that weakened their will and blurred
their goals — if it made them vulnerable to a reasoned and
predatory elite. Then his squad took fire from a building off
the highway and called in the airstrike. The building collapsed,
and they walked to where the hole revealed a network of tunnels. Cautiously, they climbed down to search for any intelligence left by the insurgents. Though pillared and reinforced
with concrete, most of the passageways had collapsed, but one
ended in a low, square room. Four bottles of Jim Beam were
wrapped in disintegrating plastic, their labels as thin as tissue
paper. They agreed that if this place had housed an insurgency,
it had been against Saddam Hussein or his predecessor a long
time ago.

Check this out, Hitch called. He swiped dust off a stack of *Playboy*s.

They lit up the stiff pages with their flashlights. A blonde woman knelt on a beach, her legs wide, the tuft of her pubic hair prominent beneath the taut skin of her abdomen. She had natural breasts, modest and pear-shaped, with delicate pink nipples.

Like what fucking year is this? Hitch asked.

They guffawed as he squinted at the cover. Holy shit. Nineteen seventy-eight.

Daniels was pointing a gloved finger at the *Playboy*. Open back to that page, he said. There! He put his finger to the blonde's pubic hair. What the fuck is wrong with her?

Briefly, no one spoke.

That's au naturel, Clay told him.

Like that? You mean —

Yes, Hitch said, all pussies, left to their own devices, will eventually look like Don King.

Jones sucked in his cheeks and spoke in the voice of Yoda. Young Daniels, in the age of Brazilian, born you were.

They laughed, stomping, decades of dust rising around them.

Daniels admitted he was just messing with them, and they reluctantly calmed long enough to change locations and set up camp. Then they cracked the whiskey, joking that it was aged, and worth thousands, maybe millions of dollars.

Authentic *hajji*-aged bourbon, Hitch had called it after taking a swig and spitting it out.

Clay tried to hold some of that pathetic joy. That's where he'd go back to.

He turned in his seat. Alexandra didn't look up. She held

Justin's face, not like something she loved but the way a child might carry an heirloom across a house to deliver it into steadier hands. Justin's eyelids twitched but didn't open, refusing to take in any more of life.

In the desert, Hitch reminisced about his favorite whores — he called them saints, since they often supported their extended families with what they earned, unlike the bitches back home who married for diamond rings and suvs. He gave a soliloquy in the night, and they all agreed it was as good as Shakespeare. Eventually, they slept.

Clay was the last to take watch and joined Daniels, who'd gone before and sat half-asleep, his rifle propped before him. At dawn, the world came into focus: plowed fields and a distant village where a narrow stream widened before a small dam.

The wildness and joy, the way he'd lain smiling at the moonlit sky so hard it hurt, ebbed out of him. It felt like someone slowly pulling back a sheet. The sun clipped the horizon. He squinted and came to, his senses converging. A figure was nearing, almost to their camp, wavering in the onslaught of light like a flame on a wick.

Clay felt Daniels see the stranger a second later. If he'd acted, if he'd been fully inside himself, he could have pushed the barrel of his friend's rifle aside. Daniels's finger pulsed. The silhouette jerked, his long hanging shirt snapping behind him the way wind catches a sail, before he fell into the furrows.

Clay fired a few shots to confuse the landscape with bullets. Then the others were there, weapons raised as they shouted questions. The sun kept rising. People ran from the village. The light burned into his eyes, and he closed them and sat, holding the shadow of fire in his head.

The car drifted to the roadside. Idris said there'd been a

problem, a loose spark plug cable. He got out and stood, drawn and pale, briefly so motionless Clay knew that fear pinned him in place. He tried to move through his confusion to the ache in his gut.

The sun shone with such force that the edges of buildings seemed to evaporate, everything in the city a dark nucleus with a burning outline.

He turned, wanting to see what he had done.

Justin's eye was open, the other eyelid sagging. This was his real face, no hate in it, dissolving as light filled the breathless air.

IDRIS

THE DETONATION DROPPED him to his knees. Even protected by
a wall, he fell, though he didn't know if this was because of
the shock wave or his horror at what he'd done. When he and
Justin had driven to Clay's, desperation had finally taken hold
of him, and he'd had no clear plan — just a thought that he
could park near a car of foreigners somewhere. Instead, he had
Justin, Alexandra, and Clay with him. When he pulled off the
road and told them to wait, they did. He'd gotten out and put
up the hood. Hidden by it, he'd walked away in a straight line,
past a concrete wall. He'd pressed send on the cell. He hadn't
made up his mind. The finality — that he couldn't return to
rethink his choices — nauseated him. The blast reverberated
in his bones. People were crouching in the street, running in
different directions, and he ran too.

He caught a taxi to his hotel, changed into his suit, and put
on his overcoat. There was money in its lining, in his jacket, his
briefcase, his suitcase. He called a private taxi and went to the
airport, stayed calm through security, handed over the passport
and took it back.

On the plane, he told himself Jalal Hafiz would never have
the shining eyes of a fanatic. His first enemies had been his own
people. Foreigners became enemies later, and *enemies* wasn't
even the right word.

His first months in Dubai, living in a modest apartment that he furnished carefully, he found himself seeing his life through violence. Walking the city, he considered that it was the closest thing the Middle East had to a New York — a haven where ambitious youth could aspire to stable careers and establish homes, meet with friends and go to the beach, or walk beneath the palms in the warm night air and enjoy light and water shows in the plaza fountain beneath the Burj Khalifa. And yet he envisioned the buildings being destroyed by hordes that had come out of the desert, hungry and fearful and vengeful, sustained only by faith. For hours, he lay by the small rooftop pool of his apartment complex, his face to the sun.

He made no friends, just read books on science. Each word was a black raindrop cutting away an exposed earth, eroding his faith. If humans were less like other animals, the divine could make sense. But they hungered and shat, fought for territory, needed each other desperately for comfort and survival while carving out their empires. All this suffering had to have meaning. He took the elevator to the roof and lay in the sun and slept.

He wasn't sure what he'd dreamed, but he woke with an image of a jungle like the one in his book, plants unfurling from swamp, immense ferny growths, each topped with a head — a bulb with two eyes to study the sun and rain and soil that nourished it.

Maybe human life was simply nature evolving so that it could study itself. The book said that mutations endured because they conferred an advantage. Each trait could be read into a past where it allowed an organism to survive. So why God? Why did men stare at the sky with longing?

The question stayed with him for weeks as he read, searching for a reason to believe humans were special. But just as nature expanded relentlessly, consuming and growing, tribes and nations fought for resources and land. And if nature was greedy to fill all spaces, it must also long to move beyond the planet. It was this thought that grew in him, finally destroying his faith. Maybe humans were simply a better spore, capable of understanding their habitat and re-creating it so they could carry it with them. Maybe there had never been a God, just an impulse for expansion so powerful it imbued inaccessible territories with mystery, conjuring an image of humans as the deities they would have to be to live in unconquerable spaces.

But in the encroaching, exterminating glory of his species, he was a broken filament, a struggling, inconsequential rodent. And yet he woke to the blast's reverberations aching through him, filling him, the way he imagined the universe beginning, exploding, rippling outward.

Daily, he stood before the mirror: the starved boy was disappearing, putting on weight. The gravitas of self-reflection and even sorrow made him older and more handsome. His eyes had lost their eagerness and credulity. He'd once believed in others without reason.

To break his solitude, he began taking classes at a private technological institute, his level remedial — math and basic science. He befriended Fathima, who'd come from Sri Lanka to study there. Her English was perfect, and they met at the mall or had dinner together, and talked about books. She was a moderate believer, and when he told her his ideas, she listened but said that men must not become enamored of their ability to explain. His romance with her seemed, but for their accents and the color of her skin, like the TV shows he'd loved.

Though he tried to stop justifying his survival and enjoy his life, he often could not help but remember what he'd done. He should have killed Frank, who treated Afghans like children, who believed his presence was needed for them to rise. But there had been too many hopes with Frank. Idris wanted to argue with him, to prove him wrong.

In Dubai, whenever he heard Afghans speaking Dari or Pashto, he avoided them, glancing only to make sure he didn't know anyone. He read the Afghan news online and people's Facebook pages, though he never again logged into any of his former accounts. Tarzi had been returned, and Rashidi got Faisal back and sent him to America. Soon after, Tarzi was shot in the street while getting out of an armored SUV. Other than the mullah and Noorudin, the only people who knew about Idris's involvement were Rashidi and Clay's partner, and they all thought he was dead.

Idris went to the mall to buy a present for Fathima's birthday. He crossed the marble floors, past tourists from around the globe, past two sheiks in white robes and checkered headscarves, on their way with their families to Ralph Lauren Kids or the aquarium. In a mirrored wall, he saw himself, older and more resigned, and behind his reflection, in the crowd, a young Afghan man dressed in jeans and a beige hoodie, with familiar Hazara features. Idris pretended he hadn't noticed, struggling to remember.

Idris, the Hazara said — the voice was a woman's, and not an Afghan's at all — I need to speak with you.

He didn't move. He tried to place her, and then he did. He'd seen her occasionally among Justin's friends, though he didn't know where she was from.

Not here, she told him. You're in danger. Walk with me.

He took a step. Why? From whom?

For years he'd watched movies, never expecting to hear someone speak their lines in any way that would be relevant to him.

People are watching you, she said. Please trust me.

美智子

WE TOOK OUR time through the crowds in the raised walkway back to the metro, caught the train and then jumped out at a station, ran across the platform, and traveled in the opposite direction. We did this several times, neither of us speaking. When Idris suggested we go to his place, I told him they knew where he lived. We left a station and took a taxi and went into a small café in a quiet neighborhood. I chose a table near a window that faced a largely deserted side street awash with harsh, late-morning light.

"Who is after me? How did you find me?"

"I want an exchange."

"What exchange?"

"I want your story. I want to know how you escaped Kabul and why you killed them. Then I will tell you who is after you and give you all the files they have on you."

"And what will you do with this story — send me to prison?"

"No. Nothing will happen to you."

"But you will write it then? You must be a journalist like all the others."

We stared at each other, my eyes looking into his to transmit by emotion what I knew would be difficult to unravel in words.

"I will never mention your new name," I said, "or even your old one."

"And how will you know if I am speaking the truth?"

"I will be able to tell."

We considered each other a while longer before his expression softened and he nodded.

"I will give you the truth," he said, "because really, outside Afghanistan, who cares? You can tell the whole world. No one will do anything. So I will tell you, and then you will explain why you are here and you will help me if you can."

"I promise," I said.

Maybe he was thinking that he'd been caught after all and should at least give his version of the story. He had nothing to lose. If I were to divulge his existence, he would soon be in prison and, in all likelihood, dead. But once he began speaking, describing his childhood, his words broke into a flood. Like Frank, he'd been arguing within himself, justifying his actions.

We sat for hours as he deciphered his decisions during his final weeks in Kabul. He annotated each of his choices with the experiences of his youth.

"A future," he said. "What would a person not do for a future? They had their dreams — Frank, Justin, and Clay — but I had mine, and they did not know that."

"And Alexandra?"

"When something is set into motion, how can you stop it? No one is in control of this war. So much has been moving for so long. That is what I learned. We can grieve for those who are destroyed, but there is nothing else to do. She went to Afghanistan. She and her people were part of the war. She put her life in the way. I chose myself."

In the course of those hours, Idris became familiar, an individual not beholden to the laws of the family or the tribe. I sensed that he, like so many people I knew, no longer saw his life as a turn of the wheel, as the carrier of the next generation, but now lived as if his were the last, as one soon might be.

"And what will you do now?" I asked.

"I will stay here or move to another country, and maybe I will someday go back to Afghanistan. The Americans will be gone. No one will remember me, and everything that happened will be forgotten. This story, if it even matters, will be mine to tell.

"So now," he said, "you tell me why I should be afraid."

Steve's interest in him finally made sense. If he could give the Afghan police Idris — someone who was supposed to be dead — he could draw the attention from himself. He could say he'd been investigating Idris as part of his K&R contract to get back Tarzi, that Idris was involved in the kidnapping and killed everyone in the car. But for that to work, Idris couldn't give his side of the story. If Steve wanted exoneration, a dead body would be better than a living one.

I explained all this, and with my laptop I showed Idris the photos.

"Is your money at your home?" I asked.

"That would be foolish."

"Do you need to go home?"

"I do not. But I will."

He lifted his eyes, dark, shining irises framed by black lashes, absent of malice.

"You think I am going to run, that I will spend my life escaping from country to country." He shook his head. "Do you still have your Afghan cell?"

"Yes."

"May I use it?"

He took it and called a number. He spoke in Dari a long

time. I made out repeated apologies and Steve's name. He hung up.

"Do you want to know what I have done and how simple it is?" he asked. He popped the back off my phone, took out the battery, and removed the SIM. He slid the phone to me.

"I have called Rashidi and told him that Steve worked for Tarzi's family and kidnapped Faisal. I said that I discovered who Steve was before I fled the country, that I had to leave because I would be killed. I told him I am a refugee, but that I read about Faisal's safe return. I told him that if Faisal is alive now, it is because of me. And I told him that Steve knows about Rashidi and the mullah, and his involvement with the attack, that Steve is going to reveal both me and Rashidi to the police, and that I gave my life for his family."

"So it is that simple?"

"It is. Steve will be taken care of."

"And me?"

"I would not go back to Afghanistan if I were you, or mention my name, or write it."

I said nothing. I'd known the danger this presented and, in a way, it was satisfying: to complete this journey that had existed until now in my imagination and face its challenges, to be part of the story that had almost taken my life and place it back into history. All I had left to do was determine its ending. I just had to stand and walk out of the café, into the light of the street.

IDRIS

MAYBE THIS TIME the murder was merited, if such a thing was possible. He would have to decide later. He'd acted with tired determination, unsure of what he was defending. Rashidi's voice — his astonishment and then his warmth, and his promise to deal with the man who'd kidnapped Faisal — had been reassuring, cathartic, like a sense of freedom, like sunlight on his skin — the way it would feel, he knew, when he finally got up and stepped out the door.

Speaking to the young woman had felt strangely good, as though his story mattered, no matter how much he was afraid of being found out. He'd been surprised by the insistence in his own words, the tone he used as he justified himself — by how much it sounded like Frank.

They'd been sitting in silence, his nerves ringing in his ears. The way they evaluated each other was tense, almost menacing, like a standoff in a desolate street somewhere, in front of a saloon maybe — that sort of thing.

So, he said, you have finished your investigation?

Yes. I think so.

Then I would like to ask you a question.

Please do.

Am I guilty? Do you think, after everything you have learned and seen, that I am guilty?

Slowly, appearing to hold herself in place, she looked him over as deliberately as he did each day before he went out, studying himself in the mirror: a young, grave man, his shirt open at the collar, ease in the cut of his hair. She lingered on the hints of sadness around his mouth, at the edges of his eyes.

This thin, unreadable person before him would leave with a secret he could not contain, and everything in his past would not be neatly shut away. She must know this, must be afraid he would decide she presented too great a risk.

He wanted her to stay, to speak and tell him her story now, her own reasons for being here.

She inhaled, slightly lifting her chin, her gaze relaxing, as if she'd come to the end and whatever she'd needed or been holding was gone — and seeing her expression, he breathed too, believing suddenly and without reason that he would be safe, though uncertainty lingered in the muscles of his chest. But maybe there is always a little fear just before the moment of release.

You are alive, she told him.

He inclined his head faintly and closed his eyes.

Yes.

ACKNOWLEDGMENTS

I would like to thank the following people for their generous support during the writing of this novel: Austin Lin, Nancy Romer, Lew Friedman, Bonnie Huang, Mark Preston, Kevin Lin, Patrick Thomas, Joey McGarvey, Aoife Roberts, Joanna Demkiewicz, Abby Travis, Christy Edwall, Leza Lowitz, Shogo Oketani, Meredith Dees, Tristan Malavoy-Racine, Linda Pruessen, John Sweet, Emily Mockler, Alysia Shewchuk, Liz Sherman, Donna Brodie, Greg Foster, Dominique Fortier, Antoine Tanguay, Alim Remtulla, Ziaullhaq Maliky, Rauf Meraj, Emma Graham-Harrison, David Gill, and Shannon Galpin. I would like to thank my mother, Bonnie Ellis, for believing in the work I do, despite the risks.

Thank you to the MacDowell Colony for a two-month residency during a crucial writing period and to the Writers Room in Manhattan for a quiet working space. I am also grateful to the Canada Council for the Arts for financial support over the past decade.

In the novel, I quote, in slightly altered form, the Twitter feeds of ISAF and a Taliban spokesman. On page 234, I quote Richard Slotkin's *Regeneration Through Violence*. On page 392, Frank attempts to quote a line from Cormac McCarthy's *The Crossing* and largely fails.

It would be difficult if not impossible to name all of the

journalists whose writing helped inform my own research in Afghanistan. Among them are Jason Burke, Dexter Filkins, Emma Graham-Harrison, Nathan Hodge, May Jeong, and Graeme Smith.

I am especially grateful to the many Afghans who shared their stories with me between 2009 and 2014, or who helped me during my stays there.

At Milkweed Editions, I would like to thank Daniel Slager for his editorial support and for taking the risk to finance an unwritten book on the basis of several long conversations. At House of Anansi Press, I would like to thank Sarah MacLachlan and Janice Zawerbny, for her editorial guidance and patience in discussing the minutiae of the novel's language.

DENI ELLIS BÉCHARD is the author of the novel *Vandal Love*, winner of the 2007 Commonwealth Writers' Prize for Best First Book; *Cures for Hunger*, a memoir about growing up with his father, who robbed banks; and *Of Bonobos and Men*, winner of the 2015 Nautilus Book Award for investigative journalism. His work has appeared in numerous magazines and newspapers, including the *LA Times*, *Salon*, *Pacific Standard*, and *Foreign Policy*, and he has reported from India, Iraq, Colombia, Rwanda, the Congo, and Afghanistan.